Praise for
The Beginner's Guide to Loneliness:

'Sweet, funny, engaging – and *[illegible]* kle
really rather wise. The *[illegible]*
V*[illegible]*

'A total hug in *[illegible]*,
honest and touc*[illegible]* utiful story
of love and fri*[illegible]* ip. I loved it!'
Miranda Dickinson

'What a read – rollicking fun and emotionally satisfying!'
Michele Gorman

'This book will leave you with a big smile'
Mandy Baggot

'Genuinely moving, beautifully told and really funny!'
Christina Pishiris

'Funny, warm and brilliantly uplifting'
Claire Frost

'Full of warmth, depth and unexpected turns,
plus a cast of characters I wish I knew in real life,
Laura Bambrey has written a beautiful debut'
Lucy Dickens

'Although it's a love story, it's even more a tale of
friendship . . . I recommend it most highly as a beautifully
written guide as to how we should live our lives'
T.A. Williams

Laura Bambrey was born in Dorset but raised in Wales. She's worked as a trapeze choreographer, sculpture conservator and stilt walker, among other occupations, and spent most of her time collecting stories from the people she met along the way. She has spent many years as a book blogger and reviewer of women's fiction and now lives in Devon with her very own romantic hero and a ridiculously fluffy rabbit named Mop. *The Beginner's Guide to Loneliness* is her debut novel.

LAURA BAMBREY

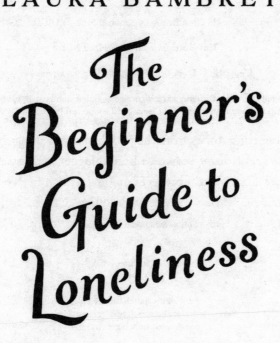

The Beginner's Guide to Loneliness

**SIMON &
SCHUSTER**

London · New York · Sydney · Toronto · New Delhi

First published in Great Britain by Simon & Schuster UK Ltd, 2020

This paperback edition published 2021

Copyright © Laura Bambrey, 2020. All rights reserved.

The right of Laura Bambrey to be identified as author of this work has been
asserted in accordance with the Copyright, Designs and Patents Act, 1988.

3 5 7 9 10 8 6 4 2

Simon & Schuster UK Ltd
1st Floor
222 Gray's Inn Road
London WC1X 8HB

Simon & Schuster Australia,
Sydney

Simon & Schuster India,
New Delhi

www.simonandschuster.co.uk
www.simonandschuster.com.au
www.simonandschuster.co.in

A CIP catalogue record for this book is available from the British Library

Paperback ISBN: 978-1-3985-0053-2
eBook ISBN: 978-1-4711-9577-8

Typeset in the UK by Hewer Text UK Ltd, Edinburgh
Printed and bound in Great Britain by CPI Group
(UK) Ltd, Croydon, CR0 4YY

MIX
Paper from
responsible sources
FSC® C020471

For Jules

Prologue

Tackling the Taboo

Dear Readers,

Today marks the second anniversary of The Beginner's Guide to Loneliness. I can't express how grateful I am for all of your messages telling me how my blog has helped you navigate your own personal journeys. It makes me incredibly proud to know that so many people have benefited from this site.

Admitting that you are lonely remains one of the biggest taboos in our society. That's why all of the recent publicity the blog has received has been so welcome. The mixture of newspaper, magazine and online coverage has helped thousands of new readers to find their way here. If you're one of them, then welcome! The more able people feel to talk about being lonely, the easier it becomes to seek the support that's needed.

One of the greatest misconceptions is that loneliness stems from a character trait, or even a character flaw. Listen to me: **you don't have to be broken to be lonely**. I've heard it so many times: 'But you're so friendly . . .' 'You seem to get on with people so easily . . .' 'But you know lots of people . . .' etc. I hope I am friendly, but that doesn't mean I can't feel isolated at times too; it doesn't mean I don't find it difficult to connect with people.

The truth is, you can be alone and not at all lonely – happy and content in your own company. Or you can be at the centre of a huge crowd and feel so lonely it's like a physical ache.

Sudden life changes can sometimes cause connections with other people to fall away. A bereavement, change of job or even the disintegration of a relationship are just a few of the catalysts. Should more than one of these things hit you at the same time, as they did for me, you can end up feeling not just lonely, but completely stuck, searching for the way out.

So no, you don't have to be broken to be lonely – but loneliness can, eventually, break you.

Let's keep talking about it. Let's keep looking at ways to heal. Let's keep supporting each other. Here's to the next two years of TheBeginnersGuideToLoneliness.com.

Thank you for being here.
TBGTL

P.S. A note to the press: thank you so much for your interest in the site! Should you wish to reach me about my work, please use the contact page. I will, however, be maintaining my anonymity. From this point onwards please note that I will not respond to any communications that include the request to 'come out' to my readers.

Chapter 1

True Friends Will Always Be There

Warriors Chat Group. April 30. 10.48pm

WriterTori: Guys, help!

Nathalie33: Hey Tori! What's occurring?

WriterTori: Gah. Gah. GAH!

Nathalie33: Drama. Drama. DRAMA ;) Come on. Tell Aunty
Nat . . .

WriterTori: Are Sue and Hugh online?

Nathalie33: Who knows . . . who cares . . . ?

WriterTori: Nat!!

Nathalie33: Kidding! Anyway, talk to me. What's up?

SueSue52: Oi, Nat, you cheeky mare! I'm here Tori. Managed to
place any of your articles yet?

WriterTori: No, and that's half the problem.

Nathalie33: What's the other half?

WriterTori: Paying my rent! My landlord is being patient, but he said
he wants the money the next time he sees me.

SueSue52: Ah, the joys of life as a self-employed writer. I thought you were going to look for a part-time job?

Nathalie33: Nah, she gave up that idea to focus!

SueSue52: How's that working out?

Nathalie33: How do you think it's working out? Her landlord's chasing her . . .

WriterTori: Jeez, thanks guys . . . But seriously – I'm skint. I have a million ideas for articles out, but so far, no interest. AND I'm struggling for rent, hence the landlord issue. Also, I haven't been paid by puddle.com, even though I wrote six weeks' worth of content for them before they went under!

SueSue52: Nightmare! Wish I could help you out, but with the twins' birthday coming up and OH's hours cut, we're tight too. Maybe think again about getting that part-time job?

WriterTori: Cheers Sue, but I wouldn't want to borrow from you guys anyway. And I don't want to give in and look for a job yet. Would seem like admitting defeat . . . Anyway, this one opportunity has come up, and I need your advice about whether or not to go for it.

Nathalie33: Spill . . .

WriterTori: You know I don't accept any advertising on the blog?

Nathalie33: If you did, you wouldn't be having these problems. The Beginner's Guide to Loneliness is so insanely popular – you'd be raking it in, especially after the recent publicity you've been getting. And don't get me started on all the interview opportunities you've turned down . . . !

WriterTori: That's not what the site's about! The blog's anonymous and I want to keep it that way. But, this place in Wales called The Farm made contact a couple of weeks ago. They run wellness retreats and they've offered me a spot on the latest course in exchange for a review.

SueSue52: What's the course?

WriterTori: It's a mixture of mindfulness and counselling, designed to teach people how to improve their mental health and wellbeing. You work on building authentic relationships, self-acceptance, with a bit of yoga thrown in there for good measure. They reckon my readers are their target audience.

Nathalie33: Erm, yep – I can see their point! So are they going to pay you?

WriterTori: No, but it's a free three-week course that normally costs £3k, and they provide food, somewhere to stay and they'd cover travel costs too. What do you think? I'm not sure if I should go . . .

Nathalie33: Why the hell not? It sounds like it's practically tailor-made for you!

WriterTori: 1. Because the site's *anonymous*! 2. Because it feels a bit like I'd be selling out.

SueSue52: The anonymity thing is easy enough to get around. Just contact them via the blog's generic email address and say you'll send 'one of the site's reviewers'. Stops them knowing that you're the face behind all the articles.

WriterTori: Oh. Actually, that's a good plan.

Nathalie33: And you wouldn't be selling out by writing about an experience that could benefit so many of your readers.

SueSue52: Have you got a link?

WriterTori: Sure, two secs . . .

I paste the retreat's website address into the chat for Sue and Nat to peruse and then slump back on my sofa. With my computer balanced precariously on my lap, I reach over for my glass of wine and take a gulp. It's not just my need to stay anonymous that's making me hesitate. The thought of sharing my problems, face to face, makes me feel a bit sick. That's why I need the Warriors' second (and third and fourth) opinions.

I really don't know where I'd be without this lot. Nat, Sue and Hugh have been my one constant for the past two years, ever since I lost my mum. Things got . . . desperate. I didn't have anyone I could talk to about how I was really feeling, so I went online and found a grief support group. Nat came to my rescue within minutes of me posting to the communal chat. We talked so much that we were clogging up the thread, and it was gently suggested by a moderator that we shift over to our own private message channel. We chatted for hours on end, and she was just amazing. I credit her with single-hand-edly saving my sanity that first week.

I was still posting to the communal chat too, desperate for as much support as possible, and that's where I met Hugh and Sue. Sue had lost a baby the previous month and Hugh's brother had end-stage terminal cancer. We clicked so well that I invited them into the private channel too. I don't think Nat was very happy that our chats were now between four of us, but I'd found my life raft. I could be completely open with these three, and within just a few weeks, they became my family.

That was two years ago, and we've been inseparable ever since. Online at least. I've never met them in real life as we're spread all over the country. I've tried to meet up with Nat a couple of times as she's not that far away from London, just along the south coast, but something always crops up at the last minute and we still haven't managed it.

But just because we've never met in person doesn't stop me classing Sue, Nat and Hugh as my best friends. They held me together after Mum's accident. They were there through the long nights of tears when my relationship with my fiancé, Markus, imploded. They stop me from feeling completely alone and are my loudest and best cheerleaders.

Nat's actually the one who encouraged me to start up The Beginner's Guide. It started out as my way of coping with everything that had happened to me, but it's grown way past that. I write anonymous essays on grief, loss, depression and loneliness. I know – they hardly sound like the most cheering of subjects, but losing myself in the research and looking at the behaviours and patterns that everyone shares helps me to see that I'm not completely alone. Or, at least, I am, but everyone is at some stage.

Anyway, the site has really struck a chord. I receive an astonishing number of hits some days and, like Nat said, even the glossies and newspapers have picked up on my pieces recently – though they rather went to town on the whole 'who's behind the blog?' angle. This makes me even more grateful that I kept it anonymous – I'm not sure I'm up for becoming 'the face of loneliness'. As it is, I'm safe in the knowledge that it's only the Warriors who know that I'm the one behind the words.

My computer makes a chirruping sound and I nearly spill my wine in my haste to see what they both think.

Nathalie33: Sorry, I don't get why you're hesitating. This looks incredible!

SueSue52: It does look like an amazing opportunity Tori. But no pay? Not sure how that's going to help your current situation . . .

Nathalie33: Of course it is! She'll get fed and watered for free so won't need to spend any money, and she'll have the chance to take a break from everything else, including the big bad landlord. Tori, it'll give you some really interesting new content for the blog on top of the review they've asked for. And, let's face it, you could do with the help, what with everything you've been dealing with. Get some of that shit sorted, and all sorts of good things could happen for you.

I feel like I've been slapped. I shoot to my feet, plonk the laptop down unceremoniously on the coffee table and start to pace around my tiny living room.

Maybe Nat's got a point. I do need a break from everything, and getting some help to keep my head straight would be a massive bonus.

My heart's hammering, and I pause in my stomping to steady myself against the wall. I suck in a deep breath and try to calm down.

The laptop chirrups. They can wait. Just for a moment. I flop back down onto the sofa and, ignoring the chat, click back onto the tab for the retreat.

The words jump out at me: Healing, Mindfulness, Relationships, Grief. I scroll through some of the photos and gasp. Their beautiful stone farmhouse is set among green fields and wild flowers. There are photos of orchards in bloom, cosy campfires and a table laden with a gorgeous feast.

Three weeks.

What if other work comes through during that time? I'd risk missing out on paid jobs by being away. I drain my wine glass.

Perhaps I need to sleep on this. Again. The request's been in my inbox, unanswered, for at least a couple of weeks.

I click back through to the email and scan it again. Shit. I can't sleep on this. The bloody thing starts on Monday. It's currently Thursday – *night*. Balls. I'm *so* not good at making snap decisions. *Any* decisions actually.

Chirrup.

Nathalie33: You okay?

Nathalie33: Tori, I'm sorry. I didn't mean to upset you. Just thought it could be good for you.

HughTypesLikeAFlamingo: Subtle as ever, Nat! Nice job.

HughTypesLikeAFlamingo: Hi by the way :)

Nathalie33: Get lost, Hugh! Tori? Come back! Don't leave me hanging . . .

WriterTori: Sorry, I was just having another look at that link.

SueSue52: So? What do you think? Gonna go for it? These guys look like they know their stuff.

WriterTori: Don't think so. I can't afford to be out of action for 3 weeks.

Nathalie33: Ah, come on Tori, what have you got to lose?! It's the 21st century. You can keep on top of emails and everything while you're there, and if something new comes in, just fit it in around the course. Isn't that the joy of being self-employed?!

WriterTori: I don't know . . .

HughTypesLikeAFlamingo: Do it do it do it!

WriterTori: You really think so?

HughTypesLikeAFlamingo: Hell yeah! Like Nat said, you've got nothing to lose!

WriterTori: Okay, okay. Three against one. I'm in! I'll shoot them an email in the morning and see if it's still available.

Nathalie33: Why wait? Let them know now. You've been sitting on this long enough by the sound of it. Then they'll get it first thing tomorrow and you can organize everything ASAP.

SueSue52: Woohoo! Good for you Tori :) You have to promise to share all the gory details with us though . . .

WriterTori: Of course – you guys have to promise to be my lifeline.

HughTypesLikeAFlamingo: Aren't we always? ;)

WriterTori: Well, yeah. You're family and I don't know what I'd do without you.

Nathalie33: Let me know as soon as it's all confirmed!

WriterTori: Of course! Right, I'm off to write the email and then to bed . . . Looks like I'll be spending the weekend packing for a trip to Wales.

SueSue52: Whatever you do, don't forget your wellies!

I grin as I close down the chat tab. The smile feels unfamiliar on my face. It's been a while. Firing off a quick email to The

Farm, I tell them that one of the blog's reviewers has agreed to attend the course if their offer is still open. I hold my breath as I hit send.

Scrolling through the photographs of the retreat for one last time, I gaze at the beautiful countryside, fresh food and all that green. Yes. This could be perfect. Out of the city, away from my grumpy landlord and away from all those crappy memories.

I pad through to my bedroom, determined to get a decent night's sleep for once. If this works out, I've got a seriously busy couple of days ahead of me, and an even busier three weeks. I need to be ready to head off and leave everything for a while. But, then, that's the joy of still being footloose and fancy free at the grand old age of thirty-three.

Just as I'm snuggling down into my pillows, my phone buzzes with a new email alert. I fumble for it in the dark and glance at the screen, fully expecting it to be junk about erectile dysfunction or offering me hot sex with a Colombian beauty.

But no. It's the retreat centre. I sit up and swipe it open.

They're looking forward to welcoming the reviewer on Monday, and they want said reviewer to call The Farm in the morning to confirm details.

Holy shit, what have I let myself in for?

Chapter 2

Positive Is as Positive Does

'Every dawn brings a new challenge, but by going into the day with a positive mindset, you'll colour everything that follows with positivity.'

©TheBeginnersGuideToLoneliness.com

I hate trains.

Do you want to know what I hate even more than trains? Coaches.

I had to swap to what must be the most uncomfortable version of public transport available when my train terminated in Carmarthen, and for the past hour I've been trundling through the soggy depths of deepest, darkest Wales as if I'm on some kind of urgent mission.

I really don't want to be here.

'*Rhyn-Yr-Eithin* will be our next stop,' the driver mumbles into his microphone. 'Make sure you gather all your belongings, ladies and gents!'

About bloody time. I reach up and stretch out my spine, wincing slightly at every single crackle and pop that comes from sitting in one position for too long. Catching sight of my reflection in the grubby window, I rake my hands through my hair and try to tame my wayward mop.

Oh God, where have I landed myself?

All I've seen from the windows for the past hour has been green, green, green, sheep, more green . . .

Green is a highly overrated colour in my opinion.

As we come to a standstill, I struggle to my feet and thrust the course handbook I've been trying to binge-read into my handbag. I yank it roughly onto my shoulder and try not to bash people on the back of the head as I struggle down the narrow aisle. I manoeuvre my feet gingerly down the steep steps, conscious of my high heels and the looming gap between the coach and the kerb edge.

I really should stop taking fashion advice from people I've never met.

Sue thought it would be a good idea for me to turn up looking professional so that they take me seriously when I arrive. I've opted for a smart, slightly funky outfit. I haven't worn heels since I left my job at the ad agency and, frankly, if I'd had my way, I'd be in a pair of grubby Converse, but Sue nearly had a meltdown at the idea. As usual, I'd ended up trusting someone else's judgement above my own and Sue won. Hence the ridiculous heels that, right now, couldn't be more out of place if they tried.

Landing safely on the pavement, I look around to see the

driver hauling my little wheelie case out of the hold before dumping it onto the tarmac. I totter over and thank him. He simply raises his hand, hops back on the coach and, without ceremony, closes the door and drives away.

I can't help but quietly fume as I make my way over to the crumbling wooden bus shelter and lower myself down onto a cracked, plastic seat.

I sigh. This is exactly why I hate being given lifts. You always end up waiting around for hours for people to turn up. Plus, it's cold and I'm hungry and . . . well, I just feel like whining right now. And I need to pee. Why would anyone leave the comfort of London and come to bloody Wales? It's cold, it's raining and people are late.

I called The Farm as soon as was polite on Friday morning. I'm not too proud to admit that I begged them to be allowed to drive, and when that was refused because they're 'trying to do their bit for the environment', I tried arguing against being picked up from the bus stop, telling the man that I'd be happier getting a cab. This caused so much hilarity that I'd had to give in and agree to the lift. Now I can see why it was quite so funny: the idea of there being a taxi anywhere near here is . . . remote.

It's so quiet it's almost scary. Quiet, but very windy. I may as well have been airlifted into this green, hill-lined valley, because apart from this little shelter, there sure as hell isn't any other hint of civilization to be seen.

For what must be the hundredth time already, I glance back down the road, which snakes away between two grey-green hills that are clearly hoping to be mountains when they grow up.

There's a small cloud of dust, but nothing much else to see. I huddle down into my collar, trying to escape the chilly wind, and cross my legs tighter. There's no way I'm going to pee in a hedge, not on my first day living wild, and not on the last day either. I'm just not an al fresco pisser. The day that happens, this little trip has gone too far and I'll be making a break for freedom.

Ah, wait a minute, I think, *that cloud of dust is getting closer.* Could it be?

As I watch, a beaten-up Land Rover materializes and swings itself gracelessly onto the patch of gravel next to the bus stop.

'Victoria!' A huge smile followed by an awful lot of white whiskers appears from the driver's side of the vehicle.

'Yes, that's me. But it's Tori.' I smile tightly at this ill-groomed Father Christmas. I hold out my hand as he steps towards me, my heels causing me to tower over him. He catches my hand in both of his and gives it a rough-skinned squeeze.

'Great shoes!' he smiles down at my feet as if mesmerized.

'Erm . . . thanks.'

'I'm Ted. This is Frank,' he pats the side of the Land Rover. 'Let's get you back to the ranch,' he says, grabbing my case.

When they'd said 'Land Rover' on the phone, I'd pictured a lovely shiny Chelsea Chariot, the kind of vehicle that glamorous, platinum-blond mums use to drop their kids off at their very expensive private schools.

This is not one of those. There are only two words to describe it: Rust. Bucket.

It used to be khaki green, but has been repaired and patched so many times that the surface looks like it has bad acne scarring. There are patches of rusty red paint and blobs of white, presumably covering some botched mending. It looks as though there may be a fair bit of household gloss paint on there too. The canvas back is just as bad and appears to be mainly held together by moss and gaffer tape.

'Your carriage, madam . . .' To my horror, Ted yanks at the handle, throws open the door at the back of the vehicle and waves me in. 'Don't worry, it's not too far. I'd let you sit up front, but Dennis is in there and he won't move for man nor beast.'

'It's fine, no problem.' I force a smile. *He's got to be kidding?!*

The floor is covered with bits of straw and, well, poo. Dried poo, but still. Waving and nodding at me are four other people. Okay, so three are waving and nodding and the fourth one has his head back and appears to be fast asleep with his mouth open. Either that or he's dead and no one has noticed the smell yet.

'Everyone, this is Tori. Tori, everyone.' Ted smiles at me and swings my case up onto the floor.

'Do you need a boost?' asks Ted.

'Oh, right . . . err . . . no thanks, I'm fine.' I can't find any convenient handholds, so I try not to pull a face as I rest them on top of the filthy floor and attempt to get a foot up. But the shoes aren't helping, slipping and sliding on the rusted metal, the heel threatening to snag at any moment. I'm really starting to struggle when a hand appears in front of me. Without looking up, I grasp it. Just as it gives me a tug, I feel Ted's palm plant firmly on my behind and he gives me a hefty shove upwards.

I practically fly into the back of the Land Rover and land straight on top of the owner of the helping hand.

There's a grunt from the warm tangle of clothes and skin from underneath me.

I scramble backwards hastily.

'Hey, watch it!' comes an angry growl from a skinny teenager I just managed to pin against the canvas side.

'I'm so sorry!' I mutter, trying to keep my head down and my sweaty, horrified face to myself. *Shit, shit, shit.* Not the calm entrance I'd been hoping for.

'Hey. It's okay. Here, take a pew.' The pile of clothing I winded moments ago takes shape, shifts a beaten-up rucksack from the seat next to him and dumps it on the floor.

'Thanks,' I mutter. 'And sorry.'

'Don't worry.'

I'm relieved to hear a smile in his voice.

'I'm Bay.'

'Hi . . . I'm sorry about . . . your . . . uh . . .' I tail off. I am sorry, but I'm not sure which part of his anatomy I should be sorry about.

'It's fine. Stop apologizing. Frankly, I blame your shoes.'

'So, what—?' I start, but I'm interrupted by the spluttering of the engine being forced into life. And then the rattling starts. Bone-splintering vibrations run through the decrepit metal skeleton and threaten to dislocate my coccyx.

'Brace yourself!' shouts Bay, and I wonder what he means. 'For what?'

I can barely hear him over the engine, but, glancing around at the others, I can see that they're all stiffening in their seats.

Catching on just a moment too late, I pitch sideways as Ted guns the vehicle into a dizzying reversed arc.

'Twice in one day?' Bay yells in my ear, an amused look on his face. I peel myself out of his lap and resolutely try to anchor myself to the hard metal bench.

'Sorry . . . again!' I yell. My face is so hot it feels like it's on fire.

Bay rolls his eyes at me and shrugs good-naturedly. I look away, mortified.

In a desperate attempt to distract myself from the constant rattling playing tom-toms on my bladder, I look around at the other passengers.

The guy in the corner still has his head tilted back against the canvas, mouth wide open and fast asleep. The woman next to him looks to be somewhere in her late seventies. Her long silver hair is plaited and coiled all the way around her head. She is wearing an oversized, bright yellow jumper with a massive daisy on the front. Beneath this is a pair of faded, threadbare cord flares. Her hands are busy knitting something in a repulsive bright green, the yarn snaking from her needles and down to a huge ball that lies nestled in a wicker basket at her feet.

I look cautiously towards the girl I managed to trample and meet a pair of very stroppy brown eyes. I smile at her, but she simply blinks at me and continues to stare, her eyes wandering leisurely down over my fitted blazer and skinny black jeans. She lingers on the offending shoes that caused her the grievous bodily trampling just now.

Oh God, oh God, oh God! What have I let myself in for? I'm going to get Nat back for talking me into this, if it's the last thing I do.

Twenty minutes and six aborted attempts at conversation later, my knuckles have turned from white to blue in a bid to stay put in my pew-of-torture. My bum is completely numb, in beautiful contrast to the base of my spine, which is on fire from the continuous vibrations and multiple bashings, courtesy of every bump and stone on this godforsaken stretch of road. I'm considering screaming for mercy, or maybe even making a mad dash for the back door and hotfooting it back to Carmarthen in time to catch the next train back to London, when Bay leans in close.

'ALMOST HOME!' he yells in my ear. I nod and bite down firmly on my lip, letting out a tiny moan that instantly gets lost under the hammering of the engine.

Ted swings sharply to the right, hits the brakes and abruptly kills the engine. Two seconds later his face appears at the back of the cab.

'Okay, campers. I need two willing volunteers to walk the

rest of the way. Frank can't take this amount of weight on his suspension going down the track.' He grins as if this is the best news he has given all day. Bay immediately jumps down.

'Of course, when I say volunteers, I mean you, Tori. It's all in the handbook.' He glances at my feet, looking a bit concerned.

'Come on,' Bay says, holding out his hand to me.

'Handbook? Wait! What?'

'New arrivals walk the driveway. It's important that they enter the aura of the place in peace, so that their spirit fully integrates with the new surroundings,' Ted recites by rote. At least he has the decency to look a little bit sheepish.

'But . . .' I look down at the muddy puddles surrounding my perch. Two seconds ago I would have given anything to get out of the Land Rover. Now, I'm not so sure.

'Have you not read your handbook?' Bay asks me, a definite twinkle in his eye.

'Of course I have . . . most of it, anyway,' I say. Perhaps it would have been a good idea to spend less time arguing about clothes with Sue and more time reading all the material The Farm sent through to me after I spoke to them on Friday. I mean, I did scan through it on the way here, but I'm guessing I missed a few key points.

Ted's smile slips. 'Oh dear. Well, you have to walk on your first time. It's really important.'

'Come on,' Bay says impatiently.

I will be fine. My shoes, on the other hand, are about to die a horrible, muddy death and my Converse are buried right at the bottom of my bag.

'Here, borrow my boots.'

A pair of grim wellies land in my lap. Dead-guy is awake and in his socks. The boots reek and are covered in . . . crap. That's the only word for it.

'Um, thanks. I don't think these will fit you though,' I waggle one of my heels for him to see.

The guy peers curiously at me, obviously trying to figure out where I've come from and whether I'm sane. He seems to come to a conclusion fast enough as he starts to howl with laughter, his head thrown back.

An eerie sound echoes his howl from somewhere in the front of the Land Rover.

'Dennis!!!' bellow five people as one. The howling stops.

'Great. You have boots. Job done.' Ted beams and hurries back to the driver's seat. As he coaxes the engine back to life, my spine instantly sets up a protest. Slip-sliding to my feet, boots in one hand and handbag in the other, I shuffle across to the doorway, but before I can even begin to negotiate my way down, Bay reaches up and jumps me down like a five-year-old.

Chapter 3

A is for Approachable

'One of the biggest challenges in escaping isolation is breaking free of habits. What started out as useful defence mechanisms are now patterns that play a large part in keeping the world out – and may be preventing you from forming new bonds and friendships.'

©TheBeginnersGuideToLoneliness.com

'Come on then, princess, let's be having you,' Bay grins as he sets me down. 'Do you need a hand?' He holds his arm out, ready to steady me so that I can slip the wellingtons on more easily.

'Thanks, princess, but I'll be fine on my own!' I snap. Why does my inner bitch always show up when I meet new people? I really wanted to start out on a better note. Too late now.

'Fine. Holler if you need me. I'll go on ahead.' Bay shoots me a tight smile that really doesn't reach his eyes. Oops. He turns his back and trudges off, following the trail of blue smoke from the Land Rover.

For a second, I just stand and stare at his departing back. Half of me wants to call after him, to apologize, to introduce myself properly and let him get to know the real me rather than this prissy little madam that seems to have body-snatched me. The other half of me, however, the one that *is* that prissy little madam, is still desperate to show him that she's fine without his stupid help. This part of me wins, like it always does when I'm feeling nervous and out of my depth. It's my version of body armour.

I dump the disgusting wellington boots down into the mud in front of me and wobble as I prize one of my hot, over-travelled feet out of a heel and plunge it into the loaned boot. I manage to gather a decent toe-scoop of mud while I'm at it. Great. Just bloody great. Go it alone and get covered in mud. Typical.

Thrusting on the other boot unceremoniously, I cuddle my heels to me and follow Bay. I really don't want to get lost on top of everything else. Slipping and sliding in the mud, I keep my eyes firmly on the ground to stop myself from going arse-over-tit. I'm so intent on what I'm doing that I suddenly slam with full force into something solid.

'Do I have "hurt me" stamped on my forehead or something?' asks Bay as he catches hold of my arm, stopping me from face-planting as I lose my balance.

'Sorry! Sorry!' I wheeze, winded from the impact. I glare at him, unsure whether to let rip with anger or give in to giggles, as both seem to be bubbling. A pair of moss-green eyes are twinkling at me from under his mop of dark, wavy hair. I quickly decide anger is the safest route. 'I wasn't expecting there to be a human pillar in my path, doing absolutely nothing.'

'See, that's the problem with you city girls. Your eyes are always down, watching your feet or your phone.'

'What's that supposed to mean?' I snap. Like he knows anything about me. Git.

'It means that you run headlong into a lot of trouble without seeing it coming. And, worse than that, it means you miss the view.'

I scowl at him and then look around. The lane is flanked on one side by a steep wall of slate and mud, with the occasional tree just about managing to cling to it. But Bay is looking in the opposite direction, to where the ground just seems to disappear. What looks like a cliff edge is actually the side of a steep valley. I find myself looking out over a rooftop of trees that must be growing on the lower edges of the slope. Piles of steely clouds march off into the distance, creating a blanket under which nestles a patchwork of fields. A narrow, leaden ribbon of river snakes its way across the valley floor. I shiver and rub my arms. As if in response, a ray of sunshine pierces the clouds just for a second, turning a bend in the river to silver and illuminating everything around it.

'You see, I wasn't "doing nothing". I was looking. It's a perfectly wonderful thing to be doing. Until you're walked into by an angry Londoner.'

I choose to ignore the dig. I can't believe I almost missed this.

'Thank you.' The words come out of my mouth, but, trust me, they are completely unintentional. I quickly make up for them: 'Do you mind if we get on with it though?' That's more like it.

Bay rolls his eyes at me. 'Sure. Come on. It's not far.' He continues his trudge and I slide along behind him, desperately trying to keep one eye on where I place my feet while I continue to sneak peeks at the view.

Pretty soon, the lane begins to descend steeply, carving its way through an avenue of giant trees. I catch up to Bay's side.

'So, is this your first time here too?' I ask, trying to start again.

He laughs. 'Nah, I've been coming here for years, at least once every six months. It's the perfect way to reset myself.'

'So you walked because . . . ?'

'Because I didn't want Frank to fall apart on the lane,' he smiles back at me.

'So the others have been before too?'

'Moth has – she was the one knitting. And Russ, the guy who lent you the boots, he's one of the instructors.'

I nod and swallow nervously. Surely I'm not going to be the only one new to this?

'So . . . ah . . . where are all the others?'

'Oh, they've been arriving since yesterday morning. I think they're only waiting for one more newbie now that you're here, and then everyone's present and correct.'

As we come to the edge of the woodland and reach the valley floor, we pass through a huge, five-barred gate.

'To keep the inmates in?' I ask with raised eyebrows.

Bay grins at me. 'To keep the world out, more like.' He swings the gate back into place and secures it with a loop of plaited, orange twine.

'So this is it? We're here?' There's a note of desperation in my voice. My bladder is now officially at breaking point. I need to empty it in the next two minutes to avoid sustaining a horrific injury.

'Almost. This path runs straight up to the main house. You carry on. I need to head off this way to sort a few things out,' he points to a field to our left.

'Oh. Okay. Thanks for your help.' *He's leaving me alone now? Seriously?*

'Sure thing. See you later!' And with that, Bay strides off, following the line of the trees.

I watch him go and shift my weight from foot to foot. It would be great to take a look around while I've got a moment to myself (who knows whether I'm going to get any peace over the next three weeks?), but the call of my bladder has now gone from an annoying mutter to a constant scream. I let out a defeated sigh and head off up the pathway in search of the house.

It's not long before I spot it. It's absolutely massive and looks a bit like it's grown straight up out of the ground. Built from heavy grey stone, it's two storeys high with a navy front door that stands open underneath a slate-roofed porch. This is flanked by stone pillars, and at either side of the porch are large mullioned windows. The top floor boasts three more windows in a straight line. As deep as it is wide, this is a proper, old-fashioned farmhouse like something straight out of a kids' book, an impression that's only strengthened by the fact that the place is surrounded by brown and white chickens, all scratching around on the front lawn.

I wander up to the front door, side-stepping a couple of the braver birds who aren't about to get out of my way, and pause. What should I do? Knock? Go straight in? Call out? Deciding on two of the three, I hammer on the open door and shout.

'Hello? It's Tori!'

No one appears. Oh, for heaven's sake.

'Hello?!' I yell a bit louder. *I can't just walk in, can I?*

There's a creaking sound behind me followed by a crash that makes me jump in fright. I take a shaky step backwards to see what made the noise and notice that the window to my left has just been thrown open with so much force it bashed straight into the wall and is now swinging on its hinges. Ted's smiling face appears and regards me with some curiosity.

'Hello. Can I help?'

I laugh. 'Oh, thank God, it is the right place!'

Ted raises his eyebrows. 'Right place for what?'

'It's Tori?' I say slowly. 'You just picked me up from the bus stop?'

He stares at me blankly. *What, does he have amnesia or something?*

'Yes?' he sounds unconvinced.

'I'm here for the retreat?' I say.

'And what do you want to do that for?'

Good question, Ted. Right now, all I want is to be back in my flat where the world makes sense behind my computer screen. I chew my lip and consider my options for escape.

'Well?' Ted asks, watching me closely, as if I might trample his flower beds and steal a chicken or two while I'm at it.

'I want . . . I want . . .' Oh shit, what was that line I spotted in the handbook earlier? I wrack my brain. 'I want to . . . to find inner peace?' Nope, that wasn't it. 'I want to start moving mountains by picking up the small stones in my life.' Yes . . . that was it.

Ted is beaming at me. 'That is a good answer. I know because I wrote it . . . Well, actually, Confucius did first and I borrowed it . . . But what's *your* answer?'

Oh great. A comedian. I let out a long sigh as it dawns on me in a rush exactly what I've let myself in for. I'm actually going to have to share stuff with these people. Personal stuff. The stuff that hurts. Something deep inside me feels like it caves in.

'I would like to find out what you're all about here. And if I can learn even one tiny thing that makes my life better, I'll count it a worthwhile stay.'

'That is an honest and humble answer, Victoria. Welcome. Come on in.'

I bristle at the use of my full name, but as I go to correct him, I find that the window has closed and the smiling face has disappeared.

Not wanting to be the one to tread inches of crap into my host's house, I'm just slipping off my borrowed boots in the porch when a figure looms in front of me.

'I'm sorry about Ted,' says a soft voice. 'He can be a tad overly dramatic at times, but I guess that's why I love him! I'm Lizzie.'

I straighten up and come face to face with a breathtakingly beautiful woman. She has a mass of strawberry-blond hair that tumbles around her face and down her back. Here and there I can see combs in it that appear to be losing a desperate battle to keep the heavy strands in some kind of order. She has clear, blue eyes and is absolutely massive. At least eight months pregnant. So pregnant, in fact, that I find myself holding my breath just in case breathing might set her off.

'I'm Tori,' I smile at her. It's impossible not to, really. I hold out my hand, but Lizzie grabs it and pulls me in for a hug. Unused to random strangers demanding physical contact, I stiffen in the awkward embrace, desperate to avoid the unexploded time-bomb between us.

Lizzie laughs. 'Sorry, this is getting in the way more and more.' She pulls away and pats her bump affectionately. 'Do you have little ones?'

'No. No. Not really.' *Not really? What kind of answer is that? What, are there imaginary kids following me around?* 'I mean, no. I've not met the right man and I'm just not ready and . . .' This is getting worse. *Stop. Talking.* 'Erm, how long . . . ?' I stare worriedly at the bump.

'Due any time after the end of next week. Hey, you might be here! That's so exciting!'

My smile freezes on my face. *What? I'm going to be here?* Okay . . . I'll be here. That's got to be at least thirty miles away from the nearest hospital. That's a decent distance from all the pain and screaming. Thirty miles should just about muffle the noise.

As if it's responding with advanced sympathy pains, my bladder gives an agonizing twitch.

'Sorry . . . do you mind if I use your bathroom? I've been on that coach for what feels like an eternity . . .'

'Gosh, you poor thing. And then Ted's driving! I'd have peed myself. I'm in there every five minutes at the moment. When I was pregnant with my first . . .'

Argh, I'm going to have to gag the woman before I find the bloody toilet. 'I'm kind of desperate,' I interrupt, mortified, but I guess a puddle would be a lot worse.

'Sorry! Just at the end of the hall there. Read the instructions!'

I shoot off as fast as my desperate waddle will allow.

'Come and join us in the kitchen and meet the other guys as soon as you're done,' I hear her call after me.

Desperately hoping my bladder hasn't ruptured, I push my way through the doorway and plonk myself onto the loo with a sigh of relief.

The relief is short-lived, though. I do up my jeans and turn to reach for the flush . . . which isn't there. What on earth? Lizzie's words come back to me. *Read the instructions.* Peering around, I spot a hand-painted wooden sign hanging from a nail in the wall. It reads: 'Lovely visitor, you are relieved. Press the orange button for pee, the red for poo. This system uses rainwater harvested from our roof.' *Orange button . . . orange button . . .* Ah, there it is. I press it and an almighty racket of groaning pipes forces me to cover my ears and back away as a torrent of slightly discoloured water pours into the bowl.

I catch sight of myself in the mirror as I carefully wash my hands and sigh at the bedraggled reflection that stares back at me. I hastily pull my hair back into a spare elastic from my pocket.

While I'm here, I may as well let the guys know I've arrived safely.

WriterTori: Here safe. What a palaver!

Nathalie33: What's everyone like?

WriterTori: Don't know. Haven't met them yet. Currently hiding in the loo. Flushes with rainwater!! ;)

SueSue52: Too cool! Go on then, Tori, get out there and meet all the other weirdos.

WriterTori: Calling me a weirdo?

Nathalie33: Well, if the shoe fits . . .

WriterTori: Don't talk to me about shoes, I had to borrow a pair of wellies.

SueSue52: I told you to pack some!

WriterTori: You also told me to wear heels to make a good impression, so you don't get to comment! Wish you guys were here.

SueSue52: We'll be with you every step of the way.

Nathalie33: Heads up, busy few weeks ahead of me, will be a bit quieter on here than normal.

WriterTori: You're going to abandon me in my hour of need?!

Nathalie33: Of course not, I'll be right by your side. Just didn't want you to worry about me if you notice I'm not online as much :)

WriterTori: Thanks, Nat!

SueSue52: Have fun!

Nathalie33: Good luck, keep us posted!

WriterTori: Catch you later.

I slip my phone back in my pocket and unlock the door. Here goes nothing . . .

Chapter 4

Be the Change

'To make a change, you have to be the change. Do something differently. Take a different route, visit a new coffee shop, speak to someone new. Every little change you make is an opportunity to set your day on a different path.'

©TheBeginnersGuideToLoneliness.com

I head back out into the hallway and follow the muffled hum of conversation to what I assume must be the kitchen. Taking a deep breath, an all-too familiar sensation washes over me and settles in my chest: nerves. Horrible, crippling nerves. I swallow down the urge to run and, pushing open the door, step into a large kitchen.

It's like something straight out of a magazine's design pages . . . or it would be if it were tarted up a bit. As it stands, its beautiful slate floor is almost entirely covered with old rag-rugs, thrown down higgledy-piggledy between the mismatched furniture. There's an ancient Aga sandwiched between cupboards topped with different work surfaces, one side marble, the other an offcut of melamine. The cupboard doors have a random assortment of handles, from intricate wrought-iron affairs to small lengths of rope. Here and there, just a bare, rusty screw sticks out.

Over in the corner is a hulking, dark wooden dresser, groaning under the weight of family photographs, thank-you cards and assorted odds and ends.

My heart flutters uncomfortably as I turn to meet the dozen or so pairs of eyes trained on me from around the long, scrubbed pine table that dominates the centre of the room. This is it then.

I'm not really sure where to look, but I force a smile, painfully aware that it probably looks like I've got a bad case of wind.

'Everyone, this is Victoria,' says Ted from his perch at the table. 'Budge up and make room for her so we can get started.'

I flinch. Mum was the only one who ever used my full name, and it still makes my skin prickle. Now's not the time to start thinking about Mum. I've already got enough to deal with. I wipe my sweaty palms on my jeans.

'Hi,' I squeak, and slip into a chair that has been pulled up to a tiny gap at the table. 'It's Tori . . . at least to friends,' I say. God, I sound like such a knob.

'Tori it is then,' says Lizzie, coming up behind me and passing a mug of some kind of strong-smelling herbal tea over my shoulder. 'We're all friends here from day one.'

'Okay, guys,' Ted says, drawing himself up, his hand-knitted, bobbly brown jumper pulling tight across his rounded stomach. 'I'm not going to go around and introduce everyone now; we can save that for our welcoming circle this evening. But just so that you're all aware, we're still missing one person from our group, but he'll be here in time for this evening's session. Oh, and Bay is off sorting out a couple of last-minute errands – but you've met him already. He's done this course so many times that he could recite this little meet-up by heart!

'Now, I just want to go over a few practicalities about your stay with us. There shouldn't be too many surprises as it's all in your handbooks, but there are a couple of things I'd like to clarify.'

I clasp my hands tightly around my mug of tea. Truth time. I wonder how many more little gems I managed to miss during my skim-read earlier.

'Lizzie,' continues Ted, 'why don't you start, my love, and we'll take it in turns?' Ted smiles at his wife and I can see that he's glad to be at the start of a well-rehearsed routine.

'Okay then,' says Lizzie, easing herself down into a chair. 'Number one. As you know, you won't be staying in the house with us. This retreat is all about self-discovery and self-acceptance – re-connecting with yourself so that you can move forward in your relationships and forge new, authentic connections. To start to do this, you need to live in the wild with your own thoughts. I know some of you have opted for the camping option, which is lovely. We've gone through your course questionnaires and have allocated sites for you.

We've done our best to match up your location with your personal and emotional needs.'

A buzz of excitement runs around the table. Moth, the long-haired knitter, nudges my elbow and grins at me. I smile back.

I wonder if she can see the pure terror on my face.

'Sam and Emma,' Ted smiles at an extremely young couple that exude the kind of shiny, happy beauty that only comes from being in your late teens, 'as you guys are here on honeymoon, you've been given the eco-build. We hope that this special space will help you connect for a long and happy future.'

Emma throws her arm around Sam's shoulders and snuggles her face into his neck. Sam flushes bright red, looking decidedly uncomfortable at the public display of affection.

'You three will be in South Wood,' continues Ted, gesturing to the three guys directly opposite me. All of them have impressive beards, two have dreadlocks, and there's an awful lot of hemp and leather on display. 'The materials you need to create your own shelters are there, as requested.' A cloud of patchouli wafts across the table as all three of them quiver with excitement.

Heart. Now. Hammering. *Build* our own shelters? Holy crap . . . there's no way I'm up for that. It's probably going to be even worse for me, I was so late getting back to them. Ted did mention on the phone that they might need to make some special arrangements. *Oh no, it's going to be sharing a sleeping bag with the chickens, isn't it?!*

36

'Tori, I know you don't have the energy for camping . . .'

They got that from my questionnaire? I bristle a bit as my natural competitive streak starts to kick in, but then I give a little mental shrug. Does it really matter as long as it means I don't have to build my own earth hut or sleep in a leaky tent?

'We've decided that the best thing for you is to take the yurt in Seven Acre field. You won't be on your own, though, as we'd already offered the space to one of our regulars, so you'll be sharing.'

'Sharing? Oh, okay . . . um . . . okay . . .' Shit, I wasn't expecting that. Then again, maybe a bit of company isn't the worst thing in the world, considering I'm going to be stuck in the middle of nowhere for three weeks.

As Lizzie and Ted continue to dole out the camp sites, I brood on how I'm going to cope with the whole sharing thing. I haven't lived with anyone since I left home, and I did that as promptly as I possibly could, so you could say that it's been quite a while since I've had to deal with anyone in my space. Markus and I never quite got around to actually living together before everything went tits up.

'Okay, so that's everyone!' Ted smiles. 'When we're done here we'll go for a walk and drop you off at your sites. Then you can make yourselves at home, or, in some cases, *make* your homes, before we all meet up again this evening.' I roll my eyes as he beams at his own joke. 'All food is supplied, and you will be expected to cook together at the outdoor station most evenings. You will not be permitted entry into the house again during your stay, except for in an emergency. There are basic facilities located close to all of your sites, except for those of you in the woods – you will make your own.' The trio opposite me, whom I promptly dub the Beardy Weirdies, all nod eagerly, clearly excited at the thought of crapping in a hole.

'We would like to request that you refrain from using any scented deodorant, antiperspirant, perfumes or chemical-based lotions while you're here. No cosmetics please. These will impede your progress and are disrespectful to the land and to each other.'

No. Nonononononono. Just as I think they can't get any worse, I feel my nerves ramp up another notch. I guess I could deal with the lack of make-up – after all, it's not like there's anyone here who's going to care what I look like, but moisturizer and deodorant? Surely they are basic human rights?

'Finally, I need you all to turn in your phones, blackcurrants, laptops . . .'

'Ted, love, I think you mean BlackBerries,' Lizzie interrupts, rolling her eyes.

'Right, right. Well, turn in all electrical gadgets, whether named after fruit or not.'

My eyes widen in shock. *What? WHAT?*

'*What?*' Damn, one of them has escaped.

Everyone's eyes swivel in my direction, and I'm pretty sure I spot a few raised eyebrows. I definitely spot a look exchanged between Ted and Lizzie.

'Sorry, I . . . erm . . . I meant to say, could you tell us a bit more about what made you decide to bring in this rule?'

There. I think I've just about managed to cover my behind . . . maybe.

'First of all, we don't really do rules. Think of them more as suggestions that we hope you'll take on board while accepting our hospitality,' Lizzie says, sounding a lot less earth mother and a lot more like a slightly pissed off librarian. 'But yes, I can certainly explain the idea,' she continues, her voice settling back into its honeyed tones. 'Each of you is here for some form of healing. You all have blocks that are preventing you from connecting fully and authentically to your lives. These might be emotional, creative,' she looks around the table, 'or mental,' she adds, turning back to me.

Way to out us all in one breath! I peep around at the others, and pretty much everyone is fixated on the table in front of them.

'You have decided to take this retreat from your lives in order to concentrate on your healing. It is our responsibility to remove the uncentring influences of the outside world. We do not want your progress impaired by the constant flow of bile that runs through communications devices. Whether you're watching the news, talking to work colleagues or being harassed by family members, your thought processes are changed by each interaction. And so we remove this interruption to your healing.'

'What if we need to check on someone . . . family . . . ?' asks a woman from across the table. She looks decidedly out of place with her tight perm and fuchsia lipstick, sandwiched in between one of the Beardy Weirdies and Ted. A few of the others shift uncomfortably. Seems I'm not the only one who's not completely thrilled with the idea of being cut off from civilization.

'The handbook says to leave the main house number here as your emergency contact,' says Lizzie smoothly.

'I did. But my mother's in a home. She often gets confused. They might need to call us,' says the woman tremulously.

'If they do call, we are here to help,' smiles Lizzie. 'If someone calls for any of you, we will decide if it's a matter of importance strong enough to interrupt your healing process.'

The woman smiles and nods at Lizzie, visibly relaxing in the knowledge that someone else is taking the responsibility out of her hands. I'm not so sure I'd be so chilled about it if it were me, but then I haven't got a single soul who'll worry about me while I'm away other than the Warriors. Crap. I hadn't thought of that. How am I going to keep them updated without an internet connection?

Ted stands and makes his way around the table, handing everyone a cotton bag and a paper luggage label. 'Okay, before you all head back outside, please make sure that all of your gadgets go in here. We advise you to leave all of your valuables in these bags too. We can all trust each other here, but we can't guarantee the safety of any belongings apart from those stored in these bags, which will be placed in our safe this afternoon and returned to you when you leave.'

Everyone starts to rummage in pockets and bags, placing items in the little cloth sacks before handing them over and heading back outside. I heave a huge sigh and place my wallet, mobile and iPad into the sack. I'm not wearing any jewellery, but I reach down, pick up my shoes and place them gently on top of the gadgets. Then a flash of inspiration hits. Glancing around me to double-check I'm not going to be overheard, I edge my way over to Lizzie.

'Erm, I know you said you'd supply stock photos to protect everyone's privacy, but as a reviewer, will I be able to keep hold of my iPad to take notes?' I ask hopefully.

'We've thought about that,' she says with a smile and passes me a bag. I take a quick peep. *Seriously?* I've just been handed a notebook and pen.

'There you go!' she smiles at me triumphantly.

Damn. Well, I'll just have to figure it out later. There's bound to be a computer somewhere around here that I can sneak onto to send a quick message when no one's looking.

Chapter 5

Go with the Flow

'Isolation can cause you to overthink. Every single step of
the day is inspected for anything that might go wrong.
Ultimately, this can mean that you don't take many steps at
all. Learn to go with the flow, take one step at a time and
set yourself free.'

©TheBeginnersGuideToLoneliness.com

The group ahead of me comes to a halt. We've reached a
wooden cabin which sits in a small clearing at the edge of the
apple orchard. The sight and the scent of the apple blossom is
quite something, and we've all been wandering along, looking upwards with smiles on our faces. Smiling's not something I was expecting to be doing quite so soon after being
forcibly parted from my phone. But this really is beautiful.

The hut looks a little bit like a rustic woodshed, but, in
comparison to a leaky tent, it's practically a palace. In front of
us are the remains of a little outdoor fire within a ring of

stones, over which hangs a blackened kettle from a metal frame. Perfect, as long as you're not after a quick cuppa . . .

'Geoff and Doreen, welcome to your new home. I hope you'll find everything you need for a very comfortable stay with us. There's running water just around the side of the cabin.'

The woman with the perm and the fuchsia lipstick hurries forward to take a look around, her husband following at a more leisurely pace. Around me, there's a lot of excited muttering and nodding. It's clear that everyone's looking forward to seeing their own quarters if they're all going to be as nice as this.

'Ted, it's lovely,' Doreen grins, coming to stand at the doorway after a quick scout around her new home. 'One thing. Where's the loo?'

'Very good question. I always forget that part. See over there?' he points off into the trees a little way. 'There's a little hut? That's your toilet. It's a composting loo. Just dump a handful of wood shavings in after . . . well . . .'

'Dumping?' provides Doreen, her perm quivering.

'Precisely,' Ted beams at her. A little titter runs around the group. I don't see it as a laughing matter, frankly. What did I say about al fresco pooing?

'Right, we'd better get going. Everyone needs to be settled in with enough time to spare before this evening's session. You two get comfy. See you later.'

As we leave Doreen and Geoff behind, I somehow feel like I've lost my last link to the real world. Rather than gossiping with the others, I walk quietly, trying to keep my bearings while tuning in and out of everyone else's conversations.

We soon head uphill and make our way through a patch of woodland. It's a little bit like the newly planted woods we walked through earlier, but fast-forwarded by twenty years. The grass between the trees is gone and the ground is covered by a soft, leafy litter, dotted here and there with clusters of tiny flowers.

Soon we're in a circular clearing with a fire pit at its centre, but there's no hut to be seen.

'Right, the three of you who've opted for the self-build option, this is where we leave you,' Ted says. He looks over at the Beardy Weirdies.

'There are only two rules. Set up more than fifteen paces away from the fire, and absolutely no felling of any live wood. I planted this woodland by hand over twenty years ago when we first came here. It's my first love and anyone who damages it will feel my wrath.'

I force down a giggle at the thought of the smiley, slightly distracted Ted smiting anyone down with his wrath. It's not an image that comes to mind readily.

Ted's still glaring around, and he does briefly seem to lose his fuzzy, hand-knitted edges, but still, hardly the thing of nightmares.

'There are plenty of stacks of seasoned firewood and brash piles for you to make your homes out of. Next to the fire pit, there's a limited supply of rope and a few tools to get you started. I've marked the site for your bog over there. I didn't want you to accidentally come across the one from the last group! Have fun, guys. See you later.'

Next we drop Moth off at a campsite, where there are already a couple of tents pitched, followed by Emma and Sam at their eco-build cabin. Finally, I'm left on my own with Ted.

'What if the weather changes?' I ask. It's something I've been wondering about as we've been walking. 'What will those guys in the wood do if it gets bad?'

'The closeness to the elements adds a deeper note of connection to the soul for those who choose to look for it.' He clears his throat and I see him glance sideways at me. 'We've found that if the weather gets really bad, everyone makes very good friends very quickly, as the loan of a cabin floor becomes rather sought after.' He grins at me, eyes twinkling, evidently aware of the mischief that these sleeping arrangements can lead to.

'Now then, let's get you to your abode.'

'Great,' I reply lamely. I've still got to meet my roommate, and I've got a knot of anxiety building in my stomach.

'It's a big space, and can easily be divided up by hanging some sheets if you need to.'

'Great, that's great.' I seem to have got stuck on a loop.

We come to the top of a little rise and I spot it: my home for the next three weeks. I let out a breath. I can handle this. It's a large round tent with a domed roof covered in canvas. In front of it, a collection of handmade, wooden furniture sits around the obligatory fire pit.

As we approach, I spot another little hut some distance away. That must be the toilet.

45

'You should find the yurt very comfortable. There are a couple of rules that come with living here, but I've got quite a bit to do before this evening – Lizzie can barely waddle at the moment! – so I'm going to leave you in Bay's very capable hands.'

WHAT?

Ted turns and begins to head back in what I assume is the direction of the main house. I'm too shocked to say anything and so I just stare, open-mouthed at his retreating back, digesting this new piece of information. *Bay?* As in, the guy I've already managed to injure *three times*?

'Ted,' I call, 'did you say Bay?'

Ted swings around, looking anxious. 'Yup. He said that he wouldn't mind sharing, and as we had no more cabins left, it was either this or make you camp. We thought you'd be happier staying here.'

'Is there no way I can stay in the house with you guys?' I'm aware I sound a bit pathetic, but there's no way I want to share with Bay.

'Nope. Sorry. That would completely undermine the whole purpose of this exercise. This is perfect for you. Unless you really do want to camp? We have spare roll-mats, tents and sleeping bags . . .'

I can see his eyes twinkling, and for a second I'm tempted to accept, just to wipe the smile off of his face. But I can't. Composting toilets *and* a tent? Not happening.

'No, this is fine,' I concede gracelessly.

'Great.' Ted twinkles at me, turns and continues on his way.

'I promise I won't bite.'

The new voice makes me jump. I swing around and see Bay's head sticking out of the little front door flap of the yurt.

'You'd better not, or I'll sue!' I shoot back. It's meant to be a joke, but comes out of my mouth more like a spear. Bay doesn't seem to care, though. He shrugs and gives me an easy grin.

'Come on in and make yourself comfortable.' His head disappears back inside, leaving me with no other option but to follow him.

Great. This is just *great*. No sooner have I got my poor little brain around the fact that I'm going to be sharing my living space with another human being, I find out I've got to share with a man. Okay, I'm an adult, I can get over that fact. But why does it have to be *this* man, who's already made it clear that he finds me incredibly annoying, and . . .

Oh wow.

As I stick my head through the flap, my jaw drops, cartoon style. It is absolutely beautiful in here. The curved sides are made from a concertina of honey-coloured wood and the roof is held up with a hooped structure of the same stuff. The floor is covered by about fifty brightly patterned rugs. There are sleeping areas at either side of the space complete with two futon-style beds. In the middle of the yurt, there's a squashy old settee with a low table in front of it.

'Welcome to my humble abode!' smiles Bay, noticing that I've let my guard down. 'Your humble abode too for the next few weeks.'

I smile at him weakly, not really knowing what to say or do next. 'Uh, thanks . . .' I start, rather lamely. 'Sorry, I didn't realize I'd be staying with you . . . I mean . . . I . . .'

'It's fine, don't worry,' he cuts me off. 'It was all a little bit last minute and this was the best solution.' He smiles at me warmly and I just nod.

'Ted said there are some rules?'

'Sure. It's simple really. Don't wear outdoor shoes in here because of all of the rugs. A bit of chicken shit takes forever to locate. Don't smoke inside. Don't go to the loo inside. That's about it. Oh, and preferably don't wake the dog. He hates being disturbed.'

'Dog?' I squeak.

'Ah. Didn't they check that with you?'

'Um, no.'

It's not that I'm scared of dogs, I just have a healthy respect for them. I respect the fact that they'll bite me if I go anywhere near them. When I was little, I begged Mum over and over again for a dog. I had no brothers or sisters, and it was just me and Mum in the house. I was desperate for someone to play with, and the idea of a furry friend took root in my imagination. That lasted until it got on my mum's nerves and she decided to tell me all about the horrors of rabies, scaring me senseless with tales of infected dog bites and horrific injuries that needed stitches. All of her stories ended up with the dog being shot. I went off the idea pretty quickly after that.

'You're not just sharing with me, I'm afraid. You're sharing with Dennis too,' says Bay. 'He's usually a big softy, but I think he's going to be a bit put out. See, your bed is usually *his* bed. I keep trying to get him off of it, but he's stubborn like that.'

'Oh great. So which one's supposed to be my bed?'

'The one with the great big dog on it?' he smiles at me apologetically and nods to the far side of the yurt.

I hadn't spotted him before because he is stretched out on a brown blanket and is so relaxed that he has moulded into the bed and has become a part of the furniture.

'Dennis! Here!' Bay pats his leg, but the dog doesn't budge. 'Dennis, don't make me come over there!' Bay lets out a sharp whistle, making me jump. Dennis deigns to lift his head. His piggy little eyes glance in our direction, his tail thumps on the blanket once and then he flops back down and appears to be asleep again almost instantly.

'Ah, what can you do? He knows who's boss here, and it sure as hell isn't me,' Bay smiles indulgently and shrugs.

Great. I'm going to have to do battle with a canine road-block. This is hardly going to be 'restful on the spirit'.

'What kind of dog is he?' I ask, not because I'm that interested, but because it seems like the polite thing to say.

'English bull terrier. Beautiful, isn't he? I couldn't resist that much attitude piled into one dog. Anyway, make yourself at home.'

I smile tightly at him, cross over to the bed and stare down at the unwelcome guest.

Correction: *I'm* the unwelcome guest.

He's a chunky mish-mash of brown and white splotches, with a bent snout and funny little eyes.

'Bay, why don't we just swap beds? At least then you'll be sharing with someone you know,' I say hopefully.

'I can't sleep on the west side. Sorry.'

'Oh. Um. Okay.'

'It's fine, don't worry. I'll make sure he gets down when you want to go to bed. He's house-trained, you don't need to worry about that. And he's been in the river today, so he's fairly clean.'

I dither around, wondering what exactly I'm supposed to do until the mythical welcoming ceremony in a couple of hours. After the initial, obligatory small talk with Bay, we've both fallen silent. I don't want to bug him. After all, I'm in his space and he's probably far from happy about it, even though he has been pretty gracious so far.

Eventually, Bay makes his excuses, saying that he'd better go and help Ted get everything ready. Before he leaves, he checks that I'm going to be able to find my way back to the little courtyard behind the house in time for six o'clock.

After he's gone, it's a couple of seconds before I realize that, as well as telling a complete lie about knowing my way back to the house, my only method of telling the time was my phone. I hotfoot it back outside and shout after him.

Bay looks back at me, amusement dancing in his eyes.

'Don't tell me you've already forgotten how to get back down there?'

'Of course not.' I'm not going to give him any such pleasure. 'You don't have a clock in any of your stuff, do you? My phone's in the safe . . .'

'You don't have a watch?'

'Uh . . . nope . . .'

'And I'm taking it that you can't tell the time by the position of the sun?' he continues, the corner of his lips twitching up into a half smile.

'See previous answer,' I huff.

Bay raises his arm and begins to fumble with the battered strap of an old-fashioned man's watch. 'Here, wear this. Look after it, though. It used to be my father's.'

Before I have the time to register my surprise, he's reaching for my hand and proceeds to gently fasten the worn leather around my wrist.

'How will you know when it's time?' I ask, my voice all husky. I cringe. Oh, for heaven's sakes. A little bit of physical contact and I'm all wibbly? *Really?*

'See previous question,' he shoots back cheekily, and sets off again.

'Thank you!' I call after him, but rather quieter than is necessary to actually reach his ears.

As I turn back to the yurt, my mind is racing. I'm not used to random acts of kindness, especially not from a complete stranger whose home I've invaded. I gaze around, still trying to fathom how on earth I'm going to manage to share the space with Bay for a whole three weeks. We've got nothing in common and nothing to talk about. The last few hours of almost complete silence have proved that.

Maybe I should ask him if we can divide the space like Ted suggested earlier. It was an absolute nightmare trying to change just now without giving him an eyeful.

And then, of course, there's the dog.

Shit! The dog! Dennis is still asleep on my bed, completely oblivious to the fact that his master has gone off without him. How could Bay forget him?

I dash back out of the tent to call Bay back again, but he's long gone and nowhere to be seen.

'Damn!' I turn and stomp back into the yurt to face my newly inherited, rather hairy problem . . . who is now wide awake.

Okay, this is going from bad to worse. Or maybe not. At least now I don't have to decide whether to wake him up or not.

'Hello. Hi, boy,' I croon, my voice wavering. I try to stay as still as possible, but he's now regarding me with grudging interest through those piggy little eyes. 'Hi, boy . . .' I say again, edging one step in his direction.

The dog thumps his tail twice on the bedspread and, yawning widely, begins to pant, his tongue leisurely flopping out of the side of his mouth. He looks exactly like he's grinning at me, and I can't help but smile back. Maybe he's not going to be so bad to have around after all.

Chapter 6

Finding Friends in Unlikely Places

'Often we are guilty of having an inflexible image of what new relationships might look like, usually as a result of unconscious expectations that lurk in the mind, narrowing our chances of new and exciting connections before they've even started.'

©TheBeginnersGuideToLoneliness.com

'Get off you idiot, get off!' I yell, not sure if I want to laugh or cry. I quickly realize that I don't have the energy or breath left in my body to do either. 'Dennis, bloody well get off!' I wheeze, pushing at him and trying to lever myself up off the multicoloured rug at the same time. He bounces straight back on top of me.

'Help! Help!' I shout. I start to giggle, but it quickly becomes hysterical as I struggle to get the mutt off me.

'Dennis, HEEL!'

The shout from the doorway makes us both jump. The reaction from the dog is amazing. He immediately slinks away from me, giving me these little backwards glances as if I'd started the game just to get him into trouble.

'Don't give her that look, you naughty hound. I'll tell Bay and then you'll be in trouble. Are you okay?'

I scramble to my feet, wondering who this angel of mercy is. Whoever she is, she's only about thirteen years old. Thirteen and extremely sure of herself. Standing in the doorway of the yurt, petting the ears of a now cowering Dennis, is the teenager I nearly sat on in the back of the Land Rover earlier. With her long, shiny black hair drawn over one shoulder, her large, melting brown eyes stare back at me as I struggle to my feet and attempt to dust myself off. She may be dressed like the bad fairy out of a pantomime, but there's something in the girl's look that makes me feel incredibly inadequate.

'Erm. Hi there. Thanks for that!'

'S'okay.' She leans against the wooden prop, jutting out a bony hip. 'You okay? Not hurt?' She doesn't look particularly worried, more like she feels like she has to ask.

'I'm fine, a little bit damp around the edges. I'm Tori by the way.' I hold out my hand. The girl simply stares at it until I start to feel mildly stupid, and let it drop to my side. Please can I go back to being mauled by the dog now? That was way more comfortable.

'I'm Rowan. I thought I'd come and say hi and just let you know that if you need anything, I'm your man.' She gives a tiny, casually indifferent shrug of the shoulders.

'Rowan? You're Ted and Lizzie's daughter?'

'Yep.'

'Oh, well that's really kind, thanks. Your parents have been great so far.' I feel wrong-footed.

'No, I don't think you get it. If you *need* anything . . .'

Is this kid trying to sell me drugs? I stare at Rowan, mouth open slightly, wondering what to say next. Rowan rolls her eyes at me.

'I mean, if you want to send an email, want some decent shampoo, a bit of non-perfumed deodorant. Basically, anything on the banned list.' She smiles, obviously proud of herself. 'Course, I don't offer my services to everyone, only a chosen few, but when I saw your shoes I knew you'd be interested. Just don't tell anyone else unless you clear it with me first.'

I smile. I can't help it. Rowan is going to make an excellent businesswoman. Identify a niche, find your captive audience, make your products available.

'Here's my price list. I can get you practically anything that's not on the list too, provided that it's legal, but there'll be an extra charge.'

I take the handwritten photocopy, plainly done in a stolen moment at school, and glance down the list. Coffee, deodorant, mobile phone use billed by the (extortionate) minute, email checking and printing service, mobile internet access. There's no end to the everyday needs of the average product-deprived, technology-starved guest that Rowan isn't catering to.

'Tell my parents, I'll deny everything and you'll likely be lynched by my other customers.' She treats me to a brief moment of the pure evils before giving me a quick smile. 'Anyway, if you need me, let me know.'

'Uh, right. Great. Thanks . . .' I'm so taken aback by this old, cynical head on such young shoulders, I find myself at a loss for words for a couple of seconds.

'And if I do need you?' I finally ask.

'Leave me a note in the crack of the gatepost at the bottom of the field. Oh, and don't let Dennis give you any shit. Bay makes out like he's such a big, scary dog, but he's a complete softy . . . like any man if you know how to handle him. See ya!'

With her piece said, Rowan turns on her heel and heads out again, no doubt to continue making the rounds of all the most likely candidates to take her up on her offer. I'm guessing that she's well-versed enough to avoid the open-air sleepers like the plague. They seem so diehard about the whole experience that they'd probably drop her in it straight away and try to forcibly cleanse her aura while they were at it. As for me, I've got a feeling that Rowan's services might come in handy at some point in the very near future.

I glance over to where Dennis is still sitting, gazing out of the yurt entrance, tail slowly wagging from side to side.

'So, you're a softy after all. Who'd have thought?' I murmur. I wander over to him and place a tentative hand on top of his head.

I spend the next couple of hours curled up on my bed and, with Dennis snoring away on one of the many coloured rugs, I finally read the course handbook properly, from cover to cover. By the time I've finished, the knot of fear that has been lurking in my chest ever since I arrived seems to be trying to throttle me. I thought knowing exactly what I was in for over the next three weeks might calm me down. I thought wrong.

I mean, I knew when I accepted the offer to come here and take the course that parts of it would be challenging, but what these guys do is serious. Basically, it's a chance to reprogramme any behaviour that's holding you back. I somehow thought I might be able to get away with watching it all unfold for everyone else without really having to deep-dive into my own issues too far. But, from what I've just read, and with such a small group of us, there seems to be fat chance of that!

The retreat is divided up into three themes, one per week. Week one is spent getting to know and trust each other; week two is all about discovering where we're stuck and breaking down barriers; and week three looks at how we can use what we've learned in our day-to-day lives. I mean . . . gulp.

Of course, I also came across all of the bits I'd missed before about handing over phones and iPads, and the fact that you have to walk down the lane the first time you come here. The other major discovery is that every day there's a session called 'Bodywork'. Yes, it's exactly like it sounds. These guys are fans of exercise – especially first thing in the morning. *Gah!* I take a deep breath and try to stem the wave of panic. I just need to take all of this one step at a time.

I check Bay's watch and realize that I'd better start trying to find my way back towards the house and, as Bay hasn't reappeared, I guess I'd better take Dennis with me. It's not like I can just abandon him here.

I look everywhere for a lead to attach to his collar. Either Bay doesn't own one, he's got it with him or he doesn't believe in them and will give me grief about imprisoning his dog. I quickly give up the search, mainly because Dennis is shadowing my every move, wagging his tail madly and pushing his nose into everything I touch. I pull a long, silk scarf out of my case and wind it around his collar a couple of times to use instead.

To my huge surprise, Dennis instantly becomes a model citizen. He doesn't pull, sits at my feet waiting patiently until I give him the nod that we're leaving and then trots daintily to heel. He looks so incredibly snooty on the end of his scarf that I can't help but laugh. Maybe I could learn to love dogs after all.

I'm finding it surprisingly difficult to navigate my way to the farmhouse. Just as I consider retracing my steps and starting again – or calling out until help finds me – Dennis begins to pull very decidedly to our right. I've got nothing to lose at this point, so let him take the lead and follow his nose. I'm guessing there's a good chance that he's heading in the direction of food, which makes it likely that he'll find the farmhouse a lot faster than I will.

Pretty soon, instead of ending up where we need to be, we're crossing yet another muddy field, completely lost.

'You idiot, Dennis!'

The dog carries on pulling ahead and, to my relief, I spot a tall figure climbing the gate at the opposite side of the field. I might be lost, but the dog certainly isn't.

'Dennis, what on earth are you wearing?' laughs Bay as he strides over towards us. 'Tori, I see you two've made friends? I'm glad. If Dennis likes someone enough to let them put him on a lead, it usually means I'll get on okay with them too.'

'I think we've called a truce, but only after he pinned me and practically drowned me in slobber!'

'I'm sorry, he does get a bit overexcited sometimes. How did you get out of that? It's his favourite game . . . usually goes on for hours.'

'Rowan saved me.'

'Ah. Well no doubt she'll bill you for it later,' Bay laughs. 'Poor old Dennis is terrified of her. So am I a little bit!'

'I don't blame you!' I laugh.

'So what services did she offer you then?' he asks, giving me a sly look.

'How do you know about that?'

'Oh, come on, I've been doing this for years,' Bay grins.

I just shrug at him.

'Anyway,' he says, 'why on earth are you all the way out here? Surely it must be about time for the meeting? If not, I'm completely out of whack and need my head seeing to.' He reaches out and takes my hand, raising the watch up to take a look. 'Yup, just as I thought, time to be heading homeward. And don't let Dennis lead you astray, he'll take you off on a jaunt any time of the day or night, depending on what he fancies!'

'You are a bad, bad dog,' I smile, bending down to ruffle his ears. Dennis raises his chin for a tickle and thumps his tail on the ground.

'I still can't believe you managed to get him on a lead. All joking aside, he usually goes ballistic and then refuses to budge an inch.'

I've been so focused on finding my way back to the farmhouse, and then actually enjoying the quiet stroll with Bay, Dennis trotting along between us, that I'd briefly forgotten where we're going and the fact that I'm completely dreading this evening. After reading the handbook, I know that the welcoming ceremony is an important part of the process. But right now, I'd much rather be back in the yurt than headed towards an evening with a group of people I don't know.

'You're really quiet. Everything okay?' Bay asks, dragging me out of my rapidly spiralling panic. I realize that I've been walking along, chewing my lip in silence for a good ten minutes.

'Just a bit nervous about this evening.'

Bay nods. 'Fair enough.'

Silence lands heavily between us again, and I feel like it's my turn to try to make some kind of small talk.

'I thought we weren't allowed back into the main house?' I ask as we reach the field gate and head into the yard.

'The meeting's not in the house. It usually starts in the old hayloft and goes on from there,' he says, leading the way around behind the house and into a cobbled courtyard. Directly opposite us, a wide flight of stone steps runs up the side of one of the barns. The rest of the group are already gathered below, and there's the hum of low conversation as we head towards them.

'Are you going to be okay?' Bay asks gently, lowering his voice.

'Sure, fine.' I bend down and rub the top of Dennis's head. He really is better than a teddy bear right now.

'He never misses the welcoming ceremony, you know,' Bay says, nodding at the dog. 'He likes to know who's around as much as the rest of us.'

I nod, feeling oddly relieved that my newfound friend will be a part of the proceedings. I hand the lead over to Bay and he unwinds it from Dennis's collar.

'Thanks for the loan,' he smiles, handing the scarf back to me. I stuff it in my pocket, feeling a bit daft. Clearly Dennis doesn't really need a lead, and there he was trotting to heel all the way down the field.

'Sorry, I wasn't sure if he was allowed to roam free or not.'

'It's fine, and probably a good job you did, otherwise he'd have just pottered off and left you up in the fields. He's pretty much got the run of this place as he's so placid, and he always turns up when he's hungry.'

As if on cue, Dennis looks up at us both, wags his fat little tail a couple of times and disappears off to check everyone else out.

'I'd better go and see if they need any last-minute help setting up.'

'Of course,' I nod, swallowing.

'Catch you later, then,' Bay smiles and jogs lightly up the steps.

Just as my nerves ramp up another notch, I feel a warm hand on my shoulder and turn to find Doreen grinning at me, though she looks so different I do a bit of a double take. She's removed her fuchsia lipstick and what must have been liberal coatings of foundation, mascara and eye shadow. She looks soft, and friendly, and so much younger.

'Hi! Tori, isn't it?'

I nod.

'I'm Doreen, and my hubby's called Geoff, though goodness knows who he's gossiping with at the moment!'

'Nice to meet you,' I croak.

'So what's your place like? I've been dying to ask but didn't want to interrupt you and that rather tasty young man . . .'

'Tasty?' I laugh. I can't help it. 'I booked my spot right at the last minute, so I'm sharing a yurt . . .'

'Oh, gorgeous! That'll be really cosy, I bet. Who're you sharing with? What's she like?'

'Erm. That was him. Your tasty little morsel. And that little devil polishing your hand is his dog.'

Doreen looks down at Dennis and pats him on the head. 'That's so unfair. I get landed with Geoff for three weeks in a tiny wooden cabin and you end up in a luxury canvas palace with a sex god and his minion . . .'

'What's this?' chuckles Geoff, materializing at my side.

'Tori was just telling me how she's living in a palace with a sex god, while I have to put up with you!'

'I never said . . .'

'Don't mind her, love. She reads a lot of steamy romance,' Geoff stage-whispers in my ear.

Doreen sticks her tongue out at him good-naturedly.

'But you're all right, are you? Happy with where you're staying?' Geoff asks.

'Sure, it's okay. Me and Dennis are already friends.'

Everyone around us seems to have teamed up into little groups. There's a great deal of earnest talking, nodding and beard-scratching going on over in the Beardy Weirdies' corner. It seems these guys are serious about being serious and, by the sound of the snatches of conversation I'm able to pick up, they're playing an eco version of 'who's got the biggest willy?'. In this instance, 'who's got the smallest carbon footprint?'.

'Hello, Tori. How are you settling in?'

I jump. Lizzie's standing right next to me. How is it that this woman, who is currently the size of a house, is able to sneak up unheard? It's unnerving.

'Very well, thanks. It's a beautiful place.'

Lizzie swells with pride. I wish she wouldn't. I really don't want her to explode.

'Thank you. We try. We pride ourselves on the energies we have encouraged from the land. All our visitors leave us in a better place than they arrived. And you're happy in the yurt?'

'Yes, thanks,' I reply on autopilot.

'And the company?' Lizzie's voice seems to take on a slightly sharper edge.

'It'll be great to have someone around who knows what direction he's going in,' I reply.

Lizzie claps her hands like a three-year-old. 'That's what I told Ted. You need a strong, warming influence. Someone who knows their place in the world and their spirit's destination. You are very perceptive, Tori. Bay has exactly what you say: direction.'

I smile tightly and keep my mouth closed. Lizzie smiles back at me, nods happily and floats off to interrogate the Beardy Weirdies.

'Not quite what you meant, that, was it?' Doreen asks, grinning wickedly.

'Erm . . . no. I just meant that it'll be great to have someone around who knows which direction the bog is in and where to find the next session.'

'Thought as much. So, have you finally read the handbook?'

'How did you know I hadn't already?' I demand.

Geoff laughs. 'You should have seen your face when they told you to hand over your phone.'

'I tried to cram it in on the journey here, but seems I missed quite a few important details. Anyway, I had the chance to read it all the way through this afternoon.' Just mentioning it makes the butterflies start to swoop in my stomach again.

'That's good . . . You'd be in for a few shocks over the next couple of weeks otherwise!' says Doreen.

I reckon we're all in for a shock or two whether we've read the handbook or not, but I keep that thought to myself.

Chapter 7

Learning to Trust Again

'There are a lot of factors that contribute to loneliness. Some come from inside us, and some come from external influences beyond our control. It's natural to withdraw into yourself after being treated badly. How can we trust someone not to hurt us like we've been hurt before?'

©TheBeginnersGuideToLoneliness.com

'Friends. Welcome.' Lizzie pauses, staring around at us all from her precarious perch halfway up the steps. She lets the pause drag on just that little bit too long, until we're all collectively shifting our weight. 'We are now going up into the loft to start our work in earnest. Each of you will begin your quest tonight.

'Before coming up these steps, please ask yourself one last time if you are truly committed to changing your life. In this moment, right now, you can still walk away and return to your life the way it is.' She pauses again. 'If you stay, and climb these steps, things will start to change.'

I look at Doreen, who raises her eyebrows at me in amusement. I can't help but shake my head.

Geoff bends his head and murmurs in my ear, 'Run, Tori, run . . . save yourself!'

I swat playfully at his arm, but I can't help but feel a bit of a nervous twitch. There's a tiny part of me that wants to listen to him and hotfoot it straight back up the lane. What on earth am I about to let myself in for? But then I think about my empty little flat. Do I really want to go back to that right now?

A bell rings and my attention grudgingly shifts back to the stairs. Ted has joined Lizzie and they stand together, side by side, watching us all. Then Ted speaks up.

'Come on up and let's learn about how we can help each other fulfil our quests.'

We all shuffle towards the bottom of the steps, forming a queue in classic British fashion. I make sure that I'm somewhere near the middle. A thrill flares in my belly. Now that I've decided not to make a break for it, I can't help but feel curious as to what's about to happen next.

I inch forward as each person disappears through the dark, curtained doorway at the top of the steps.

'So, what do you reckon? Ready for this?' Doreen asks from behind me.

'Sure . . . It's not like anything awful can happen, is it?' I say with way more bravado that I'm actually feeling.

'Tori,' Ted smiles at me as I step forward. He is out of his scruffy jeans and bobbly jumper. Instead, he's wearing a pristine, white cheesecloth shirt over wide, white, floaty trousers.

On his feet are little green velvet shoes and under his chin is fastened a heavy brown cloak which is pushed back over one shoulder. I smile at him, my lips twitching as I struggle to contain a giggle. He looks like an extra from *The Hobbit*.

'It is now time for you to commit yourself fully to this process and to surrender any guilt you feel for being here. Can you do this?'

'Sure,' I reply. Well, they certainly enjoy repeating themselves. I'm still here, aren't I? If I was going to make a break for it, I'd already be halfway down the M4 by now. And I'm certainly not feeling guilty about being here . . . I might make sure Nat does when I get back online though!

'Step through,' says Ted.

I push the curtain aside, take a step and come to an abrupt stop. It's pitch-black in here. The back of my neck tingles. I stand still, waiting for my eyes to acclimatize, but nothing happens. I still can't see. My breath starts to come quicker as my heart rate goes into overdrive. Can I hear the sound of water, or is that my imagination? I start to turn my head, searching for any movement or chink of light.

'Come, turn to face me.'

I let out a squeak of fright as Lizzie's voice, soft as silk, sounds in my ear. I turn to it, trying to breathe quietly and stop my hands from shaking.

'You don't need to be afraid. You need to trust us. Trust us enough to let us guide your unplanned steps into dark places. We will always be there to guide you through to the other side if you get lost.'

I let out an impatient sigh. I can feel my momentary fear turn to anger. I try to shove my emotions back down inside me.

'Do you trust me?'

It's a direct and blunt question, and I'm not going to answer it. *No, I bloody don't.* This is a completely random stranger who I've only just met. I take a deep breath. Seems my inner bitch has come out to protect me again . . .

'You're right to be cautious. But I will not let you fall. I will not let you get lost. I am here to guide you through your troubles, not to guide you around them. Do you trust me?'

I get the sinking feeling that I'm not going to get any further until I say something.

'Fine. Yes, I trust you,' I huff.

'Good. Please step out of your shoes.'

Not the bloody shoes again? These people are fixated. I use my heel to slip out of one oversized welly boot and then the other. Bending down, I grope around in the darkness to pick them up.

'You can leave them here. Do not be afraid. I am going to place a blindfold over your eyes and lead you through to the next step.'

Before I know what's happening, a strip of material is being tied over my eyes. She may be gentle, but I jump as she makes contact in the dark and stand rigid until she's finished. At least the blindfold takes away that unnatural darkness, but still, the sooner this bit's over, the better.

A warm hand takes one of mine and I jump again. I'm going to be a nervous wreck by the time this is over. A gentle pressure on my back and a tug on my hand coaxes me forward.

I stumble as I take an uncertain step in the dark. I know that they can't let me get hurt, but there's an irrational part of my brain currently on high alert, telling me I'm going to fall down a big, dark hole any second now.

After an eternity of being led in what feels like circles, we stop.

'Your next guide is here.'

A new hand takes mine. It's large, rough-skinned and warm. This time there's no pressure on my back, just an insistent tug at my arm, and I follow, trying to catch the pace of this new person. Whoever it is is walking faster, and I have to concentrate on the pressure on my hand and nothing else to stop me from tripping. I start to relax into it in spite of myself. After all, I've not been led straight into a brick wall. Yet.

Finally, we come to a halt and the hand lets go of mine. I stand there expecting someone to take my blindfold off, but nothing happens. I'm just starting to get jittery again when two hands land on my shoulders and I give a little shriek. I'm sure I hear a snort of laughter from behind me, but my heart is beating so fast I have no idea if I imagined it or not. I feel a gentle pressure and realize that they want me to sit down. Without being able to see what I'm doing, I brace myself to drop all the way to the floor, but hit something squishy that feels like a giant marshmallow.

This could be the library definition of uncomfortable. I wait for someone to come and take my blindfold off, but nothing happens. I'm getting a bit fidgety on my marshmallow and shift my bottom slightly, but end up almost tumbling onto the floor.

Of course, there's nothing to stop me from taking the blindfold off myself, except for self-consciousness. At least like this I don't have to take any responsibility for what's going on.

'We're all here!' Ted's voice rings out.

I shift my bum again as my legs threaten to go to sleep on me, this time careful not to disappear off the edge.

'You might be wondering what's happening; what this is all about. You are here with us to challenge your comfort zones. What better way to start than by trusting a stranger to blindfold you and lead you into unknown territory? While you're here there will be moments when you will need help. Remember that you are each a part of this – you need to be able to trust us and each other.'

There's restless shuffling and the sounds of breathing all around me. Someone clears their throat.

'We will now come around and give you the gift of your eyes once again. Please don't speak yet. Just hold in your heart your experience so far and what it means to you.'

The restlessness increases. I close my eyes tightly underneath the blindfold. I'm not sure I really want to see what's going on around me. What if my inner cynic decides to come out and party?

There's a gentle touch on my shoulder, letting me know that someone's standing behind me. I hold my breath. They remove my blindfold and, to my surprise, brush my hair away from my face with gentle fingers. My eyes fly open and light seems to flood in after being in the dark for so long. It's not the harsh light from an electric bulb, but the soft flicker of candles set in dozens of glass jars around the room.

I look around me, wondering if I'm going to be able to figure out who just decided to play with my hair. Ted's to one side, then I notice Lizzie the other side of me with Moth. It could have been either of them. Or the guy over there who lent me his wellies earlier. Good. This is a good thing. If I don't know who it was, I can't feel awkward about it.

We're all sitting in a circle under the eaves of the old barn. Doreen grins at me, but Geoff isn't looking quite so happy. His eyes are darting around furiously, as if trying to catch someone out. So it's not just me who's a tad uncomfortable with the situation then . . .

Directly across the circle from me, one of the three Beardy Weirdies is sitting in the lotus position. Despite having his blindfold removed before me, his eyes remain closed and he has a little smile playing on his lips. I have to forcibly stop my eyes from rolling. It's all well and good to give yourself a couple of seconds to suck up the ambiance, but this guy is clearly just making sure that everyone notices his superior state of enlightenment before he deigns to join the rest of us in the room. Bloody muppet.

There's a dark-haired guy next to him that I don't recognize. This must be the late arrival, and much to my amusement his shoulders are shaking with suppressed giggles. He catches my eye and his whole face is a picture of someone trying not to laugh out loud. I bite my own lip in response and he winks at me, shaking his head.

Maybe it's all the candles, but it suddenly feels rather warm in here. Thank goodness for the soft, low light, though, as the look he's giving is making me melt and blush at the same time.

Chapter 8

Cracking the Nut

'As you work to forge new connections, starting friendships and finding your community, you're going to have to open up and reveal a bit about yourself. That first crack, the first glimpse of the soft and beautiful inside, is hard-won, but so worth it.'
©TheBeginnersGuideToLoneliness.com

'Now, let's get to know each other a bit; find out what brings us all here and what we each hope to get out of the experience,' says Lizzie, easing herself onto a wooden chair next to Ted. Her hair is now hanging long and loose down her back and she's wearing a simple white dress with a short grey cloak over her shoulders. I sit up and try to concentrate rather than eyeballing the newcomer, who still seems to be fighting a losing battle with laughter. He's threatening to sweep me along with him if I'm not careful.

'We know,' Ted joins in, 'that this might be extremely difficult for you. And that's fine. It's okay to figure things out as you go along. But try to state what you feel right now in this moment. All we ask is that you are open. This evening is all about creating bonds of trust with each other.'

I drop my eyes to the floor, and when I look up again the new guy waggles his eyebrows at me. The yellow smiley-face badge pinned to the front of his shirt glints in the candlelight. I smile at him, but hastily straighten my face and tune back into what Lizzie is now saying.

'These bonds are likely to outlast your stay here with us. This is a time for making new connections. Don't be afraid. Embrace the experience fully. So, friends, be open, be truthful and be brave. That is all we ask.'

'First, names.' This comes from the guy who lent me his wellies. 'Let's go around the circle. I want the name you go by among friends; we don't care about official tags here. I also want one word to tell us all how you feel right now. I'll start. I'm Russ, and I'm feeling calm.' He turns to Bay, who's flopped on a beanbag next to him.

'I'm Bay. I'm excited. Oh, and this is Dennis,' he adds, patting the dog next to him on the head. 'He's usually happy.'

'Hi, I'm Doreen. I'm . . . um . . .' she picks at her thumbnail.

'It's okay,' Ted smiles at her. 'Whatever comes to you first!'

'Terrified!' she squeaks with a little smile.

'Sam. Lost.'

'Emma. Excited.'

'Than. Curious.' It's the newcomer, and there's a little smile on his face as he speaks. It might be just me, but I swear he managed to make those two words sound just the tiniest bit sarcastic.

'Geoff. Hungry.' A titter of appreciation runs around the circle. Ted smiles but Lizzie's face pulls tight into a little frown of disapproval, which is hastily hidden under her love-for-all-mankind look.

'Moth. Open.' She turns to me. Ah. Shit.

'Tori. Erm . . . empty?' *Empty? Where the hell did that come from?* Now they're going to think that I'm some kind of emotionless robot! Why am I worrying about what this lot think of me anyway? Of course it would be lovely to make a few friends, but let's face it, the reality is I'll probably never see any of them again after the three weeks are up. I've just got to remember that I'm here to check out this course and write a review for the blog. And if I'm going to manage that, I'd better start concentrating. While I've been obsessing and staring at the floor, I've managed to miss a bunch of names. Bugger.

'Brilliant,' Lizzie smiles at us all. She peers around the circle, taking his time. I cringe, realizing that I've probably just been caught daydreaming. 'You've all been guided through your initiation and shown that you're willing to trust us to help you reach your goals. You are ready. Know that no thought is wrong, that no action should be considered incorrect and no reaction invalid. Allow yourselves to question – that's fine – but never halt in your journey. Follow your instincts down whichever paths you need to explore, safe in the knowledge that we are here to support you.'

A buzz of excitement runs around the group like bad wiring. This is already exceeding the wildest dreams of most of them. I don't join in. I'm frightened. Truly, little-girl-style scared at the thought of becoming close to a group of people who I stand to lose in a couple of weeks. And as for sharing my issues with them, right now I'm struggling with the idea of even sharing my breakfast preferences.

'Now, let's hear from each of your tutors. Ted, why don't you start?'

Ted nods. 'Okay, so most of you already know a bit about me, but just to level the playing field, here it is again. The Farm is my home, along with my wonderful wife, Lizzie, and our daughter, Rowan. I have no doubt you'll all meet her soon if you haven't already.

'We started this retreat because it's never been more important to learn how to safeguard our wellbeing and manage our mental health.

'I'm really looking forward to working with you all. I'm a registered counsellor as well as a certified fire-walk instructor, so I'll be the one leading that session when we come to it.'

Ted sits down and I join in with the applause on autopilot, my brain busy freaking out over the words 'fire walk'. When I saw that bit in the guidebook, I thought it was a metaphor for dealing with the scary stuff, not a literal burn-the-soles-of-your-feet-off session. Before I can panic too much, however, someone else around the circle speaks.

'I'm Claire.'

Claire is one of those women you just can't put an age on. She's wearing loose black trousers with a flimsy white shirt, and I can't help but stare as I notice that, even in this light, I can see straight through it. It appears she doesn't believe in bras. I look away as soon as I realize what I'm doing and catch Doreen's eye. She winks at me and nods over at one of the Beardy Weirdies, whose mouth is hanging open. As Claire raises a hand to run her fingers through her thick, dark hair, I swear the concentration levels in the room ramp up.

'When you're dealing with deep-seated emotions and working through your innermost desires and fears, these can work inwards unless they are fully expressed and let out of your body. In fact, many people find that the root of their issues is stored as muscle memory; your body remembers things that your mind has managed to lock away.

'So, every day I will be running some form of bodywork. I will lead you in yoga, Pilates, dance and meditation. I work closely with Russ, but as he's up next, I won't spoil his bit.'

Claire sits down and Russ gets to his feet. 'Thanks, Claire. I'm Russ, and I'll be your mindfulness instructor. As Claire said, the purposes of our sessions will often cross over. There's a lot of evidence to support the use of mindfulness in combating depression and isolation. Learning to be fully present in the moment, no matter what you're doing or where you are, ultimately makes you more comfortable and confident, as well as more connected within your relationships.'

I jump as something cold and wet nudges my arm. Dennis is pushing his nose under my hand, attempting to sidle his considerable bulk up onto the beanbag beside me. I can't help but smile at him, and shift over as quietly as I can to make room. He clambers up, turns around twice, swiping me both times with his tail, and plonks down with his head resting on my lap. I place my hand on top of his hot head. I look up and lock eyes with Bay. I don't know how long he's been watching me, but he smiles. I smile back and glance down at Dennis. Well, if I can get over this particular fear so quickly, maybe there's hope for me yet.

Lizzie is the last of the instructors to speak, and she does it from the comfort of her chair, clearly a little bit worn out by this point. As well as being a trained counsellor like Ted, Lizzie will be working closely with us in the third week to guide us on the practicalities of taking everything we've learned and applying it to our real lives. I can't help but think she's being a bit optimistic. I've no doubt that she'd be more than up to the task, but somehow I wouldn't be surprised if the baby appeared before she's had her chance to shepherd us all back into the big wide world.

As soon as she's finished speaking, there's another round of applause and everyone looks around expectantly. Ted stands up.

'So, you all know what's to come while you're here. There will be a lot of surprises, not laid on by us, but generated by each of you. You will get out of this experience as much as you put into it, so I urge you to put aside any reservations and fully commit.

'In a moment, I'm going to ask you all to present your wrists so that I can bind us all together.' He pauses to show us a coil of silver-grey cord that he's just pulled out of his pocket. 'This is to symbolize our commitment to ourselves and the group as a whole.'

Okay, so this is it, my last chance to back out. I look down at Dennis again, who's now quietly snoring in my lap. What's waiting for me if I walk away now? An empty flat, a lacklustre life and a shitload of bad memories. It's not as though they can force me to do anything I really don't want to do. I lift my hands off of the dog's head and present them in front of me, looking around at the rest of the group.

To my surprise, I'm one of the first to do it. All of the tutors have their arms outstretched, but it's not as though they have any choice in the matter, is it? Doreen and Geoff give each other a little nod and follow suit. Than thrusts his hands out and grins across the circle at me. I feel a blush rise from my toes and reach the roots of my hair in seconds. Is it my imagination or is he trying to woo me over to the naughty corner he appears to have singlehandedly started?

Very soon, everyone's hands are in the circle. Well, all but one pair. Chief Beardy Weirdy, lotus-position plonker himself, is now looking mildly green. Ted turns to him with a questioning look.

Beardy shakes his head. 'You can't bind me, man! You can't make me commit! I'm a free spirit, man!' He scrambles to his feet and bolts for the doorway. Ted dashes after him.

'Don't touch me, man! I'm a free spirit! I am one, not one of a group, man!' And with that he practically falls out of the door, with Ted in hot pursuit.

There's complete silence until Doreen breaks it with a nervous giggle, followed very quickly by an apologetic mumble. I'm starting to feel pretty uncomfortable with my arms outstretched.

'It's okay.' Claire gets to her feet and takes hold of the cord. 'Not everyone is ready, and it's a big undertaking.' She starts to work her way around the circle, pausing in front of each person to ask 'Sure?' and waiting for a reply before gently looping the cord around their wrists.

'Sure?'

She's standing right in front of me, looking straight into my eyes. I want to look away, but I can't. I feel Dennis raise his head from my lap to greet her. Great. Just in my moment of need my newfound friend is going to abandon me. I gaze at Claire. What the hell am I doing here? What am I doing full stop? What choice do I have?

'Sure,' I whisper. She smiles faintly as she loops the cord around my wrists.

Claire has just completed the circle when Ted returns, looking a little bit pink around the eyes. He's alone. He takes the cord with a grateful nod and loops it around Claire's wrists and then his own.

'Friends' – Ted's voice wobbles slightly – 'we are all one. We have committed. This cord flows between us, symbolizing our connection. Feel and cherish this bond. Learn from each other, help each other and support each other. That way the circle will never be broken.'

I can't believe it . . . I've got an actual lump in my throat.

Whatever they've got going on here, it's very clever. There's a tiny, cynical part of me that wouldn't be surprised if the guy who just bailed on us is a ringer that they use every time just for effect, just to make the rest of us feel like we're being brave because, miraculously, that's how I'm feeling right now.

Chapter 9

To Boldly Go

'It's all well and good looking at the big picture and knowing where you need to get to. But it's important not to worry about how many steps it will take to get there. Just breathe deep and take that first step.'

©TheBeginnersGuideToLoneliness.com

I wake up with a start and shoot bolt upright in my bed. *Where the hell am I?* Oh yeah, that's right. Canvas roof and a duo of snores coming from the other side of the yurt. Both master and dog are still dead to the world.

I slump back against my pillows. What time is it? I go to reach for my phone, my usual port of call first thing in the morning, but it's not there. Of course it's not. Bloody great. I lift my arm and check Bay's watch. Old-school, but at least it'll give me an idea of how long I've got left in bed. We're meeting at seven for a communal breakfast. That gives me . . . oh crap, a full two hours to hang around. Why on earth am I awake so early anyway? I usually struggle into a cold shower at about eight thirty, followed by a litre of tar-strength coffee to kickstart my brain.

For a start, it's already ridiculously light. Also, the birds are tweeting loudly enough to wake the dead . . . Maybe that's their plan? And it's worse than just hanging around for a couple of hours. I need the loo. Pretty desperate too.

I'm going to have to risk the inadequacies of the composting bog.

What a great way to start the day. I don't know what else I was expecting though. It's not like I can just turn the tap off for three weeks.

I scramble out from under my mound of bedding and get to my feet as quietly as possible. Maybe it's for the best that I'm awake before anyone else. At least this way I'm going to be able to check out the facilities without being spotted. As I shuffle a pair of trousers on over my pyjamas, one line of snoring comes to a halt. I look over at Bay's bed just in time to see Dennis open his eyes sleepily. He thumps his tail and lifts his head as soon as he sees that I'm on my feet. I shake my head desperately and point at the bed, hoping against hope that he'll go back to sleep before he manages to wake Bay up.

Dennis gets to his feet, tail wagging sheepishly. *Damn it!*

'No, Dennis, bed!' I whisper sharply. If it weren't for my mission, I'd be glad of the company, but the dog is not a welcome addition to this particular party.

Dennis pauses in his tracks. Then he turns and, with a scathing look over his shoulder, makes straight for my recently vacated bed and flops down onto the rumpled pile of blankets.

I roll my eyes. I know that I should chuck him off straight away, otherwise I'm going to lose ground in the turf war we've got going on, but I'm so grateful that I'm not going to have an escort to the toilet that I leave him to snooze. I'll just have to deal with that particular problem later.

Sliding my feet into my loaned wellies, I push the flap of the yurt open. I'm just about to step out when a sound comes from behind me. *Now what?* But it's only Dennis snuggling down and starting to snore again.

I stride away from the yurt in the direction of the little hut, following the line of the hedge. I keep my bleary eyes on the ground, watching my step on the slippery grass in my oversized boots. There's dew on everything, so much in fact that I'm surprised the inside of the yurt didn't feel damp. There's a crash directly overhead and I jump and swear as a fat grey pigeon almost falls out of the tree above me.

'Idiot,' I grunt at it, heart hammering against my ribs. I watch as a second one joins it, and can't help but laugh at how it flies at the branch and hopes to stick in an act of faith, rather than trying to make any effort to land gracefully.

I've never really seen this time of day before. The light is silvery-blue and the sun's not quite up yet. The air is chilly and heavy with the dew that's half on the ground and half hanging in a low mist around me. I shiver as the dampness reaches the bare skin beneath my clothing, reminding me what I'm doing up at this godforsaken hour in the first place. I badly need to pee.

I stride forward, this time keeping my eyes up, half watching out for the little hut I'm making my way towards and half enjoying the novelty of feeling so alone. You never feel like this in London. Lonely, yes, but never this depth of silence. Perhaps that's the wrong word, considering the racket the birds are making. 'Stillness' is probably nearer the mark.

Just thinking about London brings everything I'm trying to escape rushing back. I shake my head impatiently, but it doesn't dislodge the familiar, icy feeling in my chest. I haven't always been lonely, so at least I know it's not something that comes from an in-built part of my character. Or, at least, it never used to be. I had friends. There was a large, sprawling group of us. We went through school together, and then through college. Of course, that was before Mum died. Before things between me and Markus ended. Before everything went so very wrong.

I swallow hard and, giving myself a mental shake, push it all to the back of my mind again. Now isn't the time or place to start opening that particular mental file.

I spot the small wooden hut in front of me and hurry towards it. There's a short ramp leading up to the raised doorway. Its base is surrounded by what look to be pieces of old paisley carpet like my grandmother used to have in her living room. One thing that really takes me by surprise is that it doesn't smell terrible. There's an odd, earthy, pine smell, but not the kind of sewer stench I'd expected. It doesn't make me feel any more comfortable about going up there, but not wanting to puke while I do it is a bonus.

Glancing around me, I check to see that the coast is clear. It doesn't matter how desperate I am right now; I can't do this with any kind of audience.

It's completely still, so I gingerly make my way up the wooden ramp, my hand white-knuckled on the railing. There's no way I want to be the one found outside the bog in a heap with a broken ankle.

The door is a simple, slatted thing and there's a little sign hanging from a nail in the frame that reads 'Vacant' in narrow, charred writing. I flip it over so that it reads 'Busy' and step inside. I jump as the door bangs shut behind me and hold my breath as I search for the lock. There isn't one. Damn it! There's no way I'm going to be able to do my business with just a 'Busy' sign for protection. I look around for something to wedge in front of the door. There isn't anything apart from a bucket of sawdust, and that wouldn't be enough to stop man nor beast. Typical.

I stand there for a second, torn. It's just gone five in the morning. The likelihood of anyone else turning up mid-pee is tiny.

I look down at the toilet with some fear. It's just a wooden plank with an old toilet seat attached to the top of it. Sitting down, I breathe a sigh of relief and look around me. There's a small slit in the planking to my right-hand side directly at eye level. I peer through it and am met with dancing, golden beams as the sun makes its way above the horizon and peeps through the trees on the other side of the field. The light dapples and flickers as a breeze catches the branches. This view has to be the best I've ever had while sitting on the throne. A draft rushes up from under the toilet seat. *Eww.*

I finally locate a slightly damp, rough roll of loo paper and send up a silent prayer of thanks, having vaguely expected a pile of dried leaves. I look around for some kind of flush, but of course there isn't anything. My eyes rest on the bucket of shavings. It has a sign attached to the side that I didn't notice before. It says 'Sprinkle me. Two cups should do.'

Reaching in, I use the tin mug to throw pine shavings down the recently vacated hole. And that's that. I feel strangely proud of myself.

There's a tap attached to a fence post at the bottom of the ramp and I wash my hands with a lump of yellow, gritty soap from a little saucer next to it.

I'm just starting a leisurely stroll back in the direction of the yurt when it occurs to me that this is the perfect time for a little look around down by the farmhouse. No one in their right mind will be awake at this time of the morning – apart from me of course.

I head down the hill, retracing the path I followed yesterday with Dennis and Bay.

The farmhouse looks dark and sleepy. There's no one here silly enough to let the birds and early morning light cause them to lose sleep. I head past the house to take a proper look around the courtyard we gathered in last night. The room we used for the evening's ceremony is only a small part of this complex. It's essentially a courtyard surrounded by various barns and rooms that, I'm guessing, used to be the cow sheds. Now they're being used for the far more lucrative job of farming people's souls. I shudder at the image and creep across the silent cobbles.

I try one of the doors. It's locked. Huh. Maybe not such a caring, sharing and trusting community after all! I peer through the small window set in the wooden framed door, but all I can see are benches and a few other bits of random furniture. Nothing that interesting in there, then.

I retrace my steps back out of the courtyard and wander across the small front garden of the farmhouse, before winding around to the back.

Oh. My. God.

Ted is in the back garden.

And there is a whole lot more of him on display than I saw last night.

I freeze, but that doesn't stop the blush from starting in my toes and washing up over me like a wave. I go to run, but realize that Ted has his eyes closed. Thank goodness for small mercies.

I turn away and hurtle back around the corner before he has the chance to spot me.

I know it's lame, but that's more than enough snooping for one morning. And besides, I've learned something very valuable: do not, under any circumstances, go near the back lawn of the farmhouse early in the morning.

★

I arrive back at the yurt panting, having rushed back with my head down all the way. I flip open the flap without a moment's pause and am treated to my *second* full frontal of the morning.

Bay is standing right in front of me, stark bollock naked.

Unfortunately, this one doesn't have his eyes closed.

'Shit, sorry, I thought you were out!' Bay quickly grabs a blanket from his bed, fumbles and drops it before managing to secure it tightly around himself.

'I was. I'm back . . . I—'

'I'm so sorry!'

I stand and stare at him, the image of his naked body seared into my brain. Two naked men on my first morning is a little bit too much to handle.

'Don't you people believe in clothes?' I huff, trying to cover my pure, unadulterated embarrassment with bluster.

'I'm sorry, I'm not quite used to sharing—'

'Well, neither am I, especially with butt-naked men. So please put some clothes on.'

Dennis is cowering on my bed. I stride over to him. 'Dennis, OFF.'

He scuttles straight off the bed and over to Bay, who promptly bends down to scratch his ears, almost losing his blanket again.

'Hey, don't take my nakedness out on Dennis. It's not his fault.'

'Unless you also smell of dog, I'm taking it out on the right man.'

'Well, you're pretty hideous first thing in the morning, aren't you? Good thing I learned this early on.'

'You don't look that great yourself, you know,' I mutter.

Lies! All lies. He actually looks toned and tanned, and kind of cute in his rumpled, early morning state. But that's beside the point.

'I didn't mean how you look . . . I mean . . . well . . . *you!*' says Bay.

I do a great impression of a landed goldfish for a couple of seconds before shooting back: 'Okay, try being me. I've got a coffee habit and I haven't had a coffee. I'm not even allowed to *get* a coffee because it's on the banned list for some reason. I've seen *two* naked men, and there's a bloody great big dog in my bed! All this before six in the morning!'

Bay smiles at me. 'Well, turn away for a minute or you're going to get another eyeful.'

I groan and throw myself face down on my bed. *EWW!* It smells of warm dog. I fume silently into my pillow, listening to Bay rustling around on the other side of the yurt. Seriously, this guy takes longer to get dressed than anyone I've ever met.

'Are you done yet?' I mutter. It comes out slightly muffled by my pillow.

'Hang on,' he calls.

For goodness sake, how long does he expect me to stay like this? And what is that noise? What's he doing now? Having a complete strip wash while I suffocate in the aroma of dog?

'Oi!'

I get a nudge in my ribcage. Swinging around, I come face to face with Bay, who is now fully clothed and proffering a cup of something that smells suspiciously like coffee. 'For you. To help you get over the shock.'

'Oh. Thanks,' I grunt, taking the cup from him and sniffing it. He gets up and retrieves his own mug from the table.

'Hang on,' I say suspiciously. 'I thought we weren't meant to "alter our pathways" with mind-enhancing caffeine? Don't tell me this is made from sheep poo?'

'Nope. Not sheep poo. You have the very fortunate luck of landing yourself in a tent with another hard-core caffeine addict. This is purest Columbian. Should set you up for the day!' he smiles at me. 'And I was on the course the year that convinced Ted and Lizzie to add coffee to the banned list . . . Turns out that having a bunch of people working through their issues while they're souped-up on enough coffee to keep an entire city running can be a pretty explosive mixture. They decided they'd be better off dealing with a bunch of caffeine-withdrawal headaches than vulnerable people at exploding point.'

I take a tentative sip and groan in ecstasy. *Coffee, my old friend!*

'Thank you for breaking the rules,' I say gratefully, and carefully transfer the cup to my other hand so that I can sit up.

'Pleasure's all mine,' smiles Bay, taking a sip from his own cup. 'Can't leave a fellow addict to suffer now, can I? There's a price though . . .'

Oh great. Mind you, I'll happily pay just about anything right now for the few precious sips I've already had. I can feel myself becoming more human by the second.

'Give me the gossip!' Bay grins, watching me intently.

'What gossip? I only just got here.'

'Exactly. You were here when I went to sleep and gone when I woke up. And you've seen *two* naked men today. I've clearly got the dubious pleasure of being number two. Who else?' He waggles his eyebrows at me.

I shake my head. I've always suspected that men are worse gossips than women, but this is ridiculous. 'It was Ted. I went for a walk. He was naked in his garden.' I cringe at the memory.

Bay chuckles. 'That sounds about right. Damn, I thought there was some juicy gossip to be had, but Ted gets his kit off all the time. He likes to greet the day that way.'

'Can't he just put some boxers on before he pokes someone's eye out?'

'In his own back garden?'

'I was lost,' I say defensively.

'At five thirty in the morning?'

'I went to explore. I found the loo – got that sussed. Then I found Ted and Lizzie's back garden. Trust me, I don't much fancy revisiting either place.'

'Hey! I can understand you not wanting to get a second eyeful of Ted, but I'll not have you say a word against my shitter. I put blood, sweat and tears into building that.'

I laugh but stop abruptly, wondering if he's being serious. The usual rules of conversation simply don't seem to apply here. I bury my nose in my coffee again and inhale deeply.

'I'm surprised they didn't confiscate your grounds when you got here.'

'Oh, they did. They've been locked in the safe since I arrived. I should have learned by now!' he says with a smile. I don't know whether to take him seriously or not.

'Honest! These were sourced at a very high price by a very handy Rowan. And this was my last lot. Time to get her in again if you want anything?'

'Thanks, I'll think about it.' I don't fully trust Bay yet and I think I'd prefer to keep any smuggled bars of soap a secret for now. It's definitely time for me to leave my first note in the gatepost for Rowan. I could do with checking my emails and sending a quick message to the Warriors for starters.

'Just don't go accepting coffee from anyone else,' Bay says. 'It'll most likely be acorn coffee. Tastes about as good as Dennis smells!'

Chapter 10

Courage Conquers Fear

'Find the thing that you're most scared of – you know, the
one that haunts you – and find a way to face it head on.
The courage it takes for you to face your biggest fear and
conquer it will help you realize that you've got this. That
courage came from you. You just saved yourself . . . and you
can do it again and again.'

©TheBeginnersGuideToLoneliness.com

On my way back down towards the farmhouse, I pause to leave
my letter for Rowan in the fence post. I check around me
before wedging it firmly into the crack. I've decided there's no
way I'm doing three weeks without chocolate or deodorant.

Hoping against hope that Ted has put some clothes on by
now, I make my way around to the courtyard. I'm in luck.
Everyone's gathered around a long wooden table that has been
lifted into place since my early morning visit. On it there are
jugs of juice, massive bowls of fruit, porridge and large jars of

honey. I sigh inwardly. No chance of my customary Pop-Tart here, then. I smile at Lizzie, who's brandishing a huge jug of what looks like coffee. Oh, thank goodness for that – Bay was just kidding earlier. She offers me a cup and I nod gratefully, eyeballing my large mug greedily. Bay flops down onto the bench opposite me with an odd smile on his face.

I ignore him, pick up my mug and take a sip.

And stop.

Abruptly.

I. Must. Not. Spit. This. Out.

Swallow, Tori, swallow.

It's like scrapings of burned Marmite.

'Acorn coffee,' Bay smirks at me. 'Delicious!'

I grab an apple from the bowl nearby and take a bite, desperate to get rid of the awful flavour. Damn that man for being right. I turn my attention away from him and smile as Doreen heads towards me looking pale. In fact, she looks shattered, and her hair is about three times the size it was yesterday.

'Hey, how was your first night?'

Doreen gives me a wan smile. 'Dark. Dark and very, very quiet.'

'Same. Until five, when I was so rudely awakened by the birds,' I nod sympathetically.

'I wouldn't know. That's just about when I drifted off, I think. I need coffee . . .'

'Oh no you don't,' I mutter in a low voice. 'That's not coffee. It's burned acorns pretending to be coffee. It tastes like shite and has zero caffeine. Steer clear!'

'Oh.' Doreen pushes her hair back and rests her head on her hands. Her eyes instantly begin to droop.

I grab a mug, fill it full of juice and push it towards her.

It's not long before everyone has joined us at the table, though the level of chat is fairly low. Half of us seem to be experiencing caffeine-withdrawal symptoms already, making me feel like I've got a terrible, guilty secret. The other half are enjoying the Zen-like calm of the early morning.

I hate this half.

'Morning, everyone!' Ted smiles around at us. 'Good to see you all up and ready to go!' He catches my eye as he looks around the table and I blush and look away.

Crap. I wonder if I'm ever going to be able to get that image of him out of my head!

'Now,' says Ted, clapping his hands and making me jump, 'I'm aware that a lot of you aren't used to the early start. Your bodies will be adjusting, so it's a nice, easy session this morning. You're all off for your first wild swim in the river. It'll wake you up like nothing else and wash away the cobwebs.'

Easy session? I can hear my pulse loud in my ears and my breathing is getting faster. Too fast. I put my apple down and focus hard on the edge of the table. The thundering in my ears is getting louder, and for a couple of minutes I zone in and out, trying to get my breathing back under control. I soon realize that everyone's chattering again, excited by the fact that their time here is about to kick off properly.

'Love, are you okay? You've gone very pale!' Doreen is staring at me, worry on her face.

I just nod at her. This isn't anyone's problem but mine, and I'm not about to mess up Doreen's first morning as well as my own.

Pretty soon, breakfast is over and we're all set to reconvene in ten minutes with our swimming gear. Bay is quiet as we head back to the yurt, and I'm glad of the silence.

My heart rate is still erratic and prickles of panic are rushing down my arms and pulsing in my fingertips. As long as I don't have to set foot in that river, I'll be okay. I keep telling myself this over and over again but it's not making any difference. I can't even bear to be near a bloody river. Lies . . . they're the only way to go, and no one needs to be any the wiser.

'I can't swim,' I blurt as we push our way inside.

'I thought you looked worried when Ted announced it. Don't worry, there are plenty of people who don't get in on their first visit to the river. Most just paddle in up to their knees and that's plenty for them. Just do that,' says Bay.

I swallow. Sure. I can do that. Can't I? Of course I can't. Who am I kidding? Even the word 'river' makes me feel sick.

I drag my feet getting ready. I didn't bring a swimming costume, for obvious reasons, but with Bay's quiet eyes on me, I feel like such a cop-out that I fling an old T-shirt, pair of boxer-knickers and a towel into a canvas bag. Not that I'll be using them. The closest I'm going to get to that river is the bank – if I don't pass out through panic before then.

We rejoin the others and set off across the fields. The sun is just starting to climb higher in the sky, and for a second I relax as its warmth hits my face. I'd even enjoy listening to the excited chatter around me if it weren't for the ice block of pure fear in my stomach. This is a morning so far removed from what I'm used to. Where are the four grey walls of my quiet flat and the inbox full of nothing but spam? Yet another essay waiting to be finished, only to disappear into nothingness the moment I submit it? That's all a very long way away.

Right now, I'm stuck with a bunch of excitable nutters who want to solve their problems by jumping in a very cold river. It's not fair! It really isn't. I'd be very happy to bare my soul, chant away my evils and visualize my chakras being cleansed of all pollution. But jumping in a river is just not going to happen. It's not the fact that it's going to be cold that's the problem. I'm just as rough and tough as the Beardy Weirdies – at least the two that made it through the welcoming ceremony anyway. But I really can't do this. No chance. No way.

'Are you all right, Tori? You're very quiet!' It's Emma, looking pretty and fresh with a pink polka-dot bikini peeking out from under a voluminous white shirt. Why is it that happy, outgoing people think it's helpful to check quiet people are okay by calling them out on their silence?

'Sure. Just . . . you know?' I'm not sure what to say, and I realize that this is the first time we've spoken. We're such a small group it makes sense to chat to her and get to know her at some point, but right now doesn't quite feel like the ideal moment for small talk. Not when I'm about to have the mother of all meltdowns.

She looks at me expectantly and then, giving up on any more of an answer, carries on anyway. 'It's so exciting, isn't it?

I just knew when I read about this place for the first time that it had to be our honeymoon. I mean, it's perfect, isn't it?'

'Uh, sure. I'm sure it'll be great . . .' I'm not sure at all, but it's not like I can admit that, is it?

'And, of course, they've had celebrities here you know?' Emma drops her voice slightly as she says this, grinning at me like the excited teenager she probably still is. 'So I just knew it was going to be brilliant!'

'Wow, seriously? Real celebrities? Like who?' I try to match Emma's wide-eyed, secretive tone. If I can keep her going on this topic, maybe it'll stop her from noticing the pure, unadulterated terror that must be oozing from my pores.

'Well, it's just gossip, but apparently they've had a girl band member, a footballer and a chef with anger issues . . . I dunno exactly who, it just hinted at their professions in the piece I read. And I just knew that it would be perfect here!'

'Right,' I smile brightly. I've already noticed that Emma talks about things being perfect a lot. I overheard her last night, talking about how perfect the welcoming ceremony had been. I already feel a bit sorry for Sam, poor lad. From what I've seen of him so far, he spends his entire time listening while she goes on about the 'aesthetic' of her Instagram feed, how important it is that each photograph is perfect and bewailing the fact that she can't update it while she's here. He also seems to spend as much time as possible sneaking away from Emma, or looking sheepish as he's dragged back for yet another public love-in.

Finally, Russ rounds up our staggered group at the edge of the third field we've crossed. We're at the top of a steep hill that presumably leads down to the river's edge. I give a little shiver even though there's no breeze and the air is starting to warm up in the early morning sunshine.

Than ambles up and comes to a standstill between me and Emma. I turn to look at him, but my face can't seem to muster a smile. I'm pretty sure I must look like I'm headed to my death.

'Okay, folks, we're almost there,' says Russ. 'When we get to the bottom of the hill, just head under the trees and you'll see the bit we're aiming for. It has hollowed out over the years into this fantastic natural pool. Perfect for everyone's first wild swim.'

The group shifts with excitement, bustling forward en masse a couple of inches. I, however, shuffle backwards a few feet. With a wry smile, undoubtedly thinking this is a bit of a game, Than copies me, giving me a wink.

'So let's get down there, get in and just enjoy it. This is one of those things that you won't understand the magic of until you've tried it. Trust me, as soon as you get in that water, you'll get it!' Russ grins around at us. 'And don't worry, I've been swimming here for years and have never had any problems. The water is beautifully clean and clear.'

The group starts to surge down the hill. Emma breaks into a run and I can hear her giggling as she navigates the steep slope. The others follow at a more leisurely pace, Bay and Russ striding together side by side. I don't budge and, for a second, I think I'm going to be the only one left at the top of the hill. After taking a couple of steps forward with the others, Than turns and looks at me with his eyebrows raised.

'Wanna get out of here?' he grins at me, and I'm instantly back in the naughty corner I found myself drawn to last night.

I nod.

'Come on then, quick, before they spot us.'

Before I've had a chance to think about it, he's grabbing my hand and towing me away, back through the gateway. We run hand in hand across the field, away from the rest of the group.

We don't stop until we reach the edges of the orchard. I can just spot Doreen and Geoff's cabin in the distance between the neat rows of trees. The blossom smells amazing in the early morning air. As we come to a halt and lean on the wooden fence, I try to catch my breath.

'Thank God we escaped that embarrassment!' Than laughs. 'I didn't much fancy replacing caffeine with cold water as a new way of waking up!'

I smile awkwardly at him. 'Me neither.'

Than quirks an eyebrow at me. 'I thought you were going to puke there for a second, you know! I mean, I know the others are a bit much to take, but that was quite some reaction you were having . . .'

Damn it! Now I don't actually have to go through with the whole water torture thing, I want to enjoy my freedom. I definitely don't want to talk about it. That's almost as bad as having to get in the bloody river.

I duck under the bars of the fence and take a couple of steps into the little orchard. 'What are we going to do now?' I say. All well and good doing a bunk with a guy I don't know, but now what do I do with him?

'How about we find somewhere to sit down, wake up properly and enjoy . . .' – he pauses and rummages in the little rucksack he's carrying – '. . . some of this!' he cries, triumphantly waving a little purple packet at me.

No. Effing. Way. 'Chocolate? Seriously? How on earth did you manage to smuggle that in?' I gasp.

'I have my sources,' he winks at me again, and I can't help it – my insides squeeze a little at the cheeky look he's giving me. He's all dark, messy hair and early morning stubble. Let's just say that I've seen much worse sights.

'Rowan?' I ask, swiping the chocolate from his hands. *Mmm*, fruit and nut, my favourite.

'Yep. But don't you dare tell her I told you.'

'Blimey, you got in there fast! And don't worry about me blabbing,' I say, falling into step next to him as we make our way down a little avenue of trees, 'I've got the full price list back at the yurt!'

Than points to the remnants of a fallen tree, much older and larger than the part-grown ones now gracing this well-tended little haven. The grass has grown up around it so that it looks like an outdoor settee. We both head over and, slumping down side by side, rest our backs up against it.

I hand Than back the bar of chocolate and without a moment's hesitation he rips it open, snaps it in two and hands me half.

'So,' he says around a mouthful, 'what was all that about back there? Why the need to escape? Desperate to get away from Emma, the vacant wannabe influencer?' He nudges my leg with his knee. The feel of his warm leg against mine sends a wave of butterflies through me.

'Nah, more like I couldn't handle much more of the inane smile of Doreen the bored housewife,' I joke. Than grins at me, but I instantly feel sick with myself. Doreen and Geoff have been nothing but nice to me. 'Actually, it's just that I don't like water,' I say curtly. End of subject please.

He blinks at me. 'Well, no one would when it's cold and—'

'No. I *really* don't like water,' I say.

'What, *all* water?' he asks, and I can't help but notice a strange look on his face as I peep at him. What is it? Amusement? Disbelief?

'No. Running water.'

'So, rivers . . .'

I nod. I want to get off the subject.

'What is it about them?' he asks curiously.

'Everything,' I say. My mouth's gone dry and the chocolate feels like it's about to lodge in my throat.

'I didn't even know that was a thing, fear of running water.'

I spot that look again. I know what it is. It's scepticism.

'Well, it is,' I snap.

'Sorry, I didn't mean it like that!' he says.

'No, I'm sorry,' I sigh. 'I get . . . panicked. I usually manage to avoid it pretty well. This morning was just a bit too close. It makes me—'

'Anxious?' Than supplies.

'Oh yes. And that makes me bitchy!' I say.

'How bad is it?'

How do I answer that when I've barely admitted it to myself yet? I started off being frightened around rivers. Now

I can't even bear to have a shower because the rushing sound can kick my anxiety off.

'Pretty bad,' I say. 'Put it like this, showers are out – I'm a bath girl all the way!'

Than shoots me a naughty look. 'Well, they're much better for the whole candlelit experience, aren't they?'

I blush. 'That's exactly what I always say.'

It feels strange to be sitting here with the sun on my face, stuffing myself with chocolate and admitting these things to someone face to face for the first time. I've told the Warriors online, and I've discussed it a lot with them, but that's not the same as having to say it out loud and deal with the questions and reactions that follow. I feel a warm ball of pride blossom somewhere inside me. This morning's session might not have been exactly what the powers-that-be had planned for me, but it's definitely doing me a lot of good.

'Thanks for rescuing me,' I smile at Than.

'You're welcome.'

My butterflies are now going completely nuts, but I'm not sure if it's Than or the tail end of my river-induced panic that's causing their over-excitement.

Than stands up and offers me his hand, pulling me up from my soft, grassy pillow.

'Next time, snacks are on you . . . and they'd better not be dried acorn cookies!'

'Okay, deal,' I say, holding on to his hand just a couple of seconds longer than is strictly necessary.

Chapter 11

No Man is an Island

'Asking for help is a good thing. Seeking professional support and advice can help you recognize and break bad patterns, setting you on the path to making new, authentic relationships.'

©TheBeginnersGuideToLoneliness.com

'Well met, my friends,' says Lizzie, gliding into the centre of our circle. We've all piled into the small space that Lizzie has chosen for her classroom. It's dark, stuffy and womblike, especially given the low, red-tinged lighting. Taking her time to rotate slowly on her axis, Lizzie peers at each of us in turn.

This afternoon, she's wearing a long, Grecian-looking dress in flowing white cheesecloth. Its twisted straps snake over her shoulders in a halter, and swathes of extra material cover and frame her massive bump.

When her eyes land on me, I shift uncomfortably. It's like she knows what happened this morning. Maybe one of the others said something. There's a part of me that feels bad for disappearing, but another part that's still excited by what happened instead. Lizzie smiles at me and moves on. I wish I were back out under the apple blossom right now.

'Something that you might already be learning about your stay is that things happen here. Unexpected things. Small things. Momentous things. Not one of you will be able to ride out this process as a passenger or observer. Not every realization or awakening will feel positive at first and not all of them will make sense straight away.

'You will all face fears while you are here, and this is a safe place for you to do so. However, you need to listen to yourselves and to each other to make this process as productive as possible.'

I feel Than shift on his cushion next to me and I peep at him. He winks at me and nudges my shoulder with his. The room gets even hotter, and I feel my face flame. Why? Why do I have to blush so easily? Maybe it's my guilty conscience . . .

I managed to grab Rowan and use her phone for a couple of minutes at vast expense before this session kicked off. I wanted to let the Warriors know that I've had my phone confiscated so that they don't worry where I've disappeared to. I may have also just dropped a quick mention of Than and his cheeky smile while I was at it.

I look back up to find Lizzie's eyes fixed on Than. Poor guy. She's pretty scary when she wants to be.

'Something else you all need to understand is that you need to be present in order for this process to work for you.

You need to actually *face* your fears, not keep turning away from them. You each need to take responsibility for yourself. You need to show up to each session, both physically and mentally. Be there and make every second count. It might not always be comfortable, but it will always take you one step closer towards your destination.'

Than shifts again, clearly uncomfortable. Lizzie nods once, finally looking away from him and moves slowly to sit in a chair at the far end of the small space.

'Right. Forgive me, I won't be able to get up if I join you all down there on the cushions.'

A little laugh runs around the group, breaking the strange atmosphere for a moment.

'This afternoon will be a deceptively simple session, but I think you'll be surprised how much it will help you over the next few weeks. We all need to be able to ask for help openly and without any fear, and to do this we need to be able to trust each other fully.'

My eyes start to droop in the warmth and soft, dim light. If it wasn't for the fact that I'm sitting bolt upright, making sure that no millimetre of me comes into contact with Than, who is positively lounging on the cushion next to me, I think I'd drop off. I stifle a yawn, and hear Than snigger quietly. I shake myself. All that fresh air this morning and the adrenalin surge at my near miss with the river have left me exhausted.

'First things first. Please clear the cushions to the sides of the room,' says Lizzie, 'then pair up, and try to aim for someone who's not the obvious choice for you!' she adds, catching Doreen eyeballing me from across the room.

Than grabs my arm as we struggle to our feet. It feels a little bit like being back at primary school, as we giggle at our naughtiness and chuck our cushions onto the pile with abandon. Suddenly I'm wide awake again.

As we turn, grinning, back to the rest of the room, there's not much other movement going on. There's plenty of uncomfortable shuffling and eye-contact-avoidance though.

'Come on, it's not that hard, is it?' laughs Lizzie. 'Just aim for someone you don't know much about; someone you haven't spoken to yet.'

There's more muttering as everyone starts to make awkward pairings around us. I know I'm getting disapproving looks from Lizzie right now, but if I refuse to look in her direction I can pretend they don't exist.

Before long, the whole room is paired off. Bay is with Emma, Moth has teamed up with Bob, one of the Beardy Weirdies, and Doreen is standing with the other Beardy Weirdy, whose name I still don't know.

'Good. Right, today we'll be facing some pretty ingrained stuff about ourselves. The thing is, if you're able to do this with a stranger, it should make it easier to open up to people who are close to you.'

Than turns to me and rolls his eyes. I clear my throat awkwardly. This sounds like the stuff we had to do at those interminable team-building days when I was working at the advertising agency. I used to hate every second – throwing myself backwards into the arms of someone who'd given me a bollocking the day before was never going to be fun.

But it turns out to be a very different experience with Than. We've been at it for a full ten minutes and we haven't stopped laughing the whole time. Things just feel so easy and simple between us, and I have to admit, that's quite scary in itself.

'Take a look at Bay's face!' he sniggers in my ear as he hauls me back up to my feet for the third time in a row. 'Do you think he's worried that Emma's going to drop him? Fluffy idiot!'

I sneak a peek over at the pair, and wince as Bay throws himself backwards into Emma's waiting arms. Miraculously, she manages to take his weight before he hits the floor, and I can't help but smile when I spot the look of relief on his face.

'Okay, my turn,' says Than, throwing himself backwards and grabbing my attention only just in time.

I like this feeling. It's like we're in our own little club, and the rest of them don't matter because we're having such a great time.

I instantly feel bad for letting this thought even cross my mind.

Once I've set Than back on his feet, I look around the room to see how everyone else is doing and watch as Beardy Weirdy catches Doreen. He doesn't seem to have the upper-body strength to set her back on her feet though, and both of them end up on the floor in a heap. I'm not surprised to see Doreen's in fits of giggles, but it looks like she's managed to unearth the little boy in the heart of the stoic hippy. He's laughing so hard that he's wiping tears from his eyes as Doreen punches him playfully on the elbow.

This signals the end of the serious part of this particular exercise, as their giggling is contagious and sweeps across the room, catching everyone unawares until we're all clutching at our sides, trying to avoid each other's eyes as we attempt to catch our collective breath.

I jump as Than flings an arm around my shoulder. The gesture feels too intimate in the moment, especially with everyone else around. I don't like it.

Doing my best to appear natural, I take a step away from Than and stretch, forcing him to drop his arm. When I catch his eye again, he smiles, completely relaxed. *Phew.*

I watch as Lizzie tries to regain some kind of control over the rest of the giggling group, and see that Bay is staring at us from the other side of the room. I'm not sure why, but I feel like I've been caught doing something wrong.

'Okay, guys, great work,' Lizzie slips back into her chair, a little out of breath. 'You all look like you're working as a team. Can you feel the difference?'

There's a bit of nodding around the room. I hear Than tut next to me.

'Let's test this newfound teamwork out a bit, shall we?' she grins at us wickedly. For the next ten minutes, with Lizzie instructing us from her chair, she guides us into a circle, and then, on her command, has us all sit down so that each of us is sitting on the lap of the person behind us in one unbroken loop. I've got Moth sat on mine while I'm perched on Than's.

I can't stop grinning. This is a bonkers exercise, and totally dependent on us all working together and trusting the person behind us to support our weight. It only gets a little bit chaotic when Lizzie instructs us back to our feet. We're all a bit slow to react, meaning that some people try to stand before the rest, resulting in half of the group landing in a giggling mess on the floor. Then we all shift around the room and try it again. This time I'm sitting on Doreen's lap and Emma's sitting on mine.

'Next,' calls Lizzie, clapping her hands to get our attention after we've all struggled back to our feet again, 'I want you to tell your partner from earlier a secret. This should be something that you haven't shared with anyone else here yet. They will hold this secret for you and, in return, you'll hold their secret for them.'

Crap. There goes the nice, relaxed feeling, then. I don't want to tell Than a secret. I don't want to tell *any*one any secrets. That's why they're called secrets! I look sideways at Than and see that he's looking pretty wary too.

'Take a moment,' Lizzie's voice cuts in again. 'Think about what you're going to share with each other. Make sure that it's something that will be equal in the exchange. It has to be worth trading, and something that you truly care about.'

'Come on,' I mutter to Than, 'let's find a bit of space.'

We drag one of the cushions out of the pile and head towards the back of the room, as far from the others as we can get. We sit facing each other in complete silence, looking anywhere but at each other.

'Imagine,' he says, and I jump after the long silence, 'just imagine if someone here admitted to an affair!' He looks at me, his eyes alight with mischief.

'Or murder!' I whisper back. 'But you couldn't tell anyone, because you promised, and they'd know that it was you who dobbed them in.'

We stare at each other in wide-eyed amusement for a second before I snort, a laugh escaping against my will. Than chuckles.

'Please focus on your own secrets for a moment and how you plan to share them!' Lizzie's voice cuts across the room, and I duck my head down.

'Oops. Rumbled!' laughs Than.

'So, who's going to start?' I ask.

'I don't mind . . .'

'Okay. I'll go . . .' I take a deep breath, and I see his shoulders relax a bit, knowing he's been let off the hook for a few minutes. 'One of the reasons I'm here – something I'm trying to come to terms with – is that my mum passed away.'

Than nods in encouragement but doesn't say anything. My heart is starting to hammer. What am I going to tell him? How much? 'She . . . she died in a car accident.'

'I'm sorry.' Than puts his hand out, like he's going to take mine. I pull my hand away before he has the chance to make contact. Every ounce of me is focused on sharing my secret, and if he touches me, I'm scared I'm not going to be able to get the words out.

'It was raining and the roads were really messy. Apparently, the car hit a patch of water and skidded. There was a river right next to the road. The car flipped and landed on its roof in the water.'

'Tori . . .' Than whispers. His hand is up to his mouth, his eyes wide.

'She drowned before anyone could get her out.' I take a deep breath. Is that it? Is that all I'm going to tell him? Maybe a little bit more. Maybe . . .

'There's something else. I told you when we skipped swimming earlier—'

'That you don't like running water?' he interrupts.

'Yes.'

'Well, now I can understand why.'

'Yeah.' I sigh, sit forward and hug my crossed legs like a little child. 'Well, it's a bit more than "don't like". I have severe potamophobia.'

'Pota . . . What's that?'

'Potamophobia. Fear of running water. Because of the accident.'

He looks non-plussed.

'You know how people with agoraphobia are terrified of open spaces and situations they feel they can't escape from? Some become housebound? My terror is running water.' I take a deep breath. My hands are starting to shake and my heartbeat is starting to race. Another deep breath. 'Rivers.

Waterfalls. Showers because of the sound . . . That urgent, pounding water.' I stop abruptly. My mouth has gone dry. I feel a bit sick.

Than nods, but doesn't say anything. He's wide-eyed and expectant, like he's waiting for me to say something more.

I shrug. 'So that's it. That's me.'

'But . . . you didn't have it before the accident?' he asks.

'Nope.'

'But you . . . you weren't there when it happened?'

I shake my head. That's enough now. I can't think about it anymore. I definitely can't share any more.

'How are you dealing with it?' he asks.

'Every day. Small things,' I say evasively. That really is enough. 'Some days are worse, some days better.' I clear my throat. 'Anyway. Your turn.'

Than jumps, almost like I've scalded him. I surreptitiously wipe my palms on my trousers, and let out a long, slow breath. I did it. I told someone other than Nat, Hugh and Sue. It's the first time I've had to say it out loud and I didn't go to pieces. Probably because I haven't shared the worst part yet. The part that has stopped me from getting professional help before now. I just couldn't handle the idea of someone prizing it out of me.

'Huh. I don't know where to start with mine,' mutters Than, and my attention snaps straight back into the room.

'Why don't you tell me a bit about how it makes you feel first?' I offer. He's looking shifty, like he might do a runner.

'I can do that. Scared. Guilty. Angry. That pretty much sums it up.'

Okay, that hasn't narrowed anything down. In fact, that could pretty much describe how I'm feeling too.

'My brother's ill,' he blurts out. For some reason it's not what I was expecting. 'He needs a new kidney and I'm the only option. He's asked me and I don't know what to do. I mean, obviously I do – I have to help him. But I'm scared.'

My jaw has dropped, and I quickly shut my mouth. I'd been expecting some kind of light-hearted admission, not a life-or-death situation.

'What if something goes wrong? What if I get ill? What if it doesn't help? And I'm angry. Why me? And then there's the guilt. This is my brother. I shouldn't be feeling like this, should I? I shouldn't be doubting this at all. I should be glad that I can help him. But I'm not. I've basically got no choice in the matter.'

'And there are no other options?' I ask as gently as I can.

'Nope. There are no other matches. This needs to happen yesterday and here I am, hanging out here, trying to get my head around everything, when I should be in a hospital saving my brother's life.'

It's my turn to lean forward. I go to take his hand, but I hesitate, knowing that I didn't want this just a minute ago. Than, however, grabs my hand like it's a lifeline.

'I'd be scared too. I think anyone would be,' I say.

'No. No, they wouldn't. You hear about people doing this all the time, and they're glad to do it. Not running away like I am.'

'You're not running away,' I say, looking at him steadily. 'You're here, aren't you? You're dealing with it in your own way.'

Than nods, squeezes my hand and stares fixedly at the floor. Finally he says, 'You won't tell this lot, will you?'

'Of course not. Isn't that the whole point?' I say.

'Thanks, Tori.' Than lets out a long sigh. 'He gave this to me, you know,' he fingers the yellow smiley badge still pinned to his top. 'He gave it to me when we were kids. I thought I'd wear it . . . to remind me why I'm here, who I'm here for.'

I nod and smile at him, feeling incredibly selfish for a second. Here I am, all *me me me*, and here he is, trying to find the courage to save his brother's life.

I'm still holding Than's hand. I don't pull away, but it seems like we've said everything we're going to say. I stare around the rest of the room. It's like there's been some kind of energy shift as everyone comes to the end of their confessions.

I'm not surprised to see that a couple of people have been in tears. Emma is sitting next to Bay, looking pale and withdrawn, and Bay looks decidedly wrong-footed. He looks up at me, and I turn away just as he catches my eye.

I smile back at Than and gradually ease my grip on his hand until I can reclaim mine. I want out, now. I've shared more than enough of myself for one day.

To my great relief, Lizzie seems to agree as she claps her hands to get our attention.

'Excellent, guys. Great to see these new bonds you've started to form. I want to remind you before you go that anything you've learned here today is confidential and not something to be chatted about idly around the campfire. Thank you.'

I'm on my feet and out of the door before the clapping has ended.

As soon as I'm outside, I start to feel better. The fresh air washes over me, and the images that have been haunting me in the claustrophobic little room dissolve in the sunshine.

I've never really talked much about the accident. Of course, I've told the Warriors most of the play-by-play facts, but typing them was a lot easier than saying them out loud. The real-life friends I had at the time tried to get me to talk about how I was feeling, but their support quickly turned into suggestions of 'rejoining the real world', urging me to go out, socialize and have some fun, because it was 'what Mum would have wanted'. They couldn't have been further from the truth. To add to the fun and games, in the middle of it all, my relationship with Markus imploded quite spectacularly, and as I continued to turn down every single invitation that came my way, they soon dried up.

I was left alone to struggle with the huge weight of grief and guilt about Mum, licking my wounds over Markus, little realizing that the biggest ball-ache to come out of it all would be this crushing, intense loneliness.

'Hey, how're you doing?'

It's Bay. I swing around to find him standing just behind me, and realize that he's probably been there for a while. I clear my throat and remind myself that he's not a mind-reader.

'Good.' Completely monosyllabic. Completely rude. Told you I was all talked out.

'Good session for you?' He sounds curious.

'Yeah,' I take a couple of steps away from him as if I'm about to head off back to the yurt, but then remember the look on his face at the end of the secrets exercise. 'How about you? You must have done it a few times before?'

'Once or twice,' he says, catching up with me. 'I've done Lizzie's sessions every time I've been here. Trust me, that's a lot of sessions.'

'So, do you tell the same secret over and over again?' A stock secret would be very handy, and not so hard to share after the first time, I guess.

'No. No, there's usually something new, or at least a new aspect of something I need to share that my partner draws out of me.'

'Emma draw anything interesting out?' I ask. I'm not sure I believe him, if I'm honest.

'That'd be telling, wouldn't it?'

His words might be flippant, but a troubled look crosses his face. So, that's a yes.

'What about you, Tori?'

'Like I said, it was good.'

'Which bit, the listening or the sharing?'

'Both. Surprising. But that's all I'm saying.'

Bay frowns and lifts a hand irritably to brush his hair back off his face. He looks uncomfortable, like there's something really bothering him.

Behind us, I can hear the rest of the group emerging from the classroom, a tide of eager chatter following them into the sunlit courtyard. Bay opens his mouth as if he's about to share something with me.

'Tori! Wait up!' Than's voice causes me to whirl around. As he jogs up next to me, I hastily plaster on a smile. Behind me, Bay lets out a huff and starts to walk away.

'What's up with him?' asks Than.

I shrug. My brain's full enough after that session without adding Bay's worries to the pile. 'No idea! Come on, let's go make a start on supper.'

Chapter 12

Your Body, the Storyteller

'When you start your healing process, you can work on your head all you want, but the key to success lies in working with your whole body. Get it moving and unlock those stored emotions.'

©TheBeginnersGuideToLoneliness.com

'Hey, everyone!' Claire smiles around at us all.

It's our first yoga session this morning, and I'm desperately trying to send her telepathic messages, begging her not to torture me on my first time. I know bending and stretching is meant to be good for you, I'm just not sure how bendy and stretchy I feel right now.

I actually slept really well last night. After Lizzie's session, I have to admit my mind was reeling and I was dreading going back to the yurt and just lying there in the dark while my brain replayed everything we'd talked about in the session. As it turns out, volunteering to make a start on supper was the best thing I could have done. At first, I was worried that Than would want to carry on talking about what we'd been discussing in the session, but he was way more interested in messing around. After about five minutes Moth joined us, and we didn't get into anything heavier than speculating about how hard Claire's first yoga session was going to be.

The light conversation with everyone over dinner meant that I didn't have to say much of anything, but with Than sitting on one side, giving me the occasional wink and nudge, and Moth nattering on about knitting on my other side, I felt warm and content in a way that I haven't for a long time. I wandered back to the yurt with Bay fairly early, leaving another shift of willing volunteers on washing-up duty. Bay was quiet too, and after the bare minimum of chat, and a last-minute cuddle with Dennis, I fell asleep before I'd even registered I was in bed.

'Right,' says Claire, 'before any of you start to worry, this session might be called "yoga" on the timetable, but you can forget all about those showy-offy poses you've seen online. We're looking at gentle movement to get in touch with our bodies. A chance to find out where we might be tight and caught up, where the aches and pains are. The last thing we want to be doing is adding to them!'

I let out a long breath of relief. That sounds just about manageable. I'm sitting on my borrowed mat that smells like a hundred strangers' feet, surrounded by the rest of the group. I tried to get a spot at the back of the room, but everyone else had the same idea, and Geoff, Sam and Emma beat me to it. So I've set up as close to the side wall as possible, right in front of Emma, with Doreen by my side. I'm so grateful that she nabbed that spot before Than could. The last thing I need while I'm trying not to seize up is to be worrying what I look like. He's set up his mat directly in front of me instead.

'Now, some of you will be more flexible than others, but just do what feels good for you. The most important thing is that you don't compare yourself to anyone else – either in the room or out of it. This is all about your personal journey, and no two sessions will feel the same.'

Turns out, I love every second of it once I manage to forget about the others around me – which isn't that easy, as Doreen spends most of the session giggling from one gentle pose to the next. Her balance is appalling – even worse than mine. I know I'm meant to be fully engrossed in what I'm doing to the exclusion of everything else, but it's harder than it sounds when the person next to you periodically overbalances so badly that she hops onto your mat with you.

Than peeps over his shoulder at me a couple of times, but I'm too focused on what I'm doing to pay much attention to anything else. Every stretch and release, the curve of my spine and the feeling of my skin and muscles relaxing into the floor is new to me. I almost feel drunk with the sensations.

On the couple of occasions I look around the room while trying to get my balance back, it's Moth that really catches my eye. Claire wasn't joking when she said that some people might be more flexible than others. Moth takes this to the next level. She's moving like a dancer, graceful and full of energy. Her whole body seems to flow, and the positions she's getting herself into would be jaw-dropping for a twenty-year-old, let alone someone of her age. I make a mental note to ask her about it when I get the chance.

By the end of the session, I'm so relaxed that my entire body seems to be tingling. I'm not tired, just . . . *chilled*.

'I'm starving,' says Geoff from the back row as we all clap for Claire.

'You're always starving!' Doreen laughs as she rolls her mat up.

'It's all this exercise and fresh air we're getting!' he says. 'Swimming yesterday, yoga today. Walking back and forth to the cabin. I'm going to be like a rake by the time we get home.' He pats his stomach and Doreen chuckles.

I straighten up from rolling my mat and catch Than watching me, a smirk on his face.

'What?' I say, self-consciously.

'Enjoy that?' he asks.

I nod.

'It was brilliant, wasn't it?' says Doreen. 'Nice to have the chance to be able to join in without being out of my depth in the first couple of minutes.'

'I bet,' says Than.

Doreen just smiles at him, but I swear I hear a little growl from Geoff's direction. I turn to look at him but he's already making his way towards Bay, who's standing over by the door. It must have been my overactive imagination.

'Shall we go make a start on lunch then?' I ask the other two to break the tension that seems to have popped up out of nowhere. I don't want to lose my relaxed feeling so soon.

'We don't have to,' says Than indignantly. 'We did the food last night.'

'Yeah, but I enjoyed it,' I say.

'Okay, come on then. Let's go recreate the magic.' Than links arms with me and hauls me towards the door, away from Doreen and the others.

As it turns out, I do have fun getting the lunch ready with Than at the little outdoor cooking station. Beardy Weirdy joins us and then Moth rocks up again too.

'You know, we're going to have to watch out that we don't get lumbered with all the kitchen duties!' Than says as he passes a huge stack of plates over to Moth.

'Oh, I hope I do!' Moth laughs. 'You know, all the best parties happen in the kitchen . . . even an outdoor one like this.'

'Hear hear!' says Beardy as he tosses a green salad with gusto.

I grab a handful of cutlery and follow Moth to the table. 'You know, that's the first time I've ever done yoga,' I say.

'Did you like it?' she asks, straightening up and looking at me.

'I did – after I'd finished checking out what everyone else was up to, and worrying that I was getting it all wrong. I felt . . . well . . . like it gave my brain a chance to slow down for a bit.'

Moth smiles. 'That's wonderful, Tori! And don't worry about having a look around you, everyone does it. It's just human nature to be curious.'

'I suppose,' I say, feeling a little bit less awkward about the fact that I've clocked how bendy she is.

'You should see some of the classes I go to,' she says as she starts to arrange plates down the opposite side of the table. 'Some of the women spend more time looking over their shoulders than worrying about what they're doing with their own bodies. It's sad really.'

'I thought you must have done other classes!' I say, then realize that I've just outed myself for spying on her. 'I'm sorry, I promise I wasn't staring – I just couldn't help but notice how beautifully you move.'

Oh. My. God. That might just be the most awkward thing I've ever said to a stranger.

Moth, however, is beaming at me. 'That's such a lovely thing to say, thank you! I do love a good yoga class – it keeps me in touch with what's going on in my body. I used to dance a lot, but . . . but not so much now.' She trails off, looking a little bit wistful.

'What kind of dancing?' I ask.

'Argentinean tango.'

'Seriously?' I gasp, struggling to imagine this silver-haired seventy-something with her hand-knits in the middle of a smouldering tango.

'Oh yes. It was the second love of my life,' she smiles, 'after my husband. And it was something we loved to do together.'

'But you stopped?'

'I lost Fred three years ago,' she says, and calmly sets the last plate in its place.

My breath catches. 'Oh, Moth, I'm really sorry.'

She just shakes her head. 'Don't be. We had a wonderful life together. And I've been coming here twice a year ever since, so I've done a lot of work around my loss. But . . . I haven't been able to bring myself to dance with another partner. Not yet.'

'Oi, you two slackers!' Than appears, carrying the huge bowl of salad Beardy has prepared. 'Are you going to help or leave it all up to me?'

'My fault!' Moth smiles over at him. 'Let's get this lunch on the table.'

Chapter 13

Challenge Your Comfort Zones

'To move forward and grow, we need to venture beyond our comfort zones. Yes, we are protected there, but we're also cut off from all sorts of wonderful experiences and opportunities.'

©TheBeginnersGuideToLoneliness.com

It's Ted's turn to try to tame us this afternoon, though I reckon he's got an easy session ahead of him, given how chilled we all are after the yoga class. It has turned into an absolutely gorgeous day, so, after lunch, we all troop through to the apple orchard and sit in a circle under the blossom.

'I hope you don't mind being outside,' Ted smiles around at us all, 'but when we're given a day as glorious as this, why waste it inside?'

I smile and lift my face to the blue sky, sucking in a lungful of fresh air. I'm not sure whether Claire slipped something into our bottles of water after yoga this morning, but I've not felt this relaxed in ages. Considering that we're about to have a session of group therapy with Ted, that's a bit of a miracle. This sort of thing would normally have me tense enough to snap. But right now, what's the point? I'm sitting comfortably in the long grass with Than on one side of me and Bay on the other.

'Okay, so everyone's here, that's great.' Ted beams. 'It's a simple session this afternoon. We're going to spend a bit of time getting to know each other better as a group, and then we're going to pair up to do some one-to-one sessions.'

Than nudges my elbow and grins at me. I smile back. I really want to get to know him better, but he doesn't take these sessions as seriously as the others, and after this morning went so surprisingly well, I'm quite keen to give this wellbeing thing a real shot.

'Now, don't go jumping ahead of yourselves, worrying about the second part,' says Ted, and I stiffen a bit. It's like these guys can read my mind sometimes. I look up at him, but he's not looking my way, so I don't think that particular comment was aimed at me.

'I know you did some partner work with Lizzie yesterday, sharing a secret. This afternoon is going to be about sharing one more thing, but this time, with the whole group. Remember, this needs to be about *you*. I want you to tell us about something that you feel holds you back in your day-to-day life. It can be anything.'

Suddenly, I'm not so relaxed. Share something with the whole group? Whatever I say, I'm not going to come out of it looking too great, am I? I sneak a quick, worried look around the circle and almost let out a laugh. Every single one of us, including old-hands Bay and Moth, are shifting uncomfortably. There's a lot of fiddling with nails and scratching of beards going on.

'Anyone want to go first?' Ted asks gently.

'Me.' It's Sam, looking rather surprised at the sound of his own voice.

'Well done, Sam,' Ted nods encouragingly at him. 'So, tell us something that you feel holds you back.'

Emma looks at her young husband with worried eyes.

'Well, erm . . . I dunno if this is the kind of thing . . . if this is right . . . but, it's like, every day I'm worried that I'm not perfect.' Sam's eyes are on the ground, and he's ripping up handfuls of grass.

Worried he's not perfect? Who is? I feel Than nudge my arm, but I ignore his quiet invitation to mock the others like we did last time. I might not quite get what Sam has just said, but even I can see that it took balls for him to say it.

Ted's nodding at Sam, waiting for him to say something else, but when he doesn't, Ted asks, 'And how does this make you feel?'

Sam looks at him. 'Scared. Scared that I'm not good enough. That . . . that . . . maybe Emma might see that I'm not perfect for her . . . that I might lose everything.'

Emma's now got tears in her eyes and she's shaking her head.

'Well done, Sam. That's a big thing to share with the group. We will do more work on everything that comes up today, but for now, just stating these things and bringing them out into the sunlight is a big enough step. Emma, Sam, you'll get a chance to work together later, okay?'

They both nod, Sam's staring hard at his mounting pile of grass. Emma quickly wipes her eyes with the back of her hand.

'Who'd like to go next?'

'I will,' I say. Bay jumps a little next to me, obviously not expecting me to speak up so soon.

'Great, Tori . . .'

'There's something that really holds me back. I suffer from potamophobia . . .' I pause, looking to Ted for assistance.

'And for the benefit of the rest of the group, are you able to explain what that is?'

'Oh, of course,' I say feeling a bit foolish. 'It's a fear of running water. Rivers . . . waterfalls . . . It's been getting steadily worse over the last two years. If I go out, I have to plan around avoiding rivers. I know it doesn't sound like a big deal but . . . well, it can cause me to have pretty bad panic attacks. Anyway, that's why I didn't make it down to the river for the first wild swim. I want to get over it, to face it . . . but . . . well . . . I'm sorry I bailed out without explaining why, but I'm just not ready.'

Ted nods at me. 'Thanks for sharing that with us, Tori. And it's important that you know – that you all know – working through issues takes time. It's not like skydiving, pushing yourself out of a plane and *bam*, you're there. It's all about tiny steps, little victories, allowing you to take control of the things that are holding you back. Sometimes even the act of acknowledging that they exist is a big enough step to take. Yes, we're here to take challenges and push ourselves, but we don't want to break while doing it.'

'I'm not brave.' Doreen's voice comes from the opposite side of the circle. 'There are things I wish I could do, or say or put in action . . . and I just can't make that first move.'

'And how does that make you feel?' asks Ted gently.

'Stuck. Like a big, fat, stupid, stuck coward,' Doreen growls.

I look at her in shock. She sounds so angry. Her face is white and set. I'm so surprised at Doreen's revelation. She seems so comfortable in her own skin. So confident. But what she's just said about herself is such a harsh image it almost feels like someone has torn the air out of our circle.

'Doreen,' says Ted calmly, 'is there anything else you want to add?'

Doreen shakes her head glumly.

'We're going to keep going until everyone has shared, but we're going to be working a lot on all of this, okay?'

Doreen nods once and sits staring at the grass. I want to rush over to her and wrap her in a hug, but maybe it's a good thing I can't – she looks like she could knock out a troll right now.

'Can I go?' asks Bay next to me.

Ted nods.

'I'm realizing that I'm too quick to judge people. Too quick to form an opinion of them based on the tiniest snapshot of what I've seen. I let this get in the way of getting to know who they really are. I let it colour things.' He huffs out an irritated breath. 'I used to think this was a good thing. I prided myself on being a good judge of character . . . but, actually, it's the opposite.'

'Thank you, Bay,' says Ted.

'I'll go,' says Than quickly. 'I do too much for people. Money, gifts. I forgive over and over. I lose myself in other people and forget that I'm important too.'

The back of my neck prickles as a breeze rustles the branches of the apple trees above us.

That was weird.

Set against the backdrop of what Bay just said, Than's issue sounds almost like a good thing. The complete opposite of what Bay just admitted to struggling with. Almost . . . like a brag. Than shifts his weight next to me and as Ted moves on to the next person, the sensation passes. Maybe I'm reading too much into everything.

I tune back in to hear Geoff finish talking about how he's struggling to remember to have a bit of fun after focusing too long on keeping their heads above water financially. I know how he feels on that one. Bob nearly has me in tears as he tells us about how much he misses his partner who passed away over a decade ago, and how no other guy comes near to matching up to him. Moth nods vigorously as Bob talks, clearly understanding every word and emotion that's crossing his face.

Finally, it's Beardy Weirdy's turn. 'Mine sounds ridiculous,' he rumbles in his low voice.

'Nothing you say is ridiculous,' says Ted, his voice comforting. 'It can be the simplest or the strangest things that can hold us back.'

Beardy nods. 'Well, I've been getting really bad panic attacks.'

I can't help but stare at Beardy. Really? Someone as grounded and weathered as him having panic attacks?

'And do you know what sparks them? What the trigger is?' asks Ted gently.

'Yes. That's the ridiculous bit.' Beardy takes a deep breath and looks around at us all, as if expecting someone to start laughing. 'It's . . . well, it's whenever I think about the environment . . . the destruction of the planet. If I catch something on the news, or come across an article. I start to think about it, and that thought joins a bunch of other worries, and then I start to feel helpless . . . I mean there's nothing any of us can do on our own is there? And then it just . . . it just . . . spirals.'

Beardy stops talking. His breath is coming in short, sharp bursts. My heart goes out to him. His reaction is one of the least ridiculous things I've ever seen, probably because it's so familiar.

'Thank you for sharing,' says Ted. 'Thank you *all* for sharing. These are things we're going to be working on over the coming weeks. This is just the start. You've all taken a huge step today. It's important to be open so that we can act as each other's mirrors, reflecting back a different take on these issues and fears so that we can see them from new perspectives and start to understand them better.' Ted pauses to look around at us all.

'Right, everybody up!' Ted says, clapping loudly. Everyone jumps at the unexpected noise.

He bounds to his feet and a couple of the others follow his lead more slowly, shaking their heads and stretching as if they've just come out of a doze. I'm still sitting. I can't seem to shake the sense of heaviness that has fallen over me.

'Here, Tori!' Bay, who's already on his feet and looking about as perky as Ted, offers me his hand with a smile. I hesitate for just a second and then let him pull me to my feet. He misjudges it a bit and pulls so hard that I end up crashing into his chest. His spare arm wraps around me as we stagger back under the force of the impact.

'Thanks,' I laugh.

'No worries!'

For a second I'm caught up in his eyes, more hazel than green this afternoon in the soft light of the orchard.

'Tori, can you give me a hand? My leg's gone to sleep!'

Than's voice makes me quickly step away from Bay. We both reach down to help him up between us, but Than grabs my arm and is on his feet without even acknowledging Bay's offer to help. Bay shrugs and walks away.

'Okay, gang, I think a quick game of catch is in order!' Ted calls excitedly.

'Catch?' Emma says, looking like she's missed something.

'Yep. No home bases and I'll start!'

Before anyone has quite figured out what's happening, Ted darts straight towards an unsuspecting Bob, pats him on the elbow and yells 'Tag!' before hotfooting it in the other direction.

For the next ten minutes, all kinds of chaos break loose as we dart around the orchard in the sunshine. Bob chases me three times around the same tree before turning back on himself and catching me at full tilt coming towards him. I catch Than, who's only a couple of paces away. He promptly chases Bay around the whole orchard, zigzagging in and out of the trees with the rest of us cheering, until he finally catches him. Bay promptly dashes straight at Doreen and catches her in a matter of seconds.

Emma lets out a high-pitched squeal as Doreen makes a heroic lunge for her, catching her on the arm, only to do an unexpected commando-roll into the grass as she completely fails to stop. Emma turns around to help her up, only to yell 'Tag' as Doreen reaches for her hand. We all dissolve into a round of giggles and the game comes to a rather unruly end.

'Excellent!' yells Ted. We all gather around him, breathing heavily and grinning. 'Just a quick reminder not to get stuck in our heads. It's important stuff we're talking about, but it's just as important to play in the sunshine, have fun together and be in the moment . . .'

I raise my eyebrows. Man, he's good. He does have a point – the whole time we were whizzing around the orchard, I didn't think about anything other than whether I was being chased or not.

'Can't believe I paid for this,' mutters Than beside me.

I elbow him in the ribs. I know he enjoyed that every bit as much as I did.

'Okay, we're going to pair off for the rest of the session and carry on from where we left off earlier.'

Than links his arm through mine. I glance at him and force a smile. It's not that I don't want to work with him again, but

I'd really love the chance to get to know the others a bit too. Just hearing them talk earlier made me realize that I've hardly had the chance . . . or maybe I should say, I've hardly made the effort to get to know them yet.

'This time,' Ted continues, and I look back at him, fixed smile still on my face, 'I'm going to pair you up. It's human nature to gravitate towards the same people, but that's going to keep you in your comfort zones, and that's not what today is about. So . . .'

Ted runs through some quick pairings. Than ends up with Bay, while I, much to my delighted surprise, am partnered up with Doreen. When he's done, Ted goes through all the pairs very quickly, assigning the letter A or B to each partner.

'Okay, it's A's turn to talk today, and B, you are the set of ears, the listener and the questioner. This isn't about trying to catch your partner out; it's about listening and understanding their story. And I want all you As to tell your partner about one thing you want to address while you're here. It can be more about what you told us just now, or it can be something completely new.

'I'll be here in the orchard working with Emma and Sam, if any of you need to find me. I advise you all to stay out in the fresh air, but feel free to roam the place until you find somewhere you're both comfortable. You've got the rest of the afternoon, and we'll all meet up again to start preparing supper at six.'

Chapter 14

Ban the Snooze Button

'When you start trying to change your life, it can all feel a bit scary. You're beginning to wake up, but it's too much at times. But don't hit the snooze button on your life. Get up, get dressed and find out what life has in store for you today!'

©TheBeginnersGuideToLoneliness.com

'I seriously can't believe that they let us two pair up,' laughs Doreen as we make our way out of the yard.

'Why not?' I ask. 'Hey, do you mind if we head up towards the woods instead of that way?'

'Of course not!' says Doreen. We make a quick change of direction and set off up the field past the yurt. 'Oh, the river's down that way, isn't it?'

I nod.

'Sorry, I didn't think.'

'Don't be sorry. I don't expect everyone else to have to remember my oddities! Anyway, why shouldn't they let us pair up?'

135

'Well, you'd think they'd be worried about us gossiping the whole session away!'

'Actually, I think that's what they're hoping for!' I laugh. 'At least in a controlled kind of way. I think they were aiming to pair people up who'd be comfortable together.'

'Well, in that case, I'm surprised you're not with Than.'

I blush at her blunt, forthright approach. 'Than?' I squeak.

'Well . . . yes! You've spent more time together than the rest of us have, I think.'

'Oh . . . I . . .' I feel awkward all of a sudden. I mean, yes, I've chatted to Than, he tends to seek me out when we're all together, but I figure it's just because I'm the only one who knows what's going on for him at the moment. I don't think he's shared much with the others yet.

'Don't worry, love,' says Doreen. 'You know, it's not a crime to find a guy attractive and want to spend time with him.'

'Attractive?'

'Well, don't you?'

I can feel the heat rushing up from my feet. 'I . . . erm . . .'

'Wow, girl, slow down!' puffs Doreen. 'That game of catch almost killed me. I don't need you finishing me off!'

I've subconsciously picked up my pace and have started to route-march up the hill as if I'm trying to outrun Doreen's questions. 'Sorry,' I say, slowing down as she catches up.

'So, do you?' she prods.

'What?'

I know what, I'm just playing for time.

'Like Than? I mean . . . find him attractive . . . you know, *like* him?' She waggles her eyebrows at me.

I can't help but laugh. 'I guess,' I say. 'I mean, he's a good-looking guy. He's been really nice and I've enjoyed his company—'

'Wow, you sound like a maiden aunt!' Doreen laughs.

'Jeez, thanks very much.'

'Well, you do! Where are the butterflies and the sparks and the heart-pounding excitement?'

'The thing is, I'm not here for that. I'm not looking for someone else at the moment. I've got too much to do, too much I want to get my head around.'

'I hear you,' says Doreen softly at my side. 'Shame, though. I was looking forward to you providing me with all the juicy retreat gossip.'

'Well, sorry to disappoint!' I grin at her as we reach the top of the field. We both turn and lean our backs against the gate, gazing back down towards the yurt and over the farmhouse and yard.

'Love, it's not me you'll be disappointing,' says Doreen with a serious face.

I don't know what to say to that. Maybe there is a little flutter when I see Than and when we spend time together. I know there shouldn't be, but he does seem to understand me. It's like there's some kind of unspoken communication between us, like we've known each other for longer than the couple of days we've been here at The Farm.

'Sorry, Tori, I shouldn't have said anything,' Doreen says, patting my arm, her face a picture of concern.

'Oh, don't worry about that. I've got so much in my head, I just don't feel like I can trust my instincts on anything at the moment. Anyway, that's enough about me. This session's meant to be about you!' I say, unhooking the gate from the post and swinging it back so that we can make our way into the baby woodland beyond.

'Me?' squeaks Doreen, turning to help me heave the gate closed behind us.

'Yep.'

'I . . . You know, Tori, I don't think I'm ready,' she says.

I look at Doreen and see a cloud cross her usually sunny face.

'But you've had to put up with me wittering all the way up here. And anyway, you're group A and I'm group B. And group A gets their turn today.' I grin at her, trying to lift her out of whatever slump she's slipped into.

Doreen shakes her head at me.

'Don't you trust me?' I ask. I feel a tiny shard of hurt hit me in the chest.

'Oh, love, it's not that. I don't trust *myself* yet. You're so brave, sharing your phobia with the group . . . and I, I just can't. Not yet. Not even with you. And you'd be the first person I could tell.'

I swallow down a lump in my throat and grab Doreen's hand, giving it a squeeze. She looks at me, surprised.

'It's okay. I'll swap with you. But when you're ready, I'm here, okay?' I say.

Doreen squeezes my hand hard and sniffs. 'Okay.'

We wander through the young trees in silence for a while, my hand still in hers. The sun has come out now, and rather than feeling tense and uncomfortable, like I did when Ted told us about this session, I'm completely relaxed. I'm enjoying the warmth on my face, and the company of this lovely woman I'm coming to think of as a friend.

'So . . .' prompts Doreen at last.

'So?' I say, stopping in a little clearing. There's thick grass in between the trees here. They haven't grown tall enough to cut out the light yet, and little wild flowers are dotted like bright jewels among the green. 'Shall we sit down?'

'Sure!' says Doreen. 'Two secs . . .' She yanks a canvas tote bag that I hadn't even noticed she was carrying off her arm and draws out a red tartan blanket.

'Ooh, snazzy!'

'Well, it was in the cabin, and Bay mentioned last night that Ted tends to prefer to send us outside rather than working indoors, so I thought it might come in handy.'

'Good thinking,' I sigh as I sink down onto the blanket next to Doreen.

'So . . .' she smiles at me.

'Ah. Back to that. Now what was it Ted said we were meant to do?'

'Tell me one of the reasons that you came here. It can be anything.'

I shrug. 'That's an easy one.'

'Is it?' Doreen gapes at me, surprised.

'Of course,' I say, settling down with my legs crossed. I know Claire said that the yoga session was a gentle one, but I can still feel a faint, delicious hum in my muscles that I'm not used to.

'I'm lonely,' I say, matter-of-factly. Why is it so easy to say that to Doreen?

'You are?' She looks a bit surprised.

'Yes. That's the big thing I'm here to . . . fix? Is that the right word?'

'But how are you lonely? You're so easy to talk to, so lovely,' says Doreen. 'I thought your reason for being here was the water thing . . .'

'I guess that's part of it,' I say. *Not the part I want to talk about right now, though.*

Doreen picks a long piece of grass from the edge of the rug and starts to twist it around her finger like a ring. 'How long have you been feeling like that?' she asks.

I sigh. When did it start? When Mum died? That would be logical . . . but, if I'm honest, it was even before then. 'You know, I think it's been there since I was a kid in a way. I was always a part of a large group, but never had one close friend that really stuck. It was like that all the way through school and uni. I guess it really started to have an impact when I left work just over two years ago,' I say.

'I used to be a copywriter for a big advertising agency. I never really liked it much. The work was okay, but the whole office thing was exhausting. I felt like I had to put on a different persona just to fit in. Then there were the days when my anxiety would take over, and it was a real struggle just to face the commute, let alone deal with everyone when I actually reached the office. Anyway, in the end I plucked up the courage to go self-employed.'

'Wow, that was brave!' says Doreen.

'I guess so. But it meant I lost that connection with all those people I saw every day.'

'You didn't stay in touch with your friends from work?'

'They weren't really friends; just colleagues. And I was so busy trying to scrape enough income together that I let it slip. We'd never really socialized anyway, so as soon as I finished at the office that was that.'

'But what about your other friends? Surely you didn't only have your work colleagues?'

I shake my head and sigh. 'No, I had a big group of friends. Actually, we'd all been mates since secondary school. We managed to stay in touch through uni.'

'So what happened?'

'My fiancé, Markus, was part of the same group. We'd all been together for what felt like forever.'

'Sounds perfect,' Doreen sighs.

'It does, doesn't it? At least from the outside,' I huff. 'But then, when everything went wrong, it meant *everything* went wrong.'

'What happened?' Doreen asks, looking worried.

'Markus cheated on me.'

'He didn't!' Doreen looks horrified.

'Yep.'

'With one of your friends?'

I look at her, surprised. 'No. No, not with one of my friends. It was with a random barmaid.'

'Oh. Sorry.'

I shrug.

'So what did you do?'

'I split up with him.'

'As you would expect. That must have really hurt.'

'It did . . . but I had other stuff to worry about at the time.'

'So your friends sided with him?'

'No, not at first. They kept inviting me out, trying to help me over it with offers of girly nights out and shopping.'

'It didn't work?' asks Doreen gently.

'I didn't accept any of the invitations, and it didn't take long for them to dry up completely. And before I knew it, Markus was seeing this other girl and they were a part of the group . . . and I was out.' I let out a sigh and pick at one of my nails.

'I can understand you pulling back after it had just ended, but didn't you want to reconnect with your friends after a while? Surely they could see you were hurting and—'

I shake my head. 'I wasn't easy to be around. I do understand that.'

'I'm missing something here,' says Doreen, and my heart sinks. She's not stupid, this one, is she? 'If you've been friends with someone for that long, whether you're friends with her ex or not, you make sure she's okay. And no matter what she throws at you, you keep trying.'

'My mum had just died. They didn't know how to handle it.'

Doreen looks like I've just slapped her. 'Your mum? Oh, you poor lamb! So you're telling me you lost your mum and then Markus cheated on you – all in the same year?'

I shift my legs, stretching them out and then hugging them back to me. Now I've come this far, I may as well tell her. 'The same month,' I say.

'Son of a bitch!' Doreen spits, taking me by surprise. I look at her and can't help but smile at the thunderous expression on her face.

'You could say that,' I agree.

'And your friends were okay with what he'd done to you?'

'I wouldn't say that they were okay with it. Actually, I don't think many of them knew exactly what had happened. Markus had this interesting take on things – how I wasn't giving him enough attention and he'd been forced to look elsewhere. I was in shock, and to be honest, I was numb when I found out what he'd done. I just split up with him and then got on with wading through all the shitty practicalities that come with losing a parent. I got quite good at not feeling anything.'

'And your friends just abandoned you?'

'Like I said, they asked me out, they really tried. But I wasn't in the mood to be told that I needed to "get over it", that a couple of drinks and a bit of fun was all I needed to feel better.'

'Of course not. I'm so sorry,' Doreen reaches over and pats my hand. I smile at her.

'So that's where it started. No work colleagues, no friends, no significant other.'

'And all that grief and anger and sadness to work through.'

I nod.

'What about your dad? Do you have any other family?'

I shake my head. 'Dad left when I was a baby. He's never been in my life and I don't know him. I don't have any brothers or sisters. Mum was an only kid too, so there aren't even any aunts or uncles in the sidelines either.'

'Do you need a hug?' Doreen asks me suddenly.

I grin at her. 'I'm okay,' I say.

'I don't understand how you haven't exploded?' she says.

'I went online. I had to talk to someone, so I joined this grief support group. That was just a couple of weeks after it all happened.'

'Oh, thank God!' said Doreen.

'Exactly what I said,' I laugh. 'I met my three best friends in that group. One night, I just felt like I was sinking under it all. I needed to talk to someone who was going through something similar. Anyway, this girl called Nat started to chat with me, and we got on really well. I swear she was my lifeline. I talked poor Nat's ear off in our private chat that week.'

'And the other two?'

'I met them about a week later in the same chat room.'

'And this was all two years ago?'

'Yep! I started to chat with Nat first, and then I invited the other two into our private chat when I met them . . . and we still talk every single day. I probably chat with Nat the most;

she's always checking in with me. But we've all been able to support each other. Like when Hugh's brother passed away, we were all there for him.'

'But you still feel lonely, even with these three?'

'They are amazing, but we've never met in person, and no matter how much they mean to me, it's just not the same somehow.'

'You've never met?'

I shake my head. 'Nope, we chat every day online but we're spread all over the country. Sue has baby twins now, so she's pretty tied up. Hugh lives right up north. Nat and I have arranged to meet up a couple of times as she's not that far from me, but we've never quite managed to make it happen.'

Doreen blows out her cheeks, looking flummoxed. 'Well, now I see why you feel lonely. Two years is a hell of a long time.'

I nod. 'I'm at home in my flat all day. Of course, I meet people when I'm out shopping or whatever, but . . . London's quite impersonal, you know? Millions of people . . . but they're millions of strangers.'

I stop talking, hyper aware that I've just dumped all my rubbish on someone else who's here for help. She didn't need to hear all that. 'Doreen, I'm so sorry,' I say, slightly embarrassed.

'What for?'

'Offloading! That wasn't fair.'

'Erm . . . I think you'll find that's exactly what we're meant to be doing,' Doreen chuckles.

'I guess,' I sigh. I thought I'd feel better for telling someone, but actually, I just feel exhausted, like I could sleep for a week. I lie back on the blanket and watch a little white cloud scud across the sky. I can see Doreen, to the side of me, fiddling with another piece of grass.

'You get stuck,' I say, as if I'm answering a silent question. 'After a while, it's impossible to remember how to make new friends, how to meet people. Where to even start. And you have all this input, every day. Stuff happens, good, bad, big, small . . . life happens, and you have no one there to share it with.' I swallow hard. The backs of my eyes are prickling, and I blink once, twice, willing the tears to magically disappear. Instead they spill over my cheeks as Doreen quietly reaches over and takes my hand.

Chapter 15

Trust Your Instincts

'It can be difficult to tell the difference between your gut instinct and anxiety. This can lead to people with anxiety disorders losing trust in themselves. The good news is, there are ways to learn to differentiate between the two, and doing so will help you to learn to trust yourself again.'

©TheBeginnersGuideToLoneliness.com

It's amazing what running around together in the sunshine can achieve. Despite the fact that this afternoon was emotionally exhausting, there's a lightness to our communal meal this evening. When Doreen and I trundled back from the woods in time to make a start on the evening meal, we found it already set out on the table. Russ and Claire had decided to use their afternoon off to prepare a feast for us.

I don't think garden salad, boiled eggs and fresh herby bread has ever tasted so delicious. Being out in the fresh air all day has made me hungry, and Doreen and I tuck in with relish. The others join us as they all start to rock up in their pairs. When Emma, Sam and Ted appear, the couple look a lot more relaxed than they did earlier, though strangely younger and more shy around each other. There's a huge part of me that really wants to ask Emma what happened in their session, but I know I'd hate it if anyone wanted me to tell them about my afternoon with Doreen. I can only imagine it would be worse, and doubly as private, between a couple and one of the counsellors. Instead, I smile at them both, and pat the place next to me on the bench for Emma to join me. She returns my smile, but before she's had a chance to make her way around the table, Than slumps into the spot instead.

'Hey!' he grins.

'Oh, hi,' I say, surprised. 'I think Emma was about to sit there.'

'There's plenty of room!' Than laughs, and Emma takes the seat the other side of him. 'See, no big deal.'

I smile back at him. Sure. No big deal. I suppose. Other than the fact that Doreen's words from earlier on are playing on a loop in my head. *Than . . . attractive . . . disappointing him.* I wonder if that's what everyone else thinks too. I hadn't really considered it before. Maybe that was naive of me. I take a peek at Than's face, trying to figure it out. Yes, he's definitely attractive. Dark hair, cropped fairly short. Clear skin. Almond-shaped blue eyes.

'You okay?' he asks, shooting me a sideways grin, clearly having caught me staring.

'Oh, uh . . . yeah,' I smile. 'Away with the fairies. I'm absolutely wiped!' I reach for my glass of water. 'Have a good afternoon?'

'Oh. Sure. I guess,' he says tightly. The smile has dropped

from his face now and he fidgets a bit. Reaching for a piece of bread, he starts to break it up into tiny pieces, rolling each one into a sticky ball before dropping it onto his plate.

'You know, you should try a bite . . . that bread's heavenly!' I say, trying to lighten his sudden mood.

'Cheers!' says Russ from across the table. 'That's my speciality, that is!'

'You made it?' I ask, looking at him in surprise.

'With my own, not so fair, hands!' he says, cutting himself a thick slice and smothering it with honey.

'Honey and herbs? Really?' I say, scrunching my nose up.

'Don't judge until you've tried it!' he says, and to my great surprise, he picks up the slice and offers it across the table for me to take a bite. I only hesitate for a second and then sink my teeth into it.

'Oh. My. God.' I mutter through a mouthful of herby honey deliciousness.

'And that's what you call a foodgasm!' laughs Doreen, raising her glass of juice to me. I smack her arm as I continue to chew, and she and Russ both crease up. Next to me, Than lets out a huff and reaches out to fill his water glass.

'What's up?' I ask quietly under the cover of the rising volume of chatter as more people join us at the table.

'Would you be up for coming for a walk with me after dinner?' he asks.

'What about the washing-up?'

'I think we've done our fair share of kitchen duties for a couple of days.'

'I guess you're right,' I say, but still not liking the idea of leaving it all to the others.

'Course I'm right. And I could really do with a friend this evening.'

My heart squeezes in sympathy. That's one feeling I understand right at the core of me.

'Sure thing,' I say.

But my promise to spend some time with Than leaves me with a rather heavy feeling for the rest of the meal. You'd think we'd all be talked out after the session we've just had, but it's more like a cork has come out of a bottle. The whole group's chatting away and getting to know each other. There's a lovely sense of community, and I'd like nothing more than to take time over my meal and join in. But as soon as Than finishes eating, I can feel his impatience coming at me in waves as he waits for me to finish. In the end, I give up. I'm not even enjoying the food now that I've got someone watching me eat every mouthful and sighing every time I take another sip of my drink.

As we stand together and leave the others chatting, Doreen catches my eye and gives me a wink. I want to turn around and tell her it's not what she thinks, but Than chooses that moment to tuck my arm into his as we walk away from the group, and I see Doreen raise her eyebrows.

'So, where do you fancy going?' I ask lightly, resigning myself to the walk.

'If you don't mind, I'd really like to go back to my tent for a chat, if that's okay?'

'Oh . . . uh, sure . . .' I say uncertainly.

'I would have suggested your place, as I guess you might be more comfortable there, but Bay could turn up any moment, and I don't fancy spending any more time with him today.'

I glance at him and see his jaw clench. *Uh oh!* I'm guessing that wasn't a particularly easy session for the two of them this afternoon then.

'It's okay!' I say. 'I haven't been up to the campsite since you've all arrived and set up. I'd love to see it now.'

'Cool!' says Than, and I feel him relax a bit.

'So, what's up?' I ask, as we swing the gate to the woodland closed behind us.

'Just . . . all the questions, you know? They want to get all this personal shit out of you and I can't see the point.'

'Well . . . haven't you found it's helping at all?' I ask gently. 'The bits that you've shared already, haven't they got you thinking?'

'I don't need any extra shit to think about, thanks!' he snaps.

'Oh. I didn't mean . . .'

'Sorry, Tori.' Than stops in his tracks. 'I'm sorry. I didn't mean to take it out on you. That's the last thing I want to do.'

'It's okay,' I shrug.

'No. It's not.' He sighs and runs a hand through his hair, leaving it sticking up here and there. 'Look, can we just hang out for a bit, gossip, have a laugh . . . not get into the heavy stuff? I think that'll do me more good than anything else they've thrown at us today.'

I look at him and can't help but smile. He looks like a little boy, with his dark hair all tufty, and his ever-present smiley-face badge slightly askew on the front of his top. 'Of course,' I say, 'sounds like a plan.'

There's a part of me that's now desperate to find out what Bay and Than discussed in their session. I didn't catch which one of them was due to do the talking, but from Than's reaction to the whole afternoon, I'm guessing it was him. Still, maybe he'll tell me a bit about it later once he's calmed down.

We're both pretty quiet as we walk the rest of the way to the campsite, but the atmosphere between us is now far more relaxed. It's a beautiful evening again. The light is soft and the scent of blossom seems to be drifting up from the orchard below us. I take in a deep breath as we walk and let it out slowly. Who'd have thought I'd enjoy being here as much as I am? And on an evening stroll with a handsome guy, no less.

When we reach the campsite, it's pretty clear that there's no one else here. The fire pit is black and lifeless, and the four tent entrances are zipped up tight. They're arranged in a wide, loose circle around the fire, far enough away that there's no chance of a stray spark or bit of floating ash causing an issue.

Than beckons me over to an old-school green and orange affair that looks like it would be at home in an Enid Blyton book.

'This is me,' he says, unzipping the front.

It's a tiny space, especially compared with the yurt, which is basically a palace.

'You want to get a fire going and hang out here?' I ask hopefully.

Than shakes his head. 'Nah, let's stay in here for a bit. I'm totally knackered, and there's plenty of space for us both to crash out for a while.'

He crawls in, and I hesitate, a bit at a loss for words. Than heaves a pack from inside the tent and dumps it unceremoniously on the ground outside. Then, crawling back in, he straightens a sleeping bag out on one side of the tent and places a tartan blanket on the other side.

'There ya go,' he grins back over his shoulder. 'You've got your own blanket and everything.'

Resigning myself to saying goodbye to the beautiful, sunlit evening and hello to the cramped, stuffy inside of Than's tent, I kick off my Converse and crawl in after him.

'Here!' he says, passing one of his pillows to me.

'Ta.' I scoot around and sit in an awkward, cross-legged position as Than sprawls full length onto his sleeping bag. I tuck my ankles in even further, hoping that my socks don't stink after a day in my hot shoes. Uh oh, there's zero chance of that!

'Seriously, Tori, make yourself comfortable! You look like you're sitting on a pile of drawing pins!'

Well, it seems I can't beat him, so I may as well join him. And besides, it gives me an excuse to get my potentially stinky feet as far away from both our noses as possible. I stretch out full length next to Than, wiggling my feet under my blanket while I'm at it, and lean my head up on one hand.

'That's more like it!' he smiles approvingly, and brings his arms up behind his head.

Now I'm lying down, the epic tiredness from earlier sweeps over me and I force back a yawn.

'Boring you already?' Than says, turning his head to look at me.

'I'm sorry!' I laugh. 'Of course you're not. I'm just wiped out. It's all the fresh air, I think.'

'Yeah. That and all the questions,' Than grumbles, looking back up at the canvas roof again.

'Hey, we weren't going to talk about that, remember?' I tease, poking him in the side with my free hand.

Than squirms at my touch, and shifts over onto his side, mirroring me. *Wow*. Okay, flood of butterflies – where did they come from? Perhaps it's something to do with those blue eyes quite so close to mine. We're not touching, but it wouldn't take much for me to reach out and make contact again.

I try to breathe as slowly as possible, not wanting him to sense what's running through my mind.

'So how was your afternoon?' Than asks quietly.

I raise my eyebrows, surprised. 'You sure you want to talk about this stuff?' I ask.

'As long as I don't have to talk about mine, then we're good,' he quirks a smile at me, and for a second I can't take my eyes off his mouth.

'Deal,' I say, my voice coming out huskily. I clear my throat. I settle my head back onto my pillow and turn on my back to face the canvas ceiling. 'Well, our session was good,' I say.

'It was Doreen's turn this time, wasn't it?' he asks.

'Yep, but . . .'

'What did she have to tell you, then?' he interrupts. 'What's a housewife like her really got to worry about?'

I swallow. Well, that's one way to kill a mood stone dead. My butterflies have just dive-bombed off the edge of a cliff. I had been about to tell him that we swapped, that I'd taken the turn to talk, but something makes me keep that to myself.

'That's not very fair,' I say as lightly as I can.

'But she's so insipid. You know she is.'

'I like Doreen,' I say. I *really* like her and I really *don't* like what's happening right now.

'Well, I suppose there's not much there to dislike.'

'Than!'

'Fine, fine.' He laughs. 'I'm sure she's lovely.' He says it in his arch sarcastic voice, and I bristle.

'She *is* lovely,' I say firmly.

'So what did the lovely Doreen have to say for herself?'

'You know I can't tell you that . . .' I say. I sit up and hug my knees to me. Now I feel really bloody uncomfortable, and I'd quite like an excuse to go back to the others.

'Tori?' Than sits up beside me. 'I'm sorry, I was only messing around.'

I turn to look at him, and his face is sincere, his eyes searching mine. Maybe I'm overreacting, overthinking everything. I stare hard at the smiley badge on his chest, trying to get a handle on my feelings.

'Really, I didn't mean to upset you,' he says, and rests his hand briefly on my arm.

I shake my head and give him a small smile. 'It's okay. Sorry, Than. Maybe I'm just a bit tired.'

'So I'm forgiven?' he asks.

'Nothing to forgive,' I say, and with a sigh I slump back onto the pillow again.

Than lies back down next to me and, taking my hand, gives it a quick squeeze before letting go. 'Thanks for coming with me this evening.'

'That's okay,' I say, and close my eyes as another wave of weariness washes over me. We lie in silence for a couple of minutes.

'You know, I miss this . . .' I say at last.

'What?' Than sounds alert, perplexed.

'Lying next to someone and just talking.'

Than laughs. 'What, you mean pillow talk?'

'I guess,' I say, slightly embarrassed.

'So no other half at home, then?'

'Not anymore. Actually, not for a couple of years now.'

'You still miss him?' Than asks.

I take a second to think about it. 'You know what? No . . . I don't miss him. It's like I said, I miss this. The talking. Being close to someone.'

Than turns back on his side to face me and I move to do the same.

'Well . . . just for the record, I'm always available for a bit of pillow talk.' He winks at me and I smile back.

I find myself hooked on his eyes again, and something in the atmosphere between us changes. I'm doing the slow, light breathing thing again, and the space between us feels like it's getting smaller. I can feel the warmth of his skin radiating out from him. Our faces are so close, I can see darker flecks in his eyes.

There's a crash outside the tent, followed by the sounds of two people laughing and chattering. There's another crash, and I spring away from Than as if someone's thrown a bucket of iced water over my head.

Through the tent's entrance, I just have the chance to spot Claire and Moth next to a pile of wood they've just gathered, before a brown and white blur hurtles straight at me, tail wagging nineteen to the dozen. It's Dennis, and he's insistent on a cuddle at the same time as trying to give my face a wash with his tongue.

I struggle to my knees, laughing and trying to keep my face slobber-free. But I give in and wrap my arms around the warm dog. For a second, all I can hear is his tail beating against my legs.

'Out, dog!' Than shouts, making me jump.

Dennis pulls away from me and eyeballs Than warily.

'Go on, out!' Than shouts again. Dennis looks from Than to me, and back again, clearly unused to being spoken to like this.

'It's okay, Than,' I say gently.

'No, it's not. Out!' Than barks at Dennis for a third time, and I feel the rumble of a growl come from Dennis.

'You're scaring him,' I say. 'It's okay, boy, come on.' I go to lead Dennis out of the tent before he and Than get into a real argument.

As Dennis scuttles out in front of me, Than leans forward and, placing one hand on my shoulder, tries to draw me gently back towards him. I shake my head at him and scramble out after the dog.

Chapter 16

Permission to Pause

'You've pushed your boundaries, opened yourself to new experiences and challenged your comfort zones over and over again. It's okay to give yourself permission to pause. You're not stopping in your incredible journey, just taking a moment to admire how far you've come.'

©TheBeginnersGuideToLoneliness.com

I spot the yurt in the distance and breathe a sigh of relief. As I pause for a second to catch my breath, Dennis sits down and leans his head against my leg. From the moment we got out of Than's tent, he has glued himself to me, acting like a large, furry shadow.

I only stopped for a couple of minutes to say hello to Claire and Moth, shoving my shoes back on while they did their best to hide their obvious surprise at the sight of me and Than emerging from his tent. We've probably just managed to provide tomorrow's juicy gossip. I cringe at the thought.

Claire mentioned that everyone was going to reconvene down at the main fire pit for the evening. Than was all for us both walking straight back down there together, but I managed to wriggle out of it. Thinking about it now, I might have been a tad too firm with him about coming back on my own. I used Dennis as my excuse, but really, I just needed a bit of space. That little chat was taking a turn I didn't feel particularly in control of, and the way he reacted to Dennis's innocent appearance turned my butterflies into something that felt uncomfortably close to panic. Anyway, I'm craving some peace and quiet to work it all out a bit.

As we head down the hill towards the yurt, Dennis's tail goes into overdrive, and he pulls ahead of me and scoots inside before I get there. I flip open the flap to find Bay lounging at full stretch on the sofa.

'Oh, hi!' I say. I don't know why I'm surprised to see him. I mean, he does live here too.

Bay lifts his head off the cushions and smiles at me.

'Hey, Tori. Sorry, let me budge up. I thought you were out for the evening.' He swings his feet down, making space for me at the other end of the little sofa. Bang goes my chance of a quiet hour to myself.

'I was,' I say, flopping down next to him and leaning over to scratch Dennis's ears. 'But I thought I'd better bring this monkey home before the argument between him and Than got any more serious!'

Bay raises his eyebrows. 'Argument? What did he do?'

'Oh, just growled at Than a bit.'

'I didn't mean Dennis.'

I shrug. 'Dennis bowled into Than's tent. We were in there talking and Than told Dennis to get out . . . a couple of times . . . and poor old Dennis didn't like it. No big deal.'

Bay frowns. 'Actually, it *is* a big deal. Dennis never growls.'

'Well, he was as good as gold once I got him out of the tent, and he stuck right by me all the way home . . . or at least he did until he caught your scent and hurtled in here like a daddy's boy!'

'Well, thanks for bringing him back,' says Bay. 'You know, it sounds like he was trying to protect you.'

I laugh. 'Nah, he just wanted tickles and didn't like being told off.'

'Well, whatever. Thanks for making sure he was okay. And sorry he dragged you away from your, erm, talk . . .'

I feel my face start to redden. 'No probs. I wanted to head back here anyway.'

'Need a bit of space?' he asks, ruffling Dennis's ears.

I nod. 'It's quite intense here, isn't it?'

'Sometimes.'

'You okay?' I ask curiously, realizing that I've just interrupted his moment of peace. 'You weren't at dinner . . .'

'Yeah. I just needed some time to digest today's sessions.'

'You were with Than this afternoon, weren't you?' I say as lightly as possible.

'Yup.' Bay leans back against the sofa, looking wiped.

'Do you want me to make you a cuppa before I go?'

Bay shakes his head. 'Nah, I'm good, thanks. You back off up to the campsite?' he asks, looking pissed off for some reason.

'Nope, they've decided to have a fire down in the main pit. You fancy it?'

'I think I'll stay put, thanks. I'm not in the best of moods.'

'No, can't say I'm feeling that settled either . . . but I'm learning sometimes company is the answer to that.'

Bay smiles at me wearily. 'Look, there's something I wanted to say to you.'

I wait to see what he says next, but he goes quiet.

'What, Bay?' I laugh, eventually breaking the silence.

'This is between you and me . . .' he blurts.

'Ah, come on, I'm all secreted out for one day!'

'I'll give you this one for free, as long as you keep it to yourself. But after what you've just said, I think I've got to say something.'

I shrug and don't reply. Half of me is now super-curious to see what's getting to him, and the other half is irritated that my moment of peace is turning into something far more compli-cated. I get to my feet and cross over to my case, intending to pull out a warmer jumper to wear down to the fire.

'Watch out for Than,' he says abruptly.

I stop in my tracks, dumbfounded, and swing back around to face him.

'What do you mean, watch out?'

'I mean, just be a bit careful, Tori.' He sits straighter on the sofa and twists to look at me. 'There's something about him that I'm not sure about.'

162

'You can't say that!' I squeak, indignation oozing out of me. 'I mean, we've all got stuff going on. That's why we're here. It's meant to be a safe space to share with each other!'

'I know. But something just isn't sitting right.'

I huff and go to defend Than further, but Bay cuts me off. 'I've seen a lot, and I mean a *lot*, of troubled souls coming through here. They're all looking for an answer to something. Trust me, some of the stuff that they're looking for help with is pretty horrific. And none of them – not one – has ever caused these alarm bells before.'

'And why exactly are you more worried about me than the rest of the group?'

'I'm not blind, Tori. I see how Than is with you. He spent the whole opening ceremony staring at you. He's managed to completely separate you from the rest of the group on more than one occasion . . . like when you two skipped out on the wild swimming session, and it sounds like he managed to do it again this afternoon after dinner.'

'You're imagining things. I told everyone I was sorry about the swimming session.'

'I know . . . but why was he the one there to hold your hand? To encourage you to give in to your fears?' Bay shakes his head as if there's a fly irritating him. 'How can it be best for you to just avoid the things you need to work on?'

I shrug, and then go over to straighten my bed covers. I don't have to listen to this rubbish.

'Bay,' I say, trying to keep my voice steady, 'I did what was best for me. Than just happened to be there and noticed what

163

was going on. For your information, I got a lot out of that session. Out of the whole day, actually.'

'Oh yeah,' he says, the sarcasm in his voice is so heavy that he sounds like a completely different person. 'I'm sure you got loads out of Lizzie's session, spending the whole time staring into his eyes.'

'Me? Staring at him? I . . .' Damn and blast my bloody blush reflex. I can feel the heat radiating from my cheeks.

'I saw it, Tori,' Bay says again.

'Well, you don't need to worry about me. Besides, it looks like I'm going to have you and your bloody dog as a chaperone most of my waking life while I'm here, so there's no chance anything could happen even if I wanted it to, is there?'

'Nope,' Bay snaps. 'Not if I have anything to do with it anyway.'

I shake my head in irritation. There is literally nothing I can say to make him believe that I'm not interested in Than . . . especially as, right now, I'm not one hundred per cent certain on that point either.

The fire turns out to be a blessing. For starters, it means I don't have to hang out in the yurt, silently fuming while pretending that what Bay said about Than didn't bug me. Because it really did. A lot. And that's the other good thing about tonight. I'm not on my own with Than either. Because no matter how pissed off I am with Bay, his words of warning have lodged somewhere very deep down in my anxiety-prone brain. Between that and the weird turn things took up at the campsite earlier, I suddenly feel a little bit uncomfortable around Than.

I could curse Bay for making me feel like this, because Than is back to being his usual friendly self. But now I can't help but notice how he's . . . I don't know . . . he's zoning in on me a bit. Every time I look up, he's watching me. Whenever there's a spot available next to me on one of the straw bales around the fire, he seems to be there, ready to fill it. But the whole group is here this evening. The only glaring exception is Bay, and that's fine by me because at least it means I'm not going to constantly be on edge, worrying about what he imagines he can see between the two of us.

'Hey!'

I turn to find Doreen sitting next to me.

'Glad you made it back for the fire,' she grins. 'I was wondering if you and a certain someone might be a bit too busy to join us!'

And there I was, thinking I'd managed to escape that particular smoking gun.

'He just wanted a chat . . .' I mutter. Urgh, is everyone watching and wondering if there's something going on?

'Mm hmm . . .' She leans closer and whispers, 'Well, can't say I'd blame you if you did more than just chat!'

'Shhh!' I wince, peeping back over my shoulder at Than, who's sitting the other side of me. I can only hope he's too busy chatting with Bob to have heard anything.

'Nothing happened,' I hiss, and Doreen's perm seems to deflate a little bit with disappointment.

'Really?' she begs. 'Not even a tiny snippet of juicy gossip?'

I laugh and shake my head. I could tell her about what I think *almost* happened, the butterflies . . . but frankly, I think we're getting enough unwanted attention at the moment without fanning the flames.

'So, how are you doing?' I ask, trying to deflect the conversation away from the tangle I'm in.

'Oh, fine, you know. Geoff reckons he already feels twenty years younger, what with the yoga and the swimming.' She smiles and looks wistfully across the fire to where her husband is deep in conversation with Sam. She wipes a stray tear from her cheek so quickly it's obvious that she's hoping I won't notice.

'You okay?' I ask, shuffling around to face her properly.

Doreen nods and sniffs. 'You know I said I couldn't talk to you earlier?'

I nod.

'Can I tell you now?' she whispers.

'Of course!' I say.

'It's just so strange, being here together. I've wanted to be able to spend more time with Geoff for ages . . . and now we're here, I'm scared that we've both changed too much for it to work.'

I pat Doreen's arm ineffectually, and watch Ted haul another large log onto the fire. 'But you're getting the chance to get to know each other again?'

'Well, yes. I've been caring for my mother for ages. Geoff's a sweetheart, and has been so supportive, but having Mum living with us and being a full-time carer while Geoff has held everything together financially has put a lot of pressure on our marriage.'

'You said your mum is in a home now?' I ask, struggling to remember what she'd said at that first meeting in the farmhouse.

'Yes. Social services finally decided that it would be best for her.'

'I'm so sorry,' I say.

'That's the problem,' Doreen laughs, but I can hear that it's thick with unshed tears, 'I'm not. I feel so guilty saying this, but it's the biggest relief. It's hard enough when your own mother doesn't recognize you, but she was becoming more and more difficult to care for. She got really violent at times. You must think I'm so horrible . . .'

Doreen starts to cry in earnest. I shuffle right over to the edge of my straw bale and put an arm around her shoulders. 'I don't think anything of the sort,' I say quietly. I remember the horrible comment I made to Than when we skived off from the swim, and what he said about Doreen earlier, and a part of me cringes.

'Thanks, Tori!' Doreen snuffles, pulling back and wiping her face. 'I just . . . I'm just so scared that me and Geoff won't find that thing between us again, you know?' she says. 'He's my best friend and he knows me better than anyone else in the world . . . but . . . that's not enough, is it?'

I shrug. 'Sorry, not my area of expertise.'

She smiles at me, her lips trembling. 'Oh, don't you go worrying about that. You're sharing your tent with one guy who can't take his eyes off you,' she leans in a bit closer, 'and sharing a bale with another one.'

I roll my eyes at her and she nudges me in the ribs.

'I'll leave that kind of thing up to you!' I say. 'Sharing with Bay is like a cross between sharing with a mean older brother and a strict head teacher.'

'We'll see,' she says, gazing longingly across the fire at Geoff.

By the time I head back to the yurt, it's ridiculously late. It was just me, Than, Doreen, Geoff and Beardy Weirdy left, so I figured I'd make a break for it before there was any chance of being left alone with Than. If I'm being totally honest, I might have timed my rather abrupt departure when he and Geoff were deep in conversation to avoid any chance of him offering to walk me back. Let's face it, appearing this late with Than in tow wouldn't be the best way to keep the peace with Bay.

I feel a little thrill of pride when I spot the yurt in front of me, happy that I've managed to find my way back on my own in the dark.

I slip off my boots and sneak in through the entrance flap to be greeted by two rounds of loud snoring. I breathe a soft sigh of relief. There'll be no first degree nor the need for any more awkward conversation tonight. That'll just have to keep until morning.

Chapter 17

Extraordinarily Ordinary

'Stop looking for those big changes that scare you. Stop waiting for the lightning bolt that will change your life in one strike. Instead, open yourself up and look around you every day for the opportunities to make an ordinary moment extraordinary.'

©TheBeginnersGuideToLoneliness.com

Turns out, I'm not going to have to make awkward conversation with Bay this morning after all. Based on the racket the birds are still making outside, it's not that late, but when I peer over at Bay's side of the yurt I'm met with an empty bed. My own, however, appears to have gained an extra body. I try to wiggle my feet, but they've been trapped by a large, snoozing mound of Dennis.

'Hey, boy!' I say, reaching down and just managing to tickle the top of his head. My hand gets a thorough slobbering in response and then Dennis wriggles himself up so that his head is almost on the pillow next to mine. 'Reckon your dad's going to be in a better mood today?'

Dennis licks my nose, and I splutter. Nice. Ah well, at least someone's glad to see me. If I'm completely honest with myself, I'm a bit gutted that Bay isn't here. There's a part of me that really wants to apologize for yesterday. He caught me off guard, when I was completely knackered, and now, with a bit of perspective, I know he was only trying to look out for me, and I wasn't exactly grateful. At all. Ah well, I'm sure I'll get the chance to say something later.

Today is Russ's first mindfulness session with us, and, according to the handbook, it includes a bodywork aspect of its own, so we don't have Claire's usual session on top of it. I realize that I'm actually a little bit gutted about this. I enjoyed starting yesterday off with the yoga . . . I just hope Russ has something similar up his sleeve.

I'm not sure what I think of this whole 'mindfulness' thing anyway. It feels a bit like a buzz word – all style, no substance. I can't help but feel a tiny bit sceptical.

When Dennis and I reach the breakfast table, it seems the rest of the group have similar reservations.

'What do you think?' Geoff asks, slumping onto the bench next to me and yawning widely. 'This session going to be any good, or can I head home and grab forty winks?'

'I haven't got a clue,' I say, stuffing my face with porridge before it goes cold and congeals into cement in my bowl.

'Ah, come on, don't give us that!' says Sam from across the

table. 'You know Bay's involved in helping Russ with today's session. He must have told you about it at some point, what with you two living together . . .'

'What do you mean he's helping Russ? He's here for the retreat like the rest of us . . .' I say, looking surprised.

'Oh, it's something to do with the garden,' says Beardy Weirdy. 'Bay designed it for them and does a bit of work on it a couple of times a year when he comes down for the retreats. At least, that's what he told me. He's a bit of an unofficial volunteer here, really.'

'Well, he's not told me anything about it,' I say, feeling a bit wrong-footed. I'm just realizing that I've not taken much interest in getting to know Bay.

'Well, I reckon today's going to be complete crap.' Than's voice cuts across the table. There's something about the way he says it that makes me bristle.

Doreen catches my eye and raises her eyebrows at me. I shrug. 'I'm looking forward to it,' I say.

We're gossiping around the edge of the vegetable patch when Russ's voice makes us all jump.

'Welcome to your first mindfulness session.' He makes his way quietly to the front of the group and turns to face us. 'So, what is mindfulness? It's a practice, a meditation, a manner of truly living in the world, moment by moment, without following our thoughts down the rabbit holes that take us away from the reality that surrounds us.'

He's already lost me. Ironic really. I shift from foot to foot as Russ waffles on and catch myself staring at Bay. He's next to Russ, and the sunlight on his hair is making tiny, golden lights appear and disappear as he tilts his head this way and that. My attention finally snaps back as Russ says, 'Mindfulness can stop you chasing thoughts that lead to your fears and encourage anxiety. When you're fully in the moment, you don't worry about the past and you're not anxious about the future. You're just reacting to this moment right now.'

Well, that makes a bit more sense. I guess.

'We'll be coming back here to the garden a little later on to discuss the session and work on some jobs that Bay's got lined up, but first I want to take you all on a walk.'

A murmur of descent runs around the group, and I catch Geoff's whisper of 'Not another bloody walk.'

'I've done this walk several times with you all in mind. It passes through some really important energy points on the land,' Russ continues.

'Christ, energy points? What is this – how to be a gullible hippy using twenty simple clichés?' says Than, smirking and giving my arm a nudge.

I look at my feet. Despite what was going through my head yesterday in his tent, this morning I don't want to be a part of Than's club. It's not just Bay's warnings last night that have put me on edge . . . I can't quite put my finger on it, but there's something in the way that Than treats the others too. I noticed it around the fire last night, and then again at break-fast. I've got a feeling it's been there all along, but I've been too overwhelmed by his attention to notice.

'I have certain points on the walk where you will each be dropped off,' Russ continues. 'From there, I want you to wander at will for a couple of minutes until you feel compelled to wait and watch and listen. Use all of your senses to really be there, in that moment.'

'What are we watching and listening for?' asks Emma, sounding both excited and confused.

'For whatever comes to you. Open your hearts. Try to stay in the moment. Don't let your minds wander, but trust your senses.'

'How long for?' asks Doreen.

'For as long as it takes, and then we'll meet back here. Bay, I'll start with you. I'd like you to remain in the garden and complete your session from here. This is familiar territory for you, but I wonder how much of it you truly see and experience as you work on the garden?'

Bay nods, and sits down on the edge of one of the raised beds.

'Okay, let's go. And I want silence please. Open your ears and your hearts.'

There's a definite sense of mutiny in the air as we traipse out of the garden, through the little paddock and towards the young woodland on the other side of the valley.

Than is the first to be dropped off, and as we march solemnly past him, I catch his eye. He winks at me and does a huge fake yawn.

About ten minutes later, after both Emma and Moth have been left at separate spots, Russ says, 'Okay, Tori, this is you. Stay within about two minutes' walk of here. Good luck.'

No one meets my eye as I stand stock still and watch them trudge away. I feel quite strange, staring at their departing backs. Well, there's nothing for it but to explore my little parcel of countryside and hunt out somewhere comfortable to sit.

It's a lovely spot. I turn a slow three sixty degrees to get my bearings. I'd been so intent on watching the feet of the others ahead of me on the way here that I hadn't noticed how far up the side of the valley we've climbed. Stretching out in front of me is the patchwork of fields on the valley floor, with the farmhouse nestled in the distance, snug as a bug in its blanket of greenery. I can see the willow beds that Ted pointed out on our first trip to find our various campsites. As a light breeze blows down the valley, the slender trees throw up the undersides of their leaves, turning the patch of green into rustling silver.

I'm now at the corner of a large stretch of young woodland. The trees are small enough that they've still got little plastic guards protecting their trunks. Around the edges of this baby woodland, as far as I can see, runs a border of enormous, full grown trees. They must have formed the boundary when this was just a field. Some of them are so big that I wouldn't be able to get my arms around them if I hugged them – which, of course, I'm not about to do. I'm just not a tree-hugging kind of person. Still, they're bloody enormous trees.

I walk a little way along the bank and notice that there's the remains of a wire fence, and here and there strands of barbed wire have scarred the oaks. In some cases it runs through the centre of the tree, and in others the wire is looped right around the trunk. Clearly, in the past, some farmer has saved on fence posts by nailing the wire directly to the trees.

I come to a halt next to one that has been ringed completely. The tree has tried to grow around the wire and the wood almost looks like it has spilled over the top. It's been completely strangled. The tree is dead, and I can see that some of the others are going to follow it very soon.

I sit down heavily on the bank, my heart beating fast. What's wrong with me? They're just trees. At some point they saved a farmer all the extra work of putting in fence posts. But sitting here now, I can see how short-sighted that was. Sure, it might have saved him the extra work and cash back then, but what about now? He has condemned these beautiful trees to a slow death.

God, this is a depressing place to sit. I struggle back to my feet, deciding that I've already had enough, and start to retrace my steps back towards the farm. I'll go back to the yurt for a while.

As I reach the edge of the woodland, the wind starts to pick up. The large oaks groan and strain in the sudden gust, but the young trees just sway gently, protected by their dying rear guard.

A bank of stormy-looking clouds is marching across the sky towards me like they're looking for a fight, and the wind picks up another notch. That's it, I'm out of here. I'm starting to freak myself out. Rather than opening the gate, I climb it and jump down the other side.

I break into a run and the wind seems to chase me down the hill, catching and whipping my hair up behind me. I'm hurtling back towards the field where the yurt is nestled as fast as my feet can carry me. The mayhem of the wind is echoed in the frantic beating of my heart. I feel like a child again, trying to outstrip some unknown terror as I run, my breath coming hard and fast. At last, I spot the yurt.

I'm just metres away from the flap when it happens. The skies open and the feel of giant raindrops on my skin brings me to an abrupt halt. It's something I usually avoid at all costs, but right now, in the middle of this field, it has caught me by surprise. I'm frozen in place.

As if someone is cranking up an invisible dial, the rain gets harder and heavier, the warm drops pound against my head and soak into my hair. My heart is still hammering from the run, but for the first time in a long time, I'm getting drenched by falling rain and I'm not afraid. The smell of damp grass and earth rises up to greet me. I open my arms wide and, raising my face up to the sky, I start to laugh.

'Are you insane?'

I jump and peer through the deluge towards the voice coming from the yurt.

It's Bay, standing just inside, laughing at me.

'What are you doing here?!' I call.

'Hiding from the rain!'

'Come out! It's beautiful,' I yell. In response, whoever's controlling the rain dial turns it to maximum. Bay shakes his head, still laughing. I march straight towards him and, grabbing the front of his shirt, I drag him, barefoot, out into the rain until we're both standing, laughing at each other as we're pummelled by the downpour.

Bay reaches forward and gently pushes a sodden strand of hair off my face. Suddenly we're not laughing anymore. We just stand, staring at each other. My hand is still holding the front of his shirt and my breath is still coming too fast, but I'm not so sure that's because of the running anymore. I'm staring into Bay's green eyes, and all of the movement I felt in my soul as I pelted down the field comes to a halt as I lose myself in his gaze.

The rain stops just as abruptly as it started, and the silence that follows breaks the spell between us.

'I—' Bay says.

'We'd better—' I say at exactly the same time.

'Sure,' he says, turning away from me and striding back into the yurt. I take a deep breath and follow more slowly. In a completely useless move, I try to wipe my hands dry on my sodden jeans.

As I struggle through the dripping entrance flap, I see that Bay has already stripped off his wet shirt and is stepping into a pair of dry trousers.

I go straight over to my bed and, with my back to Bay, strip off my top. I don't dare turn around for fear he might be watching me . . . or is it hope? What just happened out there in the rain?

I tug on a pair of dry jeans and top with some difficulty and then turn back to Bay. He's now sitting quite calmly on the little settee, flipping through a book on herbs as if nothing unusual has happened. Which, of course, it hasn't. Not really. So why do I feel disappointed?

I go and sit next to him.

'So . . . did you get bored?' he asks, looking at me steadily.

'Bored? No. No, not bored. Completely freaked out may be nearer the mark,' I say.

Bay nods. 'I saw you come belting down the field.'

'Well, yes.' I don't really want to talk about this yet. I'll save it for later, I think. 'What are you doing here, anyway? I thought you were being mindful in the garden?' I smile at him.

'I was . . . until I spotted a big black bank of cloud heading my way. So I thought I'd avoid a drenching. Or I would have, if it wasn't for you. Anyway, I don't get it . . . You have a fear of water and there you are, enjoying the rain?'

I think about this for a second. 'My phobia is really specific. Rivers, waterfalls . . . running bodies of water. Rain's different somehow. It's tiny drops.'

'So is a shower,' Bay counters, trying to understand.

I shiver and rub my arms. 'A shower is more intense. It thunders at you, straight on your head and on your face . . . and there's that pounding noise.' I pause and take a deep breath. 'I mean, I do usually avoid getting caught out in the rain, but that's more about wanting to avoid any chance of having a panic attack, if I can help it. It's not about fear of the rain itself. Does that make any sense?'

Bay nods slowly. 'You get scared of having a panic attack, so that starts to make you afraid of even more things?'

I nod. Nailed it in one. It starts to control more and more of your life. But that's enough of that subject for me for a while . . .

'Bay, look, I wanted to say sorry about yesterday.'

'Why?' He looks surprised at my sudden change of subject.

'For the way I reacted, I guess. I know you were just trying to look out for me.'

Bay shakes his head and sighs. 'It's me who should apologize. I'm sorry, that was probably not the most sensitive way I could have said what I did. I was . . . I *am* worried, and I didn't think it was fair not to give you a heads-up.'

'Truce?' I say.

He nods and then chucks a towel straight at my head.

'You might need this. You're still dripping all over my cushions!'

Chapter 18

Busy Hands Calm the Monkey Mind

'Your mind is a tree; its branches are your thoughts. Imagine your consciousness is a monkey swinging through these branches. It grabs hold of one thought, only to swing to another. It's rushing, excitable, frantic.

'Simple, repetitive work that keeps your hands busy can become a tool to help calm your monkey mind.'

©TheBeginnersGuideToLoneliness.com

Even though we hang out in the yurt for twenty minutes before heading back down to the garden together, Bay and I get there way before most of the others. I'm guessing they've all had to go in search of a dry set of clothes after a good, mindful drenching. Doreen's there though, so as Bay makes his way over to join Russ, I go and sit next to her underneath the overhanging roof of the little tool shelter.

'How was it for you?' I ask.

'Well . . . uh . . . I listened to the land,' she says, avoiding my eye, 'and, well . . . I went for a bit of a walk. And it was really weird because I walked straight into Geoff.'

'Really?' I raise my eyebrows, wondering what's coming next. They barely seemed to be talking last night.

'Well, you could say that, rather than listening to the land, it had to listen to us instead,' she says, looking uncomfortable.

'Oh no. You had a fight? Are you okay?' I ask. Poor Doreen, she's so desperate to reconnect with Geoff.

'No, no . . . not a fight! Completely the opposite,' she pulls a horrified face at me.

My jaw drops. 'You *didn't*?'

'It was like we couldn't bear any space between us, and we just . . . kind of . . . melted into each other . . .' She turns the most epic shade of beetroot I've ever witnessed.

I'm not sure I really want to hear the rest of the story if I'm honest, but I am intrigued. 'You weren't worried that someone might hear you?' I say.

'Didn't even consider it. It was like everything bad and all of the rubbish times we've been through just disappeared.'

She looks at me, and pure happiness is shining from her face.

'I'm so happy for you!' I say.

'Well, this is all meant to be about new experiences, isn't it?' says Doreen with a giggle. 'And I've never done it up against a tree before!'

Argh. There it is. Too much information.

She takes in the horrified expression on my face and laughs. 'What, didn't think we were past it, did you?!'

I shake my head, as much to dislodge the unwelcome image she's conjured as to answer her question.

'Well,' I say finally, 'this makes my tiny bit of gossip feel rather insignificant.'

'Ooh, gossip! Play fair now, Tori!' Doreen's eyes have the light of mischief in them, and she looks about twenty years younger.

'Well, you know that rainstorm?' I start.

'Don't I just? In fact, I blame that for . . . sorry, you carry on!'

'Well, I was caught out in it. I got all freaked out by the wind, and then the rain came and I sort of stopped in my tracks. And just stood in the rain. And I loved how it felt,' I say.

'Nope. You were right. Your piece of gossip is crap,' Doreen says, her face falling. 'Oh and there's something else you should know,' she leans in close to my ear, 'they're turning you into a hippy!' she whispers.

I dig her in the ribs with my elbow. 'I wasn't at the good part yet,' I mutter.

'Oh, thank heavens for that. So, what else happened?'

'Bay turned up.' I swallow. Now I'm telling someone about it, the moment feels really precious, like I want to hug it close and savour it for a bit longer. But there's no hope of that. Doreen's eyes have gone wide.

'When you say "turned up" . . . ?'

'I saw him watching me from the yurt and dragged him out into the rain.'

'This place is definitely doing you good,' Doreen nods approvingly. 'Go on, what happened next?'

'Just this moment, you know? This look? And then he brushed a strand of hair off my face and it was like you said, all the space between us seemed to disappear.'

'You *didn't*?!'

'No, we didn't. Not if you mean like what you guys got up to—'

I'm interrupted by the sound of someone clearing their throat. We both look up guiltily to find that the rest of the group has rocked up while we've been chatting, and Bay is staring at us from his position up in front with Russ. They've clearly both been waiting for us all to calm down and shut up so that they can start this part of the session, but it looks like Doreen and I have managed to outstrip even chilled Russ's patience quota.

Oh God. What if Bay just heard everything I said? I feel the now familiar blush hit my cheeks again.

'Doreen, where's Geoff? Is he okay?' asks Russ gently.

'Oh, yes. He's . . . okay. Just tired. Really tired. He needed a rest. This morning took it out of him,' Doreen widens her eyes, trying to look as innocent as possible.

Russ nods. I can't help letting out a little snort of laughter.

'Tired? I bet he is!' I mutter.

Doreen chuckles and settles back comfortably against the side of the shed to let the session unfold around her.

'This morning's session was all about the senses,' says Russ, addressing the whole group. 'What you saw, heard, felt . . . maybe even smelled and tasted. It was about staying in the moment and witnessing what was happening without letting random thoughts distract you. The key to the second part of the session is getting you all grounded again.'

'Already done that bit,' Doreen whispers in my ear, and I have to bite my lip.

'We've all done plenty of sitting and talking, so this afternoon is going to be about work. Getting our hands dirty and doing something useful.'

'Great!'

It's Than. He's come to stand right next to us, slouching against the tool shed, legs crossed, arms crossed and, as I peep up at him, a truly pissed-off expression on his face.

'There's actually no better way to practise mindfulness than by doing something practical to help keep your attention rooted in the moment,' Russ continues. 'You'll find that it's incredibly balancing too.'

'So we're not going to talk about this morning's session?' Emma asks.

'Oh, we will, but we'll do it as we work. Over to you, Bay. What have you got lined up for us?'

'Well, there's always plenty to do in the garden, but especially at this time of the year. Lots of weeding,' he gestures around at the raised beds, 'and there are some tomato plants that I want planted in the bed at the back of the tool shed. We should be safe from the frosts by now, but the shed will give them a little bit of extra shelter and the warmth of the tin in the sun will create a microclimate for them.'

Microclimate? He's lost me. I pick a blade of grass and start twisting it around my fingers absently. As I watch Bay talk, I think about his fingers gently brushing the hair off my face in the rain.

'Tori?'

I jump at the sound of my name, and everyone looks around at me. It's Doreen's turn to dig me in the ribs this time.

'Um, yes?' I say guiltily.

'We were just going through jobs. Are you happy to do some weeding? We need to get the beds cleared for the courgettes to go in soon.'

'Of course. Yep. Fine!' I say. *Must learn not to daydream in public.* Mindfulness – stay in the moment . . . May need a bit more practice at that.

I feel Doreen shaking with silent giggles next to me as Bay turns to Beardy Weirdy to see if he's happy to lead the tomato crew.

'Oi!' I whisper in her ear.

'You should see your face,' she laughs. 'Thinking of a certain moment in the rain by any chance? All very *Four Weddings!*'

'Shhh!' I say. I don't like the way Than's looking at me. I could really do without having to tell him about what happened with Bay. I've got a sneaking suspicion that he wouldn't be quite as enthusiastic as Doreen.

Russ was right; I find the weeding incredibly therapeutic. Bay has designed the garden so that most of it is set out in raised beds. Huge wooden railway sleepers piled on top of each other form the edges and bring the level of the soil up by a good couple of feet. I'm perched comfortably on one of them, pulling greenery out of the wet earth to my heart's content, Bay having told us before we started that there is nothing that needs saving in this patch.

Than, Doreen and Emma are all dotted around the same bed, and we've been listening to Emma describe a tiny patch of grass she'd decided to focus on this morning. She tells us about every single little critter she'd spotted in about a square metre, and I can't help but smile at how different her experience was to mine.

Bay joins us part way through Emma's description and becomes so entranced by what she's saying, he's barely touched a single weed.

'Oi, slacker!' I laugh, tapping his empty bucket as Emma finishes her story.

Bay grins at me. 'Sorry. It's just so amazing. I've done this exercise so many times, and I've literally never heard anything like that before.'

Emma beams at him.

'It's like you discovered a whole universe in that patch of grass!' he smiles at her.

Emma nods enthusiastically. 'That's exactly it. I was there for ages, and I just kept noticing more and more.'

'And that's why this work is just so incredible. We all learn to look at the world differently through each other's eyes,' says Russ, wandering over to see how we're getting on.

I smile at his earnest tone.

'What about you, Doreen?' asks Russ. 'How did you find this morning's exercise?'

Doreen's suddenly weeding with such concentration you'd think she's performing heart surgery.

'Care to share?' I ask, grinning at her.

'It was good,' she mutters. 'Lots of connection with the land and stuff.' She clears her throat.

'Any details . . . ?' I'm laughing now. Bay catches my eye and raises an eyebrow.

'Nope. No details. It felt . . . private,' mutters Doreen.

'Fair enough. Sometimes it's too close to the bone to share,' nods Russ.

At the word 'bone', I promptly dissolve into a fit of giggles, and Doreen joins me. I almost manage to sober up at the sight of the bemused look on Russ's face, but a snort from Doreen sets me off again and we just keep getting worse. In fact, it's not long before Emma joins the hysteria, tears pouring down her face even though she's got no idea why she's laughing. We're practically unable to breathe by this point.

I've just about managed to calm down, with the occasional hiccup of mirth, when I catch Bay's eye again and notice that he's completely given up on trying to keep a straight face too. Even Russ is grinning as he shakes his head in despair and heads off to check on the tomato crew. Clearly we all needed to let off a bit of steam after this morning.

The only person who seems to be immune is Than. As I look around me, taking deep, steadying breaths, I notice his face, and there's only one word to describe it: grim.

I sober up immediately. Maybe today's been too much for him to even think about smiling.

Bay looks up at him too. 'How about you, Than? What did you get from this morning?'

'I didn't,' Than rips up a handful of weeds and lobs them into his bucket as if they're a hand grenade. He straightens his back and glares at Bay.

'Care to elaborate?' Bay asks.

I glance back at him. The mirth of just a couple of seconds ago has been replaced by barely suppressed irritation.

'How can I?' bites Than. 'I sat in a field. I got bored. It was cold, wet and windy. I came back. The end.' Than stares at Bay as if daring him to contradict him.

'So you didn't bother with Russ's exercise?' Bay prompts mildly.

Next to me, Doreen has gone back to weeding with intense concentration.

'If it had been a proper exercise,' says Than, voice full of heavy sarcasm, 'I would have bothered.'

'Obviously you didn't engage in it with an open mind.'

'How open-minded do you have to be to make up some crock-of-bullshit answer after sitting in a field, freezing your naggers off for a morning?' Than's on his feet now.

'Maybe it just wasn't the exercise for you.' Bay is tight-lipped, and I can see that he's struggling to keep a lid on his own rising anger.

'Yeah, maybe,' says Than, shrugging. 'Look, I'm going back to my tent. Like Geoff, I'm a bit *tired*.' He does scare quotes around the last word with his fingers before turning his back on us.

188

'Should I go after him?' I ask, not because I particularly want to, but because it feels like maybe someone should.

Bay shakes his head, an even darker expression on his face. I see him swallow.

'Let him go,' he says in a tight voice. 'He needs a bit of time to calm down. Someone can check on him later to see if he wants to join us for the hot tub this evening if he's up for it.'

By the end of the afternoon, I'm aching all over. In spite of the fact that I've discovered muscles in places I didn't even know existed, I feel amazing, just like I did after the yoga session. Under Bay's instruction, and with Russ's ongoing input about staying mindful and grounded as we worked, we ended up weeding four massive beds. There's only one left to finish, and that's just because the weeds are way too well established to yank out by hand. The others have managed to plant out the tomatoes around the back of the shed as well as filling two little greenhouses.

We're all just about ready to drop, so I can't believe it when Bay says he still wants to do a bit more work after dinner if anyone wants to join him. Apparently the potatoes need hoeing up in the evening because the leaves point upwards then. Who knew?

I stare straight ahead, not wanting to catch his eye. As much as I'd love to help him out, I don't think my poor back will take much more.

'I know,' says Doreen, and for a second I think she's about to volunteer, 'I'll send Geoff down to help. He's skived for long enough. Time for him to earn his place in the hot tub tonight!'

Chapter 19

Avoiding the Friendship Monoculture

'There are three friendship scenarios that can lead to a monoculture; the "best friend as only friend", the "romantic partner as best friend" and the "all my friends are in the same group" set-up. Should something cause any of these friendships to end, you could find yourself isolated far too easily. As in nature, friendships benefit from biodiversity.'

©TheBeginnersGuideToLoneliness.com

When I arrive at the hot tub, it seems that Doreen has been as bad as her word. Both Bay and Geoff are missing from the party, and I'm guessing they're hard at work hoeing up the potatoes. I would feel bad for them, but right now I'm too achy and anxious to do much about it. In fact, the aching seems to have doubled since we stopped work, and there's a part of me that is desperate to get into some hot water and soak myself. Unfortunately, that part is having to put up quite a fight with the anxious part of my brain, which is really starting to kick in. I know it's not running water, but there are so many of us that I'm not going to have much control over the situation should panic start to creep in.

I dump my bag and go to help the others shift wood from under a tarpaulin. There's a solar-heated water tank, but a little wood-fired boiler helps to top up the warm water. I can't seem to stop worrying about Than. He's not here yet and I'm starting to feel like I should have followed him earlier. Actually, I'm wondering if he was kind of expecting me to.

'Why the long face?' Doreen asks, rescuing me from one of the two large logs I'm trying to heave over to Beardy Weirdy and Bob, who're taking it in turns to wield an axe and chop the bigger bits down to size.

'I'm fine,' I say, 'just a bit worried about Than.'

'Ah, he'll be all right. Different things set us off, don't they? Anyway, I think Geoff was planning to go up to see him after they finish off in the garden.'

My shoulders sag with relief. Geoff. If anyone can talk Than down, it'll be lovely, calm Geoff.

'So, you ready for this?' I ask, as we both potter back towards the tub.

'Oh, yes! How can pulling a few weeds up leave you hurting quite so much?' Doreen asks with a laugh.

As soon as the tub's full of warm water, everyone piles in. As if by magic, Claire, Russ and Bay appear to join in the fun.

I turn just in time to see a white bum dash past me. Beardy Weirdy, keen to be first into the water, has dumped his clothes and leaps stark bollock naked into the tub. This seems to be the sign everyone has been waiting for. Before my eyes, trousers are being dropped, T-shirts cast aside with abandon and boxers are lying in the grass wherever I look.

My heart is hammering, but it's not the water that's causing it this time. I just caught a glimpse of Bay's surprisingly tanned behind as he slipped into the water. My case of butterflies has levelled up and I now feel like I've got a flock of pigeons in my belly.

To my great relief, not everyone is bearing all. Doreen is in her bra and pants, and grins as Claire and Russ shift up to make room for her.

The tub is packed like a tin of sardines. We're about to cook up a large vat of hippy soup and the water is already turning an interesting browny-beige colour. Actually, that might not be a bad thing – at least it'll cover everyone up!

I changed into my boxer briefs earlier and left my bra back at the yurt, so I just take off my jeans, fold them carefully and leave my T-shirt on.

'Come on, Tori!' Claire calls. 'Hop in while it's nice and clean . . . kinda,' she laughs.

I head over to the side where she and Doreen are lounging on a submerged ledge. I sit on the edge and dangle my legs over the side. There. That's far enough. I can handle this without any trouble, as long as no one makes any sudden movements.

'You not coming in?' asks Doreen, looking up at me.

'I'm good here for a bit.' I smile at her.

'We can make room if I sit on Bob's lap!' says Claire, winking at Bob.

'Nah, I'm good thanks,' I say. I'm starting to relax. There's no pressure here. Just a bunch of people trying to be nice to me. I look over to find Bay watching me. 'Like I said, I'm not good with water. Running water mostly, but I'm a bit weird with all water to be honest. It's just one of my oddities,' I laugh, trying to make light of it. An oddity that pretty much controls my life at times, but we don't need to go into that bit right now. I don't want this evening to turn into another therapy-fest just because of my issues.

'Oh, wow,' says Beardy Weirdy. 'This is a big step for you, then?'

I shrug. 'I'm okay.' Time to change the subject. 'You know, this is awful, but I still haven't caught your name.'

'It's Messa,' he grins at me. 'Nice to meet you!'

Everyone's in full chat mode now. There's lots of talk about the garden and how well we did with the work today. I act as main fire stoker, and every now and then hop up to add more wood to keep the water warm. The others keep offering to take turns, but I've laid claim to the role. For one thing, it stops it being strange that I'm still perched on the side of the tub, and for another, it means I don't have to see a naked butt streak past me every twenty minutes.

I feel a bit bad when Geoff turns up with Than in tow. I've been having such a good time that I'd actually forgotten they were still missing from the group.

Geoff promptly strips down to his boxers and squeezes into the water between Claire and Doreen, throwing his arm around his wife.

'Oi, you two,' laughs Sam, 'not in the hot tub!' This causes much sniggering, and Doreen does her beetroot impression again.

Than makes his way around the tub, takes off his shoes, rolls up his trousers and joins me on the edge. 'Hey,' he says with a smile.

'All right?' I ask quietly as the others noisily continue to rib Geoff for his late appearance.

'Yeah fine,' he huffs. 'It's just . . .'

'SNAKE!'

The scream comes from Emma. Everyone stares at her.

'In the water!' She's scrabbling backwards out of the tub. Both Than and I draw our feet quickly out of the water. Doreen's busy making a swift getaway too, and even Messa is retreating as fast as his little white backside will allow. There's general uproar, squealing and a lot of laughter from Bay, who hasn't budged.

'Seriously, Bay, get out!' shouts Bob from a safe distance.

'No need!' he chuckles. 'I just saw it over there next to Geoff!'

It's Geoff's turn to scramble up the side and sit dripping on the edge.

'Tori, chuck me a stick,' says Bay, calm as a cucumber.

I dash to the pile, grab the longest one I can find and chuck it across the water to Bay.

'Perfect. I should be able to get it with that!' he grins, aiming it at the water like a spear.

As one, the whole group seems to take a step back. What does this guy think he's doing? Now he's the only one left in the tub. We're all standing around, dripping, watching open-mouthed.

With a quick thrust, Bay plunges the stick into the water, then brings the point up slowly into the air. I don't understand why he's laughing, or why Claire and Russ are laughing – and now Geoff too.

'Got it! You might be wanting this . . .' And with a flick, Bay sends the snake flying through the air straight towards Messa. He lets out the most unearthly squeal, slips on the grass and falls, todger akimbo, in a heap with the dead snake on top of him. He hurriedly flicks it off of him, and then, sitting up slowly, stares at it.

He turns to Bay, whose lips are quivering. 'Bastard!' he says mildly, and, picking up the 'snake', lobs it back at Bay.

Bay catches it, wraps it around his neck and pretends to be sinking under the water, only to surface again, laughing his head off with it dangling from his fingertips.

A lone dreadlock. Clearly one of Messa's.

It takes ages for the laughter to die down. Just when it looks like it's about to stop, someone yells 'Snake!' and off we all go again. Even Than is chuckling along next to me as we take it in turns to feed the fire.

When Bay finally declares he's calling it a night to make a bit more room in the tub, he starts a kind of mass exodus, and within twenty minutes it's just me, Than and Messa left.

'You coming in now it's quieter?' Messa asks me, gazing up at the sky.

'Erm . . . maybe.'

'I'll chuck some more wood on the fire,' says Than, and heads over to the depleted pile.

'It's not just you facing your fears tonight, you know,' says Messa quietly. 'What Bay doesn't know is that I'm absolutely terrified of snakes!'

'Oh my God!'

He shrugs. 'I survived,' he smiles at me. 'Might have a bit of a bruise on the arse tomorrow, but hey, at least Bay saved my dreadlock.'

I nod. 'You know, I might get in for a few minutes before heading off. Could do with it after all that weeding!'

Messa grins. 'Atta girl.'

As Than comes back over, he slips off his jeans and tee and hops into the tub in his pants. I quickly avert my eyes until he's sitting on the bench opposite me.

'Right!' says Messa. 'That's quite enough excitement for me for one night. My roll mat's calling.'

'Night!' I say, and close my eyes quickly as he hauls himself out of the tub. I just don't need to see that again.

When I open my eyes, he's wandering away with a towel around his waist, one hand raised in farewell. All of a sudden, I'm very aware that I'm alone with Than.

'You okay?' he asks.

I nod.

'Sure?'

'I will be if you stop asking me that and talk to me about something else,' I snap.

He gives me a hurt look.

'Sorry, sorry. Inner anxiety bitch surfaces again.' He doesn't need to know that it's not anxiety about the water this time. We sit in silence for a minute.

'Anyway,' I say, 'it's my turn. Are you okay? After earlier? I couldn't really ask you properly with everyone else here.'

Than shrugs. 'I'm fine. I just had to get away before the urge to smash Bay's smug face became too much.'

'Oh.' I don't really know what to say, but I find myself wishing I'd left with everyone else.

'Look, Tori, you need to be careful around him,' he says.

I shake my head. Not again! What is it with these two?

'Than, Bay's a good guy.'

He shakes his head at me, looking angry.

'He is,' I say. 'Earlier, in the garden, he was . . .'

'Don't tell me he was trying to help,' Than growls.

'Well, he was,' I say, 'just like they all are in their own, weird ways.'

'Trust me, that's not what he was doing. And anyway, he's all over you like a rash. I mean, living with you, watching you, joking around just to get your attention.'

I laugh. 'Bay had no choice in the matter when it came to sharing the yurt. I was dumped on him because I booked last minute.'

'So did I, and I'm not staying there,' he says sulkily.

'Because you opted for camping.' I'm starting to feel cross.

'But you can't deny that he watches you.'

'Look, this is ridiculous,' I say. 'Just because you don't like him, don't expect me to feel the same way, because I don't.'

Than holds his hands up. 'Fine, fine!' He sounds huffy again, and I sigh.

'I think I'm going to head back.' I start to get to my feet, but Than jumps up and grabs one of my hands.

'Don't,' he says urgently. 'Don't go. I'm sorry.'

I look at him, shake my head and sit back down again. He sits next to me. 'Really, I'm sorry. It's not fair to take it out on you. You're still the only person I've trusted enough to tell about my brother,' he sighs.

I settle back onto the bench. Poor guy, he's got so much to deal with. I just wish he'd share it with the others, especially the instructors. Let's face it, they're definitely better equipped to deal with the fallout than I am.

'It's okay,' I say.

Before I know what's happening, he's leant forward. His face is right in front of mine. Oh my God, he's going in for a kiss. I whip my head sideways and his lips catch me on the corner of the mouth.

'Than, no,' I say, pushing him away as gently as I can.

'Why?' he says, his voice hoarse.

'Because I don't want . . . this,' I say, pointing back and forth between us. I can feel the first stirrings of panic. Time to get out of here, I think. 'This isn't the place. I'm not here for . . . this.'

'But we—'

'We're friends,' I say, standing up and quickly climbing over the side. 'That's it. Friends.'

'But you—'

'Nothing, Than. I've done nothing. Look, let's just forget it. I'm tired, I'm going to bed.'

'I'm sorry, Tori. I'll walk you back,' he says, getting to his feet.

'No. Thank you. I'm fine.'

I grab my towel, wrap it around me and bundle my clothes up off of the floor. Then I turn back to see him, still standing in the tub, watching me.

'We'll talk tomorrow, okay?' I say.

He just shrugs, so I turn and walk as quickly as I can back towards the farmyard.

Oh God, how did that just go so wrong? My first thought is to get straight back to the yurt, but I realize that I need my friends. My *real* friends. I need the Warriors, which means I need to find Rowan.

Despite everyone having headed back to their various camps, it's not dark yet. I make my way towards the farmhouse, hoping to bump into her.

As if by magic, I spot Rowan heading towards me as soon as I get into the yard.

'Rowan!' I say.

'Ye—s,' she grins at me, seeing a sale in the offing.

'I need to use your phone for a couple of minutes.'

She whips it out of her back pocket. 'Call, text or internet?'

'Internet, please,' I say.

'Knock yourself out. You know the price!'

I nod. 'Mind if I take it around to the fire pit for a minute, just so I can sit down?'

'I wouldn't. That's where Mum and Dad are hanging out. Come down to the barn with me for a sec, I've got to get some feed for the chickens anyway, and there's a bench in there.'

'Thanks!' I smile at her and pull the towel tighter round me.

'You know,' she says as we walk down the yard, 'it might be a good idea for you to put that jumper on. Don't want you catching a chill!'

As soon as I'm ensconced on a little wooden bench which is sandwiched between an old chest freezer full of chicken food and a pile of straw bales, I follow her advice and pull my jumper on over my wet T-shirt. I really don't much fancy nursing a cold here on top of everything else.

Grabbing a scoop of feed, Rowan leaves me to it. I log into the chatroom and send a bunch of messages as quickly as I can.

WriterTori: Hey, guys. Still alive. Really miss you all. Need to offload – am being charged by the millisecond though so have to be quick . . . Than, that guy I told you about before, he just tried to kiss me. Totally out of the blue. It made me feel awful. I don't think I feel like that about him. Thought for a sec I might, but I think I was just excited to have someone on my side, someone who wanted to spend time with me. I just abandoned him in the hot tub. Feel really bad. Tomorrow is going to be awkward! What do I do? Give me advice? Pretty please.

WriterTori: There's something else too. There is someone I might actually like . . . like *that*. Completely unexpected, and also awkward as it's Bay, the guy I'm sharing the yurt with. We had this moment earlier in the rain, and it made me see him properly for the first time. But we're living together . . . I think Than hates him and . . . GAH! I need to talk to you. Why aren't you online? Helloooooo?

WriterTori: Damn. Gotta go. This message has just cost me about a gazillion pounds. I love you guys. Thanks for listening.

'You done?' comes Rowan's voice as she wanders back into the barn, empty feed scoop in hand.

'Yep. Give me a sec to log off.' I do so quickly and then erase the site from the phone's history. Don't know why, I just always do.

'That'll be six quid, please.'

'I don't have any cash on me,' I say.

'No probs . . . just log on to PayPal. Make sure you add an extra fifty pence though – transaction fee.'

I roll my eyes. This girl's going to go far.

Chapter 20

Let Your Lion Loose

'For those who suffer with anxiety, it's natural to avoid confrontation, but there are moments when we have to let our lion loose. When a situation demands it, it can often be the right move to let that roar out.'

©TheBeginnersGuideToLoneliness.com

I've never been so glad to see my bed in my life. Bay is already snuggled up on the sofa under a blanket. I'm so tempted to flop down next to him, but I'm still wearing a semi-dry jumper over very wet clothes, so I drag my feet over to my bed and start to get changed into something warm. I feel strangely shy around him after what I've just told the Warriors.

'Bay . . . can I borrow a thick jumper?' I ask, cringing as my voice comes out all breathy.

'Sure.' He goes to his pack and then throws a chunky, woolly sweater to me. 'I left you something next to your notebook too,' he says, pointing at my little makeshift bedside table.

I look over and there's a travel mug. I pop the lid off and take a sniff. Hot chocolate. It's official. I'm smitten. Just a moment ago, I felt incredibly lost and lonely and, without even trying, Bay's managed to hit upon the one thing that's guaranteed to cheer me up.

'You're a saint,' I sigh, sitting on my bed and cradling the warm drink.

'Hope it's still hot? You were a bit longer than I thought you'd be.'

'Mmm,' I mumble.

'What's up?'

'Mmm?'

'Difficult evening? Was it the water? You did really well.'

'I got in,' I say. I feel a bit like a six-year-old showing off my swimming badge for the first time.

'Good for you!'

'Thanks. And it wasn't that.'

'Oh?'

'It was . . . people.'

'Bit of group dynamics come out to bite you?'

'Erm, something like that.'

'Well, if you need to talk . . . I'm always here, you know.'

I smile at him. 'Thanks, Bay. I'm okay. I think I just need my bed.' There's no way I can tell him about Than. I mean, that's a sure route to 'I told you so' if ever there was one, and right now I could really do without that.

'Not surprised. That'll be the fresh air, gardening and running around like a lunatic in the rain,' he laughs.

I feel a weight land on my feet and look down to see Dennis slinking up next to me for a hug. I snuggle back into the pillows, hot drink in one hand and my other arm wrapped around Dennis's warm body. He leans his whole weight against me, head lolling on my shoulder. It's possibly the best cuddle I could have asked for right now.

'Well, looks like whatever's bothering you, Dennis knows you need some love,' says Bay. 'You'd better be careful or you'll end up sharing that bed again!'

I wake up the following morning next to a large, snoring mound of dog, and can't help but smile. Bay's words to me last night before I drifted off to sleep seem to have come true. He must have covered me up with the blankets and taken the cup out of my hand, as I've got absolutely no recollection of doing either.

'Morning, sleepyhead,' Bay grins over at me as he bounds into the yurt carrying the kettle. 'Coffee?'

'I'd love one,' I yawn, 'but I owe you some treats, you know. All this pampering with coffee and hot chocolate.'

'Ah, I'm sure we'll figure it out,' he says, busy pouring the hot water into his cafetière. 'You look better for a good sleep.'

'I *feel* better. Thanks for last night. I felt a bit weirded out, you know?'

'I do. And it's fine, that's what friends are for.'

Friends. That word should have my little heart jumping with joy. Instead it has curled up in disappointment. *Uh oh.*

Still, I force a smile and take the hot cup of coffee out of his hands as if it's life-saving nectar.

'Warned you that would happen,' he says, nodding down at the still snoozing dog.

'I don't mind,' I say, hyper aware of my change of tune since I got here. 'That was the best night's sleep I've had in ages.'

'No nightmares,' Bay says matter-of-factly.

'No. How did you know?'

'You didn't do your usual whimpering along with the dawn chorus.'

Oh. My. God. 'I'm so sorry. I didn't realize I'd been disturbing you!' I say.

'Don't worry about it. I'm awake on and off all night.'

'You looking forward to Claire's session this morning?' I ask just to change the subject.

'Ah, actually I'm going to miss this one. I promised Ted I'd help out again. We need to do some bits in the garden and get some of the outdoor work finished before the baby comes. He's having to do more with the course than usual as Lizzie's had to slow down, and he's starting to fret that he's going to get behind.'

'But . . . surely it's not good for you to miss a session?'

Bay shrugs. 'I've done it plenty of times before. And besides, this is a part of the deal. I get to come here and benefit from the retreat and in return I make sure I do as much as I can to help on the gardens and anything else they need a hand with while I'm here. They've done so much for me over the years, it's the very least I can do.'

'Pfft, but another day in the garden?' I say, trying to hide my sudden disappointment that Bay's not going to be around today. 'I'm tired just thinking about it.'

'Ah, you get used to it,' he grins at me.

There's a big part of me that really wants to skip breakfast this morning. Because I'm a wuss, and the thought of facing Than after what happened last night in the hot tub makes me squirm. But then, that would make me a coward, and I don't want to make any bigger deal out of this than it needs to be. With any luck, he'll have shrugged it off.

Bay comes down to breakfast with me, and Dennis trots along between us. I'm grateful for the company, as it stops me disappearing into my own head and chasing my worries around in circles.

As it happens, all the worrying is completely in vain anyway. Than is nowhere to be seen. It actually turns out to be a really joyful meal. Everyone else is here, and the party atmosphere from last night seems to have spilled over into the morning. We're all just starting to tuck in to breakfast when Sam screams 'snake' and we all fall about laughing. The look of complete confusion on Ted and Lizzie's faces just makes matters worse, and my sides start to ache. Messa takes it all in his stride as the tale is told again. I get the feeling that this little anecdote is going to become a bit of a legend here at The Farm.

We're all still giggling and chatting as we head off to get started on Claire's session. As she is one of the gang from last night, there's a general sense that this morning's going to be a lot of fun. My heart is light as I follow the others up the stairs into the loft space where we had our welcoming ceremony.

'Okay, gang, pull up the cushions for a minute while I explain what we're doing today.'

Like a horde of eager toddlers, we surge over to the pile of cushions. I grab the end of one just as Emma grabs the other end. I give it an almighty tug, managing to snatch it from her and promptly beat her over the head with it. She snatches up another one, and before I know what's happening I'm begging for mercy, laughing so hard I can barely breathe as she pummels me over and over again with the supersized pillow. It's far from a fair fight, though, as Doreen and Moth have both taken their own cushions and have leapt into the fray, all three now focusing on obtaining my surrender.

We end up in a tangled, squashy heap of cushions and limbs, all four of us laughing and trying to extricate ourselves from the pile.

'All right, you lot, get your behinds over here so that we can start!' calls Claire, who sounds like she'd actually quite like to join in.

I sit up only to be met by the look on Than's face as he walks through the door. The smile drops from my lips the moment I catch sight of his expression. I know I sound like a complete drama queen, but he is looking nothing short of thunderous.

I quickly look away and drag my cushion over to join the others in the circle, plonking myself down between Messa and Doreen. Suddenly I'm not quite so excited about this session anymore. Than sits down across from me and I feel like he barely takes his eyes off me, though I guess it's likely that my anxiety-prone brain is just imagining the waves of hostility he's sending my way.

'Okay, so we're all here. Great!' says Claire. 'Lizzie usually takes this session, but as you know, she's asked me to step in for her this once. Today is going to be all about vocalizing. Now, I know that sounds a bit vague and fluffy, but it's actually something incredibly powerful. We are all here to deal with things. Emotional blocks, fears and barriers. We've started to share what they are with each other, but what we haven't worked on is saying, out loud, how these things make us feel.'

Doreen shifts uncomfortably next to me, but this might just be down to the fact that these cushions are really not that supportive.

'I hope we're now at a point where we all feel that we can place our trust in this group. You have all come to know each other, shared experiences and, from what I saw last night and this morning, have developed a lovely, playful bond. So, it's time.' She jumps to her feet in one yoga-honed movement and indicates for the rest of us to join her. We do, much slower and with a lot more groaning involved, which sends another giggle around the room.

Or, at least, it makes most of us smile. Than is still stony-faced.

Urgh, is he going to keep this up for the whole day?

I fold my arms protectively across my chest and look back to Claire. Actually, I don't much fancy sharing anything today.

Not with the group. Well, not with *one* of the group. How can one person affect the whole dynamic so quickly?

'First things first, I want you all to scream.'

'Scream?' says Emma.

'Scream. As loud as you can!'

'Snake!' squeaks Moth.

Claire grins at her. 'Exactly, but maybe more like this: *SSSNNNNNNAAAAAKKKKKKEEEEE!*' Claire screams the word using every last ounce of breath. The strength and pitch of her voice is awesome. My teeth get that feeling in them like I've just bitten into ice cream, and I wouldn't be surprised right now if the windows of the barn started to shatter. When she's done, we break into a spontaneous round of applause and she takes a tiny bow. 'Now you!' she says. 'On three . . .'

As she counts us in, I suck in a breath, but when it comes to screaming, I let it whoosh out of me with no sound attached. I'm too caught up in listening to the insane cacophony around me. I catch Than's eye again and feel a bit like I've been punched. His arms are crossed, and he is still glaring at me, his mouth firmly closed.

'Okay, great!' says Claire. 'But there's even more in there. Some of you are still holding back, and I know I was completely missing a couple of you just then . . .'

I could kiss her for not naming and shaming.

'Everyone close your eyes and choose your own words to scream. No one's going to know what you're saying. It'll all mix into one big noise.'

When I close my eyes, I can still see Than's glaring face. Right . . .

'Three, two, one . . .'

'PISS! OFF!' I scream. Over and over and over, until the words lose all sense and shape. Until my breath runs out.

I open my eyes and suck in another deep breath.

That. Felt. Amazing.

My fingertips are tingling and I feel properly, fully awake. I look over at Claire and she nods back at me, a big smile on her face.

'You know how many things your voices can do, how many emotions they can convey. It's my belief that when we feel an excess of emotion, it can get caught up in our chests. If we don't let it out somehow, this can just keep building.'

Claire could be describing one of my panic attacks. I'm so accustomed to the feeling of the build-up in my chest and not knowing how to get control of it before it leads to a meltdown.

'Of course, it's not just the scream sound we can use to let it out. In a way, you had all started working on this session before we even reached this room. Can anyone tell me how?'

'The laughter!' says Messa.

'Exactly that. The release of the joyful emotions you are all experiencing here together. So what other common ways do we express emotion by voice?'

'Anger,' says Geoff.

'Right,' says Claire, 'but how does that tend to sound when vocalized at its absolute peak?'

'Shouting. And sometimes screaming, I guess,' he replies.

'So let's look at shouting next. Describe how shouting makes you feel . . .'

'Mean?' says Doreen.

'Maybe after the fact, but what about in the moment?' prompts Claire.

Doreen looks confused.

'Forceful?' I say. I'm imagining words flying out of my mouth towards a target.

'Yes,' says Claire. 'Forceful, powerful.'

'And out of control . . .' says Emma, frowning.

'Shouting can certainly stem from feeling out of control, or let out so many emotions that it can lead you in that direction, yes,' agrees Claire. 'But let's focus on the power behind it. Take a minute to think of the main issue you want to deal with while you're here, and what element about that makes you feel angry. It could be a particular person, situation or anything about it. What do you want to take control of?'

We all look around nervously at each other.

'Okay, I think we need to move for a minute. Take a walk around the space and think about what you want to shout at.'

I move off, grateful to escape the beam of everyone's nervous energy. You can feel it in the room now; it has shifted away from self-consciousness to fear – fear that Claire is about to start taking us near the bits that really matter.

I scoot around the corner of the room and walk in a diagonal path to the other end, head down, avoiding eye contact. What am I angry about? That I lost my mother? That her death weighs me down with guilt every single day? That I'm still grieving for someone I struggled to even like and who had come to hate me in return? I swallow. That she's still managing to ruin my life even now she's gone? My heart rate's climbing and the sound of running water is creeping into my mind.

I come to an abrupt halt near the centre of the room, bend over for a second and place my hands on my knees.

'Okay, Tori?' Claire asks quietly.

I don't answer. I just take a deep breath in and let it out slowly as I stand up. The roaring water calms back down to a trickle.

'Tori?' Claire prompts gently.

I nod. 'I'm okay.' I spot Than leaning against the opposite wall watching us.

'Okay, everyone, when you're ready,' Claire calls, 'I want us all in a line, facing the wall,' she points to the far end of the room.

Than pushes away from the side and comes to stand next to Claire. As the others join us, the sense of fear builds. Most faces are pale and set. Doreen is chewing her lip. Geoff is looking petrified.

'Now remember, this is a safe space. There is no judgement here.'

Doreen stands next to me and her hand slips into mine. I give it a gentle squeeze.

'Who wants to go first?'

Before anyone can move, before there's even a second to think, Geoff bellows at the wall, 'I want my wife back!'

I feel Doreen go stiff beside me. I squeeze her hand again, but this time there's no response.

'Okay, guys, don't leave Geoff hanging, who's next?'

'I never told you I loved you.' Bob's the next to hurl his voice across the room.

'None of you really know me!' Emma yells. I've never heard her voice so strong and so loud.

'I'm not ready for this!' Sam follows her.

My heart rate is going insane. I have to get this out.

'I'm sick of feeling guilty!' The words rush through my throat, feeling like they're tearing their way out, leaving me raw, hurting and shaking.

Then Doreen's yelling, and Moth, and Messa.

'Than?' Claire prompts.

I glance across at him. He is shaking his head.

'Just yell at the wall. It doesn't matter what comes out,' she says.

Than takes a step forward out of the line. He looks like he's gearing up, and my heart goes out to him. I think he's got so good at keeping a lid on how he's feeling, it must be nearly impossible to let it out.

'Than?' Claire gently prompts again.

I watch him take in a deep breath. Then he swivels towards us and stares straight at me. In a voice that's more shocking than any of our shouts, he whispers.

'You're a fucking liar.'

Chapter 21

Control the Controllables

'It is not possible for anyone to completely control their environment. This desire for control, coupled with its inherent impossibility, can lead to anxiety. By refusing to spend energy worrying about aspects we have no influence over, life becomes ours for the taking.'

©TheBeginnersGuideToLoneliness.com

There is complete silence for a couple of seconds. It's like everyone is watching this bullet travel towards me in slow motion.

I catch the blow straight to the chest and stumble back a couple of paces.

'What the hell?' comes Doreen's voice.

Muttering breaks out along the line and everyone breaks ranks, crowding around me.

'Okay, everyone, settle down,' says Claire.

But I don't want to settle down. What the fuck was

that? I push my way past the concerned faces grouped around me and take a step towards Than. 'What is your problem?'

'Tori . . .' Claire says warningly.

'I can't take any more of this bullshit,' Than gestures around at everyone. '*Oh, look at my problem . . .*' he says, doing a whiny child's voice.

'Than—' Claire tries to intervene, but I interrupt her.

'Don't you dare question anyone else's feelings just because you don't understand them,' I say.

'You of all people have the nerve to say that? You're a hypocrite. You know it and I know it.'

I can feel white-hot anger pulsing out of him, and there's no doubt it's directed straight at me.

'What are you saying?'

'I'm forbidden to tell anyone, remember? And even I have too much integrity to blab a secret to the group.'

'Okay, Than, that's enough.' Claire's voice cuts across him. He's now glaring at her, and I can see his chest rising and fall-ing, his anger still building. 'This is not about Tori or any of the rest of the group. Please don't mistakenly direct your anger and fear at them.'

Than turns back to me and I feel the full weight of accusa-tion hit me. 'My *fear*?' he hisses. 'Seems that even if *I* can keep a secret, you can't. Tell lover boy and everyone else everything about me, did you? Well fuck you, Tori.' He turns on his heel and heads straight out of the room.

For a second, there's complete silence.

'Break time, I think,' says Claire. 'Can I suggest that you all head back to your separate camps for a while? Go home, decompress and we'll get together again later.'

She starts to usher everyone out of the door. We're all a bit slow to respond. I think everyone's in shock. I know I am. My legs feel like jelly and navigating my way down the outside steps is quite tricky.

When I get to the bottom, Geoff, Doreen, Messa and Emma are already waiting for me, but Claire beats them to it.

'Tori, walk with me for a minute,' she says, giving me no choice but to send a longing look back towards the others as I follow her. It's pretty clear they're not going to take up Claire's suggestion of separate camps.

She leads me towards the farmhouse but then, to my surprise, lets us in through the side gate and ushers me through to Lizzie and Ted's private back garden. They're both there drinking tea in the sunshine. Ted looks hot and sweaty and must have only just got back from his session in the garden with Bay.

They both look surprised to see us.

'Hi. Sorry to interrupt. Ted, you might need to bring that one-to-one session we discussed last night forward?'

This means absolutely nothing to me, but it clearly does to the other two. They both look solemn and Ted gets to his feet straight away.

'I'll just change out of this stuff,' he says, pulling at the neck of his sweat-soaked T-shirt and hurrying inside.

'Tori, have a seat and wait for me a sec?' Claire says. 'Lizzie, can I borrow you for a mo?'

Lizzie nods and looks surprised, but gets to her feet with difficulty and follows Claire inside the house, rubbing her back as she goes.

I sit on one of the garden benches against the back wall of the house and stare at a bed of early roses, their buds just about ready to flower fully. It's quiet here and incredibly beautiful, so why do I feel like I'm sitting outside the head teacher's office, waiting to be told off?

I don't get it. Is Than really so cross about the fact that I didn't want to kiss him that he decided to give me a public flailing?

I sigh. I feel like shit. That session was proving to be hard enough as it was without all his crap coming my way too. It feels like he's trying to punish me for something. Maybe just knowing about his issues is enough to make him resent me.

'Tori, Claire's asked me to spend a bit of time with you, if you're up for it?'

I look up in surprise. It's Lizzie. I notice she's still clutching her back, and seems to have quite a lot of trouble manoeuvring herself back into her seat.

'Oh, okay,' I say. She looks exhausted and far too hot. I guess that's the reality of being ready to pop at any moment, but still, I feel guilty for disturbing her downtime. 'Would you be more comfortable inside?' I ask in concern, watching as she gently rubs her stomach.

'No, no, not at all. Can't have you disrupting your progress by going in there,' she says. 'So, Claire briefly explained what just happened in the session. Are you okay?'

'Yes, fine,' I reply automatically, then instantly change my mind. 'Well, no.'

Lizzie nods but doesn't say anything.

'I felt really awkward when I came here,' I say, 'a different person.'

'A little less than a week ago?' Lizzie asks gently, placing no weight on the words.

'Yes,' I say, surprised. I thought Lizzie of all people would be pleased to hear that. 'A lot has happened and I've learned a lot.'

'Of course. But you're not a different person. Don't worry, it's a mistake that's easily made.' She winces slightly and shifts her weight in the chair, trying to get comfy.

'So you're saying the changes aren't real?' I'm feeling the prickle of tears. Maybe it's not just Than who thinks I'm a liar.

'The changes are real, but you're not a different person. We provide experiences that help you learn about yourself. But the things you learn were already a part of you when you arrived here. So no, you're not a different person, you're a person that just happens to recognize more pieces of who you truly are.'

I nod. I think that makes sense but I'm not sure how it really fits with what just happened with Than.

'Did Claire tell you about Than?' I ask.

'Than's behaviour? Yes. It sounds like it stems from a deep, personal fear. He has yet to open up and allow this experience to help him – unlike you, who are already benefiting from it.'

'But this was personal!' I say.

'Yes. About as personal as it can get. You two became very close, very quickly . . .'

'Oh, you noticed . . .'

'You don't run a place like this for twenty years and miss out on much of the hot gossip,' Lizzie laughs, before clutching her bump again.

'Can I get you some water or anything?' I ask, concerned.

She waves me away. 'You and Than were partners in crime for a couple of days, and then you started to discover things about yourself.'

'It was hard not to be drawn to him. He just seemed to really understand me, almost better than I understood myself, you know?'

'But then you started to make other friends here, and I think he's missing having you all to himself.'

'Hm. Given his behaviour in the hot tub last night, I'm not sure it's just my other *friends* he's worrying about.'

Now Lizzie looks truly concerned. 'What happened?'

'He tried to kiss me,' I say, looking at my feet. I feel incredibly awkward. I didn't mean for that to come out.

'And you didn't want that?'

'No. And I told him that,' I say. I need Lizzie to understand the whole picture though. 'It's flattering to have a good-looking guy interested, of course it is. But any feelings I thought I might be experiencing for him . . . I think they were actually just this massive sense of relief. Someone actually wanting to spend time with me.'

'What happened after you turned him down last night?'

'I left.'

'So this morning's little performance could be all that angry rejection coming out?'

'I guess so. But it felt like it was about more than that, somehow,' I say. 'I just didn't think last night was that big a deal. It was awkward, but I thought he'd get over it.'

Lizzie gets up slowly and paces along the slate path, walking over to the flower bed and back.

'Can I ask you a personal question?'

'Of course,' I say.

'Claire said he accused you of telling something to "Lover Boy". Did he mean Bay?'

Here comes that bloody blush again. 'Yes. I think so,' I mutter.

'Are you and Bay . . . ?'

'No, we're not.' I don't feel the need to mention the moment in the rain. After all, that was probably just me getting thoroughly carried away. 'Than was saying stuff about Bay last night, before he kissed me. Trying to warn me away from him.'

'He was?'

'Mind you, Bay warned me about Than a couple of days ago too, so I can hardly hold it against him, can I?'

'Oh God!' Lizzie gasps.

Have I just landed Bay in it? I look up at her in surprise, expecting to be questioned some more. Instead, Lizzie is looking down at a pool of water surrounding her feet, darkening the slates.

'What the . . .'

'Erm, I think my water just broke.'

'*What?!*'

'It's fine, don't panic.'

'Okay. Okay. I'll go and get Ted!' I say.

'No. No, he's gone over to Than.'

'Okay, I'll go and get Claire?'

'She's gone for a walk in the woods. Let's not worry, I've got plenty of time to call the midwife. Then when she's here we can sort out getting Ted back! I don't understand, I've not had any contractions yet . . .'

'Is that normal?'

'No, with Rowan I had contractions for hours before this happened.'

'Rowan. Let me call Rowan . . .'

'She's out somewhere!'

'There must be *someone* around?'

'Okay, Tori, deep breaths,' laughs Lizzie.

'Hey, isn't that meant to be my line?'

Suddenly, all the drama from this morning, my worries about Than and what Bay might think, just don't matter.

'Let's call that midwife and go from there,' I say.

'Good pl—'

The 'aaaaannn' part of her last word comes out as a shriek as she clasps her stomach and bends forward, clearly in pain. I'm guessing that this is one of those missing contractions, and it's going on way longer than I would have guessed.

Lizzie starts to pant, and I rush to her side, gingerly putting a hand on her back. Finally she straightens up and takes several deep breaths to steady herself.

'Sorry, sorry!' she says. 'Look, I'll go in and make the call and get changed. I'll be back . . .' Still holding her stomach, Lizzie disappears through the door.

I don't know what to do. I nip back through the gate to have a quick look around the yard, but typically there's no one to be seen. I can hear the vague murmuring of Lizzie on the telephone inside. I really need Ted. Or Doreen. Or maybe some professionals here right about now!

'TORI!' The yell of pain from inside the house brings me back to reality, and I rush straight back through to the garden. 'TORI!!'

Okay, if Lizzie's calling me from inside the house, this has got to classify as one of those dire emergencies they mentioned when we first arrived. I head straight through the back door and into the kitchen. Lizzie's on her hands and knees on the floor, and the old phone handset is dangling from its cord.

'What happened?'

I rush to her and go to help her up, but she shakes her head, breathing hard.

'It's okay,' I whisper, 'you're okay.'

'This. Is. Too. Fast!' she breathes.

I rub her back ineffectually until she breathes easier again.

'Let me help you up,' I say.

'No. I'll stay here.'

'Okay. First things first. Midwife?' I catch up the dangling phone and put it to my ear. There's no one there, just a dial tone.

222

'She's on her way. She's just finished a visit to someone else. May be a while though.'

'Shit,' I say, without thinking.

'My thoughts exactly!'

'Look, let's get you comfy. I'll grab some pillows and stuff?'

'Our bedroom's upstairs. End of the hall then to the right.'

I leg it straight up the stairs and along the hallway, not caring that I sound like a one-woman herd of elephants as I rush to gather things and get back to Lizzie. I don't want to leave her alone for too long.

I don't even take a moment to marvel at their epic, canopied four-poster bed. I just bundle two pillows under one arm, grab a massive bath sheet off a pile on a chair in the corner and, as an afterthought, snag a big, fluffy dressing gown from the back of the door. I hurry back down to the kitchen, dump the whole lot unceremoniously onto the floor and then take the pillows over to Lizzie.

'You're an angel!' she smiles. We place one behind her back so that she can lean more comfortably up against the edge of the old dresser. 'I'll move in a minute.'

'There's no . . .'

I was going to say that there was no rush, but Lizzie's straining forward again. I crouch down next to her and hold her hand, which she promptly crushes in a vice-like grip.

'Tori, I feel like I need to push!'

'What? Already? But the midwife's not here yet!'

She moans.

'Breathe!' I say. *That's what they all say in films, isn't it?* Lizzie instantly starts doing some weird breathing pattern. Okay, this is ridiculous.

'Phew. Okay. It's easing off . . .'

'Lizzie, I think I need to call an ambulance,' I say.

'No, we'll be fine. The midwife's on her way.'

'But . . .'

'Tori! What the hell?' Rowan's face appears, pale and worried-looking. 'What was that noise? I heard it from outside . . .'

'That would be your mum,' I say.

'The baby's coming, love!' Lizzie says.

'But . . . where's Dad?'

'He's talking to Than, I'm guessing over at the campsite?' I say.

'Do you want me to run and get him?'

'Please!' I nod.

Rowan dashes off, but before I get the chance to say anything else to Lizzie, she's scooted around so that she's on all fours and is groaning again. Right, I don't care what she says, this isn't normal. I'm calling an ambulance.

I pick up the phone and dial 999.

'Emergency, which service do you require? Fire, police or ambulance?'

'Ambulance, please,' I say, my heart hammering. There's a click on the line. I must be being transferred.

'Ambulance service. What's your emergency?'

'My friend. She's gone into labour and there's no one else

here. We've called the midwife but things have ramped up rather suddenly. She just said she wants to push!'

Lizzie promptly gives a bellow of pain.

The operator quickly takes my details, Lizzie's name, The Farm's address and a contact number, which I read off the body of the phone on the wall.

'Has her water broken?'

'Yes. And she's having really awful contractions.'

'How far apart?'

'Um . . . I don't know . . . maybe every three to five minutes.'

'Okay, and how long are the contractions?'

'Well, one started just before we connected and it's only just easing.'

'It sounds like the baby is going to be there very soon. An ambulance is on its way to you. I need you to keep me on the phone while you wait for the midwife or ambulance to arrive.'

'Okay. Can I put you on speaker?'

'Please do.'

I click a button on the old-fashioned set on the wall and cross my fingers that it's going to work. 'Hello, can you still hear me?'

'Yes. I'm still here,' comes the woman's calm voice. At least I'm not on my own anymore. 'Hi, Lizzie, I'm Georgia. I'm just going to talk to you while you're waiting for some help to arrive, okay.'

'M'kay,' Lizzie pants.

'Are you somewhere safe?'

'She's on the kitchen floor on all fours.'

'Lizzie, it sounds like the baby is going to be there soon. Now, Tori, I need you to look around for me. Is there enough space around your friend for the midwife and paramedics to be able to help when they arrive?'

'Yes, plenty,' I say.

'Okay, good. And is she comfortable?'

'I am,' says Lizzie. 'I . . . oooohhhh!'

Another contraction starts and I can barely hear Georgia's tinny voice over the handset, but I can hear she's counting.

'I need to push!' yells Lizzie again.

'Lizzie, blow out three short breaths. Did you do that pattern in your classes?'

Lizzie nods. I'm glad this makes any sense to her, because it's Greek to me. She starts a strange panting rhythm over and over.

'Tori, I need you to get some towels, and if you can find a bucket or washing-up bowl to have on hand, and some bin liners?'

I quickly get to my feet. I've already got the towel from upstairs. I locate the bin liners and a plastic tub in the cupboard under the kitchen sink and place them on the floor near Lizzie.

I lay the towel on the floor for her as she sits back down, prop the other cushion behind her back, then fetch the dressing gown from where I dumped it and hold it out to her. She just cuddles it to her.

'Lizzie, love?!' Ted flies in through the back door with Rowan at his heels. They're both completely out of breath and must have run all the way back from the campsite.

'Ted?' Lizzie pants.

'Who's arrived, Tori?' Georgia's voice comes from the phone.

'It's Ted, the baby's dad,' I say.

'Who's that?' says Ted, catching hold of Lizzie's hand and peering around, bewildered.

'It's Georgia, the 999 operator, on speakerphone,' I say. 'She's going to stay on the line with us until the midwife or ambulance arrives.'

'Ambulance?' says Rowan, looking freaked.

'The baby's coming very quickly, Rowan,' I say.

'Nothing to worry about,' comes Georgia's calm voice.

The scream that comes from Lizzie rather contradicts what Georgia's saying. Rowan goes pale so I get up and go over to her.

'Can you help me?'

She nods.

'Find me as many clean towels as possible.'

'Small or large?'

'Both. And then put a full kettle on to boil.'

'Why the kettle?'

'They always do it in films,' I say.

Rowan dashes off upstairs.

'Knock knock!' calls a woman's voice from the back door.

'Hello?' I rush over and spot a kindly face peering around the open door.

'Hi, I'm Val, Lizzie's midwife.'

'Oh, thank God!' I say, breathing a sigh of relief. 'She's over there. And we've got Georgia on the phone. I was on my own with Lizzie and she kept wanting to push, so I called 999.'

'Okay. Good. Can you get me towels?'

'Already on their way,' I say, and hurry off to check on Rowan and leave the people who actually know what they're doing to get on with it.

After delivering the towels into a kitchen that seems to be full of the sound of pain, I check if Val needs anything else, and when she shakes her head, I beat a hasty retreat with Rowan at my side. I was aiming for the back garden, but the wailing from inside the house is still way too loud. 'Fancy coming back to the yurt with me?' I say.

'Shouldn't we be doing something?' Rowan asks, looking desperate.

'We've done our bit,' I smile at her. 'Your mum and the baby are in safe hands now. Thanks so much for helping!'

Rowan shrugs, looking scared.

As we traipse down the yard, an ambulance appears at the bottom of the track. Rowan runs to open the gate for them and, pointing them in the direction of the house, tells them to go straight round to the back door.

Bay's sitting outside when we get to the yurt.

'Tori, you okay? I heard—'

I shake my head quickly to cut him off and say, 'Lizzie's gone into labour. Looks like the baby's nearly here!'

228

'What? But . . . *what?*'

'I was with her when it kicked off,' I say, pointing Rowan into one of the wooden chairs around the cold fire pit. 'We left her with Ted and the midwife, and the ambulance guys arrived just as we were headed over here.'

'Ambulance?' he says, looking worried.

'Well, we weren't sure how long the midwife was going to be, and I needed help, so I called 999,' I say a tad defensively. 'She'll be okay,' I add gently, turning to Rowan.

'I thought you got more warning than that,' she says. 'I heard that Val person say the baby's coming really soon!'

I nod. 'Well, seems your little brother or sister is in a hurry.' I sit on the bench next to her.

'I'm going to have a brother or sister,' Rowan says in amazement, and then buries her face in my shoulder and starts to cry. I pause for just a moment and then put my arm around her.

Chapter 22

Sometimes 'No' Is Enough

' "No" is an important word. Anxiety can make us feel like we're not allowed to use it. So, instead, we go against our instincts simply because saying "yes" is just more comfortable. Learning to say "no" again can be a powerful game-changer. And you don't need to use excuses to justify it. Sometimes "no" is enough.'

©TheBeginnersGuideToLoneliness.com

Val comes to find us about an hour after Rowan and I beat our retreat. After calming Rowan down, Bay and I decided that we'd light a fire and settle in for the afternoon, assuming that things might take a while to work themselves out. As it is, we've only just got the wood together, the fire going and the kettle on before our visitor arrives.

'Your mum and dad asked me to come and tell you that it's a girl. You've got a beautiful baby sister,' Val says kindly to Rowan.

Rowan starts cheering, I promptly burst into tears and Bay leaps to his feet and starts doing a little dance next to the fire, unable to keep his bum on the chair.

Val grins at us. 'They've all gone in the ambulance to the hospital. The baby came so fast that Lizzie needs a few stitches, and that's best done there. They'll be able to check baby over too.'

'But she's okay?' Rowan asks, looking worried.

'Yes, they'll both be fine after a little bit of TLC,' Val reassures her gently.

'Was that normal? How fast everything happened, I mean?' asks Rowan.

'It's unusual, but it does happen to about one woman in every two hundred.'

'Trust Mum to be different!' Rowan says with pride.

'Tea, Val?' Bay asks, grabbing the kettle.

'Don't mind if I do!' she says, and sinks gratefully onto one of the benches.

Supper tonight has turned into one great big celebration, and it's like the difficult session we all shared this morning happened in another lifetime. Of course, Ted and Lizzie are missing as they're still at the hospital, and Bay has taken Rowan in the Land Rover to meet her baby sister.

Everyone wants to hear the story, and I repeat it several times. They're treating me like some kind of hero, but in reality, all I did was use the phone. Even so, I feel so bloody proud and grateful. There's a healthy new baby in the world, and I got to play a tiny part in that.

'Can I talk to you?' Than asks, coming over to me at the little outdoor kitchen as I'm refilling my cup of elderflower bubbly.

'Erm. Okay,' I say. I'm suddenly aware of eyes following us. I glance over to the table to find Claire watching us. She raises an eyebrow, and I give her a little nod. I hope she understands this as code for 'I'm okay, no need for rescue.' She's plainly still on alert after this morning's fiasco.

'Look,' says Than, 'I wanted to say sorry.'

'Because you really are sorry, or because Ted told you to?' I ask, my voice flat.

'Come on, Tori! Because I want to. I wanted to come straight back up those stairs the minute I left the session, but I was in such a state, I wasn't thinking straight.'

'Why did you do it? I don't know what I'm meant to have done wrong,' I say quietly. Maybe I should just accept the apology, but I'm genuinely curious, and there's something about today's turn of events that makes me feel like I'm allowed to ask.

Than shrugs. 'I'm not sure.' He doesn't meet my eye, and I can't read the look on his face. 'But I'm really sorry for what I did. I guess I've got a lot more to work out than I realized.'

'I've only ever been on your side, Than. What you did this morning was really shitty. I do understand that you've got a lot to deal with—' I look at him, and he goes to say something, but I cut him off with my hand raised. 'I do, I get it. But we're all vulnerable; that's why we're here. We're all working through something. But . . . that doesn't give any of us the right to behave like you did this morning.' I peter off. I know what I want to say, but it feels so alien to speak my mind that it's coming out a bit jumbled.

'Last night was difficult for me and, I don't know . . . I just . . .' Than lets out a huge sigh. 'Look, it was a mistake.'

I shrug. This just isn't important anymore. 'Okay, let's just move on,' I say. 'Bubbly?' I ask, offering him a cup.

Than takes it, takes a sip and looks at the ground. I can't help but do an inward sigh. I was enjoying this evening, but now I feel like I have some kind of responsibility to pull Than out of the slump he's in.

'Would you like to come for a walk?' Than asks, looking up at me.

I want to grind my teeth a little bit when I spot a hint of his usual smile is back in place. I may have said we could 'move on', but I'm not a complete sap. I know that there was more to this morning's outburst than Than struggling with what happened – or *didn't* happen last night.

'Thanks, Than, but I want to stay here and celebrate with everyone,' I say, keeping my voice as light as possible.

'I could just use a friend right now. Someone who knows what I'm dealing with,' he says, and the wobble that's suddenly back in his voice is clearly designed to undo my resolve.

I shake my head. 'I can't tonight. I'm tired and a bit wobbly myself after everything. Why don't you ask if Russ or Claire have a bit of time free?'

Than makes a snorting sound, and my irritation towards him turns into full-blown annoyance.

'They just won't get it like you do,' says Than, and now he sounds like a stroppy teen.

'Well, it's their job, so I'd say they'd be a better bet than me this evening!' I say. I want to rejoin the group. Now. I've had enough of whatever game he's playing.

'But . . . we have things we need to talk about . . .' he pouts.

'No, Than, we don't. You've apologized. We're good. Now I'm going back to the others. Come with me if you want.'

'But last night . . .'

I let out a sigh of frustration and turn to face him properly. 'I said everything I needed to last night.'

'You said we could talk,' he shoots back at me mutinously.

Something inside me snaps. 'I said that so I could get away from you! I've really enjoyed your company, getting to know you, hanging out a bit. But I've got stuff of my own to deal with, and I've got to focus on that.'

'But, Tori . . .'

I hear him, but I've already turned my back and am headed over towards the others, back towards the celebrations and the food. When I've squeezed myself onto one of the benches in between Sam and Messa, I glance back over to where we'd been standing.

Than has gone.

It should have been the perfect evening, but my second stand-off of the day with Than has put a decided dampener on my spirits. When Rowan, Bay and Ted appear back from the hospital with the news that Lizzie and the baby are doing well, I feel the tiredness truly catch up with me. Now all I want is to head back to the yurt, get into bed and let my head start to digest some of the insanity that has happened today. Before I do, I decide to take my own advice and seek out Claire.

She greets me with a huge hug.

'You doing okay, Tori? I saw Than catch up with you earlier.'

'I'm okay,' I say quietly. I don't really want to go into anything with the others around. 'I didn't get much chance to speak with Lizzie before everything kicked off . . .'

'You want to chat now?' she asks, and I could hug her again for not making me ask.

'You sure that would be okay?' I say.

'Of course! Did you want to talk here, or . . . ?'

'I was thinking of heading back to the yurt soon. I'm wiped.'

'I bet! How about I come with you? We can walk and talk . . .'

'That would be perfect.'

I say my goodnights to everyone and enjoy another full round of hugs. When I get to Ted, he holds me close for a long time. Anyone would think I'd single-handedly delivered his baby the way he's thanking me.

Bay's the last to wrap his arms around me, and as I soak in the warmth of his body and snuggle my face against his soft, worn jumper, my head quietens down. Just for a moment, I stop worrying about everything.

'You gonna be okay to head back to the yurt on your own?' he asks gently as I step back from him. 'Only, I need to eat and then I'll help the others clear this lot up.'

I nod and breathe a sigh of relief, knowing that Claire and I are going to be able to chat for a while without being disturbed.

To begin with, I'm a bit halting as I start talking to Claire, but her easy manner and friendliness mean that before we've even crossed into the first field, I'm opening up to her about Than in a way that I haven't with anyone else. I tell her about the weird sense of attraction I felt at first, which I'm now pretty sure was just relief that someone liked me after I'd been on my own for so long. I tell her how he's been seeking me out for advice and support, and that although I've been happy to listen, I know it's way beyond my ability to help. I tell her about Bay's warning, and I tell her about Than trying to kiss me in the hot tub.

'And then there was this morning's outburst,' says Claire quietly.

'Yup.'

'So what happened this evening?'

'He said sorry about this morning and then wanted to talk about the almost-kiss. And he wanted me to go with him so that he could talk privately about his "stuff".' I sigh. 'Thing is, last time he "wanted to talk", he didn't actually want to talk at all.'

'What happened that time?' Claire asks curiously.

'We just went back to his tent and hung out for a bit. He wanted to gossip and just chill out and . . . yeah. To be honest, I think if you and Moth hadn't arrived, and Dennis hadn't bowled into the tent, he would probably have tried to kiss me then.'

Claire nods. 'It's not unusual for strong feelings to come out when you're at a place like this, you know. I've seen it before. It's happened to me at retreats I've been to.'

'It has?' I ask in surprise.

'Of course! You're there, opening up and clearing all these blocks. And there's this huge release of energy. I've made some of my dearest friends at places like this.'

I nod. It's actually a relief to be told that these relationships are real, even if they start in the weirdest of ways. And I'm not thinking about whatever has happened between me and Than. I'm thinking of the others. Doreen and Geoff. Messa and Moth. Sam, Emma and Bob. Even Bay. I've already started to dread losing these guys when the course is over. But why should I? This bunch of nutty buggers are becoming my friends. And I don't have to live without them after we're done here.

'Tori, I think there are a couple of suggestions I'd like to make, if you're willing to hear them?' Claire says as we come in sight of the yurt.

'Of course. Please!' I say, turning to smile at her.

'Okay, number one: enjoy the group. From what I've seen, Than has monopolized you quite a bit. But you stand to gain more from being a part of the whole group. You've got the weekend ahead of you – spend time with the others. It'll then be up to Than whether he joins in too, or whether he continues to separate himself.'

I nod. That's exactly what I've been wanting to do anyway, I realize. My instinct has been telling me to be with the others more.

'The second thing I want you to do,' Claire takes my hand and turns to look at me, 'is to trust your instincts. If something feels right, and good, deep down in your core, then you're probably right. And if something feels wrong, or awkward, or out of place, trust that feeling.'

I nearly laugh out loud. 'I think you're a mind-reader,' I say as I pull Claire into a hug and thank her for clearing my head.

Chapter 23

One Step Forwards . . .

'It's not always going to be plain sailing. Sometimes it can feel like we take one step forwards, only to stumble back by two. But the key thing is to keep moving forwards. Keep taking those steps and you will make the connections you're looking for.'

©TheBeginnersGuideToLoneliness.com

It turns out the baby's birth and everything else that happened on Friday has had more of an effect on me than I could have imagined. I know, it's not like I was there for the actual delivery or anything, but I feel like a different person somehow. If I'm honest, it might not just be the baby's arrival that has changed me. Standing up for myself to Than and asking Claire for help might have something to do with it too. I've had the weekend for everything to sink in, and I feel bolder. Braver. Like I can take on a challenge.

Funnily enough, this morning has presented me with the

perfect opportunity. The rest of the group have decided to start the week off with another wild swim. And, after everything that's happened, I'm ready to face my very worst fear. I mean, it's not like I'm about to give birth on a kitchen floor, is it?!

'So, you're coming with us this morning?' Bay grins across the yurt at me as I stuff a towel determinedly into a cloth bag. 'Not going to skive off?'

I laugh. 'I'm coming for the walk at least,' I say. 'For me, even getting near that river is a big step.'

'I know. Can I ask, what is it about rivers, exactly?'

I pause, hugging my bag to my chest. *How much do I tell him?*

'I'm sorry, you don't have to answer that if you don't want to,' he says quickly.

'Well . . .' Maybe it's a good plan to fill him in a bit. 'There was an accident two years ago . . . involving a river. And since then I've had this phobia.'

He blinks at me. 'So this is the perfect way for you to face it, then. You'll be with the rest of us. You'll be completely safe.'

'I wish it was that rational. Even the sound of a river can set me off. I don't think I'll be able to get into that water—' My voice has started to tremble.

'Hey, you haven't even seen it yet,' he says, his voice gentle.

'I don't need to. It's a river.' I thought I was up for a challenge . . .

'Okay, come for the walk. Check it out, take it slow . . . and if nothing else you get to laugh at the rest of us freezing our backsides off, right?'

★

I'm the last one to make it to the bottom of the hill, and as I stoop to navigate my way under the low-hanging branches of the trees near the river's edge, I can already hear squeals and laughter. Unfortunately, I can also hear the river. My stomach lurches and I shiver. It takes all my determination to reach the small, shingle beach where a couple of the others are standing, gazing at the water.

Objectively, I can see that it's a beautiful place. A large, deep pool has formed where the rapids meet a steep cliff. Here the river becomes so slow and lazy that it merely trickles out of the other side. The cliff itself has several small trees growing out of its rough face. On our side of the river, the shingle beach leads right to the water's edge.

The pool is so clear that you can see all the way to the bottom, apart from the deepest parts where it just turns into an inky blackness. The thundering of the river as it hits the cliff is deafeningly hypnotic, and it's taking every ounce of will power I can muster not to turn tail and run. The shards of sunlight that filter down through the leaves bathe the whole area in a strange, greenish light. I shiver again, trying to calm my breathing and slow my heart rate down.

'Take your time,' says Bay, 'you're doing great.'

I nod. I can't get a word out. I'm battling an image of a car sinking into the pool. I shake my head and focus on what's really in front of me.

Russ, Emma, Sam and Geoff are already in the water, splashing wildly and laughing. The others are all on the beach, peeling off clothes and shedding their shoes.

'Come on, guys, it's beautiful!' Geoff shouts, brushing his slicked down hair out of his eyes and grinning at us from the water.

'Idiot,' mutters Doreen, coming to stand by my side. 'He's always been like this with water.'

We stand quietly together for a moment, watching as Than marches into the pool. He makes his way straight past the others and starts swimming steadily further out into the deep water.

'Get your bum in here, Mrs McVey, or I'm coming to get you!' Geoff growls to his wife in mock serious tones. He takes a couple of strokes forwards as if he's going to make good on his promise, and Doreen squeals, making me jump.

'Don't you dare, you naughty man. Give me a second!' She shrugs off the enormous jumper she's wearing and tosses it further up the beach. Stepping as daintily out of her wellies as she can, she strips down to a violently pink one-piece. Very slowly, Doreen picks her way over the slate and down towards the water's edge.

I watch, half in admiration, half with a growing sense of horror. Part of me wants to run after her, to pull her back, away from the water. This is a brave woman. I should be taking notes.

She reaches the water's edge and comes to a grinding halt.

'Come on, love, or I swear I'm coming out to get you!' laughs Geoff, beckoning to Doreen.

'I'm not sure.' Doreen dips a toe in. 'Bloody hell, it's freezing!'

'Watch out . . . I'm coming in!' The cry comes from behind me, and just as I turn to see who it is, Bay streaks past and does an almighty belly flop right into the middle of the pool, sending up a massive tidal wave that laps right up over Doreen's knees and splashes her so badly that the water drips off her hair and runs down her face.

Bay comes up gasping and rubbing his eyes while the others laugh at him, shaking their heads like a pack of dogs.

'Oh, sod it!' mutters Doreen. She turns her back on the pool, reverses into the water until it reaches the middle of her thighs, locks her body straight and, with a shriek, falls backwards into the water.

Everyone claps and cheers as she surfaces, spluttering and gasping.

'That's my girl!' shouts Geoff.

Doreen splashes an armful of water at him.

'Hey, Tori, you coming in or what?' Geoff calls.

All the sounds of splashing have had me frozen to the spot in fear, fighting a rising tide of panic, but at the sound of Geoff's voice I automatically take a couple of steps backwards, away from the water.

'Thanks, I'm fine,' I choke. 'I'm just going to watch for a bit!'

No. *No no no.* I'm having enough trouble being this close to the water and not legging it as it is. But then I think about Lizzie giving birth on the kitchen floor. And about sticking up for myself.

I take a deep breath.

I did come here for a challenge.

I take another deep breath.

I take a couple of steps forwards again. And then a couple more, getting closer to the water. My heart's pounding, but I take another deep breath in and let it out slowly.

'Come in, Tori, you'll like it!' shouts Than as he rejoins the group after exploring the further edges of the pool.

'No. Thanks.' I gasp the words out. *I'm fine. I'm safe.*

'It's mandatory to the course you know!' he laughs.

'No.' I can feel the anger starting to rise and mingle with my fear.

'At least come in for a paddle?'

'No, Than.' My breath is coming quicker. This is ridiculous. Why can't he just leave me alone?

'Let her take her own time,' I hear Bay mutter to Than.

I bristle. I'm grateful, but I'm not a charity case. I feel my resolve stiffen. I can do this.

I bend down and start taking my boots and socks off. I fight to roll my trousers up, my shaking fingers making it difficult. I take a tentative step towards the water's edge, struggling to keep my balance on the loose stones underfoot.

Breathe in. Slowly out.

See. It's fine. It's just water. I'm fine.

Fuck. I wince as the soles of my feet make contact with the damp shingle at the water's edge. I'm not in the river yet but that's far enough. My whole vision is filling with water. I let out the breath that I hadn't even realized I'd been holding. I can do this. I can . . .

I catch Bay's eye. He's watching me with a smile on his

face. He gives me an almost imperceptible nod. I nod back curtly. See. I'm no one's charity case. I'm . . .

I gasp and choke as a torrent of water hits me in the face. I shake my head, trying to clear it from my eyes only to be hit by another wave. This time I scream and flail my arms, and as I do, my feet start to slip on the stones beneath me. I'm hit again and again. I'm aware of the others shouting, but I can't make sense of what's happening.

'No! No, no, NO! STOP!' I hear a voice screaming. It's mine, but it seems to be coming from a long way away, from the other side of the humming buzz that has started in my brain and is taking over any sense I have left.

Another wave hits me. The buzzing starts to drown me and I feel my feet slip as the stones beneath me shift.

The shouting and screaming have disappeared. All I can hear is the buzzing in my head and each breath heaving into my lungs as if I'm sucking the air in through a bathroom sponge. And then I'm back in the middle of my worst nightmare. There's water all around me. And screaming. I can see fingers clawing at the windows of a drowning car, scrabbling to be released. She's desperate to get out of there. And then the fingers go limp, and I'm screaming and screaming for my mother.

Chapter 24

The Voices in Your Head

'What kind of voice do you use when you talk to yourself? So often it is cruel and mocking. You would never talk to a friend that way, so why do it to yourself? It's time to show yourself some kindness.'

©TheBeginnersGuideToLoneliness.com

When I come to, I'm lying on the shingle beach a couple of feet away from the river's edge. Two things instantly make me want to crawl under a duvet and hide. Number one: my head is being cradled in someone's lap. Number two: I'm sobbing. Really going for it. A full-blown, howling snot-fest. As soon as I realize this, I gulp several times and try to calm down, but it's no use. It's like hiccups – completely out of my hands.

'Shh, shh. It's okay, you're okay.'

It's a man's voice. Gentle hands stroke the wet hair away from my face.

'Is your head okay? Did you hit it?'

'Put her in the recovery position.'

'Give her Rescue Remedy!'

'Is she hurt?'

'Is she cut?'

'Did she slip?'

'Okay, back off everyone!'

I recognize this last voice as Doreen's and I struggle to sit up and wipe the heavy tears away from my face at the same time. A hand supports the middle of my back. I turn to see who it is, and Bay's worried eyes stare back at me.

'Are you okay? Are you hurt?' he asks gently.

'No . . . no, I don't think so. What happened?'

'You got splashed. *Than* splashed you . . . I tried to stop him . . .'

'Drama queen,' I hear Than mutter.

'Shut up,' Bay growls.

I struggle to my feet, not quite trusting my shaking legs to hold me up. Bay quickly stands up and reaches out again to steady me, but I shake him off and move towards Than, who's scowling at me.

'What the fuck did you think you were doing?' I hiss at him, as I feel every ounce of shock and fear turn into cold anger.

'Having a laugh. I didn't think you were going to spaz out on us, did I?'

'*Spaz out?*' I spit, advancing on him. 'You know I'm scared of water. I told you about my phobia! You know more than anyone else here.'

247

'Yeah yeah, you're terrified I'm sure!'

'Okay, guys, let's have a group hug and let this go!' chirrups a nervous-sounding Emma from somewhere behind me.

'I'm not having a fucking group hug. Listen to me, you prick, do you know what I see when I'm near water and I lose control?'

'Jaws?' Than tries to laugh it off, and looks around for support, but only gets disbelieving stares from the others. 'Get over it,' he huffs.

'I see my mother's fingers clawing at the window of her sinking car. My mother, desperate to get out, bleeding and terrified. My mother, drowning.' I can't help it; I start to sob again.

Than glares at me and the others have gone completely quiet. I see Doreen wipe her eyes. Bay steps forward to place his hand on my shoulder. I shrug him off again.

'Maybe I am a drama queen, but I think I've got a pretty good reason. If you don't, then fuck you.' I grab my boots, ram them onto my feet and trudge back up the shingle bank and away from the paralyzed group behind me.

As soon as I step out from under the canopy of trees and feel the sunlight on my face, my body relaxes, my shoulders slump and my sobs ease into a free flow of salty tears. I actually don't mind the tears now that I'm away from the others. I know from bitter experience that if I try to hold them in, they'll only catch up with me later.

I stride away from the sound of voices behind me and go in search of a little bit of peace and privacy where I can get back in control of my feelings. I need to get my armour back in place.

I'm already regretting my outburst. I didn't want everyone to find out like that – or at all, really. Mind you, it's not like I had much choice in the matter.

It doesn't take long for the crying and shaking to start to calm, but all that means is that I'm now aware that my arm is throbbing. I look down at my hand and see that there's blood dripping from my fingertips. *Oh. Shit.*

Coming to a halt at the top of the hill, I twist this way and that, trying to get a good look at where the blood is coming from. There's a messy gash that runs down the back of my forearm. It looks pretty filthy too. Damn. All I want right now is a bit of peace and quiet, but I'll have to get someone to help me clean this up, whether I want to or not.

I stand still just a moment or two longer and look back down the hill to where the others are emerging from under the trees, their swim cut short by the drama. I spot Bay striking out in my direction. Thankfully it's just him; the others seem to be staying put. I really don't want to talk about it yet, so I take a couple of steps towards the field gate.

'Tori, wait! Please!' Bay calls, speeding up in spite of the hill.

'Why?'

'You're in shock. You're hurt. You can't go off on your own.'

'Right. Well. Right.' I hang my head. All of a sudden, I'm absolutely knackered.

'It's not your fault, you know?'

Great. Someone else telling me it's not my fault. Does he really think I've not tried to tell myself that before? I shrug. The tears have started again. I can feel them snaking down my cheeks, hot and heavy. I wipe my face with the back of my hand.

'Shit, Tori, you're covered in blood!' Bay gasps.

I examine my hand and realize that I've probably just managed to smear blood across my face.

'Don't worry, it's just my arm,' I sigh.

'Don't worry?'

'I mean, it's not my head or anything serious.'

'Show me,' says Bay, taking a step closer. I get the sense he's been holding back until now for fear of spooking me, like a wild deer or something. But the sight of the blood seems to have galvanized him into action. I twist my arm around to show him.

He peers closely at it. 'It doesn't look too deep, but it does need cleaning properly.'

I know this. Really I do. But right now, I don't want to go anywhere near the rest of the group. 'I might just go for a bit of a walk to calm down,' I say.

'Sorry, Tori, but you really need to come back with us. You're hurt and in shock, and that cut needs attention.'

'I think I've had enough attention already, thanks.'

'Tori, you have to—'

'I don't have to do anything! I didn't have to get in that river, and I don't have to come with you.' I glare at Bay. My arm is now full-on throbbing. I know that I'm behaving like a child, but embarrassment is now mingling with the shock of what just happened, and right now, Bay is the only available target.

All I really want to do is hide under a fluffy duvet with a strong drink at the ready, followed by some serious comfort TV, but there's no chance of any of that.

'Fine,' Bay sighs. 'Look, tell you what, give me a second to let the others know what's happening, and I'll walk you back to the yurt so that you can have a rest somewhere safe. No need for you to talk to the others yet. Deal?'

I feel like arguing, but I have zero energy left, and if I'm honest I'm starting to feel a little bit fuzzy around the edges. I don't particularly like the idea of being called a drama queen again because I fainted in the middle of a field like some drippy Jane Austen heroine.

'Okay, deal,' I say quietly.

As I watch Bay pelt back down the hill towards the others, I feel all my bravery and my desire for a new challenge dissolve. Reality is crashing over me. I'm broke, my only friends are people I've never met, I live in a damp, unappealing broom cupboard and the only man I've ever loved broke my heart in the worst way possible.

And here I am, at the culmination of it all, standing in a field with blood dripping down my arm, recovering from a panic attack and a dead faint.

As soon as Bay gets back, we start to walk quietly in the direction of the yurt. I hold my arm, doing my best to wrap it in a bit of clean T-shirt. The sense of relief when I spot the yurt is insane. All I want to do now is lie down and let the shock, which is slowly making my body feel like a heavy piece of putty, subside. I need to get some sleep and then I'll feel a lot better. After that, I'll decide how best to pay that bloody arse-hole back.

'Okay, you chill out here for a while and I'll go in search of a first-aid kit. I'll be back in a bit, okay?' Bay says, his voice gentle.

I nod and duck into the yurt, grateful to be on my own for a few minutes. I yank my boots off and, after peeling off the rest of my damp clothing, I put on some fresh, loose trousers, wincing at the dark bruises that are already starting to bloom on my legs. The blood has pretty much stopped seeping out of the cut now, but I can see a whole bunch of dark flecks stuck in it. I'll have to clean that properly, but right now, all I want to do is get warm and dry. I pull on the jumper I borrowed from Bay the other night, careful to wrap my arm in the T-shirt again to stop any blood staining it, and then I climb under my blankets.

The water is closing in on me and there's nowhere to go. The fabric-lined ceiling above me is getting closer and closer and there are only inches of air left. My fingers are raw and bleeding, but I won't stop clawing at the windows. I grab the door handle and still it won't give. The air gap is almost gone. I gasp a few more lungfuls and press as hard as I can against the window. It won't budge. My vision is filled with my mother's unconscious face, eyes gazing lifelessly through the murky water, hair floating in a halo about her head like possessed seaweed. I suck in my last breath and scream, trying to wake her up. And then it's gone, the air gap has closed.

I thrash wildly, holding my breath, but my lungs are about to burst. I open my mouth to scream again, but the in-breath just pulls in water. It streams up my nose and clogs my throat. I scream and scream but no noise comes out; there's just tightness in my chest as my lungs fill. I am drowning and no one can hear my silent cries.

Then there are arms around me, lifting me, saving me. They're pulling me upwards through the water towards the light, but I'm still screaming. Can't they see my mum is still down there? She's stuck. Unconscious. Drowning.

'Help her!' This time the cry isn't silent. It shoots through the air and tears at the fabric of my dream, waking me up. But the hands are still there, holding on to mine.

'Tori, it's all right. You're okay, you're safe.' It's a man's voice. I'm sobbing so hard I can't see. I can barely hear.

'Tori, calm down.'

'Bay?' I squeak through the tears.

'Yes, it's me. You've been asleep for hours, you know.'

I know. I can tell from the stiffness in my neck and the layers of fear that have built up inside me. I've been living that dream over and over again without the relief of waking in between.

'Tori, you need to get that arm cleaned up. And you probably need something to eat too.'

'No, no, I don't. I just need to rest. I'll be fine,' I mutter.

'No.' This time there's no arguing with Bay's tone. 'Tori, you need a rest from your nightmares. You've been tossing and turning for ages. Look, I brought you something.' He gestures over towards the centre of the yurt.

I sit up to see what he's talking about, pushing back my tangled hair and trying to unglue the strands from my damp face.

In the middle of the space is an old, metal bathtub, filled with steaming water. The air is sweet and herby.

'A bath?'

'As near as it gets. I wasn't sure about the water after . . . but you said running water?'

'Running water,' I nod, and shudder. 'Water that's fast moving . . . that's rising or . . . or comes up at me . . . unexpected.' Damn, I've started to shiver in earnest at the memory of the face full of water earlier and the torrent of images it triggered. I shake my head to try to clear it.

'So a bath is . . . ?' Bay checks.

'Perfect. Thank you,' I force a smile. 'How on earth did you fill it?'

Bay shrugs. 'It did take a few trips, but I thought it might help. Even if you can't get in, you can soak your arm and use it to wash.'

I spot a couple of buckets next to the bath, still steaming. It must have taken him ages, lugging the water up here.

'What's the smell?' I wrinkle my nose. It's not unpleasant . . . just . . . *clean.*

'Oh, just a bit of lavender and tea tree oil. It might sting a bit, but it'll help clean that cut of yours, and the lavender will help with the bruising too.'

'I don't think I'll bruise. It was nothing really.'

'Well, it won't do you any harm, anyway . . .' I see Bay looking at my arm on top of the bedcover where my sleeve has ridden up. There's already the hint of a blue-black bruise on show. 'Anyway, it'll help you relax.' Bay looks down, and suddenly seems awkward. 'I'll go. I'll be off for at least a couple of hours, so just take your time.'

'Right. Um . . . thanks. It's really kind of you.'

'I'll get Doreen to look in on you in about an hour – just to check you're okay. Right. I'll go then.'

'Bay?'

'Yeah?' His voice is low. He clears his throat, looking fidgety. I shift uncomfortably too. I'm still not very good at asking for help from people in real life.

'Do you . . . could you . . . could you help me clean my arm? There are bits in it, and I don't think I'll be able to get at them properly.' Cue a huge blush from me.

Why? I've only asked for some first-aid help . . . but after he's spent a large portion of his day trudging backwards and forwards to fill a bath for me, it somehow feels far more intimate.

'Of course!' he says, sounding relieved for some reason. 'Claire gave me a first-aid kit earlier. Come over here.' Bay helps me to my feet and gets me to perch on a stool near the entrance flap so that he's got more light.

He rummages through the little first-aid kit, pulling on a pair of gloves and handing me a couple of wrapped antiseptic wipes to hold. Finally, he pulls out a triangle sling bandage. 'Needs must!' he grins at me, dips it into the bath water, wrings it out and wads it up into a little pad.

'Okay, this is going to sting a bit . . .' He gently takes my arm in his hand.

I draw in a sharp breath as Bay swabs at the newly dried edges of my cut. I feel the sting of the cloth with every little movement he makes. He works in silence for a few minutes, but pauses briefly every time I give a squeak of discomfort.

'Okay, that looks good,' he says finally.

I stop biting my lip and heave a sigh of relief. That was worse than I expected, especially as he's had to remove the little dark bits of dirt and slate out of it too.

'Thank you – I think!'

'No problem.' He smiles at me and peels off the gloves that are so incongruous in this setting.

'And thanks again for the bath. I'll just . . .' I'm eyeing the hot water.

'Sure, sure. I'll get out of your way.' He scrambles to his feet. 'You're going to be fine, you know.' He gives me a tiny smile, and before I know what's happening, he leans over and plants a gentle kiss on my forehead before disappearing out of the yurt.

I'm left sitting on my stool, mouth slightly open in surprise, wondering what the hell just happened. Did Bay just kiss me? No. Not really. That was him just trying to make me feel better, wasn't it? That was just the weird, slightly lowered boundaries that are normal around this place. It didn't mean anything.

The question is, why am I struggling to catch my breath again? This time, it's not through terror, but something far more . . . exciting?

I shake my head again in an attempt to clear the cotton wool clouds that are drifting around my brain. I must still be in shock from earlier, that's all it is. Right. Bath.

After sticking my head out of the entrance flap to double check that the coast is clear, I place a huge towel on a clothes rack and position it in front of the bath. There. Now, if anyone does happen to peek in, they won't get an eyeful.

I sigh as I sink into the water, careful not to splash myself. The warmth starts to soothe the aches and I feel the last traces of my nightmare melt away. All that remains now is the image of a pair of strong, gentle hands, and the feel of a warm kiss on my forehead.

'Knock knock! Are you decent?' Doreen's voice calls from outside.

'Come on in!' I call. After lounging around in my bath for what felt like an eternity, the water cooled so much I had to get out.

I feel so much better, like someone has washed the inside of my head for me too. I feel like I'm free of something; it's hard to describe it, but I'm calm. My arm feels loads better too. It's stopped throbbing, but that's probably because it's not full of little bits of stone anymore.

'How're you feeling?' Doreen's face appears. 'Wow! This place is gorgeous!' She sniffs. 'What's that smell?'

I smile back at her. 'That'd be my bath.'

'Bath?' Doreen moves into the space and eyes the metal tub. 'You lucky mare . . . Though I don't fancy having to haul all that water up here!'

I feel myself start to blush again. 'Erm . . . Bay did it. He thought it'd make me feel better.'

'Ooh, get you and your special treatment!' Doreen smiles and winks. I shift my weight uncomfortably. Hmm . . . maybe not the best thing for everyone to know about. 'You won't tell anyone, will you?'

'Course not!' she says reassuringly. 'Anyway, I was just kidding. You must have needed it after that fall. Are you okay?'

A finger of fear creeps back into my mind. Am I going to have to talk everything through with Doreen? And then the others too? I really can't face analyzing it all.

'I'm fine,' I reply tightly.

'So, you're ready for the next ordeal, then!' says Doreen as she bounces around the yurt, picking things up, examining them and replacing them.

I shiver. Nope. I'm not ready for anything.

'No one really expects you to turn up, you know. I think they're all half-expecting you to disappear on us.'

I pull a face. Right now, I just want to hide out here. I can't face seeing the others yet. Maybe they're right; maybe I should bow out and head home.

'You know,' she says gently, 'if you get on with things and have some new experiences, after a while, no one's going to give much weight to what happened this morning.'

'Yeah. I know you're right.' I say. 'Anyway, I don't fancy becoming the legend of the panicking water-girl.'

'Well then, what could be better than Ted's fire walk the day after tomorrow? It'll give you a day to recover . . . But I'm not going to be able to do it if you're not there to cheer me on, you know. Say you'll come!'

'Okay, I'll be there,' I say decidedly. 'I can't let you have all the fun, can I?'

Chapter 25

Fall in Love with the Journey

'Everything about our society is set up to make us focus on outcomes; it's all about the destination, not the journey. But it's time to fall in love with the little steps that take us somewhere. Let us not forget to look around us and enjoy the view as we travel.'

©TheBeginnersGuideToLoneliness.com

How am I not *completely* freaking out right now? I'm about to help build a fire. Doesn't sound too bad, does it, a nice little bonfire? How about if I add that we're all expected to walk over the bloody thing? See, I should be freaking out!

But I'm not; I'm strangely calm about this part of the course. Cool as a cucumber. Because there's no doubt about the fact that it's going to bloody hurt and at least one of us is going to get seriously injured. It's the law of the universe. Do something stupid and you're going to get burned.

If I'm honest, I'm feeling so totally miserable right now, I'm not sure I care much. I'm still in hermit mode after everything that happened at the river. I don't really want to engage with the others, and I especially don't want to talk to Than. I managed to avoid all of them apart from Bay and Doreen yesterday. Claire came up to the yurt to try to talk things through with me, but I couldn't, and my policy for today is blanking the whole thing out. I just want to get it over and done with so that I can go back to the yurt and hide out with Dennis.

'Okay, gang! In a few hours you will all have completed at least one fire walk!' Ted shouts. He's so excited he sounds like he's almost ready to burst. 'How do you all feel about that?'

He looks around at us eagerly, but rather than the rousing chorus of cheers he was clearly expecting, all he gets are a few nervous smiles, blank nods and even a groan here and there – mainly from Doreen's direction. I just stay quiet.

Ted's face falls briefly. 'So, you're nervous? That's good.' He rallies, smiling around at us all. 'That's completely natural. If you were facing something this dangerous without a hint of fear or apprehension in your heart, I would have to call you a foolhardy idiot.' He looks at each of us in turn. 'The purpose of this fire walk is to stare fear in the face. Fear of failure, fear of pain, fear of the untried and fear of the unknown. But it's not just about staring it in the face, it's about embracing it, tangoing with it and ultimately learning that you can always overcome it.

'The fire will help you learn that life's not always about taking the long route around your troubles. Sometimes, you need to walk straight at them to reach the other side.'

I roll my eyes before I can catch myself, but it doesn't matter, everyone else's eyes are glued to Ted. I sigh. I'm not so sure that scorching the living daylights out of my feet will turn out to have all these magical, life-affirming properties.

I fidget.

No, I'm not looking forward to this, but I really, *really* want to get it over and done with. The sooner we start, the sooner it will be over. Then I can take up a nice comfy bed in the nearest casualty department. Maybe I'll even get the chance to visit Lizzie and the baby while I'm at it.

Hours later, I'm exhausted from gathering wood from the nearby coppice and hauling load after load over to the fire. The afternoon has been full of the random, lively chatter of the others, but I've kept pretty quiet. After what happened at the river, I don't feel much like small talk. Most of my spare energy has been taken up with avoiding Than. Wherever he is is where I don't want to be. I've worked mainly with Bay, as he seems to understand my need to stay silent. Being with Bay also has the added bonus that Than is even less likely to try to talk to me.

As the flames start to settle, so does the conversation. We're all grouped around the fire, staring at the glowing mound of embers in front of us.

I feel a hand in mine and look sideways to find Doreen at my side. I smile at her, but don't receive one in return. She's pale and quivering.

'All right?' I ask quietly, just as Ted begins to rake the glowing embers flat, sending a cloud of sparks dancing and snapping over our heads.

Doreen shakes her head, lip wobbling. 'Not sure,' she mutters.

'I don't think anyone is,' I reply, giving her hand a squeeze. There's no point in comforting her beyond letting her know she's not alone. Right now, I think we're all shitting our pants.

'Okay, everyone,' calls Ted in a clear voice, 'you need to listen to me. I know that this is going to sound very obvious, but you need to take this in. This is a fire. You built it, and you've seen it burning. Now, I know that it's down to embers, but they're still burning at around 1,200 degrees Fahrenheit. What we are about to do needs concentration and respect. For each other, for yourselves and for the process. It is safe if you follow my lead. If you don't, this is dangerous. If you aren't happy to follow my lead, please head back to your camps now. This isn't the time for games. There is zero tolerance here for mucking about.' Ted pauses and looks around at all of us again.

No one budges an inch, but I can sense Doreen's breathing picking up a notch or two. I'm still strangely calm. After everything that's already happened, this just isn't pushing my buttons. I glance across the fire at Than. He's standing as stiff as a gatepost, arms folded, looking mutinous as the light from the embers glints off his smiley-face badge.

'Okay then. I'll take your silence as commitment. What happens next is this: we have a damp mat here at the start of the walk. There is another one at the other side. There are tubs of water here, here and here.' He indicates at various points around the fire. 'You start from where I am, and walk straight across to where Bay's standing, in a straight, steady line.'

'How?' Bob asks, his voice completely flat.

'Just concentrate. Know that you can do this. Know that it is not going to hurt you. And know that it will make you stronger. This is not an experience that can be explained more fully to someone who hasn't tried it yet. I'm sorry.'

Bob nods, turning his eyes back to the glowing embers.

'There are, of course, some rules. Make sure that your trousers are rolled high up above your knees. If they won't do this, I suggest that you remove them. You can control your own bodies, but you can't control how your flares are feeling!'

A titter runs around the group, and it's like gas being freed from a can of Coke as the tension releases a little bit.

'The second rule is, don't run. There's no need. It means more pressure on your feet, less concentration and flicking burning embers around, so just don't.'

A few people nod. I'm starting to breathe faster. Am I really going to do this? I guess so.

'All right, here we go. Watch me first just so that you can see that it can be done safely.'

Ted steps onto the damp matting just in front of the bed of embers. He paces side to side for a few seconds, staring straight out ahead of him. I take a deep breath in and hold it. This is insane. Every cell in my body wants to shout at him to stop. To wait. To step away from the fire.

Ted strides forward. He doesn't rush or hang around. He simply paces in a steady rhythm, seven strides over the embers and onto the matting at the other side. I let my breath out in a rush as he paces side to side on the damp mat, dousing any coals that have stuck to the bottom of his feet.

We all start cheering simultaneously as Ted turns to face us with a grin, arms outstretched like he's trying to hug us all at once.

'Any questions?'

'Does it hurt?' Emma asks.

'No, no, it doesn't hurt. You can feel the heat as you walk, but it's not uncomfortable; like walking across hot sand . . . or maybe eggshells. Just be sure to pace at the end to clear your feet while you're still focusing. We're all going to try to walk at least once today, but there's no rush. Take your time and decide when's best for you.' He smiles around at us all. 'So, who's ready?'

Everything goes unnaturally quiet, and for a moment all I can hear is the spitting fire. All eyes have dropped to look at the embers.

Even if you paid me a million quid right now, I wouldn't feel ready to do this.

Let's face it, I'm never going to be ready.

And I need the loo.

It's the nerves, I know, but I can't stop fidgeting. The base of my spine is tingling and my top lip is stinging with sweat.

'I'll do it!' I say. I ignore both the surprised murmuring and the sounds of encouragement from around me. Doreen squeezes my hand and lets go abruptly, as if I might drag her with me if she's not careful. I walk over to Ted and feel the rough, damp matting cooling the soles of my feet.

'Well done, Tori,' Ted smiles at me. I nod, bend down and with a bit of a fight between my shaking hands and the stiff denim, manage to roll my jeans up securely above my knees. Bay was right when he said I'd bruise – and now they're on full display to the world.

'Ready?' asks Ted gently from beside me.

Am I ready?

I stare at the embers glowing in front of me. I can feel the heat coming at me in waves. There are encouraging shouts from around the fire, though I'm not sure who they're coming from. All I can focus on are the miniature flames licking up from the embers here and there. There's a big cheer to my left, and I glance over to see Doreen grinning at me. Next to her stands Than. He's got a strange, blank expression on his face, but I haven't got time to worry about him now. Someone has started a slow clap for me.

'Focus now, Tori,' says Ted at my side.

I pause, holding my breath for a moment, staring at the fire.

Can I do this?

My mum's face appears in my mind. I let the image float away.

Can I do this?

Than's taunts at the river start to ring in my ears. I let them go. All I can hear now is the slow clap. Everything else has disappeared.

I focus on the beat and step out.

The embers spark around me and I can feel the heat rising from below. I take a step, and then another.

Clap. Clap. Clap.

I'm doing this. I can't believe I'm actually doing this! The embers are pricking the soles of my feet, but I'm calm and completely focused on what I'm doing and where I'm going.

Clap. Clap. Clap.

I take a step, and then another.

Now I'm standing on a cold, wet mat, pacing side to side, cooling the soles of my feet. And then other sounds creep back in: a roaring that is neither coming from my head nor the fire behind me. It's my friends cheering for me. The clapping beat has gone from slow and steady to mad and cheerful.

Bay's chanting my name, jumping up and down like a six-year-old, a huge grin lighting up his entire face.

And I run.

I run back to the group and into their waiting arms, receiving kisses and hugs from each of them, including Ted, who's beaming from ear to ear.

When we finally settle down, the atmosphere becomes serious and respectful again, but this time you can't feel the fearful tension that was there before. One of us has managed to come through this and shown the others that it's possible. I can't stop grinning, and I feel like I've left every ounce of my uncomfortable, nervous energy in the fire. Now it's my turn to cheer the others on.

Sam goes next, and then Emma. Messa approaches the mat and stands there for several long minutes before setting out, but he does manage it. It's as if he's pacing across the coals that I look around the group to see how many more of us are left to go. Than's missing. He's gone, nowhere to be seen among the cheering, elated faces.

I turn to ask Doreen if she knows what's happened to him, but she's looking pale and sweaty. Before I get a word out, she steps forward and heads for the mat with a determined, if slightly wobbly, stride. I instantly forget about Than as I feel my nerves surge in support for my friend. I want to reach out to her, give her a hug and show her I'm here for her.

I watch as she has a couple of quiet words with Ted and then steps onto the mat. The others start to cheer and shout encouragement.

To my right, Bay starts a slow clap. I glance up at him and smile. It was his clap that carried me over those coals.

It's time to do the same thing for Doreen. I join in.

As Doreen steps forward, she seems to pause as the first cloud of sparks rises up around her. I feel my mouth grow dry, but she paces forwards, matching the beat of our claps, and before I know what's happened, she's already on the other side.

My cheers join the others' as we all erupt with happiness. Another one of our clan has made it through the test. Doreen just stands on the cool, damp mat with a look of complete confusion on her face. As I watch, it slowly warms to a delighted smile, and she flies towards us. We engulf her in a tangled mass of arms and cheering.

We can do this – together.

Chapter 26

Behind the Anger

'It's completely natural to be angry about your loneliness. Whatever the root cause, you can feel let down by the world and want to lash out. But in order to heal, you need to look at what's behind the anger. Your anger is a reaction, not a trigger. Look for the cause and you can work on healing it.'

©TheBeginnersGuideToLoneliness.com

I peel away from Doreen, letting the rest of the group take their turns to smother her in hugs and kisses, and look around again in search of Than. He's the last of the group left to do the walk, and as things start to quieten down again, he's rather conspicuous in his absence.

'Ted,' I mutter, coming to stand next to him, 'did you see where Than went? Is he okay?'

'He left,' sighs Ted, his smile dropping briefly. 'Happens sometimes.'

'When?' I ask in surprise.

'Just after you'd started your walk. He headed back towards the campsite I think.' Ted smiles kindly at me. 'Don't worry, he'll be fine. Sometimes this step just comes too soon for some people. You did brilliantly. Really well done!' He clasps my shoulder, and I can see pride in his eyes. It brings a lump to my throat.

'Thanks, Ted.' I smile back at him, but I can't help but feel like the air has been let out of me a little bit. I know that whatever bond Than and I had is well and truly broken after everything that's happened, but the fact that he didn't even bother to wait until I'd finished my fire walk feels a bit like someone jamming a knitting needle into my heart. It makes it personal.

'Tori, get over here!' calls Bay, holding out an arm and beckoning me into the tangle of celebrating bodies. I jog over to them, but it's with a much heavier heart than just a couple of minutes ago.

I can't get comfortable in my bed. No matter how much I snuggle down, I just can't relax. It's a warm night, and I've kicked my duvet off and retrieved it twice already. I don't really need it, but I feel vulnerable lying here uncovered, wearing just my pyjamas.

I left everyone celebrating their success around the communal fire pit and came back to the yurt early. What I really wanted to do was go in search of Than. He didn't turn up for supper and was nowhere to be seen around the fire pit either.

I don't know why, after everything he's done, but I just wanted to check that he's okay . . . or maybe I just wanted to pick a fight and ask him exactly what his problem is. Either way, common sense prevailed, and I came back here instead. Whatever he's going through right now, I've learned enough over the past few days to know that I'm not the one to help him unravel it. Doesn't make it any easier to stay put though.

Dennis reappeared about half an hour ago, and after a cursory lick of my hand and a quick snuffle around for any dog biscuits I might have hidden on my person, he turned tail, jumped up onto Bay's pillows and has been loudly snoring ever since.

I jump as the flap flips open and Bay appears. He grins over at me as soon as he sees I'm still awake, and it dawns on me that I've been waiting for him. That's why I haven't been able to get to sleep. He's the perfect person to pump for information about Than.

'Hey!' I swallow. *Hmm, how to approach this . . .*

'Hi. Nice job today leading the charge. Dennis, OFF!' He strides over to his bed and attempts to nudge the snoozing dog off his pillows. Dennis is not having any of it though, and after a quick wag of his tail promptly rolls onto his back in a full stretch and falls back to sleep. 'Honestly, hound,' laughs Bay, rubbing his belly affectionately.

'So, uh . . . did Than turn up in the end?' Damn. Not exactly casual.

'No,' Bay says shortly, the laughter disappearing from his face in an instant. 'Why are you so worried, anyway? I thought you were keeping your distance?'

'Yeah, that's true,' I say. Bay doesn't need to know that I've been lying here, repeatedly talking myself out of going in search of Than. 'I'm just a bit worried after he took off like that. He's working through some pretty serious stuff.'

Bay rolls his eyes. 'Aren't we all?'

'So, you really haven't seen him?'

Bay gives me a completely unreadable look, so I stick my tongue out at him.

'What was that for?'

'Being a loser. I know you know what's happened . . . Why won't you just tell me?'

Bay hesitates, and then sighs. 'Fine, fine. I'll tell you. He left just as you started your walk. Then, when we got back, Ted went to find him to talk things through and he'd gone.'

'What do you mean, "gone"?'

'Gone. Left. Vamoosed. All his stuff, his tent. Everything.'

'He just left?'

'Yup. And probably a good thing for him, after some of the crap he's been up to. I was so close to having a word with Ted to get him kicked out anyway, especially after that stunt he pulled on you down at the river.'

'You know, I don't need you to babysit me. I can look after myself.'

'Trust me, I know that. I'm more than aware that you're capable of making your own mistakes.'

'What's that supposed to mean?' I glare at him.

'That I know that you can look after yourself, no matter what's thrown at you . . . even if it's your own fault that it's being thrown in the first place.'

'That's so much better, thanks for clarifying,' I mutter. My chest feels tight and my eyes are prickling. I know I was spoiling for a fight with Than, but I didn't expect to have one with Bay instead.

'Look, the guy's a total shit.'

'He is not a shit,' I growl at Bay, making myself jump. Dennis sits bolt upright and stares at me.

'Tori! Why the hell are you still defending him? He was awful to you.'

'That's *my* problem.'

'Yes, it is, but that makes it everyone's problem while you're here.'

'You want me to go too?' I get up off the bed and stand staring at him. That hurt. Bay is my friend, or I thought he was. I thought . . . I thought there was something between us; that we meant something to each other. Maybe I got it all wrong.

'Of course I don't want you to go,' Bay says, running a hand roughly through his hair. 'I just don't want you to waste any more energy on an idiot.'

'Well, like I said, just let me worry about myself, will you?'

'For once, will you stop thinking about yourself and try looking at it from my . . . from someone else's perspective?' The hard lines on Bay's face are so unlike him that I take an involuntary step backwards. 'Friends look out for each other, whether it's *needed* or not. That's what real friends do. Can you get your head around that?'

I turn away from him, swallowing repeatedly, desperate to stop the tears from falling. I try to ignore the human thunderstorm behind me. Maybe Bay's right. I don't know how to have friends, how to *be* a friend. Which means my mother was right, and Markus was right.

I deserve to be alone.

I heave in a deep breath and suddenly need to put as much space as possible between me and Bay, me and this stupid, pointless fight. I turn and, as the tears start to fall, I leave the yurt.

By the next morning, I've calmed down. I slept surprisingly well on the thin strip of hard floor at the foot of Geoff and Doreen's bed, padded out with their spare blankets and one of Geoff's old sweaters as a pillow.

After the fight with Bay, I stomped back down to the fire pit, hoping to find Doreen. As it turned out, only Messa, Moth and Bob were left nattering around the flames. As lovely as they are, a lecture on which particular planetary alignment was causing my upset or how taking up knitting would help wasn't the kind of sympathy I was after, so I beat a hasty retreat. After a dark and rather winding walk, I finally ended up at Doreen and Geoff's cabin door.

If I need to take lessons on how to be a friend, I know who I'll be taking them from. I might have interrupted their evening by turning up snot-nosed and tear-stained, but Geoff and

Doreen couldn't have been kinder to me. We talked for hours. Doreen gently helped me to see that maybe, just maybe, I was defending a version of Than that I hoped existed, rather than the real version; the one who was publicly cruel, snide and downright mean.

And Geoff? Well, Geoff was the biggest eye-opener of the evening. I was mid rant about Bay when he interrupted and gently but firmly told me to give the guy a break. He pointed out that it couldn't have been easy for him to watch as I stood up for a guy who was trying to break me. Of course I argued, but Geoff was having none of it.

As I settled down to sleep, all talked out, I had to admit to myself that maybe Geoff did have a point. Bay was on my side. He had been the good guy in all this. And to have that thrown back in his face had to hurt. I drifted off to sleep with one thought in my mind – Bay was right; I did have a lot to learn. But maybe I was finally ready to admit it and start trying.

This morning, it's time for yoga again, and I'm thankful it's not a more chatty kind of a session. As soon as we reach the studio, I set up my mat and am ready to get started before Claire even arrives. I'm nervous to see Bay after our argument, but I'm excited too.

So a small part of me wilts when he doesn't turn up. I'd forgotten that he was due to be helping Ted out again this morning. The group feels strangely small with both him and Than missing. As Claire makes a start and I let my mind sink into the movements, I realize that, despite what happened last

275

night, I'm way more relaxed this morning than I have been in a while. It takes a moment or two for me to realize that this is because Than isn't here, and I'm not waiting for today's dose of drama to hit.

Come lunchtime, however, my newfound sense of calm has deserted me, and my brain's up to its usual tricks, hopping all over the place from problem to problem. I'm trying to listen to a story Bob's telling the group, but I've missed most of it as I'm too busy staring over his shoulder, planning how I'm going to apologize to Bay when he finally turns up.

'You okay?' Emma asks me quietly.

I snap back to the present and stare at her uncomprehendingly.

'You've been staring at Bob's ear for the last ten minutes and you haven't eaten anything. Are you missing Than?'

I shake my head. 'No . . . no . . .'

'No, you're not okay, or no, you're not missing him?' Emma smiles at me.

'Erm, both?' I say with an apologetic grin. 'Sorry, Em, I'm not very with it.'

'Brain too full,' she says. It's not a question, just a simple, understanding statement.

'Exactly!' I say, relieved she knows what I mean.

'I get that. This place throws up so many questions and changes, I think there are these moments where you just have to slow down and let it all sink in, you know?'

I nod at her. 'You know, I really don't miss Than,' I say, just to make sure she understands.

'No, I bet. Not after what he was like with you.'

'Well, he was going through a lot,' I say like a stuck record.

'So what? That's no excuse.'

For some reason, hearing it from Emma makes it sink in. No, there really isn't an excuse for treating anyone like that, is there?

'Anyway,' she says to me, 'I find when my brain does what yours is doing, I head off and follow some of Russ's mindfulness tips.'

'You do?' I ask, surprised.

She nods. 'Does wonders for clearing the fog. I can't tell you how many times I've gone for a walk and just found a patch of grass to stare at,' she laughs.

The garden is quiet. I've left the others at the lunch table, tucking in and swapping stories. I've decided to take Emma's advice while we're still on our break. Everything is looking lovely in the early afternoon sunshine.

I wander over to the potato patch and admire the long ridges where Geoff and Bay worked together last week to hoe them up. The dark leaves have already re-emerged in tufts from the tops of the ridges. I take in a deep breath and let it out slowly, letting my shoulders drop. The beds that we weeded last week are now dotted with sturdy little plants. They must be the courgettes that Bay had planned. The bed nearest the compost heap is still half full of weeds, the ones that needed a fork to lift them as they'd taken hold a bit too strongly for weeding by hand.

I grab a bucket and hand fork from the little tool shed, perch on the railway sleepers and start methodically working away at the weeds.

'Hi, Tori!'

Bay's voice makes me jump. I've become so engrossed in clearing my little patch, I've lost track of time, and by the angry complaints coming from my back, I've been sitting in one position for far too long.

I stand up slowly and stretch as Bay makes his way over to me.

'Wow! That's quite some job you've done. Thanks.' Bay grins, inspecting the now pristine patch in front of us.

Now that he's here, I don't know what to say. Emma was right though; I had to consciously keep my head clear for the first five minutes of weeding, bringing my attention back to what I was doing and the feel of yanking each clump of weeds out from the earth . . . but it didn't take long until it completely absorbed me, and it's been a blessed relief from worrying in circles.

'Hi!' I say at last, realizing that Bay is just standing there, staring at me. I've just remembered what I was worrying about in the first place. 'Bay, I wanted to apologize . . . for last night.'

Bay cocks his head. 'So you did some gardening for me?' His smile almost looks shy.

'Well, uh . . . no . . . that was actually me trying to calm my head down a little bit.'

'Oh. Did it work?' he asks.

I nod. 'But I do still want to say sorry.'

'What for?' he asks curiously.

'For reacting like I did. Again.'

Bay nods. 'Well, for the record, help with the weeding is always an acceptable apology,' he laughs.

I smile at him in relief.

'Anyway, I'm sorry too. What I wanted to say, well, it kind of came out wrong. I didn't mean to upset you. Actually, that's the last thing I wanted to do. It's just, you're good at being a friend to other people, and I hate to see you not accepting that friendship in return.'

Damn. This doesn't feel like it's going to be a case of easy-peasy, gloss it over forgive-and-forget. Bang goes my sense of calm for the second time today.

I let out a sigh and sit back down on the side of the raised bed. Bay sits next to me.

'Talk to me, Tori. Why'd you disappear on me last night, other than because I was being a bit of a knob?'

I let out a chuckle and shake my head. 'We were both being knobs, if it helps.' I look at him and see that he's just waiting, just being my friend. There's no ulterior motive here. 'Look, I've been on my own for a very long two years. Probably longer if I'm being honest.'

'What do you mean, on your own? As in, single?'

I clear my throat. 'Well, yes, that. I spilt up with my ex, Markus, just after Mum died in the accident. We were both part of this huge group of friends. We'd all been close since school, you know?'

Bay nods, but stays quiet, waiting for me to carry on.

'After we split up, our friends did try to make me socialize, but I was so cut up about the accident. I was numb and completely confused. The last thing I wanted to do was party – and their sympathy had a really short shelf life. Anyway, it didn't take long for the invitations to dry up, and basically, Markus ended up inheriting our friends in the break-up.'

I feel a bit foolish saying all this out loud, but if Bay really wants to understand what last night was about, this is where it came from.

'But you must have had other friends, work colleagues, family who stuck by you?' Bay asks quietly.

I shake my head, feeling the usual sense of shame, as if it's somehow my fault that I ended up so isolated. 'Nope. I'm self-employed, work from home and am an only child. Suddenly my life was quiet and pretty empty.'

'Shit, that must have been tough.'

I nod and shrug at the same time. Tough. Nearly impossible. 'I think it would have eventually broken me if it hadn't been for a couple of friends I made online. They helped.'

I stop again, but Bay's still quiet.

'Anyway,' I say as the silence starts to feel uncomfortable, 'that's why I disappeared on you last night. You made me face something I've been trying to hide from – that I don't know how to be a friend anymore.'

'That's bullshit,' Bay says, and he turns to face me full on. 'You've supported every single person here when they've needed it. You know how to be a friend—'

'But when you said—'

'I'm sorry for the way things came out last night. What I *meant* was, perhaps you struggle to accept friendship in return. And after what you've just told me, I'm not surprised that you might be a little bit . . .'

'Rusty?' I laugh.

' "Hesitant" was what I had in mind, but I think they both work,' Bay says a little sadly. 'Anyway, I'm sorry that it all came out in the way it did. I was angry and, well . . .'

'What?' I ask curiously.

'Jealous, Tori. I was jealous.'

'Of me?' I say, confused.

'No, not you. Than and you. And the way that, no matter what he threw at you, you still stuck up for him.'

I stare at him, mouth open.

'Sorry. Maybe I shouldn't have said that,' says Bay, looking a bit sheepish.

I close my mouth and shake my head. 'Actually, it's fine. After talking to Geoff and Doreen last night, I think I know where you were coming from. They've helped me see that the version of Than I've been busy defending is nothing but a figment of my imagination.'

'For what it's worth, I'm really sorry I was right about him,' says Bay, digging his heel into the mud.

'No, you're not,' I smile, giving him a nudge with my elbow.

Bay grins at me. 'Okay. Maybe not.'

Chapter 27

Issue Deep Dive

'Working through issues is never easy. When you first seek external support you will experience breakthroughs – but you're not done! Now is the time for an issue deep dive. Don't cheat and use this moment as an excuse to stall in your progress – keep pushing through.'

©TheBeginnersGuideToLoneliness.com

'I'm so sorry I'm late!' I puff as I rush into the little, light attic space that Ted uses for his one-to-one counselling sessions.

'No problem.' Ted looks up from a book on his desk and smiles at me. 'Oh, by the way, I take it Bay managed to catch up with you yesterday lunchtime?'

'Bay?' I ask, surprised. I drop into the seat at the little coffee table in the middle of the room as Ted turns to join me.

'Between you and me, he was extremely anxious that he might have upset you, so when you weren't at lunch, I suggested he went to look for you.'

I look at him, surprised. I thought counsellors were usually more woolly than this rather direct approach.

'Yes, he found me. I was doing some weeding.'

'Good for you! I find the garden's a good place for sorting your head out.'

'I . . . well . . . Bay and I had an argument the night before.'

Ted just nods.

'About Than,' I continue. 'Well, that's where it started, but it became more about friendship, and, well . . . how to give it and how to receive it.'

'And when you say you argued . . . ?' Ted nudges me.

'It was my fault,' I say quickly. 'I was defending Than, and Bay got annoyed.'

'It's hard to see someone we care about being treated badly.'

'I don't really care about Than . . .'

'I didn't mean him. I meant Bay seeing the way *you* were being treated.'

Oh. I didn't see that coming. I don't know what to say, so I plough on.

'Anyway, we both got a bit . . . cross . . . heated . . . you know? And I thought Bay was saying that I didn't know how to be a friend.'

'And when he found you, did you discuss it?' Ted asks gently.

I nod. 'That's not what he meant. He . . . well, he said that he couldn't stand that I seemed not to be able to accept friendship even though I could give it.'

'And what do you think?'

I look at my hands in my lap and pick at the skin around my nail. 'It's not the first time someone has said that I'm a crap friend,' I mutter, thinking of my mum and Markus again.

'But that's not what he was saying, is it?' says Ted.

'No. It's not. But . . . I mean . . . I've been on my own for so long now, maybe that's the case. My only friends are online and . . . well . . . yeah, I'm lonely, and I've enjoyed having people around while I've been here. But it's not real, is it? When I go back to my life, this isn't real?'

'Everything you do in life is real. Every experience changes us, shapes us and will impact on how we think and what we do in the future. So yes, I'd say this is very real. And only you can decide how much it will affect your day-to-day life when you leave here. It might be just a memory – a happy one, I hope. Or it might have a profound effect on every moment of your life from here on out. Or it could land somewhere in between.'

I swallow as the words lodge in my mind and take root. These friendships, the things I'm learning here . . . I'm the one who decides how important they are to me.

'Now, I'd like to touch on how you're doing with your phobia. Sharing it with the group was a huge step. Have you talked it through with anyone since your visit to the river?'

I feel like I've just swallowed an ice cube. I shake my head. 'I've been focusing more on the loneliness and where that's coming from,' I say.

'And it sounds like that's bringing you some great insights and understanding. But I think it might be important for you to remember that one issue doesn't sit separately from the other. They're interlinked; both a part of you.'

'Okay . . .' I say. I don't like where this is going. I've become comfortable with the idea of talking about being lonely. Sounds strange, but after writing about it on the blog for so long and discussing it openly here several times now, I've got the talking points all mapped out. Quitting my job. Losing Markus and my friends. Grief making me pull back. It's like a safe little list I can work through.

'You mentioned that your fear of water is linked to your mother's death?' Ted asks gently.

'Mentioned' is a very polite way of describing how I screamed this at Than after the disastrous swimming session.

'Yes. She drowned in a car accident,' I say tightly.

'And you weren't involved in the accident?' he prompts.

I shake my head. My hands have started to sweat and I rub them on my trousers. I don't want to tell him. I can't tell him. I couldn't bear to see the look on his face if he knew that it was all my fault.

'Tori,' Ted says, looking at me steadily, 'I think, this week, it would be good for you to use the sessions to talk more about your phobia. Have you sought professional support before? Did your doctor ever refer you to a grief counsellor after your mother passed?'

I shake my head again. 'I just . . . no. I've not been to the doctor . . . or anyone. I just . . . deal with it,' I mutter.

'I'm afraid your body's way of dealing with your grief is via this phobia and your panic attacks,' says Ted seriously.

I swallow. 'I just want to focus on the loneliness. Tackle one thing at a time.'

Ted leans forward in his chair, placing his elbows on his knees. He peers at me intently.

'Sometimes prolonged isolation is a defence mechanism, you know. Your subconscious thinks it's protecting you by keeping you away from other people. You keep yourself stuck there because you're afraid of anyone coming too close, and finding out too much. Essentially, without working through it you will keep sabotaging your new connections.'

I feel a bit sick. Actually, very sick. I swallow hard. Ted pours me a glass of water from a jug on the table and pushes it towards me without a word.

I take a sip. 'But I've admitted I'm lonely and I want to do something about it,' I say shakily.

'You have,' smiles Ted. 'Now all you've got to do is believe that you deserve these new friendships. You've got to start letting people near the scary bits.'

I nod, although my lips are quivering. I feel pretty close to tears.

'But surely . . . I don't have to share everything with everyone. I don't want to be *that* person.'

Ted laughs. 'No. You don't. It's not so much about "having to share"; it's more about not feeling the need to hide. It's about coming to terms with who you are and where you've come from.

'Loneliness isn't always about a lack of people. It can be about a lack of communication and connection. And that disconnect? That's the bit you need to work on.'

By the time I'm headed back towards the yurt, my heart is in my shoes. I thought I'd feel better after Ted's session, but it's the opposite. I thought I was doing really well, that I was sharing with the others and forming bonds. But Ted's right. There's something that's holding me back. I know exactly what it is. The problem is, I know that if I share it, it's not going to be this miraculous, healing moment. It's just going to mean that I'll be back to square one, because no one is going to want to know me after they find out what I've done.

I'm so thankful to find the yurt empty when I get there, and I fling myself down onto my bed and let out an almighty groan into my pillow. Why couldn't I be reviewing a spa instead? And not the 'back to earth' kind. Oh no, I want the kind with hot water jets, Jacuzzis and fluffy towels. If only my blog was all lifestyle and interiors, I could be comfortably wrapped in some seaweed and sipping bubbles right now. Instead, I'm tired to my very core.

I sigh and flip over on my blankets to find Bay staring down at me with a very strange look.

'Did you just mutter something about a Jacuzzi?' he grins.

'What? No, of course not!!'

'Sounded like it to me!' he laughs.

I rub my face and sigh again.

'Hey, are you okay?' The laughter disappears and is quickly replaced by a look of concern.

'I guess. Just . . . well . . . knackered.'

'Tough session with Ted?' he asks, dropping down to sit at the end of my bed.

I sit up and face him, cross-legged, and nod.

'Want to talk about it?'

I shake my head.

'Sure?'

I shake my head again.

'Well, if you do, I'm here. Anyway, you'll probably feel a bit better after dinner with everyone. I always find that food gets me grounded again after a difficult day.'

'I don't think I can face food with everyone,' I say. 'I just need a bit of time here. Just quiet.'

'You want me to disappear for a bit?' he asks gently.

'No, no! I didn't mean you,' I say quickly, because I really didn't. 'I just . . . there's something different about the whole group. It can be quite a lot to take, you know?'

Bay nods.

'Where's Dennis, by the way?' I ask, realizing I could do with a cuddle.

'He's gone to spend the night with Claire in her tent. I think she was in need of a bit of company.'

'Oh,' I say surprised. 'Is she okay?'

'She's fine,' Bay nods, getting to his feet and crossing over to his side of the yurt. 'Just in need of the therapy mutt.'

I smile. It's true. Sometimes Dennis is the best medicine going.

'So,' says Bay, 'if you're not going to join everyone for dinner, what do you fancy? I'm assuming you haven't got any food lined up?'

'How far do you reckon the nearest bacon sandwich is?' I ask hopefully.

'I'd say about ten miles that way,' he says, pointing over his shoulder.

'Balls,' I say, my heart slipping another notch. 'I could kill for a bacon sandwich right now.'

'Don't shoot!' Bay laughs, holding up his hands. 'Look, I've got a plan. How about I head down and rustle us up a picnic? I'll let them know we're okay, and bring our dinner back here so we can have a quiet evening?'

'That sounds amazing,' I smile at him gratefully. 'Is there anything I can do to help?'

'Just chill out till I come back with the picnic,' says Bay, disappearing out of the yurt at high speed.

Two minutes ago I was at full-blown get-me-out-of-here overwhelm. Two minutes chatting with Bay and I've got a smile on my face and everything magically feels that little bit better.

While Bay's gone, I tidy all our bits and pieces off the little round table in front of the sofa so that we've got somewhere to sit and eat. Then I change into my pyjama bottoms and a soft T-shirt and, curling up on one side of the sofa, I make a valiant effort not to drift off to sleep before he comes back.

The delicious smell of herbs and hot tomato reaches me before Bay's even back inside the yurt.

'Sorry I took so long!' he says, bustling in through the flap and plonking a wicker basket onto the table in front of me.

I stretch in an attempt to wake up properly. 'To be honest, I think I nodded off!'

Bay chuckles. 'Well, I hope you're in the mood for pasta? I knocked up a quick herby tomato sauce. I cooked up a vat of it so that there's enough for the others too.'

'Sounds perfect,' I say. I lean over and lift plates and cutlery out of the basket and set them down for us.

Bay then takes a tub of hot pasta and divvies it out between us before pouring a deep red sauce over each portion. Then he lifts half a loaf out of the basket too. Heaven.

'Not quite a bacon sandwich, but I did my best,' he smiles.

We eat in silence, and when I've finished mopping up the last of the sauce from my plate with my bread, I sit back with a contented sigh.

'Better?'

I nod. 'Thank you so much.'

'It's amazing what food and a bit of peace and quiet can do,' he says, placing his own plate carefully down on the table, and leaning back on the sofa.

We sit quietly for a few minutes, but the companionable silence we've just eaten in seems to be morphing into something different. You could cut and layer this silence onto a piece of toast, it's that thick.

'You okay?' he asks, his voice sounding strained.

I nod. I can't get Ted's words out of my head. This isn't real. This friendship I have with Bay can't be real because I'm hiding something. I need to trust him. But . . . I can't bear to lose him, and that's what would happen if he knew.

'Tori, what is it?' he asks quietly.

I can feel my tears building, and that deep, aching pain at the thought of losing all of my friends here. Bay reaches over and covers my hand briefly with his.

'There's so much you don't know about me,' I say, my voice thick.

Bay smiles. 'I should hope so too.'

'But talking to Ted today . . . I need to open up, I guess.'

Bay nods, looking thoughtful. 'You know, there's plenty about me that you don't know too.'

There's a look on his face that I don't recognize. Is that nerves? Whatever it is can't possibly be as bad as what I'm keeping secret.

'For example, you don't know much about my work yet.'

'Okay,' I smile.

'Well, I'm pretty good at it,' he says.

'I bet!' I say. I've seen the gardens here. I can see how much he loves what he does, even if it doesn't exactly make him a go-getting high-flier.

'There's more to it than you think . . .'

'I'm sure there is.'

I'm not sure where he's going with this, but I'm too tired to get into anything serious right now.

'Tell me something I don't know about you,' he prompts.

'I'm tired,' I sigh.

'I already guessed that,' he chuckles.

'Can we do this another time?' I ask, sounding a bit like a moody toddler.

The food has managed to offset my extreme drowsiness for a couple of minutes, but the longer we sit here, cocooned on the sofa, the more my eyelids are drooping. I don't quite know how I manage it, but my head dips to rest on Bay's shoulder.

Bay shifts a little next to me, and I feel his arm reach around my shoulders, pulling me gently towards him. I let out a sigh. I know this is the point where I should really sit up and move away, but I don't want to. Instead, I reach across and take his free hand in mine, lacing my fingers through his.

His intake of breath is like a question mark hovering between us.

The question is, what do I want?

All I want, right now, is this. I want to thank him again for the food. For the company. For the friendship. But this is the point where my exhaustion finally body-snatches me, and my eyes drift closed.

I wake up with a start, then snuggle back into the arms wrapped around me and bury myself deeper into the soft mound of blankets.

Hang on. *Arms? Whose* arms? Where on earth am I?!

My head is resting on someone. *Bay.* I'm snuggled up in Bay's arms, my face against his chest, and I'm pretty sure that that's his hand resting against my hip. It feels so bloody lovely, I can't help the pang of regret as I start to wiggle away as slowly and quietly as I can. Gently, inch by inch, I try to put as much space as possible between us, which is a lot harder than it sounds on this tiny sofa. Every movement makes me less comfortable, and I sigh. Why couldn't I have just pretended to still be asleep and stayed put?

Bay's eyes open. He stretches and sleepily comes to as I fidget away from him. He breathes in deeply and tightens one arm around me, undoing all my good work by bringing us face to face.

I hold my breath, my heart hammering as I wait to see if he'll just drop back off to sleep. But his eyes are focused on mine, and I can see he's just figured out where he is and with whom. I shiver. I can feel every hair on the back of my neck stand to attention as Bay holds my gaze. Very slowly, not blinking, his face comes closer to mine, until he's so close, his breath is tickling my skin. So close that we're almost touching. I hold my breath again, waiting for him to cover that last tiny distance between us . . . but he doesn't. He is completely still, his eyes locked on mine.

Slowly, very slowly, I close the gap between us until my lips gently touch his. And then I'm still, just letting this new touch flood through my whole body. Seconds. Minutes. Maybe an eternity. My whole world is focused in on the tiny contact that feels like the most important, most amazing thing ever.

We shift at exactly the same moment, and the kiss deepens. Our lips move over each other's. My hands fight through the layers of blanket and slide up under his soft, moth-eaten T-shirt to rest against his skin. He cups my face and kisses me harder.

Chapter 28

Wish, Dream, Act

'When we're caught in the vortex of grief, loneliness or anxiety, we can lose sight of our dreams. Simple survival can feel like a super-human effort.

'But, as we begin to heal, it's important to start making wishes again, to dream new dreams and then – act.'

©TheBeginnersGuideToLoneliness.com

Bacon. It has to be the best smell in the world to wake up to. The salty aroma reaches me before I've even opened my eyes. I yawn and stretch luxuriously.

'Morning, sleepyhead,' Bay smiles at me as I struggle to sit up. 'I come bearing gifts,' he waves a grease-covered white paper bag under my nose and my taste buds cry out in longing.

All I want to do right now is hide in a slightly darkened cupboard and figure out what happened last night. I mean, I know what *happened*: we kissed on the sofa, and eventually tumbled off in a giggling heap onto the floor, then we kissed in Bay's bed – for most of the night. It was wonderful, like being a teenager again. But what does it mean? I'm not quite so clear on that part.

I want to retreat, but there's not much chance of that given that I'm still in his bed, and he's just plonked himself down right next to me. I surreptitiously try to wipe away any traces of dribble and eye-snot and quickly figure out what I'm wearing. T-shirt and PJ bottoms are still firmly in place. I'm decent. At least that's something!

'How? How on earth . . . I mean? Where?' I wave the paper bag at him, bacon fumes wafting deliciously in its wake.

'I borrowed Frank and went on a clandestine bacon bap mission.'

'For me? Just like that?'

'Okay, so I might be making it sound riskier than it was. I promised Ted I'd do a grocery shop to help them out a bit – I just snuck in a quick stop for a bacon sandwich on the way back! Anyway, you said you wanted one.' He laughs, peeling the paper off his own sandwich and taking a huge bite.

I can't take my eyes off him. I feel a hot blush start at my toes and sweep right up through my body. I mean, I knew he had beautiful eyes and a nice bum and . . . and . . . *Gah!*

'You've not turned veggie on me since last night, have you?' asks Bay, one eyebrow raised.

'No, no, of course not!' I say, ripping into the paper bag. 'Bay, I . . . we . . . do you . . . last night . . .' I'm not really sure what I'm trying to ask him. I just need to know what he thinks about us, about last night.

'What, Tori?' he asks.

I swallow. I seem to have lost the power of speech.

'Last night? Last night was . . .' he pauses, and this huge smile spreads over his face. He doesn't need to finish the sentence for me to know exactly what he thinks about last night, and a flood of warmth spreads through my chest.

He clears his throat. 'What about you?' he asks gruffly.

I stay quiet and look down at my sandwich. What about me? I'm excited and terrified and happy and I can't wait to kiss him again. But that's not what I say.

'What about Than?' I say quietly.

'What?' Bay looks like I've slapped him. 'Are you serious? You want to talk about *him*? Now? After everything . . . ?'

'No! No, that's not what I mean!' I feel a dead weight in my stomach. Nope. Not what I mean at all.

'Then what, Tori? Because now's not a brilliant time to drop another guy's name, especially not that little f—'

'I *mean*,' I cut across him, 'I mean, what if everyone thinks that I've just hopped straight from him to you?'

Bay sighs. 'But there was no "him and you", was there?' he says, his voice gentle again. 'As long as we know the truth and we're happy, what does it matter what anyone else thinks? Not that they would anyway!'

I shrug. Of course they'll think it.

'If you're going to take anything away from this place, Tori, you need to stop worrying about what other people think of you. It's your life. You can live it exactly the way you want to.'

I swallow. And then nod.

'So. What's the answer, then?' he prompts.

'Last night was . . .' I pause and smile. 'I want to find out what this is,' I say, pointing at him and then back to me.

'Well then,' says Bay, 'what's so bad about people knowing that?'

'Nothing,' I shake my head, 'but there are things you don't know about me—'

Bay laughs. 'And there's loads of stuff that I want to share with you too. We've got all the time in the world to get to know everything about each other.' He leans forward and gently kisses my cheek.

'Guys!' Rowan's voice outside makes us jump apart. 'Knock knock!'

'Don't tell me you haven't paid up for something?' Bay mutters, jumping up from the bed and heading towards the yurt entrance.

'Not guilty,' I reply under my breath as I roll off the other side and quickly straighten my pyjamas.

'Thank God you're here,' says Rowan as she bursts in. 'All hell's broken loose!'

Bay looks worried. 'Is Lizzie okay? And the baby? What's happened?'

I move to stand next to him. I can feel the waves of worry coming off him, so I reach over and take his hand, which he grasps out of instinct.

Rowan raises her eyebrows, a smirk on her face. 'Looks like you two've been having fun.'

'Rowan!' I squeak in horror, though I can't help a smile escaping. 'Tell us what's happened. Is everyone okay?'

'Oh, sure,' she says. 'Everyone else is fine. It's you we're worried about.'

'Why?' Bay asks, clearly as confused as I am, though the relief is evident in his voice.

'There was this piece written—' Rowan reaches into her back jeans pocket and draws out a folded printout.

'Knock knock?'

This time it's Ted's voice, and Bay lets go of my hand and heads out to greet him. I follow closely, wondering what the hell is going on.

Ted claps Bay on the shoulder then turns to Rowan.

'Back to the house. Now!'

'Oh, come on, Dad, they don't know anything. I was just going to fill them in—'

'Now, Rowan!'

I wince at the sharp edge to Ted's voice and realize that whatever this is, it must be fairly serious to cause this level of reaction.

'Tori,' he turns to me and smiles faintly, 'you need to come up to the house. We need to talk.'

I feel a chill wash over me. What on earth is this all about? I look up at Bay and he takes my hand again. 'I'll come too,' he says.

'Actually,' says Ted, raising an eyebrow at our clasped hands, 'I need you to do me a favour, if you don't mind? Could you go and find Russ and ask him to come down to the farmhouse? I need to talk to him and Claire before this morning's session. I'd go find him, but I really need to speak with Tori first.'

'Of course,' says Bay. 'You'll be okay?' he looks at me.

'Yep, you go. I'll catch you later.' I smile at him and he squeezes my hand and walks away.

There, on the screen of Ted's iPad, is a photograph of me. My face is tear-streaked and grimy, hair dripping, T-shirt soaked. This must have been taken during my disastrous trip to the river. Questions ping into my head: how? And by who? And what the hell am I doing on the Reflect Online gossip site?!

I can't take this in. After getting dressed, Ted led me down to the private back garden of the farmhouse and brought his iPad out. He gently explained that a piece about The Farm had been posted – a piece that was mostly about me. Then he handed me the tablet so that I could see for myself, but so far, the shock of the photographs has completely consumed me, and I've not actually read any of the accompanying words.

'I know this must be a huge shock,' says Ted. 'We wanted to let you know that this was out there as soon as possible, but remember, you're completely safe here with us.'

I don't say anything but keep scrolling down. There are more photographs of me here at The Farm: there's one of me at the fire walk, one of me being comforted by Doreen and Geoff, one of me and Messa sat side by side in the hot tub. And one of me and Bay in the rain, my hand wrapped in his T-shirt as he pushes a strand of hair out of my face.

I gasp and place the tablet down on the table.

'Tori, I think it's best if you read the whole thing, so that you're prepared,' Ted prompts gently.

I nod and pick it back up reluctantly. There seems to be acres and acres of text, and for a moment I can't focus as tears of shock blur my vision. Then sentences start to jump out at me . . .

'. . . *at best, deadly dull, at worst bordering on the cultish . . .*'

'. . . *a haven for drama queens like thirty-three-year-old Tori Williamson . . .*'

'. . . *hunting for the affection of any man to ease her sense of loneliness and guilt surrounding the death of her mother . . .*'

'. . . *her life empty after losing her fiancé, Markus, to another woman . . .*'

Who would want to do this to me? I rub my eyes and stare closer at the screen, zooming in on the name and tiny author's photograph at the end of the article.

Dark hair. Handsome face. It's Than.

Or, as it says in the byline: Nathan Jones.

Okay. Deep breath – read from the start.

'. . . *a dangerous combination of vulnerable and predatory . . .*'

'. . . *a messed-up fraud . . . self-absorbed and cruel to others, including her so-called closest friend at the retreat, Doreen McVey . . .*'

'. . . *I can reveal the identity of the anonymous author of popular blog The Beginner's Guide To Loneliness . . .*'

Oh. My. God. He's outed me. The one thing I would never, ever tell anyone.

But how did he even *know*? How did he get all those photos? It doesn't make any sense. And he's written what I said about Doreen. I didn't even mean it; I was just caught up in my fear of the river and desperate to make him change the subject.

I bury my head in my hands.

'Tori?' says Ted gently. 'Are you okay?'

'How can I be?' I ask. My voice is low and flat. Something inside me feels like it has broken. 'How did he get those photos?' I say. It's probably the smallest detail, but right now, I can't face the more serious questions.

'I've been thinking about that,' Ted sighs. 'He handed over a mobile when he arrived, but when he left, he left without it. He must have had a second one, or some other camera.'

I look at the photos again and shake my head. 'No. He would never have been able to hide using a phone in some of these. Anyone would have seen if he'd had one at the fire walk. And we'd have seen him at it in this one of the hot tub too. And look how close I am in this one,' I say, scrolling to a close-up of me, lying back against a pillow. It's me in Than's tent. I close my eyes and picture that evening.

'Well, he must have had a hidden camera or something, then,' says Ted sadly. 'In his clothing, or a pocket . . .'

Hidden camera. 'Or that badge he was always wearing?' I say, thinking of the yellow smiley badge he told me his brother had given him.

'Could be,' sighs Ted. 'The sad thing is, that means he planned this from the start.'

That makes me feel sick. Than has taken everything I shared with him, every little detail, and twisted it to paint me as some kind of monster. He's used some of the most private, painful details about my life and turned them into cheap entertainment to feed the trolls.

I feel like I've been thumped in the chest, and my breathing is suddenly coming too fast. *Oh God, not this again.* I take a couple of long, steady breaths. I feel Ted's hand rest gently on my shoulder. Everything's going to be okay. *Breathe in. Deal with the issue in front of me.*

'I'm so sorry,' I sigh.

'*Sorry?* What for?' asks Ted, surprised.

'This,' I say, pointing at the tablet.

'Did you *ask* Than to follow you around, take photographs of you and pretend to be someone he wasn't?'

'No, but—'

'Did you *ask* him to share your secrets with the world?'

I look into Ted's eyes. 'No.'

'Well then, nothing to apologize for.'

I take another deep breath and try to take everything in as Ted watches me. I need to read that article again. My mind is racing. What I don't get is how Than even knew about some of the stuff. I must have shared way more than I realized while my guard was down.

'What am I going to do?' I say it out loud, not really expecting Ted to have any kind of answer. 'How am I going to find out why he did this? *How* he did this? How am I going to deal with the blog and everything else?'

'Well,' says Ted, 'I'd suggest starting with the bits that you're in control of right now. You're not directly contactable and you're not online while you're here with us, so you've got some space to work out what you're going to do.'

I nod. 'Thank you,' I say shakily.

'If you want my advice, I think you need to start by talking to Doreen. You two have become really close, and there are some pretty horrible quotes in that piece about her. No doubt made up, but even so . . .'

I nod. I wish they *were* made up, but Than is too clever for that. I said those words; he's just managed to twist them out of context and make them sound ten times worse.

'Tori, I'm sure you understand that we're going to need to share this article with the whole group. The photographs include nearly everyone here, and it's our duty to make sure that they are aware and to support them through this, if they need it.'

'Of course,' I say.

'I asked Claire to head over and fill Doreen in while I spoke to you. As it mentions her by her full name, we had to tell her and Geoff before the rest of the group.'

My heart is pounding. I can't bear the thought of Doreen having to hear this. The things I said about her, the fact that I hid who I really am.

'I'd like to suggest you and Doreen head off on a one-to-one together. Find some space and peace and quiet and talk this through.'

I swallow hard. I know he's right, but my heart feels like it's going to break at the thought of losing my friend. Perhaps all my friends. 'Thanks, Ted. For everything,' I say, quietly.

He pats my shoulder. The sense of comfort from this friendly little gesture brings tears to my eyes.

'Dad!' Rowan's voice calls from the back door. 'Dad? Phone for you!'

'Can you take a message?' He shouts.

'It's Mel. She said it's urgent!'

'Sorry, Tori,' Ted says, hastily getting to his feet. 'I have to take this. Claire should be here with Doreen any moment, then you two can head off. Claire and Russ will be speaking with the rest of the group a bit later on. There's going to be plenty of time to talk this all through and work it out, okay?'

I nod, but I'm not sure he catches it as he rushes indoors to take his call.

Chapter 29

Allow Joy

'Happiness, hurting and healing can happen at the same time. Just because you're grieving, or feeling lonely, suffering from anxiety or stress, doesn't mean that moments of pure happiness can't co-exist in your day-to-day life. It's so important to allow yourself to feel that joy.'

©TheBeginnersGuideToLoneliness.com

My heart sinks at the sight of the grim expression on Doreen's face as she rounds the corner into the garden.

'Hi!' I leap to my feet and try to smile at her, but it feels unnatural. My eyes are stinging. I wish I'd got a bit more sleep last night.

'Claire said we should go for a walk. Somewhere quiet. To talk,' Doreen says. There's not a hint of her usual smile. She looks so worried, it feels like my heart might break.

I nod glumly. 'Ted said the same. You up for it?'

'Okay,' she agrees, quietly.

I can't stand seeing Doreen like this. It's so . . . unnatural. She's usually so warm and funny and bubbly, not this pale, scared person. But as much as I want to blame this all on Than, I can't. This is my fault. *I* said those things about her.

Mum and Markus were both right. I don't deserve friends. And this – this absolute fucking disaster has proved it once and for all. I want to crawl back to my flat and hide. But I can't. I have to try to fix this. The least I can do, right now, is apologize and explain everything to Doreen. She deserves that.

'Doreen, I'm so sorry.'

'Come on,' she says, and, taking my hand, she leads me out of the garden.

I can feel the tears prickling and threatening to spill over, but I can't give in to them, not yet. This isn't about me.

We head out of the farmyard and follow the same route that Russ took us on for our first mindfulness session – up the side of the valley and away from The Farm. I trudge alongside her and we walk in tense silence for what feels like hours, but is actually probably only about five minutes. The words – the need to apologize and explain everything – are bubbling up inside of me so insistently I feel like I'm about to burst.

'Doreen, I—' I start.

'Are you okay?' Doreen says at exactly the same time.

We come to an abrupt halt and turn to stare at each other. My hand is still firmly clasped in hers.

'Sorry,' I say.

'No, no, you go . . .' she shakes her head.

I look into her face and feel the tears well in my eyes again. I try to will them back, but no luck this time. They spill down my cheeks. I let out a sigh that comes out more like a sob, and sink down into the long grass at the side of the path and rub my face hard.

I feel a soft arm around my shoulder. Doreen is next to me in the grass. I look at her and try to smile, but I can't keep my bottom lip from quivering as more tears spill down my cheeks.

'Hey. Hey . . .' Seeing my tears, she scoops me into her arms and rocks me back and forth like a baby as I give in and soak the shoulder of her jumper.

'I'm so, so sorry,' I sob into her neck.

'What?' says Doreen, pulling away from me gently so she can see my mess of a face.

'I'm sorry for what that piece said. About you.' I shudder, trying to get control of my tears and gulping in air. I feel her stiffen slightly, but she doesn't pull away.

'Don't be silly. I'm sure what he wrote was complete rubbish. He was clearly putting words in your mouth.' She goes to stroke my hair away from my face, but I pull back from her a little.

'I said those things,' I sniffle. 'I was a mess when I got here. You were so kind and I just didn't know what to do with that, with your optimism and openness.'

'But, Tori, you said I was dull . . . a bored, insipid housewife . . .'

'I know, and I really didn't mean what I said. I was just being a bitch. Lashing out, and you were the most obvious target. It was during that first swimming session when we skived off? I was just desperate to get Than on side, trying to get him off the subject of why I'd legged it from the river . . . trying to make him like me. I did say it, but if it helps, I hated myself the second the words left my mouth.'

Doreen stares at me and sits back. She looks pale and thoughtful. 'It's okay,' she says quietly, staring at her feet for a couple of seconds. 'On the first day here, I told Geoff I thought you were a spoiled little brat with no life.' She grimaces. 'Lucky for me, he's not the type to publish what I said online.'

I shake my head. 'Well, you're pretty much spot on about me. Or, you were. You've been one of my closest friends here, which basically means my closest friend full stop. And now . . . now I can't imagine my life without you in it.' I swallow hard as the tears threaten to reappear.

'You're not so bad either, apart from your terrible choice in confidantes!' She smiles at me and pulls me in for a hug.

'I have to say, you're an amazing writer,' says Doreen after we've sat quietly next to each other for several minutes, just watching the sky and the clouds and letting things settle. 'I can't believe you're the one behind Beginner's Guide. Geoff and I read it religiously! I mean, I'd noticed that there were similarities in your past, but I never for a second imagined that it would actually *be* you!'

My heart flutters and I feel a tingling rush of panic course through me. 'I can't believe he told everyone who I am.'

Doreen pats my arm. 'It really is a terrible betrayal to go public with such an important secret – especially one you told him here.'

'That's just it. I didn't tell him,' I say. There's a slight growl to my voice as my panic veers dangerously in the direction of anger.

'Oh. Goodness,' says Doreen, looking surprised. 'I just assumed that you'd shared it with him in one of the sessions.'

I shake my head. 'Nope.'

'Well, he must have done some serious digging.'

I can't take it in. I can't even begin to figure out how he knows. Right now, I'm more worried about what it means. Everyone will know everything. Everything I've written on my blog is so personal. All my fears and hopes, tied to my research. The reality of living like I do. How low it has taken me. My heart is racing and a river starts to pound in my head.

I close my eyes, but all I can see is the caption under the photograph of me and Bay in the rain. *Tori Williamson, the blogger behind The Beginner's Guide to Loneliness: not so lonely after all.*

I want to be sick.

'Tori? Love?' Doreen's voice is worried, but I can't look at her right now. But then her hands are in mine. 'Look at me.'

I shake my head, eyes still firmly closed.

'Look at me, Tori.'

I do as she asks.

'Don't be frightened of letting people know how amazing you are. Your writing is so powerful. I bet you can't even begin to imagine the number of people you've helped by being so honest, by sharing everything with them.'

'But you don't know everything,' I say, my voice shaky.

'I know some awful things have happened in your life. And I know how brave you are. That's what people will learn about you from reading your site. Nothing more or less.'

'So, tell me,' she says after a couple of minutes, 'where were you at dinnertime last night? Both you and Bay were missing.'

'Oh . . .' I'm grateful to think about something aside from Than and that stupid article for a moment. 'I had a one-to-one session with Ted yesterday afternoon, and by the time we were finished, I was absolutely wiped. And . . . well, I just couldn't face chatting with everyone over food.'

'I can understand that,' says Doreen, peering at me, 'but why was Bay missing as well?'

I can't stop a smile from creeping onto my face. 'Erm . . . well, he got us dinner and brought it back to the yurt.'

'*Aaand . . . ?*'

'And we ended up kissing.'

Doreen squeals and claps her hands excitedly. 'Tori, this is so exciting!' she says, grabbing my hands. 'So you and Bay are . . . ?'

'I'm looking forward to finding out what we are.'

Doreen sighs and swipes at her eyes.

'Don't be such a sap,' I laugh.

'I can't help it. I'm a sucker for happy endings.'

'Well, you'd better hold that thought for a sec. I need to go and find Bay. I'm not sure whether he'll have seen the article yet, but you're not the only one with shit written about you.'

'Tori! Tori! I've got to talk to you!'

As soon as we reach the farmyard, Rowan skids to a halt in front of us and clutches her ribs, bending over double. Apparently she doesn't do much cardio in among the wheeling and dealing.

'Me first!' I say before she can recover. 'Have you seen Bay? I really need to talk to him.'

Rowan just holds one index finger out to me, indicating to give her a second.

I smirk at Doreen and cross my arms until Rowan finally straightens up and gasps out, 'He's gone.'

'What do you mean "gone"?' says Doreen, raising her eyebrows in surprise.

'He grabbed Dennis and headed off not long after you guys left for your walk.'

'Oh.' I feel completely wrong-footed. This isn't how this bit is supposed to go. 'When's he back?'

'He's not coming back.'

'What? Don't be silly. Where'd he go? I have to talk to him!'

'London. Something to do with work. He borrowed Frank.'

'Work?' I feel like someone has stuck a pin in me and I'm slowly deflating.

'I don't know. Some kind of emergency. Anyway, forget about that for a minute – this is serious.' Rowan throws a quick look over her shoulder and rummages in her jeans pockets, pulling out the same wodge of computer printouts she was waving at me earlier. 'It's about Than.'

Rowan looks uncharacteristically worried, and my heart swells with warmth for this clever little cookie – even if she has pretty much emptied my bank account single-handedly since I arrived.

'Don't worry, Rowan, I know about the article. Your dad told me everything.'

'No, that's not—' Rowan shakes her head impatiently but is interrupted by Ted bellowing her name from the farmhouse.

Before she's had a chance to say anything else, he's come into view and looks decidedly less fluffy than usual.

'Rowan Myrtle Mullins, get back up to that house this instant. I told you not to bother Tori. Go and get ready. We're off to see your mum and little sister in ten minutes!'

Rowan tuts and looks sulky. 'But, Dad, I—'

'*Now*, Rowan.'

'Here.' Rowan thrusts the wad of paper at me. 'You need *all* the facts. Make sure you read it *all*.'

'Thanks, Rowan,' I smile at her. 'I've read it all, but thanks.'

'No, you might've missed bits in the shock.' She looks at me, eyes wide, before retreating back to the house.

'What was all that about?' asks Doreen, watching them go.

'I don't know . . . Maybe she was hoping to get a nice little payout for the printout!' I laugh. 'Anyway, right now I'm more worried about Bay. I don't get it. Why'd he just disappear?'

'Maybe something really did come up for him.'

'Something that meant he couldn't wait around for an extra ten minutes to talk to me? Especially after last night. It's got to have something to do with this,' I say, waving the printout pages crossly.

'Bay's got to finish off the course, hasn't he? And he's got to return Frank . . . I'm sure he'll be back soon.'

'I guess you're right.' I shrug and kick at the ground. 'Shame Ted turned up right at that second though. With Bay gone, I could have done with asking Rowan for some coffee. I'm dying for a cup.'

'Tell you what,' Doreen says, linking her arm through mine, 'let's head back to my place. Geoff will be desperate to catch up with you and know you're okay. I've even got some teabags – proper PG Tips and everything.'

Chapter 30

The Mirrors You Can't Avoid

'Friends are the mirrors we can't avoid. We might be able
to hide certain things from ourselves, but good friends will
always find a way to reflect them back at us. Go ahead and
take a look.'

©TheBeginnersGuideToLoneliness.com

As I sink onto the little settee inside Doreen and Geoff's
cabin, I feel completely knackered. It's probably not even
midday yet, but today has already been one of the weirdest
days of my life so far, and that's saying something. There are so
many thoughts whizzing around in my head, I'm not sure
which one to grab hold of and examine first.

'So. You two worked everything out, then?' Geoff asks
lightly as he plops onto a wooden chair opposite and hands
me a mug of strong tea.

'Oh, yes,' laughs Doreen, settling herself down next to me.
'I'm a bored, twittering housewife and she's a spoiled little brat.'

I snort into my mug and Geoff grins at us. 'Oh good. At least that clears that up.'

'Point is,' I say, 'we all say stupid stuff we don't mean at times.'

'Oh, I meant it,' Doreen smirks, and I dig her in the ribs with my elbow.

'So, you're okay, Tori?' Geoff asks.

'Not really. I don't know where to start with all this. I think I'd feel better if Bay hadn't buggered off on me too.'

'What's this?' Geoff raises his eyebrows.

'Bay's gone to London, apparently. Some kind of emergency,' says Doreen, quickly filling him in while I sip my tea.

'When did he say he'd be back, Tori?'

'He didn't,' I say. 'He'd already left when we got back from our walk. Rowan told us.'

'Ah. Well . . . I'm sure he'll be back before you know it.'

'Question is, why didn't he wait and tell me himself?'

'Well, if it was an emergency, maybe he couldn't wait.'

'Not even for half an hour? I don't know . . . Something's off. I don't even know if he's seen Than's article.'

'He will have,' says Geoff. 'When Claire was here earlier, she said that they were going to have to share it with the whole group. There's no way that Ted would have let Bay leave without filling him in.'

'You're right,' I sigh. 'I just hope it wasn't something to do with the article that made him leave so suddenly . . . or maybe it was because of what happened last night.'

'*What* happened?' Geoff asks curiously.

'They had a moment!' Doreen says, waggling her eyebrows. 'And there's no way it would have anything to do with that, I'm sure.'

'A moment, eh?' Geoff smiles at me. 'So that's what the kids are calling it these days . . .'

'Well, I almost managed to screw it up by mentioning Than at a critical moment . . . *Shit*, I hope it wasn't that.' My brain is throwing worry after worry at me and I can't keep up.

'Tori, Bay's a really straightforward guy,' says Geoff, taking a sip of tea. 'If everything felt right, then it was right, so don't worry about things that you're only imagining. It'll all work out, you'll see. But on the subject of Than – *Nathan* – whatever we're calling him now, what are you going to do?'

My heart sinks even further.

'If I'm honest, I don't know.' I shrug helplessly. 'You know, this is my biggest fear come true.'

'What's that?'

'The whole world finding out.'

'What? That you're an amazing writer?' asks Geoff. 'Because you are, by the way!'

I shake my head. I have to do this. This is exactly what Ted was talking about – I've got to communicate the things that scare me the most. 'No. That I'm guilty . . . for my mother's death.'

Doreen looks at me with her eyes wide. 'Tori, that was an accident. I've read your posts and you told us about it that day at the river. A car accident. Horrific, but not your fault.'

'It was,' I say.

'But, love, you weren't even there.'

'No. And that's what makes it my fault. I should have been driving that day.'

My breath is coming hard and fast, but this isn't the usual sensation of panic returning. This is something else. Like a dam inside of me has burst.

'Tell us,' she says steadily. 'If you want to talk about it, we're here for you.'

Geoff nods. I take a deep breath.

'Mum and I had a very strained relationship. She had a drinking problem. No matter what I did to try to help her . . . it was never enough. It had come to the point where she only called when she was drunk. She called when she needed help – whether it was money, or when she got in trouble with the police, or wanted me to act as her unpaid taxi. And I'd had enough. I loved her, of course I did, she was my mum, but she was so difficult to deal with. I know . . . I *know* that it was an illness, and I did try to be there for her. But sometimes, she was just awful.'

Doreen and Geoff are both listening intently, but neither try to comfort me nor interrupt, and I'm grateful. Now I've started, I'm not sure I can stop.

'She was emotionally abusive. I guess that's what you'd call it. She was like that when I was a kid, but it just got worse as the drinking got worse. On the night of the accident, I'd had enough. I was up to my eyeballs in work, trying to keep myself afloat, trying to keep Markus happy, and I just couldn't face bailing her out of whatever shite she'd landed herself in again.

When I saw her name flash up on my mobile, for the first time ever, I just ignored the call.'

'Oh, Tori,' Doreen says gently as I pause for breath, for a beat of calm before I have to say the worst part out loud.

'Because of me . . . because I was so *selfish* . . . my mum got behind the wheel when she was so far over the limit it was a miracle she was even conscious. I wasn't there for her when she needed me. I ignored her call. I'm responsible for her death, and I have to live with that guilt every single day for the rest of my life.'

Now that I've finished, I can't look at them. I stare hard at my hands, trying to keep my breathing steady. Then I feel the warm weight of a comforting hand on my shoulder. I look up to find Geoff smiling gently down at me. Doreen takes my hand from the other side, and I look at her. Her eyes are pink from the tears that have snuck down her cheeks while I've been talking.

My biggest fear is out there, and the world hasn't ended.

'What can I do?' I ask, my voice breaking.

'Talk about it,' says Geoff. 'Talk to us. Talk to Ted and Lizzie. You're in the perfect place. Work through it. You're surrounded by friends.'

Doreen nods.

'I always thought that . . . well . . . that this means that I don't deserve friends,' I say, my voice coming out low and husky.

'Well, we're not going anywhere,' Doreen says quietly.

I smile shakily at them. 'Thank you.'

Geoff shakes his head as if to ward off my thanks and Doreen squeezes my hand and shrugs. 'What are friends for?'

'You know, I can't believe you told Than about your blog,' Geoff says, sitting back down. 'You've always been so clear on there that you wanted to remain anonymous.'

'She didn't tell him!' says Doreen, raising her eyebrows at her husband.

'Oh,' says Geoff, looking confused. 'Then how did he . . . ?'

'No idea,' I sigh. 'The only people I've ever told were the Warriors – the three people I'm friends with online. It was actually one of them, Nat, who encouraged me to start the blog.'

'Well then, he must have contacted them somehow. One of them must have let it slip,' says Geoff.

'Do you think? How would he have even known to contact them?'

'You two were very close, briefly,' says Doreen. She looks at me quizzically.

'We were. Sometimes it was like he understood me without me having to say anything . . .' I trail off.

'Maybe you mentioned the group at some point and he went from there?' asks Geoff.

I shudder. Maybe I did. 'But even if he did that, and somehow managed to get hold of them, I *know* those three. They just wouldn't have told him.'

'Have you still got that printout of the article Rowan gave you?' Doreen asks. 'Maybe there's something we missed?'

I yank the pages out of my pocket and hand them over to Doreen.

'*Rowan*,' I say. It's a light-bulb moment that brings me absolutely no relief. 'I promised to let the Warriors know how it was going here, so I paid her to let me use her phone to get online and send them a couple of quick messages.'

'You don't think Rowan . . . ?' Geoff looks shocked.

I shake my head. 'No, not her, but maybe I left it logged in. It's a possibility, isn't it?'

Doreen stops reading the article and stares at me. 'And Than somehow found it, you mean?'

'It's a possibility, I guess,' says Geoff.

'I need to talk to Rowan, now!' I get to my feet, but Doreen grabs my arm.

'She'll be on her way to the hospital by now.'

I give an impatient huff, but flop back down onto the sofa. Doreen's right.

'Tori!' Doreen squeaks, making both me and Geoff jump. 'What's that group of yours called again?' she asks me, wide-eyed.

'What, the online one? The Warriors. I know it's a bit naff but—'

'Look!' says Doreen, thrusting a couple of pages under my nose.

I take them on autopilot, bracing myself for something I missed earlier, but this is something completely different. It takes me a couple of moments to figure out what I'm looking at.

'I don't believe this!' I gasp as it sinks in.

'What? What is it?' asks Geoff, leaning forward in his chair and looking ready to snatch the pages out of my hands.

'It's . . . it's our conversation. The Warriors chatroom, I mean!' I say.

'But why would Rowan give this to you?' asks Doreen, looking as nonplussed as I feel.

I rifle through the pages of conversation. It's all the most recent stuff over the past month or so. I peer at the last page, and the very last entry from me is the one where I told them that Than had tried to kiss me, and how I was feeling about Bay. Then there are a couple of replies to my message from Hugh and Sue, telling me to enjoy a bit of holiday romance while I can get it, and generally joking around about my supposed love triangle. Then they start tagging Nat as she'd gone quiet. Right at the bottom, in pink biro, is scrawled one word, underlined three times.

Catfish.

Chapter 31

An Attitude of Gratitude

'It's all too easy to focus on how difficult life can be. The problem with these negatives is that they can spiral out of control. The solution is very simple: making conscious gratitude a part of your daily life will help you reframe your day. Don't know where to start? Find just one thing, right now, that you're truly grateful for.'

©TheBeginnersGuideToLoneliness.com

Someone hammers on the door of the cabin, making us all jump.

'*There* you are!' says Rowan as soon as I answer the door. 'I've been looking for you everywhere!'

'What are you doing here? I thought you were at the hospital?' I say.

Rowan shrugs. 'They rang to say Mum and the baby can come home, so I said I'd wait here so that there was more room in the car.' She swaggers into the cabin and plonks herself in my vacated seat. 'Well? Did you find my note?'

'Note?'

'On the printouts. Tell me you read them!'

'Oh, I read them. Rowan, how did you get those print-outs? Did I leave myself logged in or . . . ?'

'*You?* Are you kidding? You clear your browser history every time you're finished!' Rowan laughs. She catches my eye, sees that I'm not joining in with the joke and continues hastily: 'It was Than. *Than* left himself logged in.'

My mind is reeling. This isn't making any sense.

'I think he's a catfish, Tori!'

'Slow down and explain,' says Doreen gently to Rowan.

'Catfish! Oh come on, surely . . .'

Geoff and Doreen look perplexed.

'A catfish is someone who pretends to be someone else online, to get people to like them, or to trust them, or get information from them . . . from *you*, Tori!'

'Okay, but I'd never met Than before I came here,' I say.

Rowan rolls her eyes. 'But you'd met *Nat*, or "Nathalie33",' Rowan says, watching me intently.

'Nat's one of my best friends.'

Geoff has his hand over his mouth and Doreen is looking back and forth between me and Rowan like she's watching a game of ping-pong.

'Nat. Than. *Nathan* – Tori, they're all the same person. Look, I can prove it.' Rowan quickly grabs her phone out of her coat pocket and swipes it open. 'I left it logged in. He's logged in as Nathalie33. He *is* Nathalie33.'

I take the phone from her and peer at the familiar chat screen. The only difference is the avatar in the bottom left corner isn't my own face; it's a little silver quill pen on a black background. Nat's avatar.

'I can't believe this,' I say faintly.

'Dad was ranting on about Than's article, and how he wasn't who he said he was. So I went online to read it. Then I thought maybe there might be something in my history. I mean, he paid me quite a few times to go online. I had all these different tabs open. I spotted this one and didn't think anything of it until I saw your username. That's what got my attention, because you're always so careful about closing everything down. So I had a bit of a closer look and saw that it wasn't you logged in, but someone called Nathalie33. And there's no one called Nathalie here, and so I just put two and two together.'

I'm watching her with my mouth open. 'Two and two?!' I say.

'That it must have been him. If I'd known what he was doing, I swear I would have warned you!'

'But it doesn't make any sense. I've been friends with Nat online for years! She's the one who convinced me to come here.'

Rowan shrugs. 'Most people do it to lure their victims into some kind of relationship.'

I shudder at the word 'victim'. 'So why pretend to be a woman?'

'So you'd trust her . . . I mean *him*,' says Geoff, looking horrified. 'He must have wanted to meet you, so convinced you to come here and then booked his place after you'd confirmed. I mean, it's the perfect way to meet up with you without blowing his cover.'

'At least you know how he got all those details about you,' says Doreen, looking shocked.

The hairs on the back of my neck are prickling again. I feel like I'm being watched. This is horrible. One of my best friends isn't even real.

'Can I ask you something?' Rowan says slowly. 'Have you ever met the other two you talk to on there?'

'Hugh and Sue? No. None of us have ever met up.'

'If you've never met, how do we know that they aren't in on it too?'

'Oh God, don't say that!' I say.

'But I'm right though, aren't I?' Rowan asks, looking between Geoff and Doreen for backup. 'They could be anyone . . . or they could all be the same person.'

I think for a moment. No, that doesn't feel right. 'They've always been really genuine on there. Sue's shared photos of her kids with us, and holiday snaps. I email her separately sometimes too as she proofreads some of my work for me.'

'What about the other guy?' Geoff asks.

'Hugh? Actually, I've voice chatted with him a few times, as he gets bored on long drives, and he knows I'm around during the day.'

'Okay,' Rowan says slowly. 'And it never seemed weird to you that Nat never did this?'

'I never thought about it. We message on there. We message privately sometimes too, and that's always been . . . well, just normal.'

'I still think it would be a good idea to check the other two out. You thought Nat was genuine until about five minutes ago,' she says, looking a bit worried.

'How on earth am I going to do that?' I ask. This is so much worse than I could have ever imagined.

'We've got time to come up with something,' says Doreen calmly.

Rowan blows air into her cheeks then lets it out in a great huff.

I lean forward and rub my face. This is too much to get my head around. Nathan, Than, Nat – they're all the same person. For whatever reason, she, I mean *he*, orchestrated it so that we were both here at the same time. Then he befriended me, tried to kiss me, and when I turned him down, he just . . . imploded.

Now he's disappeared and gone public with details about me that were never meant to be shared. Even though I'm starting to see that it's not going to ruin my life, it's definitely going to change it.

There's still something that isn't adding up though. Why lure me in and try to start something between us with that kiss if he was just going to completely change direction and betray me?

'Hang on a minute!' I squeak.

'What?' Rowan jumps.

'I know why he was so randomly shitty in Claire's session! That was the morning after I . . .' I clear my throat, trying to swallow down the embarrassment. 'After I sent a message to the group about liking Bay and not Than. After Than had tried to kiss me. He must have seen it.'

Rowan nods. 'Probably. He did ask to check his emails in the mornings a couple of times before the sessions kicked off.'

'He wasn't checking his emails. I bet you anything that was him logging on here to check if I'd sent anything to the group!'

'Probably hoping for a juicy update about himself,' says Doreen, looking mildly sick.

'And instead he got to hear that he was turning into a bit of an irritating pain in the bum and that you had the hots for Bay,' says Rowan.

'I never said that!' I snap.

'Okay, you never used the actual words, but your feelings were pretty clear.'

'Well, at least that explains why he had that massive blow-up in Claire's session,' says Doreen.

'It's almost like he was trying to punish you,' says Geoff.

Rowan's eyes grow wide and I can see that this is starting to freak her out.

'He was always trying to get me onside,' I say, 'like we were in some kind of private little club. I wonder if any of the stuff he shared with me was even true . . .' I say. I don't know if he told anyone else about his brother, and I'm certainly not going to share it, but the fact that he might have made up something so serious makes my skin crawl.

'Well, he certainly wanted you all to himself, didn't he?' says Doreen. 'Looks like he reacted pretty badly when things didn't go his way!'

'Thank God I didn't go there,' I sigh. 'So, what do we do now?'

Doreen, Geoff and I instinctively turn to Rowan.

'You know, I think it's time to remind you that I'm only thirteen. Time to bring in more adults.'

'You've got a point!' I say. 'When are your mum and dad due back?'

She looks uncharacteristically worried for a second. 'You're going to tell them, aren't you?'

'I need all the help I can get to work this mess out.'

Rowan nods but still looks worried.

'What's up?' asks Doreen.

'They're going to find out about my business.'

'Ah. Of course,' says Geoff. 'I'm sure we can figure something out.'

Rowan looks at him hopefully.

'I've got it!' I say. 'Okay . . . it's not going to get you completely off the hook, but it might mean you don't get busted.'

'I'm listening!' she says, raising one eyebrow.

'Well, we're going to have to tell them that it was your phone we were accessing the internet on . . .'

Rowan's face falls.

'*But* we tell them that I convinced you to lend me your phone so I could check in with my friends. Just so they knew

I was safe. No mention of money; you just did it out of the goodness of your heart.' I raise an eyebrow at the very thought of Rowan doing this, and she smirks.

'What about Than?'

'Your parents know how close we were. We'll say I told him, so he asked to borrow it too. Simple.'

'It might work . . .' she says.

'Of course it will!' Doreen chips in. 'They've got no reason to doubt Tori, and it's not like Than is around to dispute it. The only other people who know are me and Geoff, and it's not like we're about to dob you in!'

'I'll still get in trouble for lending Tori my phone. After all, it's my fault all this happened. If he hadn't got onto the chat, you guys wouldn't have blown up and he wouldn't have written that article.'

'Listen to me, Rowan. None of this is your fault. He'd already targeted me, for whatever reason. Without you, we wouldn't have worked any of this out. Who knows what might have happened! We don't know why he did what he did or what he was planning, but it's definitely better that we know about it.'

'Mum and Dad won't see it like that,' she mutters and, much to my surprise, her lip wobbles.

'I'll make sure they do. Look, I know it's a lot to ask,' I say, turning to Geoff and Doreen, 'but would you guys mind helping us explain everything to Ted and Lizzie when they get back?'

'Of course!' says Doreen at once.

'Absolutely,' agrees Geoff.

'Thanks. Because it's not just a case of explaining it, but figuring out what needs to happen next. I wish Bay was here.'

'I'm sure he would too, if he knew the full story,' says Geoff.

'I'm dreading having to see everyone else,' I say.

'Well, I'm sure they'll all be right behind you,' says Doreen.

I nod, feeling a little glow of love for the group of oddballs that I'm now lucky enough to call friends. Every single one of them, from Emma and her insane enthusiasm to lovely Messa, giver of hugs and wearer of the finest beard I've ever met.

I just hope they will still think of me as a friend after all of this.

Chapter 32

The Four Faces of Loneliness

'Loneliness has four faces: social, situational, emotional and chronic. No matter which of these you struggle with, it's important to tear off the protective mask you wear to fool the rest of the world and take a long look at the face underneath.'

©TheBeginnersGuideToLoneliness.com

I don't know how she does it, but Lizzie still manages to look like a goddess as she emerges from Ted's rusty little Micra bearing the sleeping baby in her carry seat.

Rowan, Geoff, Doreen and I all rush towards them, and we're suddenly one huge tangle of arms and happy tears and hugs and congratulations.

'It's so good to be back,' Lizzie smiles as Rowan finally pulls back from her mother.

'How're you feeling?' I ask. We've all come to the conclusion that there is no way we should burden Lizzie with the news the moment she's back.

'Great!' she replies. 'Tired. Sore. But, just look at her!' she beams down at her brand new daughter who is, miraculously, still asleep. 'But never mind me, how are you all? Ted's been filling me in. Tori, how are you holding up? Sounds like we've got a lot to talk about!'

I catch Rowan's look and Doreen stops in her tracks. Hm. Maybe our plan of letting Lizzie and Ted rest a while before dropping the next bombshell on them isn't quite going to work out as we planned.

'Oh, I'm fine,' I say with a smile. Maybe I can gloss over it until later.

'What's that?' Lizzie says, stopping to look at me properly, popping the carry seat down on the grass for a moment. 'Freaked out. Insecure. Neurotic and Emotional?'

'Mum!' gasps Rowan.

I shrug. 'Yep, that pretty much nails it.' I laugh.

'Well, if we're sharing,' says Doreen, 'I'm afraid there's quite a lot more that we need to catch you and Ted up on, when you've had a bit of a rest.'

'Rest? I've been in bed for days. Other than having a baby, I've been bored senseless. Rowan, help me get these things indoors and then put the kettle on. Sounds like it's time for tea and cake.'

My heart leaps at the mention of another cup of tea – actually I'd kill for a cup of Bay's coffee. Just the thought of Bay makes my heart twist painfully. I mustn't think about him. I can't go there. Not yet. Not with so many other things I need to figure out first.

★

It's about half an hour before we're all sitting around the long dining table in the courtyard. Between them, Rowan and Ted have managed to heft a high-backed armchair outside and have dragged it up to the head of the table for Lizzie. She's now ensconced as comfortably as possible, supported by many cushions, and is busy feeding the little one while the rest of us squabble over the homemade biscuits that Doreen just produced, having nipped back over to the cabin to get them. The tea, however, is the usual brew of hedge clippings, so I opt for some mint in hot water instead.

The rest of the group are nowhere to be seen, and Ted tells us that they've all gone off on a walk with Russ and Claire so that they can share Than's article with everyone at the same time.

'Do you want to start?' I ask Rowan, who's been sitting next to her mother and baby sister, uncommonly quiet.

Rowan looks up at me with a startled expression on her face and shakes her head.

'What've you done, Rowan?' Lizzie asks, looking serious.

'Nothing. She's . . . well, actually, she's pretty much saved me from something quite nasty,' I say, not quite knowing where to start. Doreen and Geoff both nod their agreement and I relax a little bit. 'It's about Than. Nathan.'

'Is it about that article?' asks Ted sharply.

'No, no, this is something else. Something worse, in a way. At least, worse for me.'

Rowan looks up at me, glances at her mum and then her dad, and rolls her eyes. 'Oh for God's sake, this is going to take hours if I leave it to you!' she huffs. 'That Nathan bloke has been *friends* with Tori online for years, by pretending to be a woman.'

'Huh?' Lizzie looks completely confused and I almost let out a laugh when I see the expression on Ted's face. I jump in quickly before Rowan manages to drop herself in it in her impatience to tell the story.

I tell them about the Warriors and our friendship. I navigate carefully around how I talked Rowan into letting me contact them a couple of times. And then how Rowan discovered what Than had been up to and how desperate she was to warn me.

'Rowan! I can't believe this,' Ted says. He looks angry, and shocked, and just a little bit proud.

'Look, it wasn't Rowan's fault, and as soon as she figured out that there was something off about the whole thing, she wanted to put it right.'

Rowan smiles at me.

'But still. Why didn't you tell me?' Ted demands.

'You had enough to worry about. I guess I didn't really think Tori would be in any real danger while she was with us and had no access to the internet. I told her as soon as I could.'

'Catfish?' says Lizzie, as if tasting the new term on her tongue.

'Apparently,' I say with a shrug.

'But I just don't understand what he hoped to gain from meeting up with Tori here?'

'Nothing good,' Rowan says with a dark look. 'You should see the horrible stuff it says about some of these cases online.'

I shudder. I don't want to think about it.

Geoff spots my mounting discomfort and jumps in. 'Look, I don't think it's going to help to talk about that now. Thanks to Rowan, we know what's going on. Now we need to help Tori decide what to do next.'

'Do you mean pressing charges or something?' asks Ted

I shake my head quickly. There's no way I want to go down that route. What would be the point?

'What I'm worried about now,' says Doreen, who's been pretty quiet so far, 'is your other two friends on there.'

'What about them?' I ask. I'm not sure how I feel. I defended them to Rowan earlier, and there's no way I believe that they could all be the same person, like Rowan suggested, but do they really not know about any of this?

'Doreen's right,' says Ted. 'They're both pretty vulnerable, not knowing that "Nat" is a fraud. Whether they've seen that article yet or not, I think it's important that you warn them. After all, Than still has access to the chatroom. He doesn't know his cover's blown, does he?'

Lizzie nods. 'Actually, that's a really good point.'

'But what if they already know something about all this?' Rowan asks. 'I know you said earlier that you thought they were cool, but what if they're in on it?'

'Are you able to send them personal messages on there that don't appear for the whole group?' asks Geoff.

I nod.

'Well, if Rowan will lend you her phone again, why don't you send them both a private message and just ask if they've heard from "Nat"? You know he's not been posting on the public bit, but he might have been talking to them privately.'

'That's a good idea,' nods Lizzie, hoisting the baby onto her shoulder and patting her back. 'Then, when they get back to you, you can decide whether to tell them everything.'

I nod slowly. 'I guess so.' I can hardly admit that, right now, the last thing I want to do is put my trust in another two people I've never met.

Doreen smiles at me gently. 'Tori, just because Than has completely messed up his relationship with you from the start, don't let that ruin what you've got with the other two.'

'That's just it,' I say. 'I've realized that they're not my friends. How can they be when I've never even met them? They could be anybody.' My bottom lip quivers and I bury my nose in my mug to hide the fact that, right at this moment, even though I'm surrounded by people who want to help me, I feel lonelier than I ever have before.

Chapter 33

Journey Through, Not Around

'When faced with a tough situation, you've got two choices: find a way around it, or journey through it. No matter how hard it may seem, the journey through is the one that will work out better in the long run. Every time you avoid an issue, it finds a way to come back again and again.'

©TheBeginnersGuideToLoneliness.com

Rowan hands me her phone to contact Sue and Hugh. Even though I'd much rather scuttle off and work out these messages in private, I sit at the table with the others and log in to my account. I can see that they've been busy gossiping about some new Netflix show in the general chat, but there's nothing new from Nat.

'Okay, here goes,' I say as I pull up a chat with Sue first. I quickly send her a message to say hello and ask if she's heard from Nat recently. I keep it short and simple, and once I've done that I send an almost identical message to Hugh. 'Done.' I go to hand the phone back to Rowan but she shakes her head.

'Keep it on you. Hopefully they'll reply quickly and then we can move straight to phase two.'

I nod and leave the phone on the table in front of me so I can see any new notifications as they pop up.

'Good,' says Ted, clearly pleased that something practical is being done. 'Now, I think you must try to get a bit of rest this evening, Tori. I know that's going to be hard, but you've had one shock after another today.'

With that, I'm reminded of the other question I wanted to ask them. I feel a blush rising on my cheeks. 'Actually, there was something else, if you don't mind?'

I decide to skip straight over the sticky parts. 'Did you show Bay the article before he left?' I ask Ted. 'He'd already disappeared by the time I got back from my walk with Doreen. Rowan told us he'd gone to London, but I don't get why he'd go without talking to me?'

Ted shifts in his chair and Lizzie looks at him. Geoff and Doreen are listening intently. This is shit. I know that it's something awful and Ted just can't bring himself to tell me.

'Look, Tori . . . I did share the article with him before he left. He needed to know about it – especially as there are photographs of him,' says Ted. 'But that had nothing to do with him leaving so suddenly. He had a personal emergency. I'm sure he would have stayed to speak to you and say good-bye if it hadn't been so urgent.'

I can't believe he didn't think I was important enough to wait just an hour or so . . .

'Where did he go?' I ask.

'London,' replied Ted, not catching my eye.

'What for?'

'I'm sorry, Tori,' Lizzie breaks in gently. 'We can't tell you that. It wouldn't be fair to Bay.'

'Look, he's hoping to get back before the end of the course. You can discuss it then.'

'Can't I give him a quick call—'

'We can't give you his number, Tori. Sorry.' Ted looks sheepish, but I can tell he's not going to budge on this.

I slump my head into my hands. I feel completely defeated. I thought Bay and I had something special starting between us.

I'm just beginning to feel the spirals of panic taking hold when Rowan's phone lights up next to me. I grab it and scroll down.

'It's Sue. She hasn't heard anything from Nat,' I say flatly.

'That's one down, then,' says Ted.

'Should I go ahead and tell her, do you think?'

'I'd wait,' says Rowan. 'See what the other guy says and, if it's the same, you can tell them both at the same time.'

I nod wearily. This feels like game-playing and I've had enough. All I want to do is go back to the yurt, have a cup of coffee with Bay and cuddle up with Dennis. But, of course, both of those things are now impossible.

The phone lights up again. It's Hugh with the same news as Sue. No sign of Nat, but not to worry, as she said she was going to be having a busy few weeks. Well, he's got that bit right at least.

'That's both of them,' I say.

'Go on, Tori, tell them. Then at least you know you don't have to worry about them both being used against you somehow,' says Doreen.

I nod again. I'm starting to feel a bit like the Churchill nodding dog.

'Rowan, do you mind if I take your phone for ten minutes? I feel like I need to do this on my own.'

'Sure,' Rowan shrugs.

'Thanks.' I struggle up from the bench and Doreen goes to follow me.

I smile at my friend. I know she's worried, but right now I just need some time on my own to send these messages and grieve for this part of my life that has meant so much to me. 'I'll be back in a few minutes, Doreen. Just want to clear my head and get this right.'

'Okay. We'll be here if you need us,' she replies, sitting back down.

I walk away from the courtyard. As soon as I turn the corner and know for sure that the sympathetic gaze of the little group is no longer on my back, I relax a little bit.

I wander for a while, then find myself heading towards the garden and the vegetable patch.

When I get there, just the sight of the neat beds in the evening light calms my heart a little. This bit was real. No matter what's happened since, the time I spent with Bay here in the garden was real.

I sit down on the wooden railway sleepers and take a few deep breaths, staring around at the garden. Now it's time to deal with something that isn't real. I pull up the chat on Rowan's phone and stare hard at it.

I decide that I can only face doing this once, and as they're bound to ask the same questions, I start a new room and invite just the two of them to join it. They both accept and are there within seconds.

I'm crying by the time I've finished explaining. Not because of having to tell them about what's happened, nor their shocked, disbelieving and then angry responses, but because it feels like I'm killing something special. Something very dear and innocent.

Both of them have asked what they can do to help, but I've told them that there really isn't anything and that I'll try to pop into this new chat to say hello when things settle down a bit. But in my heart, I know it can never be like it was before. For one thing, Nat won't be there. I know she was fictional, but I feel like I've lost someone I love. And let's face it, I'm never going to be able to trust the others in the same way again. I'm always going to triple-guess everything I post.

As neither of them have seen it yet, I drop the link to Than's article and then slip the phone into my pocket. I can't bring myself to wait for their reactions.

In a daze, I wipe my face on my sleeve, then stand and stretch. Time for that early night Ted suggested. I head back down to the courtyard and wave away offers of more tea.

'Thanks for the phone. All done,' I say, handing it back to Rowan.

'What did they say?' she asks curiously.

'I think they're in shock. They hadn't seen the piece Than wrote, so I gave them that link too.'

'Bet they were pissed off!' says Rowan.

'Yup. You could say that.'

'You did the right thing,' says Geoff.

'I know. And now the other right thing is an early night. I'm shattered.'

'Aren't you going to wait to speak to them again after they've read it?' asks Doreen, a look of surprise on her face.

I shake my head. 'I've told them everything they need to know.'

'But . . . but don't they want to help?'

'Yes, but let's face it, there's nothing anyone can do.'

'Go on, Tori,' says Ted, taking pity on me, 'head back to the yurt and get some rest. We'll talk more tomorrow.'

I nod gratefully.

'We'll walk you back, shall we?' says Geoff.

'Thanks, but I'm fine,' I smile at him. 'I'm going to go straight to bed, so I won't be much company.'

He continues to look worried, so I say, 'Would you and

Doreen perhaps swing by on your way down for breakfast tomorrow?'

He smiles back at me. 'Of course.'

I had thought getting back to the yurt would make me feel better, but I was wrong. When I unzip the flap, shuffle out of my boots and let myself in, I'm struck by how bloody quiet it is. And not in a good way.

Before, when I popped back, nine times out of ten I'd be greeted by either Bay, Dennis or both. And even when they weren't around, there was always the chance of them appearing at any moment. The space is still beautiful, but without those two, it no longer feels like home.

The thought hits me in the stomach. Of course, this isn't 'home' anyway. Very soon I'll be back in my empty flat and, now that I don't have the Warriors to gossip with, my even emptier life. This place was meant to help me work things out, not make them worse. Yes, I've figured out a lot, but right now I'd much prefer to return to my state of not-so-blissful ignorance.

I throw my pyjamas on and sink onto my bed. Turning my back on Bay's side of the yurt, I wrap myself in my blankets and close my eyes.

I mustn't think about Bay. I mustn't think about Than.

I just want to sleep.

'Give her a poke!'

Rowan's voice drifts into my dreams, and I feel myself

surfacing. I don't open my eyes straight away. I was having such a nice dream.

'Don't be mean,' Doreen's voice says softly. 'Tori?' she croons, sounding like she's trying to wake a baby.

'Wakey wakey!' Rowan bellows. I'm pretty sure I hear a snort of laughter from Geoff.

I smile into my pillow and open my eyes. 'You lot should form a comedy act,' I say, sitting up and rubbing my eyes.

'Sorry, love, you weren't awake when we stopped by before breakfast, so we brought some back up for you, but *someone* insisted on coming too,' Doreen nods at Rowan.

'Like I'm going to miss this!' she says.

I shake my head, throw my blankets off and swing my legs around to sit on the side of my bed.

'We've got a surprise for you!' Rowan announces, eyes sparkling.

I look from her excited face to Geoff's beaming one and then back to Doreen's rather more worried expression.

'What?' I ask suspiciously.

'Now don't get mad—' says Doreen.

'Mad?' I say faintly. I'm completely lost. What on earth are these three up to?

'She's READY!' Rowan yells.

To my amazement, the flap of the yurt flips open and two people enter. One woman I vaguely recognize, with her long blond hair in a side plait, and then there's a middle-aged guy who has something of a Matt Lucas air about him.

'Erm, hi?' I say.

'Tori, it's us!' says the man, watching the look of complete confusion on my face.

I know that voice. *Wait . . .*

'*Hugh?!*' I gasp.

Matt Lucas, who is obviously not Matt Lucas, nods, a huge grin on his face.

'Which means . . .' I continue.

'Yep. That's Sue!' Rowan fills in for me eagerly.

The blond woman is staring at me with tears in her eyes. I stand up slowly, staring from one to the other. Then, I have no idea how it happens, but we're in a tangle of arms as the three of us hug each other so tightly that I swear there's going to be at least one cracked rib by the time we're done.

When we eventually pull away from each other, we still don't let go completely. Hugh has an arm around my shoulders and Sue is holding my hand.

I beam at them in turn. 'How? Why?'

'That would be our fault,' said Geoff from behind me.

I twist around to look at him, still holding on to my friends. 'I don't understand.'

'What's new?' laughs Rowan.

'Oi!' says Doreen sharply.

'Tori doesn't mind, do you?' Rowan grins at me.

I shake my head. Right now, I don't think I mind anything much.

Chapter 34

Be Open, Be Honest, Be You

'Shall I tell you a secret? You're pretty great. Your story is important. When we have suffered loneliness, for whatever reason, it can be incredibly difficult to open up to other people again. But that, right there, is the path that leads through to the other side. Show the true you, share your wonderful self openly, and encourage others to do the same.'

©TheBeginnersGuideToLoneliness.com

'It was actually Geoff's idea,' says Doreen, after we've all trooped outside to sit on the wooden benches around the unlit fire pit.

'I don't know,' Geoff looks uncharacteristically bashful. 'I just thought it was such a shame that that idiot had made you wary of two people who are clearly so important to you.'

'Yeah, so when I saw you'd left yourself logged in last night, I said maybe we should talk to them,' says Rowan.

'We were both frantic after reading that article,' says Sue.

I can't get enough of her voice. It's as though she's bringing to life all the lines we've typed to each other over the years.

'We tried to get you on group voice, we both sent you messages in the new room and privately, but you weren't answering.'

'Of course, once Rowan had spotted you'd left yourself logged in, we could see all of this,' continues Doreen.

'So I said,' cuts in Rowan, 'let's message them and tell them you're all right.'

'And you just messaged them as me?' I ask, surprised.

'Course not. I asked Dad if it was okay first. He agreed. Well, of course, it came out under your name, but I told them straight away that it was me, and that you were okay-ish, and that we were looking after you and that you'd gone to bed.'

Sue nods. 'I just wanted to know that you were okay. I swear, if I'd had a shock like that, I don't know what state I'd have been in. And it's so scary to think that Nat – I mean this Nathan person – basically set out to meet you without you even knowing anything about it.' She gives an exaggerated shudder. 'Anyway, both of us wanted to do something. We wanted to come and be with you. Even if it was just for company while you dealt with the shock.'

My heart feels like it's slowly being pieced back together. All of these people doing all of this because they were worried about me. Because they care about me.

'So Rowan asked them both to stay logged in and she'd see what she could do,' says Doreen.

347

'And Dad said to invite them here!'

'And you just came?' I ask, open-mouthed, staring between Sue and Hugh.

'Well, I was relaying everything to my hubby as it was happening,' says Sue. 'He was so worried about you, and said that he'd look after the twins if there was any chance I could come and support you. There was one issue though – our car is in the garage so I had no transport.'

'So I went and fetched her!' laughs Hugh. 'As soon as Rowan invited us, I started throwing things in a bag. Then when Sue said she could come too but had no transport, that was an easy fix; I just detoured to collect her on my way down. I stayed at Sue's last night and then we set off mega-early this morning.'

I shake my head trying to take it all in. Sue and Hugh are really here. They've spent hours driving here just because they knew how much I needed them.

'I – I can't believe you'd do that for me,' I say. 'Thank you.'

'Anytime,' says Hugh matter-of-factly.

'Now where's this Bay character? I'm dying to meet him,' says Sue.

The change in the atmosphere is almost comical. Geoff busies himself with his shoelaces, Doreen pulls a tragic face as if someone has died and Rowan starts to fidget.

'What did I say?' says Sue, looking around at the others.

I sigh. 'Bay's gone.'

'*Gone?* What do you mean, "gone"?'

'He had to rush off to London yesterday.'

'That's a shame, I'd like to meet the man that's finally swept you off your feet.' Hugh grins.

'How long's he gone for?' Sue adds.

'I'm not sure . . .' I say.

'Didn't he tell you?' says Sue in surprise.

'He didn't say anything, not even goodbye. He disappeared while Doreen and I were off on a walk.'

'You're kidding me!' says Sue, eyes wide.

'Nope. Just gathered up his dog and left.'

'But why?'

'Supposedly some kind of urgent work thing came up, but . . . well . . . I can't help but think it's more likely to do with this bloody article.'

'I'm sure that's not true,' says Sue gently.

'And Ted did say he was hoping to be back before the end of the course, didn't he?' says Geoff.

'Apparently he's going to try,' I say, 'but it's not definite. His "urgent business" might keep him tied up.'

'To be fair to Bay, it might,' pipes up Rowan, looking a bit cross. 'He is kinda famous you know.'

'Famous?' Sue says. 'Tori, you didn't tell us that.'

'Because he's not. Rowan's having you on!' I say.

'Am not! He *is* . . . in the world of gardens anyway. And I know it's crap he didn't wait to talk to you before he went Tori, but he's a good guy,' she finishes, looking a bit uncomfortable.

I watch Rowan as she stares at the ground and focuses on digging her heel into the mud. She's right. Bay is a good guy.

Here's me, expecting him to take it on trust that I'm not the monster Than has made me out to be, while busily thinking the worst of him rather than trusting him. But after everything that's happened, I'm not sure I'm up for giving anyone the benefit of the doubt right now.

'So have you called him, Tori?' asks Hugh.

I shake my head.

'Why not?'

'One, I don't have his number. Two, I don't have a phone. Three, I'm not really sure what I'd say.'

'But hang on,' says Hugh, 'isn't our Rowan here the queen of information?'

Rowan looks up from her muddy boots and I can practically see her ego swelling with the knowledge that her reputation has reached beyond the boundaries of The Farm.

'Exactly! Can't you tell me where he's gone? Or at least start with something simpler, like his full name?'

Rowan's jaw drops. 'You're not telling me you did whatever you did with him and you don't even know his name?!'

'We only kissed, thank you very much!' I can feel myself going red, and the fact that both of the guys start to laugh isn't helping.

Rowan rolls her eyes. 'Okay, I can give you his name, but it'll cost you.'

'It'll have to be PayPal again,' I sigh.

'Don't worry about that!' says Hugh. He whips out his wallet and hands Rowan a ten-pound note. Her eyes go wide, but she quickly recovers.

'Okay, that's a start,' she says with a shrug. 'Bay's surname is Anderson. He's actually called Bailey Anderson, and his business is called . . .'

'Anderson, Simpson and Green!' squeals Sue.

We all turn to stare at her.

'What?' she says. 'Don't tell me you haven't heard of them! They do the gardens of the rich and the famous. I mean, Bailey Anderson's practically royalty . . . he's like a gardening god!'

'But . . . but he's just Bay!' I say.

Oh great, another person in my life who's been busy pretending to be someone else.

I can't believe this. Is no one going to turn out to be who they say they are?

'See!' says Rowan, pointing at Sue. 'That reaction is exactly why Bay prefers to keep a low profile when he's here. Of course, plenty of people recognize him, but he does his best not to make a big deal out of it.'

'Now we know his name, we don't need Ted to find out his number,' Hugh says as he whips out his own phone and within seconds has pulled up the Anderson, Simpson and Green website. It's going to be that easy to call him. But now that I can, I'm not sure I want to.

'Wait. I need food and I need to let everything sink in a bit first. Anyway, it's Sunday. If I'm going to call, I'm not going to be able to do it until tomorrow when their office is open.'

★

351

As it turns out, I needn't have worried for a second about how the rest of the group were going to react to Than's article. As they arrive to find Sue, Hugh and I setting the dinner table after a whole day spent together exploring the countryside around The Farm, I am engulfed by hugs and offers of support. They are all on my side, and all desperate to make sure I know it. Emma gushes about my writing, while Messa and Bob both offer to be there to talk any time I need them, day or night. Moth presents me with a beautiful knitted hairband in the hope that it might cheer me up, and even quiet Sam throws his arm around my shoulders and tells me how brave I am.

Supper is a ridiculously happy affair, and for a while I'm able to forget everything that's happened and just enjoy the amazing company. Ted and Lizzie are still celebrating being back at home with Rowan and the baby, and their joy overflows in their welcome to the new arrivals too.

In among all their plotting and planning, Rowan, Doreen and Geoff have arranged for Hugh and Sue to stay in the yurt with me tonight. Ted tells me it's the most practical option as the little settee pulls out into a bed. In my heart, though, I know they've planned this so that I don't have to spend another night on my own, and I'm deeply grateful.

We all help tidy up after the meal. Lizzie disappears off to bed early, and Ted follows soon after with strict instructions to Rowan not to stay up too late, which she roundly ignores. She's actually pretty indignant when the rest of us decide to head back to our respective camps soon after, but, as I explain, she's not missing out on anything as we're all headed straight to bed anyway.

By the time we're all snuggled up in our beds – Hugh has taken Bay's, and Sue's on the sofa as she's so tiny – my head is whirring again. So much has happened, I'm still trying to process it all. The issue that I keep coming back to, however, is Bay. Why did he leave without talking to me? Will he come back? Should I phone him?

'You okay, Tori?' asks Hugh.

'I am thanks to you two,' I sigh. 'Thank you so much for being here with me.'

'It's fun! An unexpected adventure. And anyway, you'd have done exactly the same for us!' says Sue.

I think about this, and realize that she's right. Hugh, Sue and, until yesterday, the fictional Nat are three people that I would have done almost anything for.

It's a wonderful feeling when I realize that, since I've been here, several new people have joined that list. And right at the top is Bay.

'You know I can't just call Bay, right?' I say into the dark.

'Why not?' asks Hugh, surprised. 'You've got the number, and you can use my phone. No one else needs to know.'

'It's not that,' I say. 'I need to see him. It's got to be face to face.'

'Oh.' Hugh goes quiet.

'Well, he might come back in time,' says Sue in a soothing voice.

'I need to go back to London. As soon as possible,' I say, surprising myself. 'Do you reckon you could give me a lift down to Carmarthen tomorrow? I can catch the train from there—'

'Nope,' says Hugh. 'Think we're going to let you escape our clutches that quickly?'

'But—' I start.

'I'll drive you to London. You up for another road trip, Sue?'

'Oooh, yes!' she squeals. 'I've got a few days to play with so—'

'Guys, you don't need to do that.'

'Oh yes we do!' says Hugh.

'Absolutely. I need to know how it's going to work out with you and your sex-god gardener!'

'What about your course, though? You won't get to finish it,' says Hugh.

'I think I've got quite a lot to write about already. And anyway, if everything goes to plan, perhaps I'll get the chance to come back in time to finish it off.'

'So what are we going to do tomorrow? Say goodbye to everyone and then head off after breakfast?' asks Sue.

My heart clenches at the thought of saying goodbye to Geoff and Doreen earlier than I have to. But I have to see Bay, I just have to. 'I don't think so. We're going to have to make a break for it early, otherwise I'm not sure that Ted and Lizzie will let us escape.'

'When you say early . . .'

'Ted's usually up at 5.30am.'

'With a newborn baby in the house you might find either of them up at any hour,' says Hugh.

'Good point. We need a distraction.'

'The car is parked up at the top of the lane, so it's just going to be a case of sneaking past the house,' says Hugh.

'How about Rowan?' asks Sue. 'She could be a lookout for us.'

'How on earth are we going to ask her now?'

'I've got her number,' says Hugh. 'I took it so that I could let her know when we would be arriving.'

'Perfect,' I say. 'Oh, and ask her to break my stuff out of the safe while she's at it.'

Chapter 35

Survive vs Thrive

'Are you surviving or are you thriving? What's the difference? Surviving is an incredible achievement. You are pulling together the resources that you need to stay afloat. Surviving through some of the toughest times in life feels like a badge of honour.

'But thriving? Thriving means tapping into your potential. It's about joy and abundance. It's about growth.'

©TheBeginnersGuideToLoneliness.com

I feel kind of bad as we scuttle down the yard towards the lane at ridiculous o'clock the next morning. I should be saying goodbye to everyone, thanking them for basically changing my whole life.

I can't think like that now, though, otherwise I'll be crying again, and a tearful mess at five forty in the morning is not a good start.

Instead, I comfort myself with the thought that, if everything pans out, I'll be back soon enough to finish off the course.

'Thanks so much for everything,' I whisper as Rowan hands me the little bag with my shoes, phone and other bits and pieces from the safe.

'You owe me!' she yawns. She looks so much younger when she's all crumpled from sleep and sans make-up.

'I've already sent you twenty quid!' I say.

'You still owe me! Dad's going to do his nut when he knows you've done a runner.'

'Let us know what happens, won't you?' says Hugh.

'Sure.' Rowan yawns again, turning back towards her bed with a wave over her shoulder.

'You know, I think Ted's going to be more worried about his safe-breaking daughter than you disappearing after Bay,' Sue chuckles quietly. 'Come on, guys, let's get going.'

The journey feels like a breeze compared to the public transport marathon from hell it took to get me there. The best thing is, we don't stop talking until we reach the outskirts of the city. I may have only physically met these two yesterday, but there's no doubt that our friendship is real.

It might feel like we've talked about everything under the sun, but there are two subjects we've carefully been avoiding: Bay and Nat.

Gah, I've got to stop calling him Nat or Than in my head. *Nathan.* Catfishing, bullshitting Nathan.

'Guys, what am I going to do about Nathan?' I finally ask when there's a lull in the conversation. 'I know what I said about not pressing charges, but it doesn't feel right to just let him get away with what he's done.'

'If it were me, I'd want to get even,' says Sue over her shoulder, peering at me in the back seat.

'You know,' says Hugh, not taking his eyes off the busy road, 'I think it's about more than that. This is someone who's successfully befriended the three of us while posing as someone else. For whatever reason, it looks like he has become completely obsessed with you, Tori, and when he didn't get what he wanted, he turned nasty.'

'Actually, if you think about it, how he behaved towards you at the retreat kind of mirrored what he was like in the chat,' says Sue. 'Nat swooped in and isolated you from the main chat almost as soon as you'd joined, and I don't think she – *he* – ever forgave me and Hugh for crashing your private group.'

I raise my eyebrows. Hindsight is a wonderful thing. I can see now that Sue's right.

'But how does that mirror what he was doing at The Farm?' I ask, confused.

'From what you said, he started to get all stroppy when he saw you were making friends with the others,' says Sue.

'Yeah. I mean, he was definitely jealous of your friendship with Doreen,' says Hugh. 'And it sounds like he tried to isolate you as often as he could, and acted out when his plans didn't work.'

'Well, he got the ultimate revenge, didn't he?' I say, shivering.

'No. No, he didn't,' Sue says, her voice firm. 'The only way he will have done that is if you let him undo all the amazing things you've achieved while you've been at The Farm.'

I nod. 'So, do you think I should go to the police?'

'Not if you don't want to go down that route,' says Hugh, thoughtfully, 'but I do think that, as he has gone public about his time with you, you'd be well within your rights to do the same to him.'

'Out him?'

'Yes. And while you're at it, raise some awareness.'

Sue's nodding in agreement. 'We're three relatively sensible adults—'

'Speak for yourself,' I laugh.

'What I mean is,' she continues, 'if he's doing it, there must be others targeting kids and vulnerable people who rely on the internet as their main source of interaction.'

'More people like me . . .' I say, realizing that's probably what had drawn him to me in the first place – the fact that I'm deeply vulnerable. Desperate. A fuck-up. No, let's rephrase that. The fact that, until very recently, I *was* a fuck-up. Now . . . now I'm more of a work-in-progress.

'Well, yes,' says Hugh. 'I mean, what's to stop him from doing it again?'

'Nothing,' I say. 'But even if I do write about this, he might do it again anyway.'

'You haven't got any control over what he does, but you have got complete control of how you respond to him.'

I sit back and think about this. By outing me as the blogger behind The Beginner's Guide to Loneliness, he's forced me to take ownership and go public with my most intimate thoughts. I mean, they were already out there, but their connection to me wasn't. It should have been my choice, and he's taken that away from me.

'You're right!' I say. 'I need to respond publicly, and it has to be on my blog.'

'Perfect idea,' says Hugh enthusiastically. 'I mean, after all the extra exposure from Nathan's piece, your readership is bound to be even higher than usual now. May as well take what he's caused and use it to get your own back!'

I hadn't even thought about what this drama might have done to the site itself. Sure, most of the new readers will probably be visiting out of morbid curiosity, hoping to find out more about this man-addicted slut-bag that Nathan's presented, but then, surely, that makes them the perfect audience to reach out to with my reply.

Getting back to my flat is a bit of an eye-opener. Of course, I've invited Sue and Hugh to stay. It's not going to be the most comfortable visit – Sue's going to have to share my double bed and Hugh will take the sofa – but it's not that that's bothering me. It's the fact that this place could be anyone's. It's an anonymous, colourless space with absolutely no personality or warmth. I can't even compare it to a hotel room, because at least hotels attempt to make you feel comfortable.

I dump my bag in the corner of the living room and turn to see both Hugh and Sue looking around with something close to dismay on both their faces.

'I'll completely understand if you'd prefer to stay in a hotel,' I say quickly. 'I know it's a bit—'

'No, it's great!' says Sue, her voice too bright.

'Yeah. We want to be with you, Tori!' says Hugh.

'Well . . . thanks.' I say.

'I like what you've done with the place,' he says.

I snort. I can't help it.

Hugh's lips are twitching, and Sue clearly doesn't know whether she should join in or keep up the polite facade.

'It's just a bit . . .'

'Bare?' I say.

'No . . . just . . . I'd never know you were the person living here. You've got so much energy and personality; you're so full of ideas and creativity and this place is . . .'

'Crap,' I finish for her.

'I didn't say that!' she says, looking worried.

'No, but I did. Thing is, it's taken this break for me to be able to see it properly. Seems like I really did keep myself for "online only",' I sigh.

'But look how much has happened in such a short time. Just shows how fast things can change!' says Hugh.

I think he's trying to be encouraging, but I want to point out that having my privacy violated online, followed by Bay disappearing on me, weren't quite the changes I'd been hoping for. I keep my mouth shut. The flat is depressing enough, without me adding to it.

'Look, I know it's a bit shit. You guys sure you're still up for staying here?'

Both of them nod.

'Okay.' I take a deep breath and look around at the familiar bare walls, plain carpet and minimal furniture. 'I can't believe I was so worried about not scraping the rent together. Let's face it, not being able to stay in this place isn't exactly a big deal, is it?!'

'You thinking of maybe moving after your adventure?' asks Hugh.

'Not maybe. Definitely. I can write from anywhere, and this place doesn't fit the new me. The *real* me.'

The rest of the morning disappears in a haze as we struggle to combat the after-effects of our early morning dash from Wales. After an emergency supplies run to the local Tesco Express, we nurse ourselves with coffee and bacon sandwiches.

The question of what exactly I'm going to do about Bay, now that we've travelled across the country for me to see him, is looming large. Although neither of the other two have mentioned it, I know they're waiting for me to bring it up.

I really should get on and call that number on Bay's website, but there's something holding me back.

Our level of gossip has died right down with the wave of sleepiness that engulfs us after our lunch. I'm slumped in the armchair and the other two are on the sofa. Sue has slipped her shoes off and is sitting with her feet cosily tucked up under her bum. Hugh has his arms behind his head, legs outstretched in front of him and his eyes are almost closed.

'Right!' I say, practically leaping to my feet.

The other two jump.

'Sorry, sorry!' I laugh.

' "Right" what?' asks Hugh, watching as I start to pace the room. Exactly two and a half strides one way. Turn. Two point five strides the other.

'I know what I need to do,' I say triumphantly.

'Call Bay?' asks Sue.

'Nope. I really want to, but first, I need to write that blog post.'

'You do? First?' asks Hugh surprised.

'Yep. Close that particular chapter of crap and draw a line under it. Whatever happens next with Bay, I don't want it to have anything to do with the whole Nathan Jones mess.'

'And if it doesn't work out between you?'

'Then it was something really lovely while it lasted, and I still don't want it to get mixed up in my head with Nathan's shite.'

'Great. Okay, so . . .' Hugh's at a loss. He's great when there's something practical to help with, but I can see he's wondering what to do until he's given his next superman mission.

'Look . . . this is going to be incredibly boring for you two while I obsess over getting every word right,' I say. What I really want to ask is if they'd mind buggering off and doing a spot of sightseeing for a couple of hours. That way, I'd know my guests were enjoying themselves while I'd get the peace and quiet I need to get the job done.

'Ooh . . . do you mean we can go sightseeing without looking like we're being really rude?' Sue grins. It seems she's a mind-reader.

'If you'd like to? Or just chill out, or—'

'I'd like to go sightseeing!' says Hugh, suddenly looking wide awake. 'Of course, it won't be the same without you, but maybe we'll get to hang out together when you're done, Tori?'

'Sounds like a plan,' I grin at them, loving how excited they are.

'EEEK! This is amazing! Unexpected me-time and the whole London experience too?' Sue is on her feet, hopping up and down while yanking clothes out of her bag. 'Tori, can I use your bathroom to get ready?' she asks.

'Of course!'

While Sue's changing, I dig out a Tube map for Hugh and arrange to meet up with them this evening at the Italian restaurant just around the corner.

The minute the door closes behind them, I rush through to my tiny office and fire up my laptop. I log into my blog and let out a gasp. Hugh was right. The number of page hits since Nathan's article went live has been insane. I feel a little bit sick all of a sudden. All those people reading what I've written. All those people knowing so much about me . . .

Use it. That's all I can do. Use this platform to tell them what really happened. And anyway, there's nothing on here I should be ashamed of. There's some incredibly tough stuff, things I wish I'd never had to deal with. But this isn't an ideal world, and these things *did* happen to me. And if they happened to me, I'm certain they've happened to other people too.

There are hundreds of comments waiting for approval, but, for now, I need to get straight to the task in hand.

Dear Readers,

A big hello to all you lovely regulars, and welcome to all the new faces too.

As I'm sure most of you already know, I've recently been on a retreat to The Farm in west Wales. I'll be back next week to share more about the incredible, life-changing work they do there. But, rather a lot has happened while I've been away and, right now, that's what I need to talk to you about.

As you will have seen, the big secret is out and I am no longer able to remain anonymous. My name is Tori Williamson, I am 33 years old and currently live in London. If you don't know what on earth I'm talking about and why I've just so casually revealed my closely guarded secret, you need to have a read of <u>this</u> article by Nathan Jones before we go any further. Go on . . . follow the link . . . I'll wait.

I paste in the link to Nathan's piece and take a deep breath. Here goes.

The first thing you need to know about Nathan Jones is that we have been friends online for two years. The second thing you need to know is that I didn't know him as Nathan. I knew him as a thirty-one-year-old female called Nathalie. Nathalie was one of my best friends, and was, in fact, the one who encouraged me to start up this blog in the first place. Unfortunately, Nathalie was completely fictional – an alias used by Nathan Jones to gain my trust and friendship.

By the time I've finished writing about the chatroom, 'Nathalie' encouraging me to go on the retreat, 'Than' befriending me and trying to initiate a physical relationship, and then Nathan sharing my identity along with my inner-most secrets with the world, I'm shaking. But I've come this far, and I've got one more thing to say about him.

The questions I keep asking myself, over and over again, are: why did he target me in the first place? Why, after two years, did this catfish finally decide to meet me? And what was he hoping to achieve? I guess I'll never know the answers. The one thing I do know for sure is that a lot of his motivation for this final betrayal seems to have been revenge. What for? For rejecting him. For saying no. And for being romantically interested in someone else.

Nathan Jones tried to paint me as a deranged man-eater. When I got to The Farm, I was incredibly lonely – as my faithful readers will already know, and as you will have gathered from the title of this blog. With all his knowledge of me gathered over a long 'friendship', it didn't take much for Nathan to create a closeness between us. But at the same time I was learning how to make friends and to value the amazing people I was surrounded by. I was also opening my heart up for the first time in several years.

The lead photograph shows me with a fellow partici-pant, my friend Bay. This is not an image capturing a fling between an impressionable man-eater (me) and an opportunistic retreater (Bay) as Nathan Jones would have you believe. It's a photograph that shows a joyful moment shared between friends – the moment when a little piece of me fell back into place, and I started to see possibilities all around.

I broke The Farm rules by accessing the internet while I was there. I logged into a chatroom I share with my three best friends and told them about this amazing moment. I also shared the fact that 'Than's' advances were unwelcome.

'Than' left The Farm soon afterwards, but not before his behaviour towards me became aggressive and erratic, and he used my triggers to expose my severe potamophobia to the whole group.

Thankfully, he neglected to sign out of the chatroom while using the borrowed device, and this is how we discovered the depth of his deception.

There. Done. I take a deep breath and get on with the rest of the article, drawing attention to the dangers of catfishing and just how dark the outcomes to this kind of story can be.

When I'm finished, I read it back through several times. There's still something missing. I head out into my tiny kitchen to make a cup of tea, but before I get as far as pouring the water on the teabag, I've got it. I head back to my computer and type one final bit.

This has been a truly frightening experience in many ways, and I lost one of my best friends when I discovered that 'Nathalie' doesn't really exist. But I find that I am grateful that you now know who's behind these words and this blog. Perhaps I was wrong to remain anonymous for so long. This is my journey, and I look forward to continuing to share it with you.

Big love,
Tori
x

I stand up and stare at the screen for a moment.

'Fuck you, Nathan!' I say, sticking two fingers up at the screen. I reach over and click POST.

Chapter 36

Real, Not Perfect

'The most powerful gift you can give yourself is accept-
ance. It's time to accept all of your facets – the dark as well
as the light; your past as well as your dreams for the future.
Accept the real version of yourself and forget about the
pointless struggle for perfection.'

©TheBeginnersGuideToLoneliness.com

My taxi swings to an abrupt halt in front of a glass-fronted
building with a carved wooden 'Anderson, Simpson and
Green' sign adorning the front.

Okay, so this isn't a small, boutique kind of a company,
then? Holy crap, this place is huge!

I pull open the vast slab of a door and find myself in the
reception area, suddenly very aware of my scruffy clothes in
the polished surroundings. Staring upwards, my mouth falls
open and I come to a complete standstill.

The space is light and airy with the highest ceiling I've

ever seen. The far wall appears to be made of living plants, the greens of which create a double-room-height pattern of a giant leaf. As I move closer, I notice that the delicate yellow and orange highlights are made up of tiny flowers, giving the appearance that it's being touched by late evening sunshine.

'Can I help you?'

The words cut across my awestruck staring, and I look around. There's a girl smiling at me from behind a curved, wooden desk. It looks like the thing has grown straight up out of the floor and is a living, breathing part of the building.

'Oh, hi,' I say, returning her smile quickly. 'Sorry about that, it's just . . .'

'I know, right?' the girl laughs. 'Don't worry, it happens all the time. Gorgeous, isn't it?'

'Uh huh!' I nod, looking back at the living wall.

'This place was their first work as a team, and it's the best bit of advertising they could have ever given their new company, if you ask me!' she laughs.

I nod. And swallow. Okay, so that's the small talk done – now how am I going to approach this?

'Is Bay here?' I blurt.

There we go, that's one way. Desperate and just a little bit scary . . .

On second thought, I should probably have asked for Bailey.

'I'm guessing this is a social call rather than business?' the girl asks politely.

'Why?' I ask sharply. Has Bay told this girl to watch out for me? Maybe she's got a mugshot behind that vast desk somewhere and is, even now, gearing up to warn him to get into hiding.

'The nickname!' she smiles. 'Always a dead giveaway.'

'Oh. Oh, of course.' I shift my weight awkwardly. I'm feeling really out of place. Maybe I shouldn't have come.

'Is Mr Anderson expecting you, Miss . . . ?'

'Tori, my name's Tori Williamson. No, he isn't. I was just hoping to catch him.'

'He's not here at the moment; he's on site.'

I nod, unsure what to say next. Maybe there really has been some kind of an emergency after all. *Note to self: entire world does not revolve around you, Tori!*

'He shouldn't be too long; he's due to pop back for some paperwork. Would you like to wait?'

'Oh . . . okay. If that's all right?'

'Of course! I'm Mel by the way. If you need anything, just let me know.'

Half an hour later, I've skim-read every single brochure in the plush reception area, and I feel like I've learned about this whole other side of Bay. The side of him that is Bailey. Bailey couldn't be any further from the easy-going, warm guy I thought I'd come to know. This Bailey bloke is an award-winning landscape gardener who part-owns this globally renowned company. Together, he, Simpson and Green have become the city's leaders in ecologically sound landscaping and design for the super-rich.

I swallow down something that feels strangely like disappointment. This is definitely not the man I thought I knew.

This is someone who's all about the money. He's a stranger and, what's worse, he's lied to me about who he is. Just like Nathan did.

Coming to a decision, I get to my feet, brush down my crumpled trousers and push my hair away from my face. What am I doing here, chasing after some guy who fed me a lie and then did a runner? I need to go home. I need to go and find my friends.

'Hi, Mel? I think I'm going to head off. I'll catch up with Bay later,' I fib.

'Oh, okay,' she says, looking worried. 'I've just heard from him. He should be here in about ten minutes. I told him you were waiting.'

'He's coming? Now?' My voice comes out a bit faint.

'He was going to fit in another meeting first, but as soon as he heard you were here, he cancelled it. I'm really sorry, you should have said that it was so important! I would have called him straight away.' She wrings her hands nervously, evidently used to dealing with clients on a short fuse.

'Don't worry,' I say. 'Like I said, he wasn't even expecting me!'

'So you'll stay?' she asks, and I can hear the anxiety in her voice.

'Of course,' I smile at her, though inside I'm feeling anything but cheerful. But I may as well get this over and done with now, then I can crawl back to the others and lick my wounds.

'Come with me. He said for you to wait in his office until he arrives.'

★

I follow Mel down a hallway where the light seems to be funnelled in through tubes set in the high ceiling. The lattice-work of bare, warm wood that snakes over my head makes it feel like I'm walking under an avenue of vast trees.

'Here we are,' says Mel, pushing open a door to our left.

The room beyond is arched, the ceiling running from a high point just off centre all the way down to the floor on both sides. There's something about this beautiful office that makes me feel like I'm back in the yurt. I smile for a moment as I allow myself to imagine that the Bay I know is real, that my version of him is a part of this high-flier.

Natural light floods in through a huge window at the far end of the room and there are plants everywhere. In among the trailing leaves I spot a group of photographs, and I make my way over to look at them.

There he is: Bay at The Farm, just outside the yurt; Bay chopping wood; Dennis on his bed; Dennis trying to lick the camera.

I suck in a sharp breath: Bay – with his arm around a woman. A tall, immaculately beautiful woman.

'Have you been to The Farm?'

I jump. I'd forgotten about Mel still standing behind me. I nod.

'Oh, wow. I really want to go. Mr Anderson said he'll make sure that I can attend the course next year. I'm so excited. It's such an amazing opportunity . . . Hey, are you okay? You've gone very pale!'

'Mel . . . who's this?' I ask, gesturing to the woman in the photograph.

Mel comes to join me in front of the pictures.

'Oh, that's Imogene. Don't you know her?'

'No. I've only just met Bay. At The Farm . . .'

'Cool! So no, you wouldn't have met her, then. She never goes down there with him. Imogene is Bay's wife.'

I stare at Mel.

'I'll just go and get you a glass of water. Maybe you're a bit hot . . .' Mel hurries to the door and throws a worried look back at me.

'Tell Bay I'm leaving,' I say, rubbing at my eyes.

'Tell him yourself!' comes a gruff reply.

My head snaps up and I see Bay closing the door behind him as Mel disappears on the other side.

No, not Bay. This is Bailey.

I barely recognize him in his smart chinos, white shirt and expensive-looking shoes. His hair has been swept back and his scruffy stubble is gone. It's only the gleam of concern in his eyes that marks him as the same man I shared the yurt with.

Before I can say anything, there's a scuffling at my feet and a large, panting head plops onto my lap. Dennis is staring up at me, his grin tempting me to smile back, and his manically wagging tail reassuring me that there's someone in this room who's happy to see me. I ruffle his ears. I want to cry.

'Tori, how are you here?' says Bay, still standing by the door. '*Why* are you here?'

'You're *married*?' I ask, completely ignoring his questions.

'No, I'm not,' he replies.

'Come on!' I growl, causing Dennis to whip his head out of my lap. He slinks back to Bay's side. 'That's the most pointless lie in the history of mankind.'

'I'm not lying. I'm not married.'

'Sure. Who's this, then?' I snap, standing up and slapping the photograph of the happy couple. 'Your fucking herbalist?!'

Bay winces. 'No. That *was* my wife. Now my ex-wife. I wanted to tell you but—'

'How come Mel said she's your wife, Bay?' I interrupt, a dogged determination coming over me. For once, won't someone just tell me the damned truth? 'I don't get it. You lie about this place. You lie about your *wife*?'

'I didn't lie, Tori. Mel, as lovely as she is, is an employee. I have my reasons for being careful how much I share about myself—'

'Oh, *reasons*? Wow. Great speech,' I fume. I'm so angry, I've started to revert to toddler mode. I need to leave. 'Excuse me,' I snap, trying to push past him to get to the door.

'Tori, what the hell? Where's the Tori I know disappeared to?'

'That's a bit bloody rich coming from the award-winning, married businessman,' I say.

'I'm not married. The divorce has been finalized. And this place? This place is the reason I got divorced. It's already wrecked things for me once, I didn't want it to happen a second time.'

375

I take a step back, and all of the fight feels like it's draining out of me. 'I don't get it. I just can't believe you didn't tell me.'

'Look, it's simple. Four years ago, I married a woman I loved. She just happened to be way more interested in my career than in me. It was all about the money. She was always pushing me to take on more projects here – things that didn't gel with our vision – just because they'd pay well. Every single time I did something for love rather than money, she'd throw a hissy fit, telling me that I was wasting my training, that I was endangering our future, the future of our children—'

'You have *children*?' I gasp.

'No, our unborn children. Unthought-of children. Anyway, she didn't want me to be happy, she just wanted me to be rich.'

'But why didn't you tell me? I'm not her.'

'I know that. But you know what it's like. If you're bitten once, you're slower to trust again.'

My thoughts fly straight to Markus, and then to Than. And how I've just behaved with Bay. He might have a point.

'I'm sorry, Tori,' he sighs.

'But you're not the man I've spent the last few weeks with. You're Bailey Anderson,' I say, gesturing from his tidy hair to his shiny shoes.

'Yes, I am . . . I'm also the person you got to know at The Farm. You can't just remove one part of me. I'm a mixture of all of the above and more!'

376

'But . . . you disappeared without even talking to me!'

'No offence, Tori, but you were kind of busy at the time. You'd disappeared off to sort things out with Doreen when Ted came to tell me that I'd had a phone call. I had no idea where you'd headed off to, nor how long you'd be. Than had landed all this crap on your plate with no warning, and I wanted to be there for you – to help you work through it all. But I was needed here urgently. Greg, one of my partners, fell and broke his leg. He hit his head too. Luckily nothing too serious, but he has concussion. He's right in the middle of a huge partnership – one of the show gardens at the Chelsea Flower Show. The whole firm's reputation is at stake, so I had to step in the minute I could. I left you a note—'

'Bullshit!' I say.

'I did. In the yurt. On your pillow. Didn't you get it?'

I shake my head, not sure whether to believe this or not.

'No wonder you're pissed off . . . you thought I just left without saying anything?'

I nod. If there really is a note, does it change anything? I don't know. Right now, I just don't know.

'Tori, you know me. I would never—'

'But I don't know you, do I?' I say, looking panicked.

We're interrupted by the sound of his phone ringing. We stare at each other, and I wonder if he's just going to ignore it.

'That's you . . .' he says with a small smile.

Shit. Of course it is. I've got so used to not having a phone on me, I didn't even think about the bloody thing in my pocket. I rummage around, pull it out and, with an apologetic look at Bay, answer it.

'Tori! You HAVE to check your emails.'

'Rowan?'

'Check. Your. Emails.'

'Can I call you back in about five minutes? I'm just finishing doing something.'

'Fine – say hi to Bay for me?'

'How do you know . . . ?'

'I'm assuming that's who you're finishing doing,' she snorts, and then rings off.

'Rowan says hi,' I say faintly.

Bay smiles. 'Look—'

'I can't do this, Bay,' I interrupt. 'Not now. I need to go. I need to think. I'm sorry. I'll call you?'

Bay looks surprised, but I don't give him the chance to answer. I push past him, and with a quick look back at Dennis, I leave his beautiful office behind me as fast as I can.

Chapter 37

Discover Your Superpower

'We've all got a superpower – a gift that we can give to the world. When we're facing loneliness, grief and trauma, it becomes impossible for us to use our superpower, because each day simply becomes about surviving.

'As you begin to heal, start looking for your super-power. It will be there – and the more you use it to help others, the swifter your healing will be.'

©TheBeginnersGuideToLoneliness.com

I find a little park about two streets away from Bay's office and hurry through the wrought-iron gates. I'm on the hunt for a park bench; somewhere quiet to call Rowan back. I need her to do something for me.

Spotting a path, I follow it and end up in a small but perfectly formed rose garden. I sink gratefully onto a wooden bench and gaze around me for a few seconds, trying to catch my breath. I don't know what to think about everything that just happened with Bay. I almost don't want to think about it all, but really, what did I learn that's so terrible? If I'm honest, the thing that's bothering me most is the ex-wife and the fact that he hadn't told me about her. But should I really hold that against him? There are plenty of things I haven't told him about yet.

Well, there's one thing I do need to know. I pull out my phone and redial Rowan's number.

'Did you see it?!' she squeals by way of greeting.

'See what?'

'The email?! Catch up!'

'Oh. No . . .'

'Seriously, Tori!'

'Wait, Rowan. There's something I've got to ask you first, something important . . . a favour.'

'Another one?' she whines. 'You do know the last favour I did for you got me grounded, right?'

'What?'

'Yep. Getting your stuff out of the safe and hiding the fact that you were doing a runner. As I predicted, Dad did his nut.'

'Oh no, Rowan, I'm so sorry. How long for?'

'Ah, don't worry about it. Neither him nor Mum actually know what grounding is supposed to mean. I think they've already forgotten about it,' she laughs. 'Anyway, I blamed as much of it as I could on Sue and Hugh. Tell them it's all their fault for me, will you?!'

I laugh. 'It'll have to wait till we meet up for dinner later. They're off sightseeing.'

'Oh. You guys going anywhere special?' she asks, lightly.

'Nah, just the little restaurant around the corner from my flat.'

There's a brief pause.

'So, what's this new favour, then?' asks Rowan.

'It's about Bay . . .'

'Of course it is,' she says sarcastically.

I pick at the flaking paint on the arm of the bench. 'Look, he said he left a letter for me on my pillow in the yurt before he left, but I never got it.'

'And . . .'

'And . . . could you go and see if you can find it for me?'

'On your pillow?'

'Well obviously it won't be there now. The three of us stayed in there last night, didn't we? But maybe it blew off onto the floor or something?'

'Okay, okay. I can't right now. I'm watching the baby while Mum and Dad have a rest, but I'll text you later when I've looked?'

'You're my hero,' I say thankfully.

'I know.'

It's not ideal. I'm not going to be able to focus on anything until I know for sure.

'Right . . . about this email?' I say. 'Actually, how do you know what emails I'm getting? You've not hacked me or something, have you?' I laugh a little nervously. Somehow, I wouldn't put it past her.

'Course not,' she says, sounding offended. 'I answered the house phone earlier and it was someone asking for you.'

'Me?'

'Yeah, there have been quite a few since that knob told everyone who you are. Mostly journalists asking for interviews. Mum and Dad have been fielding them and just writing the contacts down so they can give them to you.'

'Oh,' I say, my heart skipping in fear.

'Look, I didn't tell them about this one. I thought it might be too important to wait till you got back.'

'Right . . .'

'It was this woman from a publisher. She said she'd emailed you via your blog, but she was worried you wouldn't pick it up because you'd be snowed under, so she was calling us on the off-chance she could speak to you directly.'

'Someone from a publisher?'

'Yeah. When I said you weren't available, she asked if I could make sure that you knew she was trying to reach you, and she hoped to talk to you soon. Look, can't you just check your emails yourself and read what she's got to say?'

'I'm not anywhere near my computer . . .'

'You stayed with us for too long . . . your brain is fried. Let me put this in words you might understand: Turn. On. Your. Bloody. Mobile. Data. Her name's Sarah . . . erm, hang on . . . Sarah Mack.'

And with that, Rowan hangs up.

I shake my head and can't help but smile as I faff around with my phone and open my emails.

It takes me ages to find the one she's talking about. There are hundreds of new messages. I cringe as I scroll through dozens, all with subjects along the lines of 'interview request'. Then I spot it. Sarah Mack. The subject line reads 'The Beginner's Guide to Loneliness: Book Proposal.'

Holy sainted granny pants.

Dear Tori,

I've had the pleasure, following the recent publicity, of discovering your blog The Beginner's Guide to Loneliness. Your writing is nothing short of exquisite, fresh and honest. Having binge-read all of your posts, I had to get in touch.

I am the Commissioning Editor for Farthing, a publishing imprint focusing on mental health and wellness titles. I would love to discuss the opportunity of turning your blog into a book.

Give me a call when you get back to London, and if it's something that you might be interested in, we can arrange a meeting to discuss the idea further.

Please can I also just take this opportunity to congratulate you on your article this morning in response to Nathan Jones. I feel that you have touched on a topic that needs to be under the spotlight, and I'm so sorry to hear that you have been the victim of this behaviour. I do hope you are receiving the support you need.

I look forward to hearing from you soon,

Kind regards,

Sarah Mack,

Commissioning Editor, Farthing Press

Farthing Press? They're huge! I read the email through a couple more times, let out an excited squeal, then quickly shoot a text to Rowan containing just two words: 'Holy. Shit.'

I take a deep breath, reopen the email and call the number in the signature strip.

'Sorry I'm late!' I gasp, plopping down into my chair opposite the other two.

Hugh grins at me and Sue waves a chunk of focaccia dipped in copious amounts of oil and balsamic vinegar at me.

'S'okay!' she says with her mouth full. 'We may have started without you though!'

'Wine?' asks Hugh, waggling a bottle of red at me.

I nod enthusiastically as I struggle out of my coat and tuck my bag under my chair so that no one goes arse over tit – lesson learned from bitter, mortifying experience.

Hugh pushes a large glass towards me and I take a grateful sip.

'So, what's up?' asks Sue. 'You look completely freaked! Is it the thought of having to face Bay tomorrow?'

I shake my head. Where to start . . .

'Well, I'm going to begin the evening with a toast now that we're all here,' says Hugh, unwittingly coming to my rescue. 'To old friends.'

Sue and I clink our glasses with his.

'And to your flippin' fantastic blog post,' says Sue, raising her glass again.

'How on earth have you already seen that?' I say.

'Oh come on,' says Hugh, 'she gave you all of half an hour after we left the flat and then kept refreshing your site on her phone until you posted.'

'You're kidding me?' I laugh. 'You were meant to be out enjoying yourselves and seeing the sights!'

'We were. The sights were just interrupted every five minutes for a quick blog check!' says Sue. 'I couldn't relax till I knew you'd finished. Must have been really hard.'

I nod. 'Not the easiest thing I've ever written, but definitely cathartic.' I smile to myself as the image of sticking two fingers up at my computer pops into my head.

'But where've you been since? I mean, I know you probably needed a bit of time to recover and everything, but that was hours ago. I was convinced you'd give us a call and come and join us, but you didn't . . . We were about to send out a search party,' she says.

'It's been a busy day. And I have some news.'

'Actually, we've got a bit of news for you too,' says Hugh, trying to flag down a waiter at the same time.

I catch Sue shooting a worried look at him. 'What? It can't be that bad,' I say, thinking of everything we've dealt with over the past twenty-four hours.

'Not bad for us, but definitely bad for Nathan,' Hugh mutters.

At the mention of his name, I stiffen.

'Turns out he's married,' says Sue.

Married? Why is everyone suddenly *married*? That is the very last thing I was expecting.

385

'How do you know?'

'A news site has already picked up on your post and done a bit of digging of their own.'

'Oh God, his poor wife!'

I don't know how I feel about this. Despite my little outburst in private, I didn't post my response for revenge. I posted it to warn other people of the dangers of this kind of behaviour, and in doing so I've unwittingly managed to warn his own wife.

'It's not for you to worry about, Tori,' says Hugh quietly.

I nod. This isn't happening to a friend. This is happening to a stranger who wormed his way into my life and then proceeded to do his best to ruin it. Nathan needs help, and somewhere deep down – right now, it's still *very* deep – I hope he finds it.

'Tell us your news, Tori!' says Sue excitedly.

'First, let's order,' I say, as a waiter appears at Hugh's elbow.

'Come on then, spill,' says Hugh as the waiter finally disappears with a rather full pad.

'Okay, so, big news, or *bigger* news first?' I ask.

'Is any of it to do with Bay?' asks Sue. 'Because that's the news I want first.'

'Okay. You've opted for "big" news first. I've already seen him. I went to his office earlier.'

'And?' Hugh prompts impatiently.

'And discovered that he's married.'

'*WHAT!?*' explodes Hugh, making Sue and I jump.

'Okay . . . I should have said "*was* married".'

'Didn't you know?' asks Sue.

'No. I didn't. And it was a shitty surprise. But, in fairness, I think he was going to tell me – we just hadn't quite got to that bit yet.'

'Ah. Awkward,' says Hugh sympathetically.

'Yep,' I agree.

'What about abandoning you without saying anything?' he asks.

'He said he left me a letter.'

'Really?'

'Yep. Said he left it on my pillow before he went.'

'But . . . you didn't get it?'

'Nope. I called Rowan and asked her if she'd go and hunt for it for me.'

'A letter . . . how romantic,' Sue sighs.

'If that is the case, surely it'll change things a bit?' asks Hugh.

'Hmm,' I say sceptically, 'rather depends on what it says.'

'So did you hear back from Rowan yet?' Sue prompts excitedly.

I shake my head. 'Last I heard she was baby wrangling, so goodness knows when she'll get the chance to go and look. We didn't spot anything, so there's no guarantees she'll find it, even if it *is* there!'

'But what about Bay? This afternoon?' prompts Hugh.

'Yeah, did you kiss and make up?' says Sue.

'Hardly.' I feel cold dread slide into my stomach. *What if we never do . . . ?*

'Why, what happened?'

'I just . . . I needed some time to think about things. As soon as I saw him, I realized that I needed to digest the fact that there's this whole side to him that he didn't tell me about. The business. The ex-wife. He's not the person I thought he was.'

'So when are you seeing him again?' asks Sue.

'I'm not. I just, well, I just . . . kind of left. Rowan called and I used that as an excuse to get the hell out of there.'

'Poor you, that sounds horrible.'

'It was.' I pick up a piece of bread and start to tear it into tiny chunks. 'In my head I think I had some kind of happy ever after planned out where it would all turn out to be a huge misunderstanding, and we'd fall into each other's arms. Instead it turns out that we're just two adults with a bunch of baggage, wondering if we can trust each other.'

There's silence around the table. The other two are staring at me like I'm the most depressing thing they've ever seen. I give myself a little shake, sweep the bread chunks into my hand and tip them onto a side plate.

'Anyway,' I say, 'enough of the big news. Who wants to hear the *bigger* news?!' I can't help but let a little smile creep onto my face.

'This better be happy news. You've nearly put me off my food,' says Hugh, sitting back in his seat.

'Oh, this is good news. Actually, this is *amazing* news.'

'Out with it then.'

'Well, I told you Rowan called?'

'Uh huh?'

'A publisher's interested in turning my blog into a book!' I blurt, jumping straight to the end of my story.

'Okay, WHAT?!' Sue is frozen, glass halfway to her lips.

'Um . . .' says Hugh, 'rewind please.'

'Well,' I say, 'turns out Nathan's article has massively upped the visitors to my blog. Most of them are complete rubber-neckers and just there to read about yours-truly-the-fuck-up. But, some of those new readers, well, it looks like they liked what they read.'

'Of course they did, your blog is amazing!' says Sue loyally.

'Well, one of my new visitors was Sarah Mack, Commissioning Editor at Farthing Press. She emailed me to invite me to a meeting. Then, just to make sure she reached me, she called The Farm. That's what Rowan was calling about. Can you believe it?!'

'And you just went? Just like that?!' asked Hugh, eyes wide.

'Well, it was just a coffee so we could meet – the real meeting will be in a couple of weeks – but I thought I may as well, as I had a free afternoon,' I grin.

'Oh my God!' Sue is threatening to go ultrasonic now, and I look around me, slightly embarrassed.

'Shhh! I'm meant to keep it quiet until everything's signed and sealed!' I laugh.

'Sorry . . . sorry. But WOW, Tori!'

'I can't believe it,' I say, and a wave of happiness floods through me. This is happening. 'Telling you two makes it feel real, somehow!'

'Well, that's you sorted, then, isn't it?!' says Hugh. 'Just think, you were busy melting down about work and money, and now you're going to be a published author!'

'Yeah, hopefully, and I guess I've got Nat – I mean *Nathan* – to thank for it. If he hadn't told the world who I was, Sarah might never have discovered my blog.'

I'm not sure how I feel about this, to be honest. I don't particularly want to owe him anything.

'No,' says Sue, and I'm surprised at how determined she sounds. 'You only have yourself to thank. You put in all those hours of work. Thousands of people already loved your posts, so it was only a matter of time before a publisher saw your potential.'

'Sue's right. And if they do give you a book deal, you'll be able to put the money towards a new place,' says Hugh.

I grin at him as another wave of excitement washes through me.

'What sort of thing do you fancy? Flat? House? Romantic cottage?' asks Sue. I swear she's ready to pull up PrimeLocation as we eat and start searching for my new home straight away.

'I don't know yet,' I say honestly. 'But I'm finally ready to give myself the permission to find out.'

Chapter 38

Integration and Return

'There will come a moment when you realize that you are no longer "struggling" with loneliness. It might still be there on occasion, but when you've put in the work to accept yourself for the perfectly imperfect person you are, those occasions will no longer feel so threatening. You will always be in the company of one of your best friends – you.'

©TheBeginnersGuideToLoneliness.com

By the time I've filled them in on all the gossip from my unexpected meeting, we've worked our way through two bottles of wine, three courses each and are just settling down to coffees. I'm starting to flag. I'm bloody exhausted. I'm just considering talking the other two into heading back to the flat for an early night when my phone starts to ring. I flip it over and see Rowan's name flashing up.

'Hey, Rowan!' I say, answering it before the ringing

manages to bug the entire room. I hate answering phones in public places. Maybe I should go outside . . .

'Tori, it's Doreen.'

It's so wonderful to hear my friend's voice, but I instantly start to panic.

'What's happened?' I ask sharply. Sue and Hugh stop gossiping and look at me with concerned expressions.

'Nice to speak to you too!' laughs Doreen.

'Sorry, sorry . . . it's just—'

'I know, you were expecting Rowan. Everything's fine. Well, other than the fact that Rowan's grounded!' She laughs again.

'I know, she told me earlier,' I say faintly.

'Yes, well. That was before Ted went online to read your post and decided to look up "how to ground a teenager" while he was at it.'

'Uh-oh!'

'Exactly. He confiscated her phone and gave it to me for safe-keeping, just in case you tried to make contact.'

'Wait, hang on . . . Ted gave you a phone? Is the world coming to an end?'

'No, we're just in the re-integration week, and he and Lizzie have decided that my friendship with you is an important part of mine!' she says. 'Plus, I don't think they liked the idea of it disturbing the baby.'

'Well, at least this explains why Rowan was taking so long to call me back,' I say.

'Yup. She managed to let Geoff know about your little mission earlier while she was helping him lay the table.

Hope you don't mind, but we went and had a look for you instead.'

'Course I don't mind!' I say. 'Find anything?'

'Yes. A little white envelope with your name on it. Must have blown off your bed. It was mostly wedged under one of the rugs.'

So Bay was telling the truth. He didn't just disappear on me.

'What does it say?' I breathe.

'I don't know,' she says. 'We didn't want to open it without speaking to you first.'

Sue and Hugh are now riveted, like if they concentrate hard enough, they'll be able to catch both sides of the conversation. I smile at them and point to the door. Sue looks gutted, but Hugh nods.

'Give me two secs, Doreen. I'm just going to head outside.'

I stand on slightly wobbly legs. I think it's the nerves rather than the glasses of wine that hit me and make me stagger. I make my way towards the front of the restaurant and head out into the cool evening air.

'You still there?' I say at a more normal volume as I wander down the street away from the buzz of the restaurant.

'Yep! You okay?'

'Yeah. Just had to get out of the restaurant for a second. I've abandoned Hugh and Sue over coffee,' I say.

'So, do you want me to read it to you?' asks Doreen.

'If you don't mind?' I say. Frankly I think that's quite restrained considering I want to reach through the phone somehow and rip the thing out of her hands.

I hold my breath while I hear paper tearing and much crinkling.

'Okay . . .' And she starts to read.

Dear Tori,

The outside world has come and bitten us both at the same time. I haven't told you much about my work yet, but I own a landscape and design company with two friends. We work with all sorts of insane people. I've just received a call to tell me that my partner Greg has been in an accident. He's hit his head and broken his leg. I don't know how bad he is yet, but I've got to head straight to London to take over a project for him. I don't want to rush off, but he's working on a garden at the Chelsea Flower Show and the deadline is nuts. I really want to see you before I go, but I've got no idea where you've gone or how long you're going to be.

Ted just showed me Than's article. I hope you're okay. I know everyone will look after you and I'll be back as soon as I can. I really, really want to be back before the course finishes.

There's so much for us to talk about and to share, and I can't wait for all of it. Last night was amazing. I'm a slow, cautious kind of person when it comes to my heart, and I'll tell you all about that when we see each other next. But for now, know that you're a very special person. I love spending time with you and I can't wait till I see you again.

Just remember how strong you are.

Bay

x

Doreen goes quiet, and I swear I can hear her sniffing.

I can't bring myself to say anything. There. That's the Bay I know. On that piece of paper that my friend is busy crying all over. And the best thing is, on that piece of paper is the proof that he wasn't keeping any kind of secret from me. There were no lies either. We just hadn't got round to that bit of the conversation yet.

'You still there?' comes Geoff's voice down the phone.

'I'm here!' I say, smiling to hear his voice. 'Is Doreen okay?'

'Ah she's fine, great big softy. But you could have been waiting for an age for her to compose herself!' he laughs. 'You okay, love?'

'Okay? Very okay. I've got loads to tell you both when I see you,' I say, making the snap decision that I want to share my news in person when I get back to The Farm. Because all of a sudden, I know that's where I need to go next.

'You're coming back? That's brilliant!' I can see his beaming face in my mind's eye, and hear a squeak of excitement from Doreen in the background. I turn and head back towards the restaurant.

'Look, I'd better go. I'll see you soon, okay? And Geoff? Thank you!'

'Wait! Tori! There's something else we should tell you!' comes Geoff's voice, and it sounds urgent.

'Go for it!' I say, coming to a halt outside the restaurant and peering through the windows for a glimpse of my friends at the back.

'There was another reason for Rowan getting grounded. She—'

'Oh. My. God!' I breathe.

'What? You okay?'

'Don't tell me,' I say, 'she gave Bay the details of where I'm having dinner, didn't she?'

'How on earth did you know that?'

Because I've just managed to spot Hugh and Sue at our table. And Bay is sitting in my chair.

'Gotta go!' I squeak. I hang up on Geoff and push straight into the restaurant.

What on earth am I going to say?

I stare at the little group and start walking towards them. I feel like a zombie, weaving between the tables and other diners. The poor, bemused waiting staff have to duck out of my way as I can't take my eyes off of Bay, laughing with my friends.

I manage to make it most of the way before Bay, as if sensing my presence, twists in his chair and spots me. He gets awkwardly to his feet and we stand and stare at each other for several long seconds.

Sue and Hugh just sit there, grinning at me like a couple of lemons. I still don't move.

'Don't forget these!' Sue's voice cuts into our little bubble.

Bay reaches over and takes something from her. 'I . . . I brought you something,' he says finally, walking towards me. In his arms he's holding a pair of bright yellow wellington boots, with an enormous bunch of flowers poking out of each one.

I take them and hug them to me with one arm.

'I read – I mean, I *heard* your letter,' I say.

'And?' he asks. He's smiling at me, but clearly nervous that this might turn out to be a public re-run of earlier.

'And, I'm sorry,' I say. 'I should have trusted you.'

'Well, I reckon I can let you off due to special circumstances,' he says, not taking his eyes off me.

I nod my thanks.

'But, did it . . . I don't know . . . did it help at all?' he asks.

I nod again. There's so much I want to say, but I feel like I'm going to have to choke the words out around a lump that has mysteriously appeared in my throat.

Bay seems to understand. He steps forward, closing the distance between us until we're almost touching.

'It was you,' I whisper. I can't tear my eyes off him. 'The letter. It was you. The you I know *and* this you. It was the link I was missing.'

Bay reaches out, takes my free hand and laces his fingers through mine. I feel the hard calluses of his garden-rough hand and smile up at him.

'Then, we're okay?' The little quaver in his voice goes straight to my heart.

'More than,' I say. Reaching up, I kiss him gently, the wellies and flowers squashed between us.

Chapter 39

The Beginning

'Every single second can be a new beginning. It's too easy to get caught up in the past and let your life slip by as you mourn the mistakes you've made, the decisions you regret or the paths you didn't take.

'Every single second can be a new beginning. But this time you're not a beginner . . . you start with a whole heap of experience and hope in your heart.'

©TheBeginnersGuideToLoneliness.com

As Bay swings Frank to a standstill at the top of the lane, I can't help but laugh.

'What? You don't want me to "walk the track" again, do you? This isn't my first time, you know!'

Bay grins over at me. 'Just kidding!' he says, and we carry on, bouncing our way over the rough slates towards The Farm, where our friends are waiting for us.

Friends.

That word has more meaning to me now than it did just a few weeks ago. Doreen and Geoff. Moth, Messa and the others. Even Rowan. All friends. All on my side.

And then, of course, there's Bay. Over the past couple of days, there's barely been a moment's silence between us when we've been together. Hugh and Sue decided to head home the day after their epic sightseeing session, so while Bay's been at work, I've started pulling notes and ideas together for the book. In the evenings, though, we've spent every single second getting to know everything about each other. *Everything.*

I even told him about my mum. How it really was between us, and how it just got worse the more she drank. I told him about the relief I feel at no longer having to justify my life to her, no longer having to hear that I am her biggest disappointment. I told him about how guilty this all makes me feel.

I also told him that I should have been with her the night of the accident. If I hadn't ignored her call, I would have been driving, and maybe the accident wouldn't have happened at all. Or maybe I would have died too. There it is. There's the 'what if' that's at the heart of my phobia.

Of course, sharing hasn't miraculously made it all go away, but it feels like another step in taking back control of my life. Bay is definitely the best friend I could have ever hoped for. He's the best at a lot of other stuff too.

We've both been granted our wish to get back to The Farm before the course is over. Bay's colleague Greg has already been able to take back the reins of his project, though he'll be mostly directing his team from the comfort of his wheelchair.

As Frank bounces into the yard, my attention is brought firmly back into the present by Dennis barking in the seat between us.

'Oi, hound, what're you complaining about? We're home!' I say, patting his head excitedly. He wags his tail, struggling against his seatbelt harness to stand up and peer properly through the windscreen. Then I see what he's barking at. Rowan is heading down the yard to meet us.

'Tori!' she squeals as I push the door open and struggle to hop down onto my stiff legs.

'Hey, Rowan!'

To my delight, she throws her arms around me and hugs me tight. I squeeze her back, but not for long as Dennis forces his way between us.

'Hello, idiot!' laughs Rowan, bending down to ruffle his fur. He promptly throws himself on his back, demanding a belly rub.

'I thought you were still grounded?' says Bay, throwing his arm around me.

Rowan looks up at us and grins. 'Nah, I made a deal with Dad,' she says, still tickling Dennis's stomach while he squirms, tongue lolling out of his mouth like a complete loon.

'Of course you did,' laughs Bay.

'Well, turns out that extra help around the house and with chores is more useful than keeping me off my phone, so . . .'

Straightening up, she takes her phone out of her jeans pocket and waves it at us.

'Shall we go find the others?' Bay asks me.

'Yay!' It's the only thing to say. I've missed them.

'No, wait . . . I've got to tell you something first!' says Rowan.

'Uh oh,' I say, coming to a halt. Rowan's smiling this time, but this feels a tad too familiar for my liking!

'Don't panic, it's something good. Guess what?'

'Rowan!' Ted's voice calls from the top of the yard. 'Stop hogging Tori and Bay! Your mum needs you.'

'But—' she groans.

'Now.'

'Fine.' She slouches off up the path, Dennis following hot on her heels in pursuit of more belly rubs.

Ted reaches us and with a huge, tired grin, he flings his arms around Bay. 'So glad you could make it back!' he says.

'Me too,' says Bay.

'Tori!' Ted throws his arms around me too, and I squeeze him back, bobbly jumper and all.

'What was Rowan about to tell us?' I ask.

'Oh. Well, that's not for me to say. I think Lizzie wants to tell you.'

'But it's not bad news?' I check, worried that the chaos Nathan caused has had some kind of negative effect on The Farm.

Ted shakes his head. 'No bad news here.'

Bay takes my hand and we follow Ted towards the house. For a dizzying second I think he's about to lead us straight into the house itself, but instead he heads for the main fire pit, where everyone is hanging out around a lovely fire.

There's general pandemonium as they all rush over to us, and we find ourselves caught in the centre of a very happy, very huggy pile-up. It takes a good ten minutes before we're all perched back on the bales around the fire.

Doreen's right next to me, and one of my hands is in hers. My other hand is still in Bay's. The heat of their palms in mine heads straight up my arms, and my heart has never felt so warm. Maybe Doreen was right – perhaps they are turning me into a hippy.

'Go on then, Tori!' says Geoff, waving his cup of tea at me from across the fire. 'What's the big news you had to share with us?'

No, no, this isn't right. I'm the one meant to be finding out the news first!

'If I tell my news, will you tell me yours?' I ask Ted.

He looks at Lizzie, comfortably ensconced in a chair next to him, the little one nestled into her front.

'Deal,' says Lizzie. 'You first!'

'Okay. Well, the best thing ever happened when I was in London.'

'We can see that,' Doreen smiles at me, nodding at my hand clasped in Bay's.

I grin at her. 'Okay, you're right. The second best thing ever, then . . .'

Doreen chuckles, and Rowan nudges her from the other side. 'Shhh . . . or she'll never tell us!'

'Well, it's thanks to you really, Rowan. I met with a publisher when I was there. And they're interested in turning my blog into a book.'

A massive cheer goes up, and there are questions left and right and centre. I can't stop beaming as I say, 'Well, at least one good thing came from Nathan's article!'

'More than one good thing!' says Ted. 'Since you posted your response on your blog, our bookings have gone completely mad!'

'But . . . I haven't posted my review yet,' I say, perplexed. 'I wanted to finish the course first!'

'No, but you gave us a lovely mention in your post, and it's been incredible. So, thank you. Not just for that, but for everything,' he nods over at his baby daughter.

I shake my head, slightly embarrassed. I don't deserve this praise, this thanks.

'And that leads us to our next bit of news,' says Lizzie, bouncing the baby on her lap.

I hold my breath.

'We've decided on a name for this little munchkin,' she says.

I let the breath out. Thank heavens, the spotlight is off me.

'We've decided to call her Victoria. After you.' Lizzie beams at me.

I don't know what to say, or where to look, so I turn to Rowan, who's grinning at me.

'She's going to be Vicca for short. Because you were amazing.'

That's it. They've finally broken me. I feel two huge tears break free and slide down my cheeks.

Moving back into the yurt with Bay and Dennis, even if it is only for a couple of nights, has to be one of the most joyous moments of my life so far. And given the amazing things that have happened to me over the past few days, that's saying something. This is the first place I've truly felt the sense of being at home, something I never felt for the house I grew up in, nor my London flat.

Speaking of the flat, that's something else I did while I was in London. I called my landlord. To be fair to the man, he was perfectly nice to me. I realized that I'd allowed my overactive imagination and anxiety-prone brain to turn him into the 'Big Baddy'. The poor guy was only doing what he had to do. I explained that I'd be able to pay him as soon as the advance for my book lands.

While we were on the phone, I also handed in my notice on the flat. I'm not one hundred per cent sure what my next move is going to be, but with Bay in my life, I know it's going to be an exciting one.

I wake up to the sound of birds and the soft light of ridiculous o'clock creeping into the yurt. For a second, I just lie still and listen to the interweaving harmonies of the songbirds outside and the two sets of gentle snoring inside. I'm exactly where I want to be, snuggled up next to Bay with one of his arms wrapped around me. And Dennis is exactly where he wants to be, fast asleep on my bed over on the other side of the yurt.

I'm glad they're both asleep. I've got something I want to do, and the sounds of the early morning are beckoning. I'm ready.

I carefully slip out from under Bay's arm, pausing as he stirs in his sleep – and then I relax as he turns over and his breathing becomes deep and even once more.

I get dressed quickly and quietly and am just pulling my yellow wellies on by the door when a cold, wet nose and wagging tail demand my attention. Dennis is awake, and clearly quite keen to join me on my early morning mission. I ruffle his ears and briefly consider ordering him back to bed. But I change my mind and we set off together.

The morning is crisp and clear, and the fields teem with life. Last week's rain has made the greens even brighter and everything feels full of possibility, full of hope.

When I reach the top of the hill, I pause. I don't want to turn back this time; I don't want to run away and hide. I've got one more thing to face while I'm here, and then I really will have done everything that this place has asked of me.

Coming back to The Farm in time to finish the retreat has meant a lot to me. I've been able to work with all the tutors some more, and I've had the chance to talk to both Ted and Lizzie about Mum's accident, our relationship and about my guilt and grief. I know I've still got a long way to go, but the

steps I've already taken on the journey have shifted something deep inside of me.

I glance down at Dennis. He's sitting in the grass next to
me, completely content to watch and wait for my next move.
Question is, am I ready to make it?

'Ready,' I say quietly, and together we stride down the hill.

I duck under the trees at the bottom and pause again as the
sound of the river reaches my ears. I take a deep breath in and
let it out slowly. I can see running water. I can hear the pounding of the river. But it isn't taking me over.

Bending forward, I slip out of my wellingtons and peel off
my socks. I roll up the legs of my trousers and straighten back
up to stand, barefoot, on the shingle bank.

The sound of the river fills my ears. I take a step forward.
Then another. I keep walking until my toes are right at the
edge of the water. I pause.

I look behind me. Dennis is sitting by my boots, watching
me, tail wagging and tongue lolling. I turn to face the river
again. The sound of water is all around me. I take a deep
breath in. For a brief second I see my mother's face, and then
it's gone, replaced by the water swirling in front of me. I
breathe out.

I breathe in.

I'm ready.

I breathe out and step into the river.

406

Acknowledgements

My first thanks goes to my mum for all her gentle support, and to Pops for being the biggest champion of creativity I've ever met. I miss you both very much.

To my family – Dad and Jill, Rhian and Graham, Ross and Amberina, Sebby and Echo – thank you for all your love.

Huge thanks to the Books and the City team for scooping Tori out of the #OneDay submissions pile and wanting to read the rest of her story. A special shout-out to Bec Farrell and Sara-Jade Virtue for all your support and hard work – it has been amazing working with you.

A big cheer for all the authors and bloggers who have inspired me over the years, but special thanks to Heidi Swain, Darcie Boleyn, T. A. Williams, Kim Nash and Mary Lewis for being amazing friends and cheerleaders while I've been navigating the overwhelming waters of crafting a debut novel.

Special thanks to my Sapphire family for inspiring the Warriors. Thank heavens none of you are anything like Nat!

Greg Poulos, Leah Stevens and Sara Olsson – thank you for always being there, and for all your help. I look forward to the day we all finally get to hang out!

I undertook a lot of research while working on Tori's story and would like to give Mind.org.uk a shout-out for their wonderful online resources. I would also like to thank Suzanne Olenczyn for sharing her experiences with me. Any errors or inaccuracies are all on me.

To Mop – thank you for all the company and cuddles.

Jules, I've left you until last because I know you always skip to the end first – thank you for everything. I wouldn't have been able to do this if it weren't for you.